# London: Lashed, Lacerated, Lampooned and Lambasted

# London: Lashed, Lacerated, Lampooned and Lambasted

By

Jay Dubya

Published by
Bookstand Publishing
Pasadena, CA 91101
3092_2



ISBN 978-1-58909-697-4

# Other Books by Jay Dubya

## Adult Fiction

*Black Leather and Blue Denim, A '50s Novel*
*The Great Teen Fruit War, A 1960' Novel*
*Frat' Brats, A '60s Novel*
*Ron Coyote, Man of La Mangia*
*Pieces of Eight*
*Pieces of Eight, Part II*
*Pieces of Eight, Part III*
*Pieces of Eight, Part IV*
*The Wholly Book of Genesis*
*The Wholly Book of Exodus*
*The Wholly Book of Doo-Doo-Rot-on-Me*
*Thirteen Sick Tasteless Classics*
*Thirteen Sick Tasteless Classics, Part II*
*Thirteen Sick Tasteless Classics, Part III*
*Thirteen Sick Tasteless Classics, Part IV*
*Thirteen Sick Tasteless Classics, Part V*
*So Ya' Wanna' Be A Teacher*
*RAM: Random Articles and Manuscripts*
*Mauled Maimed Mangled Mutilated Mythology*
*Fractured Frazzled Folk Fables and Fairy Farces*
*FFFF&FF, Part II*
*Nine New Novellas*
*Nine New Novellas, Part II*
*Nine New Novellas, Part III*
*Nine New Novellas, Part IV*
*One Baker's Dozen*
*Two Baker's Dozen*
*Shakespeare: Slammed, Smeared, Savaged & Slaughtered*
*Shakespeare: S, S, S and S, Part II*
*Suite 16*
*Time Travel Tales*
*Snake Eyes and Boxcars*
*Snake Eyes and Boxcars, Part II*
*UFO: Utterly Fantastic Occurrences*
*The Psychic Dimension*
*The Psychic Dimension, Part II*
*Modern Mythology*

*First Person Stories*
*O. Henry: Obscenely and Outrageously Obliterated*
*Twain: Tattered Trounced Tortured and Traumatized*
*Poe: Pelted Pounded Pummeled and Pulverized*
*Hawthorne: Hazed Hooked Hammered and Hijacked*
*THEMES*
*PLOTS*
*PLOTS, Part II*
*The FBI Inspector*
*Prime-Time Crime Time*
*The Arcane Arcade*
*Thirteen Tantalizing Tales*
*Hawthorne Hacked, Shakespeare Sacked & Thurber Thwacked*
*Homer's Odd Sea Odyssey*
*HOMER'S ILL Iliad*
*The Timeless Time Machine*
*War of the Worlds*
*The Invisible Man*

## Young Adult Fantasy Novels

*Pot of Gold*
*Enchanta*
*Space Bugs, Earth Invasion*
*The Eighteen Story Gingerbread House*

# Contents

# Description

*London: Lashed, Lacerated, Lampooned and Lambasted* is a unique collection of eighteen classic Jack London short stories that have been creatively rewritten and satirized into adult parody form featuring adult content and language. When author Jay Dubya was a New Jersey public school English teacher, he often enjoyed teaching and reading Jack London's "influential literature" to his sometimes-enlightened academic students.

Jack London (1876-1916) died at the early age of forty but the author left behind a rich collection of literature still read and admired today. London was a master at the literary writing technique known as *Realism* where he skillfully describes struggles and life-or-death situations pitting man against man, man against hostile environments, and often man against himself.

Jack London was born in San Francisco and helped to support his family at age fourteen, dropping out of school to do so. Spending plenty of time in city libraries, London was a voracious reader who studied hard and eventually passed the entrance examination into the University of California. He stayed as a student for one semester but then went to work as a sailor and a laborer. During the Gold Rush of 1897, London spent a year in the Klondike and Yukon territories where he gathered material and information about interesting characters that later would appear in his novels and short stories.

Very fascinated by the Darwinian theory of "survival of the fittest," many of Jack London's works focused on the endurance of strong men driven by atavistic instincts and primitive emotions. His two famous novels are actually direct reversals of each other. In the *Call of the Wild,* Buck, a very large dog, is stolen from a wealthy family's Santa Clara, California home and is transported to the Alaska/Canadian Yukon to eventually become the lead canine in a dogsled team. In the classic novel *White Fang,* a wolf dog is taken from the tundra wilderness and then becomes domesticated.

The settings of most Jack London stories are in California, the Klondike/Yukon regions of Canada, and the South Sea Pacific islands in and around Tahiti. London graphically described the great San Francisco Earthquake of April 18th, 1906 in his newspaper account "The Story of An Eyewitness," and two other stories in this collection take place in California. Twelve of the eighteen satirized tales in this work occur in the Yukon/Klondike territories, and the remaining three stories are set in the South Pacific islands in and around Tahiti.

# “Story of an Eyewitness”

Besides your undependable fellow man, don’t expect Mother Nature to give you a fair shake, either! On April 18, 1906, for thirty devastating seconds in San Francisco, California, the terrible up and down sensation felt worse than being a goddamned devout Quaker! After experiencing the nauseating motion, I wouldn’t ever wish to be a grain of sodium chloride inside a friggin’ salt shaker; no way!

I was not only an eyewitness to the remnants of the tremendous disaster, but also, I was an involuntary participant. And I’m still shook-up about the whole damned ordeal. ‘What the hell is this shit?’ I remember thinking as ceiling plaster fell onto my head and rudely awakened me from my deep slumber. Then, after being violently knocked out of my hotel room bed, and harshly landing upon the rumbling floor, according to my astute observations, here’s what actually went-down, besides a lot of enormous brick buildings.

Millions of dollars-worth of walls and chimneys came tumbling-down, as if Joshua’s trumpet got stuck on one very loud note outside the fabled walls of Jericho. But it was the spectacular fires that the San Francisco Earthquake had caused and rendered that generated the loss of hundreds of millions of dollars in additional property and real estate. Downtown San Francisco has very noticeably crumbled and tumbled to the ground. The city’s industrial section won’t be industrious for at least a decade; its business section has been wiped-out, and many of its social and residential areas are no longer social and residential areas. The formerly profitable “City-by-the-Bay” warehouses, factories, hotels, and whorehouses; the great stores and newspaper buildings, along with the opulent mansions and palaces of the wealthy nabobs all look like some sort of grotesque edifice wrecks. Only a small fringe of dwellings still-remain somewhat-intact on the outskirts (and on the petticoats) of what was once proud San Francisco.

Fearing the trauma of electrocution, people were afraid to touch the ground because of the great aftershocks. San Francisco’s smoke-laden atmosphere was visible a full hundred-miles away, looking like a lurid tower of ever-expanding atmospheric pollution. And the dense smoke blotted-out the sun for nearly three days, and everybody within a ten-mile-radius was running-around, gasping from smoke inhalation, with each person sounding like he or she had a chicken bone caught in his or her throat. The trouble of breathing was even far worse than living on the distant island of Mada*gasp*ar.

The formidable earthquake began its wicked destruction on Wednesday morning at a quarter past five, when most people were sleeping, and not even having intense sex (or not even masturbating), with their extreme climaxes knocking each and every person out of their respective beds. A minute later, the immense flames were leaping all over the downtown district like a goddamned blazing frog plague. Huge fires, and major Dante-like infernos, began igniting all over the doomed city, especially in the working-class ghettos, and also in the highly-flammable dildo and sexual prosthetics' factories.

The unassuming public was so caught by surprise from the unprecedented half-minute rocking and rolling, and the subsequent voracious fires, that the citizenry had no reactive organization or communication to directly oppose the mass destruction in progress. A twentieth-century modern American city was suddenly transformed into ancient first-century Roman Pompeii in a matter of minutes.

The streets and avenues suddenly became humped, and all of the afflicted residents were screwed, also. Human prosperity had ceased in a mere half a minute's duration. The instantaneous falling debris had caused artificial ridges, recessions, and depressions everywhere. Steel rails and iron beams had become twisted and tangled into horizontal and perpendicular angles, none of which was a cute one.

Two of the city's three principal communications' networks were disrupted; telegraph, telephone, but unfortunately, not tell a woman. The metropolitan water mains had burst, and the overall scene looked like thousands of sperm whales spouting their water jets, and shooting gargantuan ejaculations from their giant erections all over the damned ruined landscape. All of the shrewd scientific devices, mechanisms, and precautions of today's "modern man" had been vanquished in less time than it takes the average male to have a premature ejaculation. Even the surviving dick-less women felt so impotent that the ladies thought that they were suffering from erectile clit' dysfunction.

By Wednesday afternoon, half of the heart (along with the lungs and intestines) of the city had been demolished by nature's omnipotent fury. At the time, from my advantageous vantage point out on the bay, everything seemed dead calm, with most of the traumatized people had already evacuated. But inside the city, strong winds were fiercely gusting, and the remaining citizens were all holding their heads because they didn't want their minds blown-away.

The rising-heated air made an enormous suck that no fantastic bordello blowjob could ever come close to matching. While still in my small dinghy out in the bay, I harbored great animosity toward the incredible San Francisco Earthquake and its economic after*math*, the arithmetical monetary sum being quite astronomical.

Someone had a dynamite idea, and *that* brainstorm was to explode the walls of expendable standing structures, along with the rubble piles of former brick and mortar stores, thus forming street and avenue barricades to block the onrushing flames of destruction. Regrettably, the puny contrivances and defenses of diminutive men were easily defeated by the callous and mindless onslaught of nature gone amok.

The enumeration of buildings that collapsed and went-down during the incomparable holocaust is like a directory of San Francisco's most prominent and esteemed establishments. An enumeration of the buildings not destroyed could be listed in the footnote of a college student's term paper. And the number of cremated human bodies might never be accurately known, tabulated, or published, because even the damned undertakers had fled the city, anxiously leaving their horse-drawn funeral hearses behind to be consummated by flames.

Upon returning from the safety of the bay on Wednesday evening, I exited my miniature boat and then trekked through the downtown area. And as remarkable as it may seem, while the whole city had been leveled, no crowds were gathering in the streets, and no looters were evident anywhere, because truthfully and succinctly, there was little left to loot. There was no apparent disorder or hysteria, since there weren't any disorderly or hysterical humans anywhere in sight. Not even non-existent hospital orderlies were around to ever become disorderly. Not one woman was weeping, and not one man was angry or excited. No one was panic-stricken because in that ruinous section where I walked, only roaring flames could be seen and heard.

Before the fires arrived in the vicinity, tens of thousands of homeless victims had fled, and most of the evacuees were wrapped in blankets and in swaddling clothes, many not having time to put their regular daily attire on, or even lie-down in a manger. Other residents hurried along uprooted streets, carrying whatever family treasures or heirlooms the luggers could transport to the city's outer perimeter, where the already escaped crooks, thugs, and bandits were waiting to pounce on their prey, who were bringing personal valuables in *their* direction.

Baby buggies and toy wagons were used as improvised transportation trucks, and every other person was dragging a trunk, including the escaped and loose circus elephants. But throughout the long procession extending all the way out to the city limits, courtesy and manners prevailed, and there were few incidents of argument or larceny amongst the generally law-abiding refugee majority.

The trunk-draggers were extremely courageous, with most of them being the strongest male in each family. The hills of San Francisco are very steep, yet these brave trunk draggers persisted and continued in their monotonous, grueling plight. Trunks were everywhere, and many exhausted owners and other family members sat on their chests (and safeguarded their possessions), while some of the fatigued men sat on their wives' chests. Picket lines of soldiers that were frantically wielding bayonets tried keeping the trunk-pullers moving along, instantly making even the smallest man into a "Big Lug".

Oftentimes, the bedraggled trunk-draggers would arrive at the crest of a new hill, and witness a wall of hungry flames heading in their direction, thus causing the frustrated pullers to immediately retreat to seek-out and find a new escape route in a hurry. Many disenchanted laborers abandoned their possessions in despair; but others, particularly the ambitious workingmen, who brought-along shovels and spades, excavated holes and buried their trunks in backyards and in vacant lots, and were hoping to return in several days to retrieve their chests and wishfully, luckily finding their undisturbed articles inside, and still-intact.

At nine o'clock Wednesday evening, I walked through the center of the city, and amazingly, most of the magnificent buildings were still standing. The police were stoically patrolling the streets, and no fires were threatening either man or property. Every protected building had a watchman, a post-colonial minuteman, or a vigilant guard at its door. But much to everyone's concern and apprehension, two approaching conflagrations were damned imminent, with much-needed water being in short supply, and with the dynamite caches running low.

Just past midnight, I again ambled through those same quiet thoroughfares, and even though most of the familiar structures were still upright, ash was raining-down, despite the fact that it was now Thursday morning, and that Ash Wednesday had come and gone. The coffee and doughnut shops had all closed their doors, so almost simultaneously, the police had withdrawn, the firemen with their engines had retreated to safer areas, and the disappointed watchmen had all abandoned that particular region.

I stood all by my lonesome at the normally hectic and busy corner of Kearney and Market Street, and my disbelieving eyes perceived that Kearney was burning like Vulcan's Hades, for a full half a dozen blocks on both sides in either direction. 'This is not my idea of a hot time in the old town tonight!' I whimsically thought.

And then, eerily silhouetted against one of the converging walls of flame, sat two United States cavalrymen sitting atop their horses, calmly watching the incredible devastation. Not another person or animal was in sight, so not even the U.S. cavalry could be bugled in from the frontier to save the city from an unstoppable, relentless foe.

The sewers had been pumped entirely dry, so not even human shit and piss could be used to extinguish or battle the invincible flames. More blazes instantaneously ignited, and as a last-ditch effort, the Examiner Newspaper Building, the Call Building, the Put Building, the Grand Hotel, and the formerly majestic Palace Hotel, were all being dynamited in a vain attempt to curtail the horrendous, inevitable catastrophe from devouring everything in sight.

Earlier, I had passed through Union Square that was packed with depressed refugees; thousands of them sleeping on the grass and lying amidst the bushes and shrubs. Government tents had been erected, and some other desperate people were lining-up for free meals. At two hours past midnight, three-fourths of Union Square had been engulfed in flames, and on the fourth side, where the resplendent St. Francis Hotel had proudly stood, the palatial structure was now also heavily in flames.

Thank goodness St. Francis was away from his hotel, vacationing in Italy, and visiting *a sissy* gay friend of his, otherwise the benevolent saint's life would have been in serious jeopardy. The central square was now completely deserted. and I was trying to figure-out why I was an idiotic asshole still aimlessly standing there in its center.

Just west of nearly-abandoned Union Square. I was confronted by a man offering anyone within hearing distance a thousand dollars to rent a team of horses. The paranoid fellow had been in charge of guarding and transporting a massive wagon stacked-high with trunks from a downtown hotel currently in flames, so I curiously asked the man, "What in blazes are you doing here?" And out of sheer aggravation, the thoroughly-upset nutcase wildly slugged me in the face, giving me an instant swollen lip.

I then awkwardly staggered-over to an old gentleman (seemingly more of a gentleman than the jerk-off that had just sucker-punched me) who was leaning on crutches. "Today's my goddamned birthday!" the old geezer told me, as I impatiently held my bleeding mouth and hurting mandible. "Just last night I was worth thirty-thousand dollars. I had bought five bottles of imported port wine, some delicious aphrodisiac fish, and some other exotic erotic sex foods for my eighty-fifth birthday. Today, I have no dinner, no wine, no sex, and all that I own are these stupid-ass, fuckin' crutches!"

"That's what the fuck you get for not acting your goddamned age!" I muttered before the old codger maliciously walloped me on the opposite side of my mandible, doubling my already unbearable excruciation. Slowly and gingerly, getting-up from the dirty wet pavement to my knees, I derived some minor satisfaction from seeing the first antagonistic jerk-off's trunk-laden wagon gradually incinerating, and then I perceptibly noticed and relished the nasty old fart's left crutch igniting into flames.

On Thursday morning, just twenty-four hours after the earthquake had commenced, I sat on the hard marble steps of a Nob Hill residence, the general ridge being somewhat-shaped like a woman's breast. Near me on other step levels, glumly and reticently sat Italians, Japanese, Chinese, Frenchmen, Lesbians, and Negroes, all separate parts of the cosmopolitan flotsam of the vastly wrecked city. The distant palaces of the nabob pioneers of the 1849 Gold Rush were about to be consumed by the insatiable appetites of the advancing fences of fire. The overall effect was fantastically awesome.

Following a sudden compulsion, I trespassed inside one of the nearby abodes to take a piss, when the aggrieved owner encountered me while I was pulling down my fly. "It's no use," the idiot dejectedly announced. "No amount of water or piss can ever combat the raging fires! Yesterday morning, I was worth over six-hundred-thousand-dollars along with this paid for mansion. And in fifteen-minutes, my entire life's work and savings will all go up in smoke!"

"Sounds like you have money to burn!" I stupidly commented before then enduring a well-deserved vicious right cross to my chin, sending me tumbling onto the tiled floor, where I rolled about and writhed in total pain before involuntarily pissing myself.

And as I lay there, moaning and groaning from my facial agony, the irritated curmudgeon continued his boring speech while pointing to a large expensive china cabinet. "Over there! That's my ugly wife's ornate collection of red china. And the fancy rug upon which you're lying is also Oriental, and the dusty piece of shit cost me two thousand clams, even though I made my fortune as a lobsterman. Listen to the tone of this expensive piano," the belligerent fellow said before playing a few dissonant non-classical bars of 'Chopsticks'. "The son-of-a-bitchin' flames are rapidly descending upon us, so stay conscious you rotten bastard; so that you can rise to your feet and save your own goddamned ass from being broiled!"

Meanwhile, outside, the old Mark Hopkins residence (along with its many Johns and accompanying washrooms) was just catching fire, and the various army troops were quickly retreating along with the homeless Italian, Japanese, Lesbian, and Negro refugees. At that moment, all that was discernible to my throbbing ears was the crashing of buildings and the distant detonations of dynamite.

I hobbled out of the bellicose (formerly rich) jerk-off's house, after again involuntarily pissing my pants during my rather-crippled exit. 'Where's that nasty old son-of-a-bitch with the crutches when I fuckin' need him?' I remember thinking and wondering.

Daybreak was endeavoring to crack through the thick pall of smoke. The sun was blood red on the eastern horizon, and the orange sphere was a quarter of its normal size. And so, my aching senses were dreadfully introduced to the second day of the horrid annihilation of a previously vibrant metropolis.

An hour later, I was creeping past the partially shattered dome of City Hall, which actually looked like a nightmarish *hall*ucination. Most of the stone facade had been vibrated off of the great dome during the tumultuous quake, and only a naked and gnarled steel framework remained. The Parthenon-temple-like-pillars of the once magnificent building were now crosswise sections lying upon the street, and the remains of the structure were mind-boggling mounds of wreckage, along with abundant brick and stone litter.

Every structure in *that* formerly special section of San Francisco (with the exception of the Mint and the Post Office) had been demolished, or was in what could only be described as 'irreparable-shambles'. Whenever I saw an occasional man or woman tottering around, my fertile mind imagined that the scenario was analogous to meeting an unfortunate survivor during the cataclysmic climax to the end of the world.

On Mission Street lay a dozen steers, all apparently roasted barbecued beef without any human diners in sight to enjoy the delectable meat. The human dead had already been removed from the thoroughfare, so *that* fact, at least, convinced me that the city's humane authorities had not treated the male and female survivors as mere cattle. Ambling further down Mission Street, I witnessed where a telegraph pole had smashed into a milk wagon; its impact completely crushing the driver's seat and front wheel. 'No use crying over spilt milk!' I reasoned. 'It's time for me to get the fuck outa' here before the enraged milkman shows-up and breaks my nose, along with my glass jaw, with several stiff jolting uppercuts being administered!'

All-day Thursday, and all-day Friday, the outrageous flames raged and spread. Friday night the ravenous fires were finally conquered, but not until Telegraph Hill, Russian Hill, Blueberry Hill, and three-quarters of a mile of docks and wharves, had been consumed and licked-up. The firefighters had made a last valiant stand on Van Ness Avenue, and the brave souls managed to deflect the fire into a less disastrous direction. Thus, the fabulous homes of the second-generation lazy and indolent nabobs had been salvaged and rescued from obliteration. But lacking essential water in certain poorer sectors of San Francisco, many smaller fires had to be beaten-down by rugs and wet blankets, many of them being utilized by people who ordinarily were rugged wet blankets themselves.

San Francisco at present is similar in appearance to the crater of a volcano, and thousands of sorrowed, affected refugees are camped around the half-circumference of the smoldering city. At the U.S. military reservation known as the Presidio, at least twenty-thousand weakened survivors are camped-out; their basic needs waiting to be attended to by various relief and charity committees.

The normally greedy-and-capitalistic railroad barons have shown some new-found altruistic tendencies by offering free transportation to anyone leaving San Francisco, headed to any valid big city destination in the United States. And at latest report, over one-hundred-thousand people have already availed themselves of the generous option, and have departed from the overwhelmed peninsula.

Thank goodness there is not any evidence of famine or widespread disease resulting from the great earthquake and subsequent fires tragedy. The bankers and the downtown businessmen are already making plans to resurrect San Francisco back to its glory days as being the "Incomparable Jewel of the Pacific".

# "All Gold Canyon"

William Pocket had anxiously left the village of Cedar Brook, New Jersey, and journeyed westward to the enchantment of the Sierra Nevada Mountains of California, seeking a new life, and to try his luck at gold prospecting. The seventy-year-old man had labored on the Philadelphia to Atlantic City line of the Pennsylvania Railroad for fifty years, but because of certain ongoing family problems, the bachelor decided to live on his own out West, and attempt using his life's savings to build an isolated cabin, and perhaps strike it rich as the "shit-lucky San Francisco '49ers" had done.

'I still keep in touch with my younger sister, Madeline, and she sends me letters keepin' me posted on developments and gossip back in South Jersey,' William considered as the independent-minded pioneer fed his obdurate mule outside his small mountain cabin. 'Ma and Pa are dead, and Madeline's the only one left in my family worth communicatin' with. My other sibling I'd rather forget about, and never care to see, again. Give me fresh clean mountain air any time over the flat pinelands of South Jersey.'

William Pocket was an introverted loner, who shunned crowds of people, especially crowds of people in raucous frontier town saloon environments. Fifteen miles south of his lonesome prospecting site was Angel's Camp, but Bill shied-away from that 'boisterous California den of iniquity', populated with what the new-arrival graphically described as 'reckless, drunken, loud-mouthed, and obnoxious varmints, sidewinders, jaspers, and whiskerandos.'

The secluded canyon in which William Pocket had settled-down in, and where he had built his rustic cabin was quite pristine, featuring a narrow. fast-descending stream situated in its center, with meadows of multi-colored wild flowers growing on both sides. The ledges of the rocky cliffs were steep and precarious, and William had to ascend them without the aid of "Lazy Daisy", his stubborn, old, lethargic, uncooperative mule.

In the distance on that brisk April morning, were the higher peaks of the magnificent, majestic Sierras, towering-up into the pale blue sky, with the ice and snow at the glorious summits brilliantly glistening in the early sunlight.

'Instead of No-Man's Land, I consider this canyon One-Man's Land,' resilient William Pocket mused as the ambitious gold prospector casually prepared to venture-out on his daily morning routine excavations. 'I'm bringin' along my pick, my spade, and of course, my indispensable mining pan; that is, right after I make myself some tasty flapjacks, bacon. and beans for breakfast. And then I'm gonna' honor a brainstorm I had in my sleep, and scorch my pan and screen inside the fireplace to make them black, so that the gold dust will stick-out like shining yellow diamonds when I finally make my first big hit. Shit! It's not fuckin' easy bein' a goddamned genius!'

On his standard morning trek upstream, William's path was crossed by several errant butterflies along with three busy honey-bees, and the flying bugs had temporarily annoyed his mobile existence as Bill brushed the flitting insects away from his ears. 'Good thing those son-of-bitches weren't disease carryin' mosquitoes!' the trekker playfully imagined. 'Maybe today's gonna' fuckin' be my big lucky strike! Say, my Viejo Hombre; that name 'lucky strike' wouldn't be a bad title for a new cigarette company back east.'

All in all, the region around the prospector's Sierra Nevada canyon had a somnolent aspect to it, with every part of the physical environment appearing serene and tranquil. But then, during his morning amble, something inordinate caught the wily and paranoid prospector's attention.

'Fresh horse hoof tracks in the mud!' the neurotic old-timer observed and worried. 'Some dumb-ass cuss is snoopin' around here, and I don't like it. I came out to this remote canyon for peace and quiet, and to escape so-called civilization. People are trouble, even though I'm one of them! I have trouble getting-along with myself, let alone meetin' up with some tumbleweed drifter, or some outlaw desperado. Ah shit! There's a buck over on yonder ridge. I shoulda' brought along my rifle and got me some tasty venison for dinner!'

But not remaining pessimistic for long, the elderly gold dreamer resumed his mental reverie. 'Oh well, Bill Pocket. Let's go a-prospectin'. God; I'm sure glad I never got married. Just think how dried-up my wife's cunt-well would be by now, ha, ha, ha! And her flabby tits would be subject to that dead English feller' Newton's law of gravity, too, ha, ha, ha!'

Dandelions, wild roses, and a tangle of dense brush randomly cluttered the trail that paralleled the fast-moving stream. All the while during the remainder of his morning hike, William was concerned about the fresh horse tracks that his eyes had recently discovered only a half mile from his tiny cabin.

Fifteen-minutes later, Bill Pocket stopped and began digging-up some 'creek dirt' to predictably sift through his black-straining screen. After completing the rudimentary task, the un-thwarted searcher was happy to discover that six pieces of gold stood-out against the black background that his fireplace fire had scorched into the utilitarian wood and metal sifter. Feeling energized from his minor discovery, Bill clambered ten-feet up an incline, and tried his mediocre luck again. This time his toil yielded eight tiny amber sparkles, after the accompanying moss and dirt had been finely strained-out of the black background screen.

After each and every dig, the dauntless prospector had to take his pan down to the creek to rinse it with water, and to shake and separate the dirt and the sand from the minuscule gold specks. A third dig had produced twelve small gold particles, and a fourth effort showed sixteen diminutive specimens. 'I think I'm getting closer to discoverin' something big,' Pocket optimistically hypothesized. 'I've always been a trifle superstitious!' But then, an amazing realization flashed into old William's vacillating mind.

'Holy shit! If pumpkins ain't cauliflowers growin' in a goddamned manure patch, then I don't know what the fuck to believe!' the red-bearded man recognized. 'The five holes that I've just dug have formed a W. And W is the first letter of my first name. Now, the W is about three-feet-long and three-feet-high. I know what the fuck I'll do! There're seven letters in the name William, so I'll outline the separate letters with a stick on this gravel ledge. That'll be an asshole distance of twenty-one feet, or so. Then, I'll skip a letter just as if I'm usin' some sort of mountain typewriter, and then draw my last name the same damned way. This is a bizarre idea, but I'll give it a try, anyway."

William laughed in self-amusement, because his many days of frustrating failure simply required some form of mental diversion. 'And my last name Pocket has six letters, so I'll also sketch them out three-feet by three-feet, and then where the T ends at the end, that's where I'll dig a four-feet-deep hole! It's only a dumb-ass hunch, but this activity oughta' get me interested in something different all morning and all afternoon. I mean;' the veteran-at-failure concluded. 'I'm too fuckin' old to be thinkin' about idiotic things such as big plump tits with silver-dollar-sized dark nipples, firm curvaceous asses, and nice hairy wet pink pussies!'

After an hour of diligently mapping-out and roughly drawing the thirteen three-by-three letters to form his full name, and then also including the blank space separating "William" from "Pocket", further pursuing his fanciful hunch, the imaginative-minded prospector started digging his exploratory hole. After four hours (and four feet of industrious excavation) into the six-feet-long and six-feet-wide pit, the transplanted geezer let-out a whoop as his avaricious eyes focused upon several shiny gold nuggets. It appeared that Pocket's fondest dream had finally materialized.

"Sufferin' Sardanopolis with a sprinklin' of sassafras and sarsaparilla on top!" the old codger jubilantly shouted. "Lumps and chunks of it! Fuckin' lumps and chunks of it! Shit! For the first time in ten years, I feel like getting laid."

William held two nuggets in the palm of his callused right hand, and covetously admired the sparkling mineral objects. His heart was wildly palpitating, and his mind was swimming in euphoria. An hour of additional digging brought Bill down to a depth of six-feet, and then the discoverer exclaimed to himself, "Holy cat fish shit! There's gotta' be two- hundred-pounds of marvelous gold embedded in this one wall here, if there's a goddamned single ounce! That vein alone should be worth at least forty-thousand-bucks, and that's a lot of goddamned deer," the ancient prospector giggled to himself, and then ecstatically guffawed with delight.

'I'll separate the main chunks from the vein,' Bill determined. 'Christ! I might just prematurely ejaculate and pop my first load in ten years, because I might've just accidentally discovered a mother lode, ha, ha, ha! I'll go into town and stake my claim tomorrow morning, and then change these yellow pebbles into cash before the son-of-a-bitchin' moochers from Angel's Camp hear about my find and violate this here entire canyon, which I intend to call 'Gold Canyon'. It sure does pay to know how to spell your fuckin' name, yes it does! Ha, ha, ha! Who says that readin', writin' and book-learnin' education aren't vitally important?'

After another arduous hour of assiduous digging, William Pocket perceptively noticed a sinister shadow showing on the west side of his pit, apparently, its source originating from above. Suddenly, the suspicious old-timer's mind started thinking.

'That must be the dirty varmint whose horse tracks I had seen down by the stream,' William rationally theorized under severe emotional duress. 'I gotta' remain composed and collected, or else my fuckin' goose might be cooked. I'll just stay squatted-down here until I figure-out what to do! Of all fuckin' days for a goddamned stranger to show up snoopin' around in this remote canyon!'

William fathomed that eventually he would have to rise-up and confront the anonymous intruder face-to-face. Minutes passed, and still the ominous shadow remained reflected on the pit's west wall. Sweat began cascading down William's back, arms, and legs as the digger pretended to be working while generally acting unaware of the trespasser's encroachment.

‘I could hear the bastard breathing heavily like he’s got some sort of lung malady,’ Bill apprehensively evaluated. ‘This lazy son-of-a-bitch wants to steal my claim. I just sense it! The scoundrel probably wants to kill me to steal my gold-nuggets! What the fuck am I to do?’

Becoming frantic from his escalating paranoia, William Pocket quickly stood-up fully erect, and was promptly greeted with a loud gun blast that singed his left side between his hip and his shoulder. Realizing that his tormentor had the advantage of a handgun, Bill immediately collapsed to the bottom of the hole and played his only viable deck card, ‘the possum’.

Above the pit, a ruthless gunslinger stood holding his revolver and peering-down into the hollow at his evidently dead victim. Bill remained motionless, afraid to move a finger as much as an inch. Then, Pocket’s ears could hear the villain sit-down upon a huge rock, roll a cigarette, and then light a match.

All the while, the wicked intruder sitting above kept his eyes staring down into the six-foot-deep hole. Being convinced that the man in the hole was dead, five minutes later, the vile interloper had his two hands holding on to the top ledge of rocky terrain, while his dangling feet eventually made contact with the earth below, as the malicious encroacher entered the recently-dug hollow.

Bill’s left hand sprang-out like a crab claw, and the desperate old man firmly grasped the intruder’s left ankle. A fierce struggle ensued over possession of the revolver, as Pocket managed to gain his upward balance. Four hands frantically grappled for possession of the muzzle, when the trigger was pulled during the intense struggle, and a bullet ricocheted off the top of the pit, fortunately exiting the hole.

Bill got a leg wrapped around the trespasser’s right knee, and employing all of his strength, flipped the attacker over onto his back, and fortuitously landed on top of him. A second tussle for control of the gun ensued, and the revolver fired a third time, with the errant bullet becoming embedded inside a soft section of dirt.

The beleaguered prospector then employed his savvy, and using his good right hand, Pocket gathered a fistful of gravel and sand, and flung the grit into the assailant’s face, temporarily blinding the accosting maniac. Bill now had control of the handgun inside the limited space, and the frantic victim recklessly fired the remaining three shots into the molester’s side.

The old man slowly ascended from his knees to his feet and uttered, “Slimy skunk son-of-a-bitch! Why the fuck did ya’ have to select me to commit your evil treachery, and way out here in the fuckin' wilderness, too! Serves ya' right; you cheatin,' stealin' killin' bastard! I'm fuckin' glad I had the pleasure of killing your evil ass!"

Bill then stepped to one side, so that the sunlight could shine-down inside the now-gloomy pit. The excavator hunched-over and closely examined the dead man's face. Even though Pocket was half-crying from anger and exhaustion, the elderly gent couldn't help but reflexively let-out an exclamation of astonishment.

"Holy shit in Heaven!" Bill strenuously screamed. "I've just fuckin' killed myself!" Pocket boomed as the exhausted prospector observed a red-bearded face that was the facsimile of his own. "This no-good cock-sucker looks exactly like me! Hey, wait a minute! I know what the hell happened!"

William Pocket had a nefarious twin brother named Samuel, who was a chronic criminal back in Cedar Brook, New Jersey, and who had given the Pocket family a bad name because of a variety of felonies and associated jail terms. The pieces of the jigsaw puzzle had finally come together, and now everything again made vivid sense in William Pocket's mental universe.

'My twin brother Sam's crime record sent Ma and Pa to early graves,' William recollected and lamented. 'It's a good thing that Sam always had poor vision and refused to wear glasses, or else I'd now be a fuckin' dead duck!'

Then, another fascinating speculation entered the fatigued geezer's perplexed and erratic mind. 'So that's how my criminal twin brother found me,' Pocket conjectured. 'Madeline probably told him where I was, and the dirtbag bastard came out here to California to freeload off of me. Sam-the-scam probably thought that I was a lucky stranger, and not his bad-luck brother when the bastard shot me. And thank goodness that the bullet only grazed my left side because of Sam's notorious poor vision.'

The superstitious, God-fearing prospector thought of how he would deal with his dead brother's body, which William Pocket honestly believed was sinfully contaminating his recent gold bonanza. 'I'll go and get a long rope from the cabin, and with lazy Daisy's help, yank the dumb-shit's body out. Then, I'll gather-up all the gold nuggets, and get them up to ground level, too,' Bill soon reckoned he would utilize his problem-solving skills. 'I'll next drop Sam's body down into this hole, which by coincidence is the right depth of a normal cemetery grave. Last but not least, I'll fill the hollow, and then decide how I'm gonna' stake my claim; convert my gold to cash, and finally successfully deposit the loot in the town bank.'

After removing the embedded gold from the tremendous discovery spot, William Pocket sadly buried his diabolical twin brother. Upon scooping the last shovel-full of dirt into the former six-foot by six-foot hollow, the coy prospector's mind formulated a second sensational hypothesis worthy of his next pursuit.

'This very sad day is also my best lucky day ever! Say now,' Bill reckoned and concluded. 'The first name Samuel has one less letter than William has. I'll just sketch-out the son-of-a-bitch's full name 'Samuel Pocket', just to the right side of Sam's hastily-filled grave here, and then dig another six-foot-long and six-feet-wide and six-feet-deep hole, thirty-nine-feet west in the direction of the Pacific. Who the hell knows?' Pocket wondered. 'Who is the cynic that says that thirteen is a goddamned unlucky number? Fuck everybody over there in Angel's Camp! There just might be some platinum or gold thirty-nine feet over to my right, just fuckin' waitin' to be located and dug-up!'

# "The Mexican"

The Junta, consisting of Mexican rebels Paulino Vera, Carlos Arrellano, and Geraldo Ramos were preoccupied conspiring their imminent Mexican Revolution against the corrupt Porfirio Diaz Regime. The three plotters were meeting inside their office headquarters southeast of Los Angeles, where agile bullet evaders were either dodgers or angels. The major objectives of the notorious "Tijuana brass" were twofold: to raise money and donations to finance their planned insurrection, and to recruit willing and able members into their insurrectionist ranks.

One morning, a young, thin, muscular teenager with cold brown eyes stepped into the Junta's L.A. office to join "la revolucion". Immediately, Vera, Arrellano and Ramos became suspicious of "the strange, oddball mercenary," conjecturing that young Felipe Rivera might be *that* dreaded distrustful "double agent" egregiously working for the abusive Porfirio Diaz administration, which the Junta triumvirate instinctively loathed and feared.

And so naturally, caution became the splinter group's watchword in dealing with Felipe Rivera, who definitely had to prove his allegiance to "la revolucion" cause. Paulino Vera competently conducted the final interview of the aspiring applicant, while *his* attractive secretary Maria Torres apathetically took notes whenever *that* particular responsibility was ordered.

"Okay, Senor. You say you desire to be an integral part of the revolution, but first you must prove your damned worth to this noble organization," Paulino Vera prefaced and declared. "Take off your jacket and hang it over there on that hook. In the closet, you'll find a bucket, a mop, a sponge, and some raggedy cloths. First of all, Senor Rivera, the fuckin' floor is dirty, and it urgently needs scrubbing. The same goes for the floors in the two other offices, and the grimy windows and the hundred spittoons need cleaning, too. Now tell me. When the hell are you ready to get started on making your important voluntary contribution to *our* cause?"

"Is all this cleaning to be done for the revolution?" the applicant asked. "I'll do anything for the revolution. Even screw your beautiful, horny secretary if that is necessary!"

Paulino Vera was shocked at 'the impostor's' audacity and brazen attitude, as Maria Torres surreptitiously put the fingers of her left hand under her desk and began slowly massaging her clit' button in rhythmic, methodical masturbation.

Vera quickly regained his composure and yelled at the new candidate, "Get fuckin' started right now, Asshole! You can't charm me as easily as you have adroitly captivated my promiscuous, nymphomaniac secretary!"

Day after day, Felipe loyally performed his myriad janitorial services for the imminent revolution, and especially for the skeptical martinet Junta leaders. Obediently and without protest, Rivera emptied the ashes from the wood stoves; brought-up the kindling and the coal, and lighted the fires to adequately comfort his militant-minded, demanding superiors.

"Now that I'm officially working for the revolution, can I sleep here?" Felipe respectfully asked Paulino Vera.

The Junta head-honcho was wary and suspicious that Felipe Rivera wanted immediate access to the office's secret files and records of all members of the revolution, and its contributors, sympathizers, and supporters. Obviously, that "classified information" was labeled "confidential", and its documentation should never be made available to any agent laboring for the diabolical Porfirio Diaz (and his ten despicable cabinet members).

"You know Senor," the very shrewd Paulino Vera mentioned to the recruit. "Those revolutionaries that are arrested and taken into custody by the United States government are put into irons in federal prisons, and then sent across the border to Mexico to be shot by Diaz's firing squads against adobe walls. It would not be wise for you to sleep in our targeted headquarters; to be apprehended, and then to be wickedly executed! If you want to become a successful revolutionary, you must first learn how not to be a dumb shit!"

The budget of the Junta was meager, and plenty of times a matter of a few-hundred-dollars meant the difference between possible extinction and bankruptcy, or the continuation or discontinuation of operations. Once, when the Junta needed sixty-dollars for stationery and for paper clips, Felipe amazingly laid-down the money on Maria Torres's desk. The horny whore excitedly stood and lifted up her dress, thinking that Felipe had been soliciting her body. But instead, Rivera removed a large flaccid cucumber from his jacket pocket, dropped it upon the secretary's desk, and much to Maria's utter chagrin, marched out of the office to clean the bathroom spittoons.

And when the desperate Junta needed a hundred-dollars for stamps, Felipe Rivera nonchalantly handed the secretary a peculiar-looking vegetable (along with the cash), and laconically declared when Ms. Torres again raised-up her dress exposing her black-hairy pussy, "Here Maria! Why don't you squat on this fuckin' kumquat!

The little runt will do wonders for your cunt!" And when Felipe casually exited the Junta's main office, the lonesome, sex-starved secretary began wildly rubbing her spongy clitoris like there was no tomorrow.

One morning in early May, the Junta leaders met in Paulino Vera's office to discuss and review the performance of newcomer Felipe Rivera, who had just been assigned to clean the yellow-stained urinals and to scrub the cruddy porcelain toilets, and also the residue (both inside and outside) of the metal spittoons, in the co-ed bathroom.

"I still wonder if this jerk-off who calls himself Felipe Rivera is an undercover spy for that lousy dictator, Diaz," Paulino remarked to his two undistinguished colleagues, Carlos Arrellano and Geraldo Ramos.

"Where's that sneaky son-of-a-bitch getting all that fresh money to plunk-down on Maria Torres's desk?" Carlos Arrellano asked his equally-skeptical comrades. "Shit. If I was Felipe Rivera, I'd use the goddamned cash to get blowjobs and hot kinky sex from Maria, which of course, the three of us assholes get any goddamned time we want for free from the sexy, horny harlot!"

"I do not like his ways and means, so that's one committee Felipe will never get to serve on, once the revolution happens," Geraldo Ramos opined and commented. "Senor Rivera looks at us with those cold dark eyes, as if the recruit wants to kill someone with his bare hands, without even using any fuckin' knives or guns! I tell you Paulino and Carlos," Geraldo concluded his narrative. "Felipe Rivera scares the living shit out of me much more than any member of Porfirio Diaz's goon squad secret police does! The guy's even more ruthless-looking than the head of Diaz's crack assassination team; that evil prick bastard having the code name, Gus Stoppo!"

"Felipe has a heinous, nondescript spirit that defies description," Carlos Arrellano cryptically indicated. "That formidable punk shit-head is not human, I tell you hombres. One day, Rivera's not going to put-up with our shit, and the three of us will find ourselves sitting at Satan's table licking *his* evil demons' sweaty, smelly balls."

"I also fear Felipe and think that the name that he gave us is either a fictitious lie or an alias," Geraldo Ramos concurred. "Perhaps the dangerous jerk-off's real name is Anonymous Incognito!"

"Ha, ha, ha! That was quite a dumb-ass funny comment you just made," Paulino Vera commended Ramos. "But believe it or not, I don't think that Felipe is any fuckin' spy. I think the kid's an idealistic, naïve virgin shit-head that's never been fuckin' anything or anywhere, including Maria Torres's constantly pumped pussy. Isn't that right Maria? Ha, ha, ha!"

"Si, Boss," Maria reluctantly answered. "I've been fucked almost as often as your revolution has been! But as far as Felipe Rivera is concerned, he has no heart. And I'm now wondering if he even has a dick! His eyes are as pitiless as cold steel; and as frigid as frozen frost. And I only thought that certain ugly Eskimo and Siberian nuns were *that* friggin' frigid!"

"Felipe might not be the breath of death we all fear after all," Paulino Vera asserted. "The punk might actually be the most patriotic and dedicated rebel of us all. The son-of-a-bitch has an implacable disposition; that's for fuckin' sure. I say let's pretend to trust him and see what the fuck happens next. Quite frankly," Vera expounded. "I'm getting tired of this lowlife, stench-laden office existence, and even the barrel of an executioner's gun seems better than these lackluster, drab, piss-yellow four walls. I say we let Felipe join our illustrious fraternity and then see what the fuck happens."

"Yes," Maria Torres butted-in. "If they take Felipe to the gallows naked, I'll finally see how well he is hung!"

"But where do you suppose the jerk-off gets his money to finance our basic needs, when everything else appears grim?" the befuddled Paulino Vera asked his equally-bewildered colleagues. "Just yesterday Rivera paid a hundred-dollars for *stationery,* when nothing fuckin' ever moves around in this office except the stupid-assed people!"

"We should send a spy out to check on the spy," Carlos Arrellano suggested. "Yes; that will be our new motto! A spy for a spy; a tooth for a tooth! Ha, ha, ha!"

"To be as sure as shit in a large intestine, that young dick-head is a dangerous rattlesnake; a stinging centipede; a venomous insect; probably born under the astrological sign Scorpio," Geraldo Ramos wildly speculated and theorized. "The devious asshole loves no one and hates everybody, including himself. That's what makes this hombre Felipe Rivera the perfect revolutionary! The stubborn fuck can stay focused on committing destruction, and easily accomplish it with fuckin' facility!"

"Quiet!" Paulino Vera exclaimed, covering his lips with his right index finger. "I think I now hear our illustrious patriot coming-down the hallway. Show him your luscious tits, Maria. I just gotta' find-out if Felipe is gay, because confidentially, I've read in certain bordello magazines where the best damned revolutionaries are disenchanted, fucked-up homosexuals!"

* * * * * * * * * * * * * *

The Junta was hard-pressed to raise additional money for operating expenses from its advocates and from its secret funding sources, and the frustrated leadership was now depending on assistance from on-the-lam Mexican fugitives, destitute aliens, and impoverished refugees, who were already donating most of the cash that the subordinates had robbed and pilfered from innocent gringo Americans to subsidize "the cause".

"Across the Rio Grande, Diaz continues to pee on the peons," Paulino Vera complained to Geraldo Ramos and Carlos Arrellano as the junta head honcho pounded his fist upon his termite-infested desk, puncturing the flat surface. "The time is ripe to organize anarchists, socialists, banditos, Mexican exiles, roughnecks, smooth-necks, soldiers of fortune, and soldiers of misfortune alike, along with the flotsam and jetsam scum of the earth. We aren't fuckin' too particular now, are we, men?"

"Not if all three of us keep screwing Maria every single day, even when she's having her period. No Paulino, we aren't particular!" Geraldo Ramos verified.

"And what about our weird recruit Felipe Rivera?" Carlos asked. "What's the latest scoop on him. Is he now working nights in an ice cream parlor?"

"Let's send Felipe to the Rio Grande front, because I think that *that* fucked-up bastard is borderline insane!" exclaimed Paulino, for the expressed amusement of the Junta brass, all three hailing from Tijuana.

"I've heard that even the little dogs over in Chihuahua are barking about the upcoming revolution," Carlos Arrellano laughed, trying to boost the morale of his depressed colleagues. "Hey; I have a terrific ingenious idea. We'll make those dogs over in Chihuahua into our specially trained canine units; that's what the hell we'll do! Ha, ha, ha!"

"But listen, men," Paulino Vera declared in a more-serious tone of speech. "Speaking of Chihuahua, our main financial backer, Jose Amarillo, who incidentally looks a little like a corpulent-mustached armadillo, has been apprehended in Mexico at his hacienda, and shot against his own stable wall. I mean, where the hell is that asshole Pancho Villa when *we* fuckin' need his services to fire back?"

Virile Felipe Rivera then entered the dusty, smoky office, and coughed in response to the heavy dense cigar fumes that were swirling around. "I understand that the revolution needs five-thousand-dollars to continue its vital operations. Well gentlemen," the normally laconic Mexican/American stated. "I think I can get that sum if you three men will give me the go ahead."

"Who the hell are you, Rumpelstiltskin?" Paulino disbelievingly challenged and guffawed. "But if you can spin stray into gold, then let's make hay while the fuckin' sun still shines."

"Order your needed guns and ammunition," Felipe advised the astounded Junta chiefs. "In three-weeks-time, I promise to deliver the five-thousand American dollars. Bring your little ornery donkeys into the office that day and watch me kick some ass!"

"You're fuckin' crazy; loco en la cabeza!" Paulino Vera exclaimed. "Even fuckin' crazier than that totally crazy mother-jumpin' bandito, Pancho Villa!"

"Order the guns and you'll have your dough in three short weeks," Felipe Rivera reiterated. "If you don't order the guns, then I'm dropping out of this wimpy revolution once and for all!"

And with those austere threatening words, Felipe Rivera stepped into the hallway and slammed the door behind him, making its hinges detach from the portal's jamb.

* * * * * * * * * * * * *

A certain dilemma had been furtively concealed from the local Los Angeles sports press that had the potential to explode into an all-out scandal. Boxing promoter Michael Kelly had arranged a bout between Danny Ward, a contender for the lightweight championship of the world, and Billy Carthey, a New York brawler who had been undefeated in a dozen professional fights, accumulating a string of ten consecutive knockouts in his budding career.

The widely-publicized fight had been billed "East Coast versus West Coast", but there was one salient obstacle. The Los Angeles arena had already been sold-out, but Billy Carthey had recently broken a shoulder while sparring for the big match, and a suitable replacement had to be found in a hurry.

"Every decent lightweight from here to Philly' is tied up on the date of the scheduled fight," Michael Kelly lamented to popular trainer Frank Roberts. "You had told me a week or so ago, Frankie, that you've got a little-known lightweight who has won seven matches? Who the hell is he?"

"His name is Felipe Rivera," Frank Roberts firmly answered. "He's a Mexican, and you know how the crowd loves to see Mexicans get viciously pummeled in the ring. The kid's undefeated in small venues around the city, and I've seen this Rivera phenom' beat the crap out of Dusty Morgan, Joey Henderson, and Tommy Jackson. He'll be able to give good old Danny Ward a fair battle from what I've seen of him."

"I think you're full of shit!" Michael Kelly arrogantly assessed. "Danny Ward will put this rookie greenhorn Rivera in the emergency ward midway in the first round. But I'm fuckin' stuck sittin' on top of a saguaro cactus, Frankie; just like a turtle put on a fence post, and I need a viable replacement to get the snoopy reporters off my back. Are ya' sure you can help me out of this ugly mess? Where's the kid now?"

"Waiting impatiently out in the corridor," Frank Roberts replied with a smile. "But I warn you, Mike. Don't judge him by his scrawny, unkempt appearance. I guarantee that the kid won't disappoint you boxing against anyone inside the ring."

"Bring the neophyte in here, and even though it's not Thanksgiving, we'll talk some turkey to the turkey," Kelly commanded his gay male secretary. "Now Frank, Danny Ward's due in my office in fifteen minutes to learn of Carthey's injury, and to be advised about the change in plans. Don't expect Danny to be too fuckin' keen about the new arrangements."

Felipe Rivera was escorted into the promoter's office, and was told to politely sit-down. Hate was evident in the young Mexican's eyes as the prospective boxing challenger malignantly stared at Michael Kelly, who felt rather unpleasantly uneasy at being glared-at by an angry-spirited 'Chico chicano".

"You've got a hell of a nerve thinkin' ya' got a dewdrop's chance in Hades of goin' the distance with a fighter the caliber of Danny Ward," Michael Kelly haughtily chided the young Mexican. "You're gonna' be lookin' at more canvas than that Italian son-of-a-bitch Michelangelo ever did!"

"I can lick Ward," Felipe claimed in a low angry voice.

"Look Nino. I know you can give Danny Ward a blowjob," Mike Kelly reproved and laughed. "But I don't think ya' can whip him in the ring, unless of course you had some miracle whip, ha, ha, ha!"

"Leave the poor kid alone," Frank Roberts implored the influential-but-rude promoter. "I've seen Felipe here put-up some excellent fights, and the kid can box and counterpunch with just about any skilled palooka. Felipe could actually surprise Ward. I'm not sayin' this kid can beat Ward," Frank Roberts revised and clarified his statement. "I'm just sayin' that he's no goddamned flunky. Rivera here is pugnacious, and the boy can throw a haymaker from any standing or crouched position, whether it's a right cross, a left hook, or an uppercut. And besides," the veteran trainer added. "Felipe Rivera here absolutely hates gringos. And Mike. You can play-up the ethnic clash thing from that interestin' Mexican versus American angle. The bloodthirsty white crowd will eat it up like filet mignon!"

"Never mind the exaggerated hype bullshit!" Michael Kelly vehemently admonished the very reputable Frank Roberts. "That's *my* job! You've been trainin' and conditionin' fighters in your gym' for over twenty years, and I fuckin' trust your sound judgment. I know you haven't brought me a sheep that punches like an old bag nanny goat. What makes Rivera here tick?" Kelly rhetorically asked. "I'm askin' you *that* pertinent question, Frankie, because the surly little bastard sittin' right next to you apparently refuses to talk to me!"

"Felipe's hung around the gym', and truthfully, wasn't makin' too much progress until around four months ago," Frank Roberts noted and explained. "Then all of a sudden, a fire lit-up inside his heart, and the kid claimed he needed money. So, Rivera here began knockin' the best boxers that frequent my place around pretty damned good, until he's earned the right to be sittin' here in your office. Don't jump to conclusions, Mike! It's called 'Opportunity and Need', my Friend, and it's your need and his opportunity. That's all the hell I'm sayin'!"

Good looking and garrulous, big-mouthed Danny Ward entered the promoter's office without even knocking on the door, and "Iron Mike" Kelly introduced the flamboyant fighter to Frank Roberts. Meanwhile, Kelly's gay male secretary began scribbling-down notes.

"So, this is the scumbag I'm gonna' fight as Billy Carthey's substitute," the obnoxious, cocky lightweight stated. "I heard all about Billy's broken arm over at the corner pool hall and betting parlor across the street, so word travels fast. You ain't expectin' me to fight a deaf mute, are ya'?" Danny facetiously asked Kelly as Ward pointed at and tried to intimidate 'callow' Felipe Rivera. "This pathetic Mex' with the big chip on his shoulder doesn't seem to know five words of English; either goddamned curse words, or fuckin' otherwise!"

"Don't underestimate Felipe, here!" Frank Roberts cautioned Ward. "I've seen him throw flurries as if he's pretendin' he's a damned blizzard. This kid ain't no length of straw to snap in half. He's got some ring talent, and is capable of producin' a haymaker if ya' take him too lightly."

"Enough of the small stuff bullshit!" Danny Ward arrogantly yelled at Kelly and Roberts. "Let's get down to brass tacks, and forget the brass knuckles for a minute. According to the original contract, I get sixty-five percent of the gate take, right?"

"That's right!" Mike Kelly confirmed. "But not the gross receipts! You'll get sixty-five percent of the *net* after administrative costs and managers' commissions are deducted."

"Well now," Danny Ward qualified. "In that experienced Billy Carthey is no longer available, and I gotta' fight this dirt bag punk Mexican upstart here, I now want eighty-five percent of the net. The old deal's null and void, because now that Carthey has backed-out of the contest, I'm now fuckin' boxin' a relative nobody, who nobody wants to be *his* goddamned relative!"

"How much is eighty percent of the gate?" Felipe curiously asked, breaking his fifteen-minute abstinence from speaking.

"Around nine-to-ten thousand bucks, after expenses, includin' my standard promotional fees," Kelly wonderingly explained. "Yeah, around nine-to-ten thou'!"

"I don't like the terms," Felipe brazenly insisted. "I say if we're gonna' fight, it oughta' be winner take all!"

"Look Chico, are you fuckin' nuts?" Danny Ward verbally exploded before promoter Mike Kelly could beat him to the punch. "Now you've really pissed me off, and I'm gonna' make sure you're gonna' receive the beatin' of your life!"

"I can defeat you!" Felipe audaciously uttered in a low, somber tone of voice. "If you're so sure that I don't stand a chance, why not accept my winner take all offer? My fifteen or twenty percent ought to be a piece of cake for you!"

"Arrogant greaser son-of-a-bitch, ain't he?" Danny accused and evaluated. "Look here, you spic fool! You're fuckin' nobody with a chance of fightin' the next lightweight champion of the world!"

"Danny's right!" Mike Kelly concurred, while glancing over at Felipe Rivera. "Nobody ever heard of you, Punk, outside of Los Angeles, and come to think of it, few L.A. people besides Frank Roberts here ever fuckin' heard of you, either! Ya' have no fuckin' reputation around town, either good or bad!"

"It is a winner take all match, or find somebody else to fight this Irish gringo!" Felipe repeated. "I'll beat him like he was an egg yolk!"

"Okay, you little Mex' prick!" Danny Ward agreed. "My manager is out of town and due in L.A. tonight, so I'm gonna' make the no-brainer decision all on my own. I don't give a shit about winnin' a hundred percent of the net. I'm goin' to administer to you the most fuckin' agony that you've ever experienced in your lousy, short life!"

"Let's draw-up the papers that spell-out the exact terms," Mike Kelly yelled-over to his faggot male recording secretary, sitting in the office's far right corner. "This has gotta' be the most interestin' bout that I've ever fuckin' promoted!"

* * * * * * * * * * * * *

On the night of the hastily-arranged boxing match, no one sitting in the packed arena audience seemed to notice or care when the underdog Felipe Rivera had ducked his head and body through the ropes, and adroitly entered the ring. The rambunctious crowd was anticipating the arrival of the prima donna 7-to-1 odds' favorite Danny Ward. Felipe quickly sat-down upon his three-pronged stool in his corner, waiting for his conceited opponent to make his grand entrance.

"Now Kid, ya' gotta; be careful," the challenger's appointed second Spider Hagerty advised. "Kelly wants this thing to last as long as possible, so keep your guard-up, and absorb some punishment. Take a beatin' and earn your dough, which I've heard ya' already relinquished by making an outrageous proposal that the winner should take the whole pot. If ya' go-down too early," Spider warned, "the lousy newspapers will destroy the fight game in L.A. for the next ten years!"

"Where's Ward?" Felipe asked, squirming upon his stool. "Is he constipated or something?"

"It's an old trick veteran boxers like to use. He's makin' you wait to make ya' anxious and worried," Spider informed his fighter. "He's also getting the crowd worked-up for his grand appearance. Expect to fuckin' wait at least ten-minutes, so try your best to relax. Why don't ya' try farting? It'll make ya' feel better to release some excess gas."

Fifteen minutes later, a loud roar, sounding like a rumble of thunder, rolled through the filled-to-capacity arena. An entourage of trainers, handlers and cut-men escorted the ostentatious Danny Ward into the ring. The famous pugilist held his arms above his head in mock victory, as the cocky competitor obviously savored the abundant adulation and accolades of the cheering crowd.

"No use getting scared now!" Spider Hagerty instructed the determined underdog. "He's gonna' play his reputation and ego."

To further demonstrate his fearless audacity, Ward trotted over to Felipe Rivera's corner and said to his rival still sitting on his three-legged chair, "You little Mexican rat! I'll beat the yellow piss and brown shit out of ya' before the night is through!"

The referee signaled for the fighters and their handlers to come to the center of the ring and receive the perfunctory general rules' review. The modern-day gladiators then routinely returned to their respective corners to listen for the opening bell.

The gong sounded, and the boxers met in the ring's center and touched gloves. Exhibiting great stamina and skill, Danny Ward bombarded his foe with a series of savage right and left combinations, and the incredible barrage continued for two whole minutes. The enthusiastic, exuberant crowd became antagonistic to the challenger, because it appeared that the youngster was not showing any serious offense to counter his adversary's wicked aggression. But few spectators seated in the gallery noticed that Felipe was *not* breathing heavily, thus employing his clever strategy of making the favorite expend as much energy and stamina as possible, and simultaneously, becoming overconfident about his opponent's lack of prowess.

And then, at the two-and-a-half-minute mark of the three-minute round, Felipe unleashed a crushing overhand right that stunned the pretentious veteran, sending him sprawling onto the white canvas. The shocked audience watched nervously as the referee deliberately wasted time pointing and then walking Felipe to a neutral corner, giving the floored favorite a chance to recover from his grogginess. The count commenced, and when the ref' got to nine, Ward was able to dizzily stand-up on his wobbly feet, precisely when the gong sounded, dramatically ending the first round.

"I told you the Mex' was a decent two-handed puncher," Frank Roberts told the now-paranoid Mike Kelly. "The kid's no charlatan by any stretch of the imagination. That was no damned lucky punch we just witnessed. I assure you, Mike. It wasn't!"

"Look Frankie, baby," Iron Mike anxiously replied. "I've got thousands riding on Ward in this fight; bet with hundreds of bookies from coast-to-coast. You go tell the skinny Mex to go easy for a while, and take a poundin' the next eight rounds. Then if the son-of-a-bitch has anything left in his arsenal," Kelly ordered Roberts, "the Mex' can use whatever he's got left in the tenth. But if everything goes right, Danny will have adequately recovered, and Rivera will have been knocked unconscious before any damned last round ever happens!"

Frank Roberts delivered Iron Mike's imperative message to the challenger's handlers. For the next eight rounds Felipe Rivera honored Mike Kelly's imperial command and took an awful pummeling, but still, the courageous underdog had the fortitude to persevere into the tenth. If nothing else, Felipe Rivera had earned the respect of one Danny Ward, who had underestimated the kid's wherewithal, guile, and creativity, not to mention his devastating overhand right.

The bell rang for the final round, with the fatigued boxers touching gloves in the center of the ring, and with the capacity crowd all standing on their feet, expecting a dynamic and explosive conclusion to the highly-exciting event.

Just like in the first round, Danny Ward was expending all of his energy, endeavoring to pulverize and subsequently knock-out his valiant antagonist. Throughout the grueling bout, Ward had verbally belittled and berated the resilient Mexican during each and every clinch. And for the remainder of the fight, Danny Ward was keenly aware of the kid's overhand right that had decked him to the mat in the first round. Two minutes had elapsed into the tenth, and Felipe Rivera had absorbed all of the hostility and ferocity that Danny Ward's enviable skill could muster; all without uttering a word through his mouthpiece, or even throwing a retaliatory punch.

Ward tried to head-butt the gutsy challenger, but Felipe was expecting that dirty tactic, and blasted the aspiring champion with a right uppercut that sent the favorite falling like a boulder onto the canvas. Again, the perplexed referee deliberately stalled for time as the official unnecessarily and intentionally guided Rivera to a neutral corner, and then slowly returned to center ring, to initiate his animated count to ten; hoping that the timing bell would soon again sound.

Just when it was plain that the count of "ten" would be reached prior to the final bell, a fat police captain (at Mike Kelly's request) climbed- up to the ropes, intending to stop the fight, and have the referee declare Danny Ward the winner on a technicality; "An illegal rabbit punch."

But the bell sounded, and observing the high-ranking cop attempting to get between the second and third ropes, Felipe ambled-over and clobbered the fat officer directly on the jaw, sending the man-in-blue plummeting onto the auditorium's cement floor; thus enacting *his* own sense of ring justice while the agitated crowd gasped and jeered.

No words of congratulations were forthcoming from Danny Ward's handlers as the three astounded men anxiously tried reviving their spoiled boxer, and Mike Kelly gave Frank Roberts a very dirty sneer, and then lividly stepped into the jammed aisle, and with his head crestfallen, meandered all the way up the metal stairs to his remote second-floor office, with the intention of lifting his spirits by getting a good blowjob from his gay secretary.

As the referee reluctantly held Felipe's gloved right hand up to tacitly communicate the Mexican's triumph, young Rivera had random sensational thoughts floating around inside his head.

'Paulino, Carlos, and Geraldo will definitely know how I earn money to finance their Junta when they read tomorrow morning's newspaper,' Felipe reckoned as the victor faced the booing crowd of gringos. 'Maybe I should change my boxing name to 'Anonymous Incognito' as Geraldo Ramos thinks I should be called. Anyway,' the bruised, bashed and battered winner thought. 'I sacrificed and gave everything I had, and everything I could endure, for the cause. Fuck Porfirio Diaz! Viva la revolucion!'

## “The White Silence”

“That spoiled dog Carmen won’t last more than a couple of more days,” Mason hollered to the Malemute Kid. The disgusted man then placed the dog’s left front paw into *his* mouth, and bit-off a chunk of ice that had been embedded between the husky’s toe pads. And next, Mason proceeded to ruefully spit-out the solid matter from his dry mouth. “Never in my life have I ever seen a dog with a high-falutin’ name like Carmen that was worth its weight in chow beans.”

“Carmen sounds like a fancy foreign opera to me, instead of a powerful Alaskan dog!” the Malemute Kid answered and laughed. “But that dog’s loud bark is far from bein’ the sound of a female soprano. I wonder if Carmen can sing the *Marriage of Figaro* and the *Barber of Seville,* too. Ya’ know, Mason. I’ve always enjoyed those handsome opera fellas’ with the loud vocal cords cavortin’ around the stage in those really tight leotards.”

“Sled dogs like this Carmen just lose stamina over the long haul, and fade-away and die under the responsibility of serving their master,” Mason pessimistically continued his negative analysis, while ignoring his companion’s witty remarks pertaining to opera. “Did ya’ ever hear a dog with a sensible name like Cassiar, Siwash, Yukon, or Klondike go wrong and let ya’ down? No sir Malemute! Take a serious gander at Shookum here, he’s….”

The lean brute lashed its mouth-up, flashing its sharp white teeth and nearly decapitated Mason at the throat. But Shookum was immediately disciplined with a stout clout behind the ear that Mason administered, using his indispensable dog whip, which sent the uncooperative-temperamental animal sprawling onto the snow with a yellow slaver dripping from its ferocious fangs. Mason seemed unfazed from his near-death encounter.

“As I was saying Malemute, Shookum here’s got the survival instinct and spirit that *that* prima-donna diva Carmen lacks. Bet Shookum eats Carmen before the week’s finished, because it’s not gonna’ be the other way around.”

“I’ll take your lousy prediction one step further,” the Malemute Kid answered as the listener reversed the thawing loaf of frozen bread that had been placed before the fire. “I’ll wager that we’ll be eatin’ Shookum before the week’s expired; that is to say, a few days after hungry Shookum has consumed Carmen for dinner. What do ya’ say about that Ruth?”

The Indian woman, Ruth, who was Mason's dedicated and devoted wife, was often just as reticent and laconic as the Malemute Kid's twin brother back in Dawson, the Deafmute Kid. The woman gave no reply as she respectfully settled the pot of coffee on a plate platform situated above the fire. Ruth, who was far from ruthless, realized that the party had to travel two-hundred more miles in six days with a limited food supply, and that most of their emaciated sled dogs would not survive the grueling journey, mostly suffering from a lack of nutrition.

Out of necessity, Mason, the Malemute Kid, and Ruth grimly huddled around the meager fire with scant grub to eat, as the hostile dogs lay in their harnesses during the standard midday halt, and jealously watched the humans swallowing-down each mouth-watering food morsel.

"No more midday lunches after today," the Malemute Kid objectively commented. "And the dogs are becomin' more envious and vicious every time we have a poor man's meal. They'd have any one of us for dinner if one of us falters. Be sure to be on your guard at all times around these famished canines."

"Thank God we'll still have some tea to drink once the coffee runs out!" Mason realistically replied. "Don't worry Ruth! Ya' won't be wearin' those flimsy deerskin moccasins much longer! And once we reach our final destination, we'll be back in civilization again, and wish the hell we were returnin' here to the frozen wilderness to repeat starvin' to death."

The Indian woman possessed great love for her handsome white lord and master. And in fact, Mason was the first white man Ruth had ever seen. But more importantly, the garrulous American was the first man that had ever treated her as if she were more than mere property, or a stubborn beast of burden, although "the ugly squaw" actually looked a little like a Colombian donkey.

"Yes Ruth," Mason continued his prattling jargon, pretending that Ruth was fathoming every single word. "Once we reach the Outside Territory, we'll take the White Man's canoe and paddle-down to the Salt Water Flats. Yes," Mason fantasized and articulated. "There'll be bad water, yes, rough water, with many great mountains; forty days of sleep and no sex until we finally get there. And when we arrive, there'll be huge wigwams three-trees-high in a great village where the hungry giant mosquitoes bite each other, and remarkably, leave people, both men and women the fuck alone."

The Malemute Kid smiled upon hearing Mason's gross exaggeration, but Ruth just obediently sat there with a broad, simple smile upon her countenance, believing that her often-facetious husband had stated something grand and spectacular, although she understood less-than-half of his statement. Mason's apparent jocularity (in any language) was magical medicine for Ruth's tortured heart, which had only known misery and abuse ever since her early childhood days in the formidable North Country.

Then, just as Mason was about to whimsically invent another fanciful fairy tale involving Ruth and him, the dogs began snarling and biting each other, and the men had to separate the restless beasts and calm them down, before lashing the famished animals to the nearby sleds, and then courageously venturing-out once again onto the extremely-inhospitable snow trail.

* * * * * * * * * * * * *

"Mush! Mush-on, Baldy! Mush-on, Scarface!" Mason loudly yelled as the sled driver deftly worked his whip, and the affected dogs barked beneath his emphatic shouting. Ruth followed with the second team, and the Malemute Kid, who had helped the Indian woman get started and to set-out, trailed behind with the third. Unlike Mason, Malemute was strong and brave, and treated his temperamental animals gently, refusing to beat them. But instead, "the Kid" felt sympathy for the dogs' unenviable plight and labor.

"Come-on there; mush without you male and females getting too mushy," Malemute uttered and chuckled. "This ain't Santa's sleigh you're fuckin' pullin'. Mush-on now, you poor, sore-footed brutes, or else I'll get tired of literally killin' your pathetic asses with kindness! This Northland Trail ain't exactly Times Square that *that* storyteller Mason always fuckin' brags about at each campfire!"

A distance of forty sleeps is a distance that Ruth's native gods would surely envy. "Holy shit!" the quixotic Malemute Kid hypothesized and habitually said to his dog team, who only cared about their next breaths. "If those idols really are gods that Ruth's people tote around on those Totem Poles, they'd be immortal and invincible. Why the hell do immortal gods anywhere, in any religion, get tired and ever have to rest or sleep even a wink?"

The White Silence of the North Country had eventually descended upon and enveloped the three dog sled teams, along with their beleaguered riders. Any man or woman trapped within the general icy allure quickly realizes how diminutive and insignificant he or she really is in the grand scheme of things.

The dull-gray sky is vast and clear, the wind is chilled and cold, and the alien earth is quite frozen and terrifying. The entire Arctic world seems dead, except for the tired dogs and their fatigued masters. The traveler is suddenly reduced to the size and function of a maggot; fearful of disaster; fearful of death; fearful of one fatal mistake, and finally, fearful of meeting the Immortal Creator face-to-face. Truly, the three humans were trespassing into God's dreadful, isolated domain, and to their most-secret apprehensions, their souls were entirely at His Divine Mercy.

Days passed without major incident, and a great bend was soon evident in the river. So, Mason led his team to a cutoff across a narrow stretch of barren land. But the exhausted dogs balked and barked, demonstrating their vociferous protest to such a rigorous bank that the exploited animals had been assigned to ascend.

The demoralized creatures toiled and gasped, exerting their last strength to honor Mason's outrageous commands and demands. The rebellious pack leader, Carmen, swung to the right, and Mason's snowshoes were compromised with the surprised driver flying-off his rig with the sled then toppling over onto him. Within three seconds, everything stored aboard the sled obeyed gravity and slid downhill.

Mason rose to his feet and began wildly whipping the lead dog. "You fuckin' brute! You almost killed me, Carmen, with your fuckin' disloyalty! Obey my damned easy commands, do you hear? Obey my fuckin' easy commands!"

"Don't Mason!" the Malemute Kid entreated. "The poor creature is on its last legs! Tell ya' what I'm gonna' do. We'll perform a little switcheroo! I'll attach my dogs to your sled, and maybe they'll be able to pull ya' over the rise."

Indeed, Carmen had been the defiant offender who had violated Mason's directives, and the beaten and bleeding animal rolled-over onto its side, weakened, and piteously crying and whimpering while breathing heavily and being near "the death zone". If Carmen couldn't regain strength and make it to nightly camp, then the animal would be shot, killed, and devoured as nutritious food, unless an itinerant moose or antelope should lope across the path of the desperate human travelers, and be shot and eaten, instead.

After managing to get over the difficult rise with the fresher dogs, Mason stopped and waited for the two trailing teams and their harrowed riders to re-join him. During his pause, the cruel sled-master reached-down to adjust his snowshoe, with his movements taking place underneath a giant pine that had been weighted-down with heavy snow and ice. A large branch unexpectedly snapped-off and descended upon the already-encumbered man, who was immediately smitten and trapped beneath the burden of the heavy, snow-laden object.

The intrepid and alert Malemute Kid sprang into action, instantly leaping from his sled with his trusty ax in hand, and upon reaching the tragic scene, then diligently chopping away to free his special friend from his trapped situation beneath the fallen pine rubble. Ruth dutifully tried pulling apart the myriad branches and twigs, as Malemute continued hacking-away with his characteristic vocal "Huh!" being exclaimed with each successive downward swipe. Little was said as "the Kid" gradually managed to drag Mason's limp body from the cumbersome coniferous pile.

Since the temperature was an abominable sixty-five degrees below zero, time was at the essence. A roaring fire was anxiously built from the fragmented fallen pine tree limb debris, and Mason was gently rolled in furs and blankets to insulate him from the lethal freezing temperature, which would easily turn any Eskimo's limp brittle frosty dingle into a drooping icicle, if the delicate organ had been exposed to the harsh elements for over thirty seconds.

But a cursory inspection of Mason's injuries revealed to the Kid that the victim had been severely crushed, and had suffered a broken arm and leg. Also quite apparent was the fact that Mason's limbs were evidently paralyzed. An occasional moan was the troubled man's only sign of life.

"No more ravings of Southern Tennessee swimming holes, coon hunts, moonshine whiskey, and watermelon raids," Malemute (to no avail) told Ruth, who was still trying to comprehend the emotional impact of her husband's prescribed-by-accident fate. And in the morning, just after dawn, the Kid bent-over Mason to listen for any faint whispers of instruction being uttered from the dying man's pallid-looking lips.

"Remember Kid; four years ago, when we were on the Tanana," Mason coughed-out. "I didn't care too much for Ruth then, except that her face was pretty ugly like it belonged to a retarded jackass. But Ruth's been a good wife to me, and a very good trader, too," Mason managed to declare and praise. "Too bad the no-speaky-the-English Indian bitch can't *trade* places with me right now."

"Conserve your limited energy, Mason!" Malemute urged his hurting friend. "Stop actin' like you're dyin' to get out of this here life! Severe pain now might be much better than a possible black *nothingness* that's awaiting you!"

"Don't send her back to her people, Kid, if I should happen to die," Mason requested and then coughed. "Ruth's been eatin' bacon and beans for nearly four years now. She'll never adjust to goin' back to fish and caribou again."

"Please Mason, shut the hell up, will ya'!" the Malemute Kid exclaimed as he held-up his friend's head. "Conserve your energy! You're fuckin' getting on my nerves with all of your nonsensical, sentimental bullshit! Cut-out the stupid emotional and nostalgic crap, I say!"

"Her people's ways are primitive, Kid, and now Ruth's entitled to live a decent life in *our* so-called advanced civilization," Mason spouted-out. "If I die, promise me you'll marry Ruth and send her back to the States, along with your own stupid Alaskan ass!"

"Mason! Shut the fuck up, or else you're gonna' be left out here to perish and be eaten by the don't-give-a-shit hungry wolves!" Malemute Kid warned. "There's only so much of your dumb-ass shit my ears can stand listenin' to, even if ya' *are* fuckin' dyin'!"

"If I die, Kid, sell all my precious furs," Mason mumbled and insisted. "They'll fetch a handsome price at any market! And if you and Ruth have any children, once you get to livin' back in the States, please make sure that the little bastards and bitches never return up here to this atrocious Eskimo country!"

"You can't govern the rest of my life!" the Malemute Kid adamantly objected. "I'm an unhappy, sex-starved faggot livin' up here in these terrific gay '90s, and I don't want any fuckin' wives, kids, or family responsibilities to make me even more unhappy than I already am. If I was a knife, I'd be a goddamned gay blade, yes I would."

"In four days, I reckon that I should be dead!" Mason declared and prognosticated. "You can't deny a dyin' man his last desired wishes, can you Kid?"

"Look Asshole," Malemute angrily replied. "I'm gonna' make sure that you live through this dreadful dilemma, so that I don't have a grotesque future with an ugly wife, bratty kids, and an unwanted family environment imposed upon my ass. Just give me those four days ya' promised, so that I can rehabilitate ya', so that I'm not stuck with Ruth and your goddamned asshole last rites' requests. I'll sneak into the forest and try to kill an unwary moose, if its precious meat will see us through this fucked-up crisis!"

"One pull of your trigger should send me speeding into the afterlife!" Mason insisted. "Now send Ruth over here, so that I could say 'goodbye' to my wife, should I soon expire while you're out there killin' your imaginary moose that's guaranteed to be an illusion. And Kid," Mason further stipulated. "If I should die in the meantime, kindly shoot Carmen in the head, so that I'll have a companion-dog in the *hereafter.* Then, good old Carmen and me can figure-out what we're here after and ultimately, what we're there after in the hereafter."

"You're a crazy Fool, even when you're close to death!" Malemute muttered and complained. And then, the on-a-mission Kid escorted Ruth to be close by her husband's side, while Malemute momentarily grieved that he had always wished to have a homosexual relationship with Mason. An hour later, no itinerant moose had been located in the forest, and the discouraged hunter quickly returned from the pine tree clusters to the makeshift camp, after Malemute's ears heard the dogs howling, and normally tranquil Ruth screaming and wailing.

The aroused beasts had attacked the grub cache, and Ruth had been bravely fending them off with Mason's ax. Malemute rushed and arrived on the scene, and smashed his rifle butt against the heads of several vicious growling huskies. And frightened Ruth also dented several canine noggins with her elevated ax handle, too, as humans and beasts dramatically battled for supremacy and dominance. Finally, the defeated, still-harnessed huskies retreated to their respective sleds, licking their wounds and bitterly announcing their agony to the stars.

During their feeding frenzy, the excited dogs had devoured the entire stock of salmon, not caring one iota about contracting salmonella poisoning. And now, only five pounds of flour remained to tide the entire traveling party over the most challenging last miles of travail.

Ruth ambled over to comfort her ailing husband, while the valiant Malemute Kid sliced-up the warm body of a recently deceased dog, whose head and butt had been crushed by the Kid's rifle butt.

'I'll shoot Carmen in the head if and when Mason dies,' the gay fellow thought and concluded. 'I can't explain it. But I feel like I have to honor Mason's last dyin' request, no matter how fucked-up and how illogical his bullshit all seems to be!'

* * * * * * * * * * * * *

Renewed obstacles accompanied the following morning's sun, as the dogs were impulsively turning-onto each other, even though it was six months past the dog days of summer, and despite the fact that there were plenty of trees to be barking-up besides the wrong ones. Carmen still clung to her slender thread of life, and was savagely attacked by her furry peer mates, tearing the vulnerable husky to shreds and killing her within seconds and gobbling up her remains: bones, kidneys, ovaries, and all within one minute. The carnivorous pack refused to scatter until the last wretched remnants of Carmen's flesh, blood, and hide had been consumed.

Meanwhile, the all-too-patient and benevolent Malemute Kid listened to Mason's incessant jabbering in *his* semi-conscious state, rambling on about Tennessee, and the great bourbon whiskey that was illegally manufactured there up in the Appalachian Mountains. Next, Mason's confused mind imagined that the dying adventurer was a country parson preaching to hick hillbillies about the medicinal benefit of drinking a gallon-and-a-half of piss-tasting moonshine every day, and then repenting about their reprehensible drunken sinfulness.

Ruth solemnly watched as Malemute almost ritualistically prepared a cache similar to ones often used by frontier hunters to preserve their recently-butchered fresh meat from wolves and wild dogs. The Kid carefully and methodically bent two small pine trees towards each other, stretching the separate objects nearly to the ground. Next, the survivalist systematically and adroitly fastened the two trees with moose-hide thongs, making a suitable catapult to sling and fling a human body into the air.

And then much to Ruth's utter shock, Malemute tied her to several loose furs, bound her feet together with the remaining moose-hide cords, and next pushed her bound body upon the rigged cache catapult. And then with one wicked slash of his sharp knife (and without uttering a remorseful syllable or phrase), the cunning, goal-oriented Kid cut the binding cords, sending Ruth screaming her last words while simultaneously zooming high into the air and disappearing completely out of sight.

'I think that Mason's gonna' make it through his ordeal with some of my tender loving care, providing him with the emotional strength that he needs,' the homosexually-motivated, muscular asshole reasoned. 'Basically, it all came down to a simple choice between marryin' that fat-faced, ugly heterosexual Indian bitch, or linkin'-up with my favorite main man, Mason, whom I've adored and idolized ever since I had made his acquaintance. When Mason recovers,' the Malemute Kid scrupulously reckoned, 'we'll live together happily-ever-after in a civil union, and he can suck me off each and every morning, noon, and night; even if he's paralyzed from the waist-down for the rest of his goddamned life. And even if my hero loses all his teeth, his soft wonderful gums will no doubt still be workable!'

Then, the sex-starved Malemute Kid gently placed Mason into *his* sled, chose the best and strongest dogs among the three teams to pull the rig, covered Mason up in warm furs and blankets, shot three dogs for necessary spare meat to survive the remainder of the trip, and anxiously grabbed the gee pole. Soon, Malemute was "mushing" the sled along the seldom-traveled trail, as Mason slowly fell into a coma, not realizing that he was being kidnapped and being held hostage by a raving gay maniac that finally came-out of the closet in the middle of the Klondike, where there aren't any goddamned closets, or too many horny faggots around, either.

It is not pleasant being alone wandering about in the White Silence of the North Country. The snow-covered, God-forsaken, physical landscape is both pitiless and inclement. 'Maybe if Carmen is truly a lesbian dog as I had always suspected,' the Malemute Kid considered as his sled sped onward toward the white man's civilization, 'then perhaps Ruth and that wimpy dog can have a viable budding gay relationship in that legendary Faggot Kingdom in the Sky! Oh well, I'll have my faggot gay experience right here on good old Mother Earth, just in case that Faggot Kingdom in the Sky turns-out to be a big mythological bust!'

## “The Wisdom of the Trail”

Sitka Charley was one of the few northern Indians to be successfully assimilated into the white man’s culture. Other Canadian Indians knew the knowledge of memorizing the trail, but only *he* had mastered the white man’s wisdom and laws, and was able to incorporate the diverse entities into his own frame of reference. From his boyhood years, Sitka Charley had loyally associated with the civilized white man, and had gained an ample appreciation of the basic European concepts, technology, and traditions, which Sitka Charley evaluated as being superior to the primitive ancient Indian customs and rudimentary “shaman medicine man science”.

This is what Sitka Charley comprehended about the white man’s unique perception of things. The newly arrived pioneers to the area apparently valued each other’s lives; often helped each other through calamities and difficulties, and the extraordinary women of the species were incredibly emancipated and independent. And unlike subordinate squaws scattered throughout the valley, the Caucasian females defended their own rights and were willing to tenaciously fight for sexual equality.

And because of his dedicated adoption of, and allegiance to, the white man’s intelligent ways, Sitka Charley developed a certain condescending contempt for his own dark-skinned people’s male-dominated, chauvinistic culture, and the converted native especially despised Kah-Chucte and Gowhee, who in return, both feared and loathed their “changed” Indian comrade. The two old Indians were adamant in their beliefs, but over the years, suffered much hunger and desperation by clinging to their antiquated methods and customs.

Conversely, Sitka Charley vastly distrusted Kah-Chucte and Gowhee, and this is why the young Indian had sagaciously confiscated their rifles ten days before, leaving only Sitka’s gun, along with the soon arriving Captain Ellington’s rifle, as the only remaining visible ones in the mobile camp. From his many white tutors, over the years, the wily guide had proficiently learned how to be a competent leader and an austere disciplinarian.

“Come on you two lazy Nincompoops; get a decent fire going,” Sitka Charley commanded Kah-Chucte and Gowhee in their native tongue. “You’re basically what the white men call Neanderthals, which loosely translated into our language, means something akin to being ‘prehistoric assholes’!”

"Fuck you!" Kah-Chucte answered as the old codger obediently gathered precious dry branches and dry birch wood to fuel the flames. "My back aches from stooping over so often like a squaw woman should be doing, and my wrinkled ass hurts from repeatedly falling on it, because I lack the energy from suffering because of poor nutrition. And why the hell should Gowhee and I listen to your polar-bear-shit, you arrogant young upstart!"

"Kah-Chucte and I are both weak and tired from being exploited by you and your arrogant white bosses," Gowhee agreed. "Feed us more food, and we'll work harder for you. You seem to honor the white man more than you respect your own people, especially your elders. Here is my curse to you, Sitka Charley. May your testicles and your asshole fall-off, and instantly appear carved-onto the tribal shaman's wooden totem pole!"

"Learn and appreciate the white man's ways and laws, and stop thinking and behaving like stupid-assed Indian jerk-offs!" Sitka Charley remarked. "I'm glad I no longer think like you two narrow-minded shit-heads do. You two asshole clowns have to learn how to think inside the house, but before you can accomplish *that* high level, you must first think outside the fucked-up igloo! Look at my feet: I wear warm boots. Look at yours: you still wear thin moose-hide moccasins. Now tell me, dumb-fucks; which fuckin' feet and toes do you think are warmer? Mine or yours?"

While the two elderly Indians attended to their need to get warm, Sitka Charley surveyed the campsite to ascertain that the tents had been properly installed and anchored, and that the weapons and ammunition were safe from being pilfered. Then, Sitka perceptively noticed a group of travelers approaching from the northeast; two more elderly Indians, along with Captain Ellington and his beautiful wife.

At first, a month before, the alert scout and guide didn't want to offer his services to the pair of white trekkers, because Sitka had a stereotype in his head that Caucasian women were soft, tender, and fragile, and could not endure difficult Yukon travel or temperatures. But Mrs. Ellington was quite different from the generalization that the guide's mind had en*gender*ed. The lady was brave, strong-willed, liberated, and the woman didn't take any crap from anyone.

'Holy seal shit!' Sitka Charley thought. 'I'd love to sleep with a gorgeous blonde woman like Mrs. Ellington. Her shape is nice and curvaceous; her teeth are pearly white, and her tits are large and hard. Why the fuck did I have to born a scumbag Indian like these old asshole companions?'

And Charley could not comprehend why the children of soft, tender, white-skinned women could grow to become courageous and powerful; and could conquer the area Indian tribes; and could admirably invent and control great machines and weapons. But certainly, Mrs. Ellington was tougher than most other females of her Caucasian breed, and Sitka knew that the gorgeous lady could easily beat the feces out of the four older Indians one at a time, and that she might even be able to wrestle *him* to the ground in an out-and-out four-fisted brawl.

And that cold autumnal night, after Mrs. Ellington had serenaded her fellow travelers by singing and playing her guitar, the American female demanded equal food for supper, and at the campfire, she had the strange audacity to protest the four elderly Indians' insistence that she should *not* be given an equivalent portion, comparable to what the men had received.

"You think that just because I'm a delicate-looking white woman that I can't defend myself against your obnoxious bullying," Mrs. Ellington shouted into the four appalled elderly Indians' faces. "But your dumb-ass perception of me is totally wrong! I'll kick any of your asses black and blue, if you dare aggravate me with your obsolete primitive nonsense! I've had adequate training in boxing, wrestling, and also in an Oriental art known as karate!"

Sitka Charley was extremely proud to know 'the blonde-haired goddess', Mrs. Stephanie Ellington. She, too, knew the cultured laws of the white man, and was abundantly acquainted with the wisdom of the trail, which amazingly emphasized group cooperation and assistance, along with individual equality. Those alien-but-special foreign qualities and characteristics that had been imported into Northern Canada had remarkably transformed Sitka Charley from an aimless savage into a sophisticated, civilized human being, and unlike the four other aged Indians present at the campsite, the redeemed native felt quite superior to *them,* and consequently, treated his brethren as his barbarian subordinates.

At the roaring campfire that fall night, after Captain and Mrs. Ellington had retired to their pitched seal-skin tent, Sitka Charley laid-down the specifics of the law to the four elderly, obdurate, resentful Indians, whom the dubious expedition guide suspected might be plotting insurrection and robbery.

"Listen-up, you four delusional, stubborn, old-fart Assholes!" Sitka sarcastically addressed his elders, who according to Indian custom, should be *his* revered superiors. "A few important words, Brave Men, for your own good, so that you and everyone else in this camp might survive and live. We have passed the Hills of Silence, and are advancing west towards what the white man calls the Stuart River," Sitka lectured. "If we help each another according to the law of the trail, and according to the white man's traditions, no one will be abandoned and left behind to die. When we eventually reach the Yukon River, other white men will give us food and shelter, and reward us with furs to trade."

"Why the hell should we trust you when you now think like a self-centered white asshole?" Kah-Chucte defiantly asked and challenged. "You're a damned traitor to your race!"

"Kah-Chucte is right!" concurred Gowhee. "Why should not the law of the Indians prevail over the white man's laws? Don't you fuckin' wear war paint, anymore?"

"If any or all of you four, ancient dumb-fucks try anything abnormal that violates the laws of the trail and the laws of the white man," Sitka Charley un-diplomatically threatened and advised his elders, "then I'll personally blow your balls, your dicks, and your asses off your torsos with this trusty rifle of mine! Now, I repeat. Here again are the fundamental rules of behavior, you retarded shit heads: everyone helps one another during the trip; no one living is left behind; and we all share the food supply equally, including the beautiful white lady with the radiant blonde hair. And finally," Sitka promised the four defiant old geezers. "Any deviation from those simple rules, and you'll be deader than that seal whose skin and ligaments had been used to sew that tent over there together!"

* * * * * * * * * * * * *

Sitka Charley was a light sleeper, who knew that the vile propensities of his four elderly Indian companions were to steal, to kill, and to leave the sick or the dying behind, and those undesirable primitive native ways were the antitheses of the white man's laws, and of the white man's lucid interpretation of the law of the trail.

The trustworthy guide would instinctively wake-up every fifteen minutes, or so, from his shallow sleep, to ascertain that the four wrinkle-skinned, insolent elders were not awake, and were not conspiring against Captain James and Mrs. Stephanie Ellington, or for that matter, against him. But now, Sitka woke from his slumber and observed that two of the elderly Indians had escaped with two sacks of flour, leaving the less brazen Kah-Chucte and Gowhee behind to organize their own theft conspiracy.

‘I’ve already threatened the remaining two fossil-faces with what the results would be should the connivers ever dare to trespass against the law of the trail,’ Sitka imagined and thought as the guard fended-off weariness and stayed awake, staring at the overhead stars. ‘I’ll just silently lie here tonight on my blanket, and think about Mrs. Stephanie Ellington’s pretty face, her nice tits, her really firm ass, and her hairy wet pink, blonde pussy. I wonder if the gorgeous lady really does have a furry-fluffy blonde beaver?’

At dawn the following morning, Sitka caught Kah-Chucte and Gowhee violating the wisdom of the trail, which required swift action on the scout’s part. The pair was about to desert the camp with two large sacks of flour when their escape was interrupted by the Ellingtons’ ever-alert guide.

“So, my good mentally fucked-up comrades. You’ve been apprehended stealing and deserting those that have hired and trusted you, all done for you assholes out of the sympathy of their hearts,” the honorable guide announced to the mendacious duo. “Very good now! I must make examples of you two dumb-asses by combining the white man’s laws with the Indians’ sense of justice. Because of your greediness and fucked-up stupidity,” Sitka revealed, gritting his teeth, “now there will be fewer bellies to feed on this lengthy excursion up the river that the white men call Yukon.”

“What do you plan to do with us?” worriedly asked Kah-Cuchte. “Are you telling me that you favor the white man and his yellow-haired squaw over your own elders?”

“You two pathetic morons have authored your own death sentences, even though neither of you two dumb-shits know how to read or write,” Sitka verbalized in the local Indian native tongue. “You ninnies have acted selfishly, and in the white man’s language, you have behaved in a ‘pernicious manner’. Therefore, I must mete out your punishment, according to my keen understanding of the wisdom of the trail.”

“I can’t believe that you’re a despicable traitor to your own people!” Gowhee alleged. “Sitka Charley.  You’re now an absolute disgrace, and an abomination to Indians everywhere!”

“Stop acting like a couple of uncivilized, bratty children ignorant of the needs of others. Stand shoulder to shoulder and meet your deaths like mature grown men ought to be doing,” the determined on-a-mission frontier guide directed. “You’ve both stolen from your honest employers, and besides that, you’ve both really pissed me off like I’ve never been pissed-off before! Now then, Gowhee; hast thou a wife and children and a deerskin lodge in Chipewyan near

Chipaway? What is thy final will and testament in regard to those family matters?"

"Give my wife all of the properties I own to eventually distribute to my children when she dies, for I'm quite sure that the old bitch will not live more than another sun year," the doomed Gowhee communicated. "I'm fuckin' tired of sleeping with her dried-up, dried-out cunt, anyway!"

"And how about you Kah-Chucte? I understand that you have no wife or children?" Sitka Charley asked.

"My only family blood is my younger sister, who is the unfortunate wife of the homosexual shaman over near Chipewyan, which as you know, is not far from Chipaway," Kah-Chucte reminded his seemingly invincible nemesis, Sitka. "My last wishes are to give my doltish sister all of my possessions, and for *you* to kill her gay husband if the bastard once again abuses her and beats the total shit out of her."

"But what about Kilkachu and Red-ass?" Gowhee ineffectively argued. "Those other two elders ran away during the night, and stole their two bags of flour. They are free and unpunished, unlike Kah-Chucte and me. What about them?"

"I didn't catch those two imbeciles, but I've caught you two cretin fuck-heads!" Sitka sternly replied. "That's all the facts that really matter to me right now."

"They are free and have not been reprimanded for their actions!" Gowhee argued and reiterated. "It is not fair to Kah-Chucte and me that Kilkachu and Red-ass have gotten away without any harm, and that we're both being held as criminals!"

"But I assure you Gowhee, when I do eventually find those two senile and demented old shits, I'll take care of their wrinkled asses, too. This I promise you two retarded degenerate rogues!" the disgusted scout stated. "Now then comrades, we've established the covenants of your wills and the disposition of your properties, which the white man calls 'estates'. And I promise that I'll dispose of the gay shaman should the faggot again kick the shit out of your mentally-retarded sister, Kah-Chucte; and that I'll shoot and kill those dumb-ass bastards Kilkachu and Red-ass the next time my path crosses theirs. Are you two old fucks now ready to die?"

"We are!" both quivering senile elders answered in unison.

"Then goodbye my good comrades, for I must do what I feel compelled to do. I must honor and value the wisdom of the trail. I wish you two stupid fucks well in your new happy hunting grounds!" Sitka finished. "May you sit in your heavenly warm lodges in the highest sky, and again be young, and eat juicy pussy, and screw beautiful squaws, each and every night and day!"

"That sounds great to me!" Gowhee exclaimed. "Hurry-up and pull the damned trigger!"

"Yes. Even empty oblivion will be much better than living in this fucked-up white man's world! Hurry-up and pull the damned trigger!" parroted Kah-Chucte. "I haven't had a fuckin' satisfying orgasm, or licked delicious pussy in over three long decades! I just know it's all going to be simply heavenly!"

And so, Sitka Charley raised his rifle and blasted-away, the noise of the gun firings awakening both Captain and Mrs. Ellington from their deep slumbers. The wisdom and swift justice of the trail had been preserved, and its laws enforced. Kah-Chucte and Gowhee were now enjoying the trails and the adventures of their new happy bordello hunting grounds, existing high up in the eternal sky.

# "To the Man on Trail"

"Dump more liquid ingredients into the concoction until it approaches a hundred proof," instructed Big Jim Belden to the carefree Malemute Kid. "I've come way down here from my stake over at Mazy May, just to celebrate Christmas with you' jaspers. I mean," Belden searched for the right words to accurately express himself'. "The Yule Tide season only comes around once a year, and must be honored correctly by getting drunk any which way ya' can! Your magic formula can't be worse than any of the foul-smellin' hooch I've drunk over at the Tanana River claims. The last crap I've swallowed-down over there floated my kidneys away, and rotten-out half my asshole, too!"

"Here's some brandy and whiskey combination with a little cat piss mixed-in, too, and prepared special for *you*, our internationally famous amateur whiskey expert," Malemute Kid offered to Stanley Prince, who had been prospecting in that area of Northwest Canada for two years. "When nothin' else is available to drink, this stuff tastes like nectar and ambrosia, if ya' possess a good enough imagination. Who else wants some of my exotic poison that's guaranteed to kill every last germ in your body, before ultimately altogether destroyin' you?"

"Pour me a full cup of that lethal brew, too!" the Frenchman Louis Savoy demanded. "I got a sore throat, and need to get my vocal cords anesthetized somehow, and your rare beverage might just do the trick. If your cocktail will make me forget about the pain in my abdomen, and make me forget who the hell I am," Savoy laughed, holding-out his tin cup, "then fill this sucker right up to the brim."

"Here Padre!" Malemute Kid offered Father Roubeau, an ordained Jesuit priest. "Take a swig of this homemade moonshine! It's my secret recipe, and much more delicious and powerful than that communion wine you serve every Sunday at the altar!"

The jolly men sat before the fireplace blaze, and then reminisced past adventures and experiences; each story becoming more exaggerated than the preceding legend that had recently been described. And then, the half-inebriated Malemute Kid stood-up and proposed a dignified toast to all those audacious individuals who braved hardship driving their dogsleds through the Klondike and Yukon passages on Christmas Eve.

"To the good health of every gutsy man who is bravely traveling on the trail this frigid holiday night," Malemute requested of his assembled high-spirited comrades. "May the courageous fellows' grub supply hold-out; may his dogs keep their legs striding; may his matches never misfire, and sorry Father, but may he get happily laid and blown after reaching his ultimate destination!"

Everyone laughed and cheered in response to the Kid's witty commentary, including good-natured Father Roubeau. But then the merriment was interrupted with the sound of "Crack-Crack-Crack!" followed by the crunch of a dogsled pulling-up to the remote cabin. Everyone inside the cozy, warm dwelling wondered who the new visitor would be.

"I already trust the driver," Malemute automatically judged. "Whoever the son-of-a-bitch, er, excuse me Father, whoever the son-of-a-gun is, the dogsled driver's not only feeding his own dogs, but also not ignoring the others owned by us, and I interpret *that* considerate behavior as kindness belonging to a man with real character. Any decent traveler maneuvering-about on the barren trail will give food to all the dogs, or to none at all! That's one way I measure the true size of a man's heart!"

Then, came the expected rapping upon the door. The weary-looking stranger seemed momentarily dazzled by the bright illumination originating from the fireplace, and instinctively shielded his eyes. The mammoth traveler in the doorway was tall, around six foot four inches in height, with broad shoulders, and the cabin visitor was clean-shaven and wore a Mackinaw jacket; a fur hat, and sported two awesome Colt revolvers inside his holster belt. Immediately, the other men all understood that their beings were in the presence of a transplanted American possessing a powerful self-image.

"What sort of cheer you fellas' drinkin'?" the new-arrival asked as the huge fellow closed the cabin door behind him. "I could use a few mouthfuls myself!"

Immediately, the Malemute Kid recognized the stranger, whose noteworthy reputation had preceded him. After politely drinking-down several swallows of the weird brandy/whiskey blend, the tall strong guest had an important question to ask his temporary hosts.

"Tell me; how long has it been since that basket sled passed through here with three men and eight dogs?"

"Two days ago," Malemute sincerely answered. "Are ya' after them for some reason?"

"Yes, and I've gained two days travel time on them already," the muscular stranger vaguely replied, without specifically identifying the exact nature of his pursuit.

"Reckon those three varmints will show more spunk once the renegades realize you're closin' in on them," Jim Belden said over his left shoulder while the gold prospector sizzled some bacon in the frying pan. "Hey Kid; get the coffee pot ready to pour. That alcohol mix is already playin' havoc with my intestines, and I think my testicles are beginnin' to bounce and twist around, too! Don't want those two necessary things fallin' off my torso; no way!"

The stranger impatiently tapped his revolvers when the Kid decided to resume the rather odd, unfinished conversation. "When did ya' leave Dawson?"

"Twelve o'clock noon today!" the impressive tall visitor tersely responded. "I've gone around seventy-five miles in twelve hours, so I'm pleased with my time. I figure I'll catch-up to the others in about three more days!"

As the young-but-mammoth guest ate some chow, the Malemute Kid scrutinized the fellow's features, and upon initial observation, believed that his visitor was honest, fair, and quite determined to accomplish his still-undefined mission. Malemute also concluded that hard work and toil were evidenced on the young man's callused hands, but the fellow's steel blue eyes showed brightly, and their reflections from the fire light tacitly communicated both resolve and perseverance. The quiet stranger politely listened to the other men conversing and exchanging their good-natured anecdotes.

"So, that's how me and old Betty got spliced like we were some sort of wire or cord," Jim Belden articulated and described the end result of his failed courtship. "And it was all downhill from there, with bills to be paid, mortgages to be met, and furniture to be acquired. I knew I should've listened to my mother and become a parasitic priest, just like Father Roubeau here had done, ha, ha, ha! The Monsignor, the Cardinal, the Bishop, and the Pope pay all his goddamned expenses, ha, ha, ha! And the good Catholic parishioners around the world pay tribute in the form of donations to the Pope!"

"Any kids waiting for you back in the states?" the young stranger asked Jim Belden.

"Nope. When we were about to divorce, Betty died just before I came to this secluded part of Canada, and that's basically why the heck I'm up in the Yukon Territory. I just wanted to forget my troubles back in Seattle, and start a new life up here in the wilderness," Belden explained. "How about yourself, Young Man? Are ya' married?"

The broad-shouldered, handsome lad opened his watch and showed Jim Belden a picture of a beautiful blonde woman and a child at her breast; the photograph, having been inserted into the interior watch cover, so then the old-timer handed the watch to Louis Savoy and Stanley Prince for them to inspect.

"The boy's now two years old, and I haven't seen him since he was an infant," the Young Man informed his listeners, as the cabin guest finally got his watch back from the temporarily laconic Christmas celebrators. "Can I catch three hours sleep before I go back-out on the local trail?"

"Certainly," Malemute Kid obliged. "You can rest up in the bunk in the back room. I promise to wake ya' up at three in the morning, so that you can continue your mysterious midnight ride. You ain't a descendent of Paul Revere, are ya'?"

After the Young Man was sound asleep in the back bedroom, the other men inside the cabin were curious to know who *he* might be. "By Jove!" Stanley Prince said to Jim Belden, Louis Savoy and Father Roubeau. "That Young Fella's a frisky chap, goin' seventy-five miles in twelve hours, and then hittin' the trail again with only three hours sleep. Who is he Malemute?"

"His name is Jack Westinghouse," the Kid confidentially revealed to his friends. "The guy works like a Clydesdale field horse, but I assure you, he's as honest as the day is long, and if Jack promises to get a job done for you, most absolutely, you can be sure if it's Westinghouse doin' it! Now Guys. I know quite a bit about Jack from my buddy back in Dawson, good old Sitka Charley. Jack's hit it big twice prospecting, but both times he's had bad luck and lost his profits from his stakes. Sitka says that some pernicious villain's been swindlin' Jack over there in Dawson!"

After two hours had elapsed, the Malemute Kid excused himself from the non-enlightening company of the gossipy, merry drinking men, put on his heavy fur clothing, and stepped-outside to conduct some clandestine business. Upon reentering the cabin thirty-minutes later, the Kid ambled into the back room and woke-up Jack, got the groggy and hiccupping Father Roubeau to bless Westinghouse (along with his grueling trip south), and then escorted the goal-oriented man on the trail outside to give the harried traveler some last-minute instructions and information.

"Listen, carefully. You'll find a hundred-pounds of salmon eggs in those two white sacks I've put on your sled. Use them to feed your starving dogs and to keep them strong," the sympathetic Kid related to the flabbergasted Westinghouse. "There's no fish available in Pelly as you've probably believed, so the salmon eggs will give you an advantage in *not* having the three men you're after ever crossing you. The next available food will be at Five Fingers, but that's still two-hundred-miles away, and let me remind you, there's no five-finger discounts allowed at Five Fingers," Malemute weakly jested. "Finally, watch-out for the rapid-flowing open water on the Thirty Mile River, and make sure you take the big cut-off above Le Barge."

"Surely, the news can't be speeding ahead of me?" Westinghouse incredulously wondered and asked. "How do you know about my particular situation?"

"It's my business to know what drives good men to do certain things that others presumptuously judge, but if anybody ever asks me, I don't know a goddamned thing about your situation, even though I actually do," the Kid awkwardly expressed. "My friend Sitka Charley back in Dawson sold that team of dogs you're chasing to those three men on the basket sled, and Sitka had sized you up to me once, and his word is Gospel to my ears, regardless of what intoxicated Father Roubeau in there might think or say about morality and sin."

"Thank you kindly," Jack Westinghouse replied. 'I'm much obliged."

"Now here's a sack of gold I've been saving. Use it to buy fresh dog food, or to buy fresh dogs for that matter, should you need them at Five Fingers, at Little Salmon, or further down the trail at Hootalingua, where the trading post owner doesn't give a hoot about what language ya' speak, as long as you pay him. And finally, Jack," the Kid very clearly enunciated, showing Westinghouse that he knew exactly to whom he was speaking. "Keep traveling up to twenty-five below zero, but if it gets below that temperature, halt your team, and be sure to build a fire and change your socks! That's the best way that I know how to avoid getting pneumonia out in *that* frigid apathetic wilderness! And finally, Jack. I know you aren't chasing after three men on that basket sled! They're fuckin' chasin' after you!"

* * * * * * * * * * * * *

A half an hour later, a mounted policeman of the Northwest Territory arrived at the remote cabin, accompanied by two half-breed dog drivers. Like Jack Westinghouse, the policeman was heavily armed and showed signs of fatigue from being on the trail that cold Christmas Eve. But the police officer was little more than an idealistic, neophyte; stern, clean-shaven, adamant law enforcer, and his main objective was apprehending a dangerous suspect-on-the-lam.

"I suspect that an accused felon named Jack Westinghouse stopped here earlier! When the hell did the felon pull-out with his dogs?" the novice policeman demanded learning. "Don't lie to me now! I saw his dog team's fresh tracks outside!"

"Sir, we've been drinking some potent whiskey in here celebratin' Christmas cheer and all that," the Kid inventively prevaricated. "So, I can't cite an exact time about anything, and neither can anyone else sittin' in here! For ya' see, Sir. I'm respectfully reportin' to ya' that we're all kinda' mentally fucked-up!"

"Come on, now; you all can't be that drunk!" the truculent frontier patrolman challenged the remainder of the uncooperative group. "One of ya' has got to know the answer to my simple question!"

"You seem to want this Western House fella' pretty badly," Jim Belden declared and slurred. "He musta' been getting a little cantankerous fuckin' around over there in Dawson!"

"He held up McCormack over at the trading post for forty thousand, and then transferred it at the P.C. exchange store for a check that'll be good at any Seattle bank," the very determined vernal policeman alleged. "And who's to stop him from cashing that big check once the thief makes it down to the States? Now I want one of you all-too-sly son-of-a-bitches to tell me, when did Westinghouse pull out of here?"

"Don't precisely know!" Stanley Prince answered. "I don't study clocks for a livin', ya' understand! He shouldn't be too hard for you to catch, though! The varmint drunk-up a storm before he flew the hell outa' here! Exactly when I can't rightly recall!"

"How about you, Frenchy!" the policeman interrogated Louis Savoy. "You seem to have retained some wits about you!"

"I was stone drunk before I ever got to this celebration cabin, so please don't ask me how the hell I arrived here safely," Savoy very capably lied. "And I haven't stopped drinkin' Malemute Kid's delicious liquor formula, and I don't want to stop now! Hic!"

Then, the young policeman had a sudden inspiration. "How about you, Father? A priest would never tell a lie or bend the truth, would he? Level with me, or else I'll write a letter to your superiors! How long ago was it that the alleged criminal Jack Westinghouse left these premises?"

"Half an hour ago, but the fella' had around three hours rest for himself and his dogs," the on-the-spot priest candidly answered. "I now see that confession is just as much a part of the law as it is part of the church! I could never violate any sacred sacrament, especially Confession! Hic!"

"My God Father; even though you're not my godfather!" Louis Savoy cleverly and amusingly stated.

"Padre, excuse my inferior English, but I'll never be able to catch that sneaky bastard under the present circumstances! My dogs are dead tired, and I feel more dead than tired myself!" the disappointed keeperof-the-peace admitted. But then a flash of brilliance entered the pursuer's mind. "Lend me five fresh dogs?" the perplexed-but-obsessed-to-duty officer demanded of Malemute.

"My Siwash and my Babette are both sick, and the stubborn canines won't serve you well," Malemute creatively fibbed. "I'd feel fuckin' guilty if you got stranded out in the middle of nowhere, and then froze to death. Stay here with us, Corporal, and have some whiskey while keeping warm! I promise that you'll live to see the glorious sun rise at dawn, or is it twilight?"

"Look. I have the authority to sign a check in Captain Constantine's name for five-thousand-dollars that I can write anytime at my discretion," the frustrated policeman insisted. "I want to buy a new dog team!"

"You'll die on the trail, and I don't want to be responsible for that tragedy ever happening!" the Malemute Kid maintained. "I've been to enough funerals in the last year, and don't wish to attend another one before January 1st!"

"Then, I'll have to order you to turn your dogs over to me in the name of the Queen!" the red-faced trail patrolman angrily bellowed. "To refuse *that* command would be tantamount to treason! I have the authority to confiscate your dogs!"

"Okay, Corporal; you win our little debate! Write me the check for five-thousand-smackers, and you can have my five dogs in exchange for your tired team," the profit-minded Kid stated, feigning melancholy. "But if you happen to die out there on the trail, don't fuckin' blame me!"

After the on-a-mission Corporal and his two obedient deputies hastily departed the area, the Malemute Kid requested that the men drink to the successful escape of one honorable Jack Westinghouse, who according to the speaker's fascinating testimony, "Last fall, our new friend J.W. gave forty-thousand-dollars to that scoundrel Joe Castrell to buy-in on the Dominion Stake, and if that had actually happened, Jack would be a multimillionaire today," the Kid informed his captivated audience.

"So, what really happened that the law's after Jack?" Louis Savoy seriously asked. "It just doesn't add up!"

"Jack didn't go-off to the Dominion Stake. Instead, he stayed behind and took care of his former partner at Circle City, who incidentally had a bad case of scurvy. In the meantime," the informative Kid related to his attentive pals, "Castrell goes into McCormack's trading post and spends the forty-thousand on supplies and on accumulated gambling debts, leaving poor Jack flat busted. Jack

Westinghouse shows-up at McCormack's place, gets into an argument with the proprietor, and then steals the forty-thousand that *that* dirty bastard Castrell had lost, or had gambled away. McCormack has a heart attack and dies after the theft, but the police think that Jack's wanted for both robbery and murder, when actually that evil skunk Joe Castrell is to blame for everything. And so, Gentlemen, that's the whole blessed story that Sitka Charley had told me early yesterday morning, midway between here and Dawson."

"In the name of the Father, and of the Son, and of the Holy Spirit, Amen!" Father Roubeau remarked, and then loudly belched, blessing all present with the Sign of the Cross.

"I see what the hell you're sayin'," Louis Savoy realized and communicated. "Jack Westinghouse is a good decent man, and *that* shit-head Joe Castrell is the opposite type of jasper with plenty of malicious tendencies. And Trader Joe had meanly cheated Jack out of forty thousand bucks, and then paid off his sinful gamblin' and supply debts to McCormack and then..."

"And then the police are only interested in the letter-of-the-law, and have totally abandoned all sense of morality and common ethics," Father Roubeau logically and soberly contributed to the discussion. "Whatever happened to the spirit of the law?"

"And therefore," Stanley Prince piped-up in his rather annoying, staccato voice saying, "The Malemute Kid here is judgin' the sequence of events on Jack Westinghouse's character, his morality, and his ethics, and not on the *damned* law. But if *you* weren't standing here, Padre Roubeau," the short, fat, baldheaded hunter/fur trader qualified, "I would've said 'on the *god*damned law'!"

"So, Gentlemen," the Malemute Kid acknowledged raising his full tin cup of homemade liquor aloft. "Here's another toast to Jack Westinghouse, the noble man riding on the area trail. May his grub sustain him; may his dogs' legs hold out; may his matches never fail him, and may he get laid and blown upon reachin' his ultimate destination!"

"Here, here!" Jim Belden confirmed, clanking his cup against the other men's tin containers. "Here's another excellent salute to the valiant Jack Westinghouse! And here's also a third one directed toward the continued confusion of the misguided, by the book, Canadian Mounted Police!"

# "The Story of Jees Uck"

This is the story of Jees Uck, a swarthy-skinned, mixed-blooded beautiful Indian/Eskimo woman, who was a native resident of the Yukon Territory of Northwestern Canadian. But it is also the story of a man named Neil Bonner, whose path Jees Uck had crossed (and possibly had double-crossed), and whose life the lady had significantly touched and influenced. Although Jees Uck had never learned how to read or write, her abundant wisdom is quite famous, and her tale is told around myriad nightly forest and mountain campfires, even to this day.

Neil Bonner was the only son of a wealthy trading tycoon, but the father-son duo constantly bickered and argued over even the slightest of trivialities. In order to discipline his son and indoctrinate him into the real business world at a low entry level, the inflexible and sanctimonious Mr. Neil Bonner Sr. had a close friend hire Neil Bonner Jr. as an agent for the P.C. Company, which operated by adhering to very strict, austere, politically correct rules.

The large international trading corporation owned fleets of sailing ships that exchanged goods for furs, gold, and meat in the primitive Alaskan Klondike and in the Canadian Yukon territories. "Five years up there in the frigid north country will teach my son a good lesson in self-control, and compel him to implement sound business practices," the power-hungry San Francisco mogul told his P.C. Company associate. "It's so damned cold up there that only male polar bears get hard-ons!"

"If your son works-out well the first year in our junior management program," the father's friend explained, "then we'll really test young Neil's perseverance and mettle by assigning him to manage a small trading post up in the Yukon. I think that the one in Tanana Station will be manned next year this time, or else Young Neil will be in charge of the company's new Twenty Mile General Store. The damned trading post will be called Twenty Mile because it's twenty friggin' miles from nowhere; the nearest town being Dawson, which is nearly thirty-miles away from *that* desolate area."

"That sounds like the perfect prescription to cure my obstinate, know-it-all son of his lackadaisical business disposition," Mr. Bonner replied with a smile. "Young Neil has two college degrees; one in pharmacy and another in basic chemistry, but the ornery fool doesn't want to enter either of those two professions. Neil wants to start at the goddamned top, but just like you and me George," the avid commerce broker stated to his company executive friend, "the little prick has to start at the bottom, learn the operation from the ground level, and then through hard work and achievement, pay his dues and earn the right to ascend into corporate administration. But first, Neil has to kneel!"

The newly-constructed post at Twenty Miles was a modest-looking log cabin the size of a corner grocery store. The place had two rooms to rent upstairs, and a kitchen and bedroom conveniently situated behind the main commercial area. The post was but one tentacle of the enormous P.C. Company empire; a sort of ice-bound Devil's Island where the neophyte Neil Bonner had been dispatched so that he could impress his superiors and simultaneously placate the lad's very strong-minded and highly regimented Puritanical father's uncompromising and indomitable iron will.

Young Neil Bonner's assistant at Twenty Miles was Amos Pentley, whose brother Andy had been fired by "the Company" just three months before down in Seattle. Amos was a short, hollow-chested, bossy fellow who frequently coughed, making Neil suspect that the jealous man was suffering from an advanced case of consumption. The new post manager felt sorry for Pentley's deteriorating health condition, but conversely, Neil Bonner just did not like or trust the whiny little man.

'Shit!' Neil thought. 'I love to party and flirt with beautiful women. But there's none of that neat city stuff going on up here. The only person I have to commiserate with is this wimpy, sneaky, fuck-head Amos Pentley, who hates to talk to anyone, including me! All the annoying bastard does is talk to himself in his sleep. But now that the outside temperature is seventy degrees below zero, I might just wind-up conversing with a goddamned igloo, a totem pole, a baby seal, or a glacier, simply to keep my general sanity intact.'

In January of that winter, Jees Uck entered the remote trading post to barter furs for food and supplies. Neil instantly observed the beautiful girl, and despite the freezing temperature, immediately Bonner got a boner.

'Oh my God!' Neil promptly imagined. 'This pretty Eskimo girl wants beads, flour, beans, and bacon for her furs. I wouldn't mind putting my bacon inside her fur pelt; yes, that's what the hell my warped mind thinks. My sensitive pecker throbs and bobs like a son-of-a-bitch every time that gorgeous doll looks me in the eyes.'

Amos Pentley noticed the flirtations going on between Neil Bonner and Jees Uck, and *that* scrutiny made him became even more envious of his newly arrived boss. During the Indian/Eskimo girl's third visit to the Twenty Mile trading post, Neil Bonner courteously carried a fifty-pound-sack of flour out to the young woman's dogsled when suddenly, his neck became exceedingly stiff, even stiffer than his erect penis. A quick spasm soon had the prodigal son rolling on top of ice and snow. Bonner became tense, and his body quivered, his back arched, and his general anatomy appeared distorted and twisted as his oddball convulsions continued.

Neil's forehead began to sweat profusely, despite the fifty below zero temperature, and his mouth started to foam. The love-afflicted man attempted crawling back inside the store on his hands and knees, but as soon as he got to the door, it opened and benevolent Jees Uck immediately intercepted the aching fellow's progress and gingerly raised-up his head to promote his ability to breathe. Using all her remaining strength and dexterity, the benign girl dragged Neil back inside the log cabin, and then adroitly kicked the door shut.

"Oh Amos!" Jees Uck cried-out to apathetic Pentley. "Him die, you think? Him really paleface now!"

Pentley stood there in a nonchalant, reticent manner, shrugged his shoulders, and then uttered, "I believe he thinks he's Julius Caesar having one of his many epileptic seizures! Now I know how fuckin' Brutus must've felt!" Of course, Jees Uck was totally unaware of the historic symbolism of *those* fucked-up, malignantly-spoken words.

A minute further into the dire emergency, the tension in Neil Bonner's body eased, and during that auspicious moment of slackening, the trading post manager gritted his teeth before the onslaught of the next terrible spasm and sternly commanded, "Jees Uck; get medicine from wall cabinet. Never mind! Drag my ass over there, and I'll tell you what medicine to reach-up and get!"

Obeying the ill man's strict dragging order, even though the Eskimo doll was not a drag queen, Jees Uck tugged and pulled the incapacitated victim over toward the medicine cabinet that was hanging on the wall next to the store's wood-burning stove. Despite his hazy and cluttered mind, Bonner recalled that three of his sled dogs had exhibited similar muscular contractions, and the agonizing agent determined that he would utilize his academic knowledge of chemistry and pharmacy to alleviate his suffering. Neil pointed to a vial of chloral hydrate, and signaled for the native girl to pour an ounce of the formula down his throat, which she compliantly did.

"Listen to me, please, Jees Uck!" Bonner further instructed. "Stay by my side and guard me from Amos, but whatever you do, do not touch me!" And upon hearing what the sick man had directed, Amos Pentley retreated to the back bedroom, not wanting any confrontation with Jees Uck, who was an expert at hitting distant targets with the sharp knife she possessively kept inside her sheath. The girl also kept a sharp harpoon wedged inside her trusty dogsled. 'Neil is having regular contractions,' the Eskimo beauty considered, 'but I don't think he's pregnant. I'll check his eyes for dilation.'

A full day passed before Neil Bonner again opened his eyelids to marvel and gaze upon the pulchritude of Jees Uck, who was still loyally kneeling by his side without once having to use the bathroom. "Go into the kitchen and bring some food: biscuits, beans, and bacon," the recuperating trading post representative directed. "Take a lit candle in there because it's dark, and you might trip over some obscure object in the way. And get some coffee and the pint of whiskey on the table also, and then gees, Jees, come back in here and place those items on the trading post counter. I know you've never heard of a thing called science, but you're about to witness what we Americans call a *counter*-revolution!"

"Why all of yesterday's food? Are you going to eat like a snow vulture, Neil?" Jees Uck asked.

"Geez Jees; why the hell would I want to eat myself?" Bonner jested, finally exhibiting signs of snapping out of his lethargy. "But no; I'm not going to eat any of yesterday's food. I'm going to perform what the people in my country call 'a laboratory experiment'. I'm going to test it to determine if any of it has been poisoned!"

"What is a laboratory experiment?" the girl curiously inquired.

"A laboratory is a place where a white man often *labors* and mixes liquids together in what is called 'an experiment'," Bonner tried elaborating. "Try to pay attention Jees Uck. You will soon see what the hell I mean. All of that a scientist performs in a lab!"

'How the hell does anyone perform anything in a friggin' retriever dog!' Jees Uck wondered.

After the requested food items had been carefully arranged upon the trading post counter, the store's manager assessed his remedy theory. 'I believe that I had been suffering from a condition of tetanus,' Bonner suspiciously surmised as the science major began conducting his meticulous food analyses.

His initial research definitely demonstrated that the coffee had not been tampered with after the chemistry/pharmacy graduate had methodically mixed liquids of certain vials with yesterday's java taken from the pot. Then, after mixing other chemicals into different tumblers containing food, Bonner systematically determined that the baked beans had not been contaminated or tainted. All the while, Amos Pentley, who knew nothing of the sciences of chemistry and pharmacy, stuck his bald-head out from the kitchen from time to time, and at minute intervals, the craven asshole looked-on with abundant curiosity, and then again, retreated into the back room like a timid mouse scurrying into a wall opening.

"Is this white man's medicine a form of black magic?" Jees Uck asked. "It looks very strange and complicated. I did not know that you were a white shaman, Neil."

"I cannot speak wise words while I concentrate and mix," Bonner answered as the ailing chemist carefully studied the biscuit particles suspended in a salt solution, and then watched them change color. 'This next step is the most important part. I hope that this bullshit experiment works!"

Amos Pentley slowly and surreptitiously entered the main room, and the distrustful little man silently pretended to be concerned about Bonner's physical welfare.

"Are you feeling better Neil?" Pentley queried, feigning sincerity as best as he could. "I was worried that you'd be dead by now."

"Listen to me, you, dirty, puny, Lilliputian cock-sucker!" Bonner screamed at his new-found adversary. "You have to pack-up an outfit and hit the fuckin' trail before I fuckin' kill your ass right here and now! You can use the six company dogs out in the back shed."

"You don't mean to say that you're sendin' me out into fifty below temperatures at night to freeze to death?" the appalled assistant manager incredulously asked. "That type of irresponsible action could be construed as voluntary manslaughter, even in an Australian wallaby court of law! You might hang for it, if I die out there!"

"You fucked-up jealous bastard! Don't try threatening me with your perverted bullshit! You tried to kill me, and you failed!" Bonner accused, as the dumbfounded and confused Jees Uck listened to the dramatic exchange and attempted to comprehend what the exact nature of the white man controversy entailed.

"The company believes that Bob Birdsall had killed himself, but now I know better," Bonner vociferated to his pretentious enemy. "You, Amos Pentley, had evilly eliminated Birdsall by poisoning his ass right off the planet, you fucked-up, demented, dirt bag! In my case, my chemical analysis showed that you used strychnine in my biscuits to try to permanently send me to the Grim Reaper's happy hunting domain. Now listen carefully, Amos; if you don't want me to violently kill you right here and now. Twenty Mile is too small for the both of us to inhabit, and it's only two-hundred-miles on the trail to Holy Cross, the next company trading post," Bonner informed Pentley of *his* imminent journey. "Now I warn you, Asshole; mush the hell out of here with the six canines before I change my erratic mind and perform a fuckin' autopsy on you while you're still fuckin' alive! I attended but failed undertaking school before I ever studied chemistry and pharmacy!"

* * * * * * * * * * * * *

"You must go to bed, and I will take care of you until you're feeling better!" Jees Uck suggested after Amos Pentley got out of Twenty Miles like a fart zipping out of a challenged coward's asshole. "You, sick man, Neil; you need good squaw to nurse you."

Bonner licked his lips while peering at Jees Uck's magnificent breasts. "No Jees Uck; you go back to your camp and stay with your people for one full week," Bonner insisted. "Then come back here and by that time, you can *nurse* me into better health," the recovering fellow thought as his selfish brain contemplated sucking on the native girl's firm breasts and gorgeous nipples. 'I'll just pretend that I'm an infant again; yes, a cute little sucker with my anxious tongue greedily licking away!'

"You don't like me, Neil?" the attractive brown-eyed girl sadly asked as she slowly put on her warm parka.

"Only too well, Jees Uck! Only too well!" Bonner replied. "I promise you that by next week, I'll be strong enough for you to nurse me as you have suggested!"

Seven days later, Jees Uck showed-up at the Twenty Miles trading center with ten furs to barter for beads, food, scarlet cloths, moose-hide moccasins, Eskimo panties, and leather straps. After conversing in small talk for two full hours, Neil Bonner decided it was time for him to make his romantic move.

"I go now, Neil!" the pretty swarthy-skinned girl lowly and politely said with her eyes pointed-down. "Good night, Neil!"

"No, Jees Uck; you aren't going anywhere without my expressed permission," Bonner nebulously declared. And then the horny fellow kissed her on the forehead, and then again upon her lips, which seemed like a strange and eccentric behavior to the apprehensive native girl, who was unaware of Western Civilization male behavior.

"What do you call that caribou shit act?" Jees Uck asked her admirer about *her* peculiar experience. "Is that what white men do to white women?"

"Let me tell you all about a white man named Charles," Bonner affectionately said before kissing her again.

"Charles? Charles who?"

“A six-inch-tall fellow named Charles Dick-ins, who insists on being sucked and inserted at least three times a day!” the amorous and aroused white man stated as Bonner wrapped his muscular arms around the stunned native doll, and then planted a huge smooch upon her receptive mouth.

A month later, after Neil Bonner and Jees Uck shared a minimum of three fantastic intimacies a day, a P.C. Company employee named Sandy MacPherson showed-up at Twenty Miles with some bad news to convey to the trading post manager, which an hour later, was joyfully evaluated as ‘a blessing in disguise’ in Neil Bonner’s self-oriented mind.

“This letter in my hands, Jees Uck, says that my father has died and that I must return to a far-off big village called San Francisco to manage his affairs and settle his will,” Bonner endeavored to explain to the native girl who was ignorant of such complicated matters. “But do not worry. I will take good care of you during my absence from Twenty Miles, and one day, return and take you away to live with me in my country inside my big igloo. In the meantime,” the goal-minded man announced, “I’ll build a nice cabin for you to live in. and you can have a fine job being employed here at the trading post; yes, working with Sandy.”

“Is your mother still living?” the compassionate girl wanted to know. “You’ve never spoken to me about your mother.”

“Yes, and I must return home and help take care of her because she’s very upset that my father has passed-on to stay forever with the Great Spirit,” Bonner tried to express in words that Jees Uck could fathom. “Stay here and work with Sandy, and I shall come back and get you when everything back home in a place called California has been straightened-out!”

A week later, after the spring thaw had descended on the Northland, and the annual thick river ice had finally melted, Neil Bonner sincerely kissed Jees Uck “Goodbye” and then sauntered up the dock platform and onto the *Yukon Belle*, an antiquated steamer on its way out to the Bering Sea. “I’ll be back before the first winter snow flies!” Neil Bonner yelled to his love from the ship’s deck as the departure whistle blasted from the steamer’s main stack.

‘Shit!’ Bonner thought as the ship’s passenger again waved to his one and only girl. ‘With dad’s massive fortune sitting there for me to inherit, I can come back here and become the Cecil Rhodes of Alaska and of all the Yukon! Yes, you-con Neil,’ Bonner’s mind whimsically played and toyed with silly words. ’Yes you-con!’

* * * * * * * * * * * * *

Jees Uck was absolutely thrilled with her new log cabin, with enacting her "important job" at the isolated Twenty Miles trading post, and with her meteoric ascension into prominence among the white fur merchants and Indian pelt hunters that bartered in that part of the Yukon. The last fall steamboat left the local river dock, and the fierce winter snows arrived (including two savage blizzards), but yet, Neil Bonner had not returned to the Northland despite the native girl's admirable vigilance.

A full month later, John Thompson, who had replaced Sandy MacPhearson as the chief operator of the P.C. Company general store, tried to put the make on Jees Uck, and the impulsive Casanova almost had the blade of the angry female's dependable knife penetrate his jugular vein and nearby voice-box.

"Neil Bonner will return to me and to *our* new cabin in the woods," the faithful and vigilant girl communicated as the enraged female held her weapon to the quivering man's neck. "He is a good man, and will keep his sacred promise to me after his unknown business in his far away land has been completed."

"Look Princess Summer-Fall-Winter-Spring, I just read an article from a San Francisco newspaper that stated that your wonderful Neil Bonner has just married a very rich woman named Kitty Sherman, and that the pair intends to spend their honeymoon in a beautiful warm place called Hawaii," Thompson maintained, after the now-disconsolate native girl had placed the lethal knife back into her leather waist-belt holder.

"Neil will come back to me. And you lie to me, Mr. John Thompson. Do you think I am dumb Indian/Eskimo girl? Moon is not made of honey!"

"You have a hard head, Young Lady, and will never understand the white man's truth or the white man's reality," the new store manager maintained before gulping and then clearing his throat. "Neil Bonner will never return to this God-forsaken place, now that he's a very important businessman back in his big country. You'll never see him here again, and the only damned way you'll ever see him in the future is if you somehow travel down to San Francisco, California and witness the real truth I've just described, all for yourself; you naïve, gullible, beautiful, mixed-up mixed-breed!"

"I am, as you' white people call 'pregnant' with Neil Boner's, er, I mean Neil Bonner's child, and if you dare attack me again Mr. Mink-less," Jees Uck predicted, "I will first slice your sex organs off your scummy body, and while you're bent over and bleeding to death, then I will get great pleasure from cutting a big second asshole in your fat, ugly neck! And now John Thompson, *you* can stack the maple syrup bottles used for the white man's pancakes on the log cabin shelf wall!"

Five months after the intense argument between John Thompson and Jees Uck, the girl gave birth to a son whom she named "Neil" in honor of the child's biological father. Four long years passed by, and with each successive month, Jees Uck's hope that her lover would journey back to the Yukon to resume their amicable relationship dwindled-down to almost nil.

But Jees Uck steadfastly kept her fidelity and refused to look into the face of the jilted John Thompson whenever the two had conversations inside the Twenty Miles General Store. And then three separate native hunters gladly offered to marry Jees Uck, despite the existence of her totally "mongrel son Neil", but the dedicated girl shunned the awkward verbal overtures of 'Oche Ish, Hah Yo', and 'Why Not Babe', because Jees still believed that the father of her child would still honor his pledge to come back to the Yukon; regardless of the 'false language' about Neil Bonner's recent marriage that had been printed in the newspaper announcement that the perplexed woman insisted for all literate white man customers to impatiently and orally read to her disbelieving ears before ever leaving the secluded Twenty Mile Trading Post.

* * * * * * * * * * * * *

The sixth disappointing spring after Neil Bonner had left her stranded at the Twenty Mile trading post, Jees Uck took her life's savings and walked her son Neil down to the river dock to board the decrepit, old steamer *Yukon Belle.* Her journey took her and young Neil on an odyssey to St. Michael's; to Unalaska; to Metlakahtla, and next to St. Mary's at the terminal point of the Panhandle. Finally, she and her wide-eyed lad traveled south by ship through the strait of Juan de Fuca (which does *not* mean John the Fucker), and eventually arrived in the thriving metropolis of Seattle, where Jees Uck met-up with reassigned Sandy McPhearson, who painfully read the faded newspaper article about Neil Bonner and Kitty Sherman's wedding ceremony, about their elegant hotel reception, and about their elaborate Hawaii honeymoon. But still, despite the mounting evidence, Jees Uck refused to accept the printed truth about her former lover's new life in the all-too-modern and bewildering United States of America.

And adamant and determined Jees Uck was not intimidated by the great "iron horse" that transported her and her son along the jagged western coast from Seattle to San Francisco, nor was the Eskimo beauty overwhelmed by the masterful, industrial civilization and its attendant factories and immense warehouses that her amazed eyes were viewing outside the train window. This big train is nice, but I wonder if my good friend Neil has any loco-motives!' Jees inadvertently imagined.

With specific address information that the stubborn lady had obtained from Sandy MacPhearson in Seattle, the courageous woman and her awed son hopped-out of a hired buggy cab, and the weary travelers climbed up the white marble steps to Neil Bonner's opulent big city mansion.

A Japanese servant answered the mammoth-sized mahogany front door, and the valet escorted the woman and her child to a tile-walled waiting area. Five minutes later, a snobbish butler guided the pair through three elegant chambers (with crystal chandeliers suspended from ornate ceilings) until Jees and the wide-eyed toddler arrived inside an ostentatiously furnished parlor.

A vivacious, well-dressed, blonde-haired woman gracefully entered the room through French doors, and quickly initiated a polite conversation with the poorly-dressed but very unique Indian/Eskimo girl. "I understand that you wish to see my husband," the queen-like aristocratic lady prefaced. "Do you know my husband?"

"No," Jees Uck slowly answered, her disarrayed mind now boggled and disheveled. "I come here to see Neil Bonner."

"Neil Bonner *is* my husband!" the suddenly-amused, sophisticated woman laughed. "Neil will be arriving home for supper in about ten minutes. I presume you had known my husband when he had been stationed up in Canada. Please sit down. You've probably trekked a long way, and are quite exhausted from your long trip."

Jees Uck nodded her head in consternation, her stunned mind still swimming in a state of culture shock. A series of disturbing thoughts rushed through her mind, with the ideas ranging from salvaging Neil Bonner from certain death, to John Thompson's repelled romantic advances. And then, also, there was Sandy MacPhearson's most recent awful verification of Neil Bonner's marital activities and of course, finally, the fantastic excursion south on the "iron horse" from Washington State to Northern California. The culturally shocked, visiting woman and her amazed child sat back on the ridiculously comfortable sofa, as Mrs. Kitty Bonner resumed the rather awkward dialogue.

"You had known my husband up in Canada?" she graciously interrogated her unexpected, grimy-faced guest.

"Sure. I wash his clothes, and work in his trading post," the befuddled visitor honestly answered, obviously withholding certain essential facts from her sketchy account.

"And I presume that this sturdy lad is your boy? I have a little girl almost the same age," Kitty noted, never realizing that the two children might be kindred.

The alluded-to daughter entered the magnificent room accompanied by a manservant carrying a silver tray with a pot of steaming tea, along with two empty china cups. Soon, the youngsters had gotten over their initial shyness and began playing on the opposite side of the lavish room, while the disparate women sipped tea and continued their stilted conversation.

All the while, Jees Uck realized that she was out of her league competing with the charms and manners of the sophisticated former Kitty Sherman. A moment of silence was interrupted with a familiar male voice that featured surprise blended with an element of anxiety detectable in its intonation.

"Why mercy me! It's Jees Uck!" Neil Bonner exclaimed, not knowing exactly how to emotionally express his genuine feelings. "Kitty," the nervous man said to his unsuspecting wife. "This marvelous young woman had worked for me up in the Yukon."

The fidgety husband was still wondering precisely what Kitty had learned about the native girl and him in *their* past relationship, and so Bonner was reluctant to pursue any additional discourse with *her*.

"Hello Neil. I am fine, yes; very fine," Jees Uck clumsily replied. "You look much good!"

"Well, I can't say how glad I am to see you," Bonner declared with a degree of alarm evident in his tone of voice. "What's happened? Did you strike a gold mine? When did you arrive here in San Francisco? I love this city! I'll never leave my heart here!"

"No Neil; I did not find any gold," Jees Uck emphatically answered her former bedmate. "I saved all my money and came all the way down here just to visit you."

"To think that you knew my husband all the way up there in the primitive Yukon Territory," Kitty chimed-in. "I understand that *that* part of the world is almost prehistoric!"

Jees Uck stared-over at her handsome son harmlessly playing with his half-sister, and noticed both children enjoying themselves tremendously; and suddenly, Jees heart sank lower from the total weight of emotional pity, despair, and melancholy.

The man of both women tried filling a void in the cumbersome, three-way discussion. "Honey," Neil said to Kitty. "I've never told you this, but Jees Uck once saved my life after I had been poisoned by a diabolical fellow named Amos Pentley at the Yukon trading post. I truly owe my life to this fantastic young lady, and will be eternally grateful to this special woman as long as I live!"

"Why that is absolutely incredible to hear, Neil!" Kitty genuinely exclaimed. "I think that you should reward Jees Uck for her splendid loyalty. She should not have to live in abject poverty up there in *that* hostile wilderness. When she leaves San Francisco, I expect you to make her life more comfortable in every way possible."

Neil Bonner felt extremely guilty about his questionable past, and felt obligated (for his own good) to change the subject. "Is that your boy?" the father asked his displaced female visitor. "He's a handsome young lad, and I'll see to it that he receives a good quality education when he grows-up."

"That would only be wise and prudent," Kitty confirmed and agreed. "What is your name Young Man?"

"Neil," the boy all-too-honestly replied.

"That's dumb Injun talk," Jees Uck interposed, realizing the futility of her present situation. "Him do Injun talk. Him name is Nee-al, meaning 'cracker' in white man's talk."

"And the boy's father?" the impressed wife wondered and inquired. "His father must be a fine man!"

"Oh yes, Nee-al's father is very good man," Jees Uck answered, squirming upon the sofa and awkwardly verified.

"Did you know Nee-al's father?" Kitty questioned her husband without showing any trace of suspicion.

"Know him! I knew him personally!" Neil Bonner attested. "He's as fine a man as ever lived in the Yukon, yes he is! I knew him almost as well as I know myself!"

* * * * * * * * * * * * *

But the story of Jees Uck is not one of total disappointment and misery. Human dignity has a way of rising above catastrophe, and ultimately triumphing over all contingencies. And so, the principal characters in this saga all found satisfaction in their individual endeavors, exploits, and enterprises.

The remarkably resilient Jees Uck returned to the Northland and led a straight, decent, moral life, and the modest lady never again slept with a man, or ever again considered marrying one. The Eskimo/Indian beauty stayed for a while with the dedicated Sisters of the Holy Cross Order, who patiently taught her how to read, study, pray, and write.

Out of her lucid fond memory of unreliable, materialistic and goal-oriented Neil Bonner, Jees Uck conscientiously learned the rudiments of nursing, medicine and surgery, and the "quick read" later in life had attended to the critical needs of many prospectors and trail-weary journeymen requiring first aid treatment.

And for the next two and a half decades, San Francisco socialite Kitty Bonner had made sure that her wealthy husband generously supported Jees Uck's humanitarian activities in the Yukon, where the native woman received a handsome annual stipend (and later a pension) of five thousand dollars. And finally, Mrs. Bonner encouraged her sometimes-forgetful spouse to make philanthropic financial contributions to the betterment of the education of children in the Yukon and Klondike territories.

And as for the child affectionately named "Neil," Father Champreau took the boy under his personal supervision and guidance. With great pride, Jees Uck received weekly letters sent from the Jesuit College in Baltimore, Maryland, and later from Paris, France, and then from Vatican City in Rome, Italy. The warm correspondence was from her loving son Father Neil, who eventually rose to a very eminent station in his religious order, and who steadfastly exhibited (with noteworthy distinction) all of the worthy qualities, characteristics and virtues that *his* self-indulgent father failed to master.

# "The League of the Old Men"

The legendary, pernicious Indian criminal known as Umber was both feared and despised throughout the Canadian Yukon River Valley. The villain's infamous murders were reputed to have been committed wantonly and purposely, without any comprehensible reason or motive. And Umber's trademark was that the prejudiced murderer specialized in exclusively killing white men. That fact is what had struck immense terror in the hearts of the law-abiding citizens of Dawson, although many prospectors along the river exaggerated their estimates of the number of people Umber had savagely eliminated, with some statistics reaching as high as three-dozen white men that had been indiscriminately executed. The unassuming victims had been slain singularly, in pairs, or in some instances, in groups of three or more.

The Canadian Mounted Police had been searching in vain to capture the elusive Umber, and bring the culprit to justice, but the reputed "sly as a fox executioner" kept moving-around outside the community boundaries of local civilization, and knew the mountains and the wilderness territories all-too-well.

But even more bizarre and mysterious was why Umber one day appeared in the town of Dawson to voluntarily surrender to authorities. The heinous-minded renegade showed-up on the main street, physically weak and tottering, and the ruthless Indian staggered-over to a pile of logs to rest his weary bones. At first, the on-the-lam hobbling fugitive from justice went unidentified as the unsuspecting parade of law-abiding residents casually shopped and went about their daily business activities, for the fatigued and weary dangerous old Indian appeared to be quite drunk and harmless.

But the vagrant did not escape the attention of little Jerry Dickensen, a neurotic clerk laboring in the brokerage firm of Holbrook and Mason. Ambitious young Dickensen had, the year before, come to the northern country with a bundle of cash and high dreams about discovering gold, but after squandering his money on basic necessities, the unfortunate man now was working to pay for passage back south to the United States. It was craven Jerry Dickensen who looked-out his office window and noticed the old Indian loitering across the street, aimlessly staring at the Caucasian foot traffic that condescendingly ignored his presence, as preoccupied Dawson men and women strolled and ambled by.

'This scenario reminds me of last year during the height of winter when another Indian came into town and died in that exact same spot,' Dickensen recollected. 'It took two whole days until someone had the idea of feeling for a pulse, only to shockingly discover that the poor fellow had died leaning against that same unused cabin log heap. But now it's the height of summer, and the weather's been exceptionally hot. Maybe I should go out there and fuckin' investigate the weird matter during my fifteen-minute coffee break. Who knows? Perhaps I'll get my handsome mug on the front page of the local gazette!'

When dwarfish Jerry Dickensen stepped-outside onto the wooden platform walkway, the young American lit a stogie, and then nonchalantly sauntered across the street where the Dawson-transplant inadvertently met pretty Emily Travis, the daughter of a wealthy mining engineer that had recently struck it rich. Dickensen felt inspired to initiate a casual conversation.

"Very colorful parasol you're holding there, Miss Travis," Jerry courteously greeted, momentarily forgetting about the immobile Indian vagrant. "It matches your expensive dress quite nicely."

"Why thank you, Mr. Dickensen!" Emily suavely replied. "It's very pleasant to know that there's at least one gentleman residing here in Dawson! I mean, it's not exactly as modern as London was when I had lived there, but this town is becoming more advanced with each passing year. Ahhh! Oh my God!" Emily hysterically screamed. "Who is this hideous grotesque monster lying there?"

A gaunt and famished-looking old Indian was brazenly touching Emily's arm through her dress. Feeling threatened, diminutive Jerry Dickensen nervously squealed-out to the barbaric-looking intruder, "What do you want?"

Umber just grunted and mumbled some indiscernible Indian words, and continued to gaze-up and admire the enchanting Miss Travis, who obviously felt very uncomfortable and insulted. The manner-less native could not comprehend how women of Emily Travis's weak, soft build could produce such fierce white men that had descended like a herd of wild caribou into *his* people's valley, and had greedily confiscated the best locations, and then constructed sophisticated towns like Dawson all along the Yukon River.

Emily noticed an Indian employee of her father's company, and beckoned for the worker to walk across the street to serve as an interpreter. "Over here Jimmy!" Emily yelled and waved. "I need your indispensable assistance!"

Jimmy was a hulking native Indian, who gladly obliged the pretty Miss Emily Travis's request. The employee attempted communicating with Umber, but his efforts at first yielded minimal success, for the stranger spoke a dialect indigenous to the interior lands, and Jimmy was a Sitka, who had been domesticated by the customs and language of Western Civilization Caucasians. "Him Whitefish Indian. Not too many of the tribe is left," Jimmy informatively disclosed. "I have plenty trouble talking with him, but he say he wants to speak with chief of the white man."

"Does he wish to speak with the Governor?" Jerry Dickensen facetiously jested. "What about Her Majesty the Queen? We could always send him to England as one-way freight!"

"I think he wants to talk to Captain Alexander at the fort," Jimmy related to Jerry and Emily. "Him say he kill plenty white men; white women; white boy; white girl, and many other white people. Him say he hate white people. Him say he wants to die!"

"This frail fellow must be an insane lunatic!" Jerry confided to Emily and Jimmy. Then, Dickensen signaled to a tall, handsome uniformed Mounted Policeman, patrolling the sidewalk across the street, to come over and evaluate the situation.

Umber clumsily rose to his feet, and then pointed his right index finger at the policeman's chest and uttered some obscure gibberish in his native tongue, which Jimmy endeavored to translate. Soon, an assemblage of curious onlookers gathered around, and the various merchants, loggers, businessmen, prospectors, mountaineers, pioneers, and women shoppers all wanting to learn something about the strange conference-in-progress.

"Him still say same damned thing!" Jimmy explained. "Him say no more white fish in river, because all destroyed by white man who like to eat white fish! Him want to see Captain and die for killing plenty white people! Him say he be last of Whitefish tribe, and want to die to catch new white fish in big land belonging to Spirit in the Sky!"

"Perhaps this seemingly trivial matter requires some review by my superiors," the tall, muscular, red-jacketed Mounted Policeman recommended. "I'll escort this old fellow over to headquarters. We have an interpreter stationed at the barracks who knows the Whitefish tribe's language, and he'll be able to decipher exactly what this wrinkle-faced rascal is attempting to divulge!"

* * * * * * * * * * * * * *

When the residents of Dawson learned that the notorious outlaw Umber was to stand trial for his multiple heinous misdeeds, on the morning of the hearing, the town courthouse was packed to capacity with "standing room only" spaces all taken-up. A light drizzle was falling outside, and the suspect's apathetic-gray face matched the overcast dull sky outside the courtroom building.

Umber looked at his audience unfazed, with a somber emotionless expression upon his countenance. Everyone in attendance was expecting a decisive and quick "conviction and guilty verdict" to be rendered by the presiding judge and the hastily-organized jury.

The judge rapped his gavel on his elevated bench table, and soon the droned gallery conversations turned to silence. A district prosecutor stood, and in a monotonous voice, read the long list of charges against the defendant. And after the ten-minute long document had been verbally reviewed, Umber was surprised to hear someone address him in his native Whitefish tongue.

"Thou does not remember me, or perhaps you do!" the well-educated, fully-assimilated Indian began his remarks.

"Yes; you are Howkan, who had deserted our village and ran-away to learn the white man's ways," Umber recalled and mentioned. "Your mother is now dead."

"She was old, and is now in the hands of the Great Spirit in the Sky!" Howkan replied, showing reverence to customary old Indian beliefs. "Now then, Umber. I'll review for you in Whitefish dialect the major charges that have been lodged against you. You may say anything you wish, because I'm probably the only one in this room who'll know what the hell you're stating, so feel free to speak your mind," Howkan advised and confided. "I'll then translate your general words for all the white people sitting and standing in this room to hear and understand. This is the way that the white man performs justice. They call what they do 'democracy'!"

After Howkan narrated and enumerated to Umber the essence of the serious allegations that had been introduced against him, the aged Whitefish seemed rather perplexed and confused.

"Speak freely, Brave Indian! Please don't talk like your throat is made of lumber, Umber!" the court prosecutor confided.

"Please tell me, Howkan; *how can* the papers in your hands speak to you? You look at the white man's white papers, and then are somehow divined to speak. Those papers you are holding; are they the white man's fucked-up kind of devil magic?" Umber wanted to know. "How could the magic papers know all of the shit that I've done, and also, all of the shit that I'm being accused of doing? How can your lips know what I have done, when your eyes and ears were not present when the damned crimes had been committed? Those evil white papers you fuckin' hold in your clean and washed hands must be possessed by the devil spirits!"

"It is no great medicine or magic," Howkan assured the puzzled suspect sitting on the witness stand. "It is what the white man calls 'writing', or words that can be looked at on paper and then spoken. I realize that it is difficult for you to fully understand, but I had learned this special writing knowledge when I became a student going to white man's school. There is nothing really magical about it!"

Howkan then publicly read Umber's confession that had been given to Captain Alexander at the fort. The Whitefish Indian was astounded that all of the murders had been reviewed and accurately classified, and then orated in exact chronological order. The two Indians then discussed the major felony incidents, and next Howkan took the allotted time to translate the oral consultations for the benefit of the general audience.

"Why did you kill the old red-haired bearded man traveling alone along the river on foot?" Howkan asked the accused Whitefish. "Did he violate you in any way?"

"Hell! That was my brother, Harold!" a flannel shirted man yelled-out from the gallery. "You savage! You cannibal! You never gave Harold a fighting chance; killing him in cold blood like you did!"

The stoic-faced judge banged his gavel and ordered "Silence!" and then the hubbub of commotion within the courtroom eventually subsided. "Continue with your statement," Howkan urged the unpenitent defendant. "Everyone present in this room is very interested in what you have to disclose."

"I am proud Umber of the Whitefish people," the accused elderly villain announced. "My father was Otsbaok, a strong man and brave warrior in his youth. When I was young, the land was warm with sunshine and food-a-plenty," the dispassionate witness recalled and related. "My people did not hunger, and we all prospered with many white fish swimming in the rivers and creeks. Our tribe had over two-hundred people. But one day, a crazy-minded dumb-ass white man came with a large ugly dog with short hair. Both the fucked-up man and his fucked-up dog were sick, and my people took care of them."

"Although this accurate background seems quite irrelevant to your defense," Howkan interrupted and translated for the public to hear, "what happened after you healed the white man and his dog? Did they directly harm or injure you?"

"Well now, the damned dog became healthy and powerful, and fought with my tribe's smaller dogs, and killed-off most of them except for several bitches, with which the big alien dog mated. Soon, a new breed of dog came to be, and the new dogs were scrawny, ugly and disobedient," Umber testified and explained. "The new breed would not make good companions on the hunt, because the animals barked too much. The fucked-up thin-haired foreign dog had contaminated my tribe's hunting dogs that then refused to pull the dogsleds, and did not stay quiet in the forests during hunts."

"And what about the old red-haired bearded white man you had shot to death from a distance?" Howkan objectively asked. "Did he wrong you in any way?"

"He was a loud-mouthed son-of-a-bitch, who bragged that his people were plentiful, and that they would take-over the whole damned valley, which they fuckin' gradually did! That's how I began to hate the white man!" Umber lividly bellowed. "And then this asshole white man ran away with the chief's daughter Noda, and within five years, other Indian women slept with other white men, and soon the Whitefish Tribe had mixed blood children. Indian culture was fuckin' being destroyed slowly-but-surely. Ten sun years later, the chiefs and the elders were disrespected by these fucked-up mongrel half-breeds, who defied and disobeyed the older men's authority," the suspect vehemently insisted, finally overtly showing his livid disdain. "Everyone in my tribe except me became fucked-up, until to this day, in this room, where I proudly sit here as the last true-blooded Whitefish Indian of my destroyed tribe."

"So, I deduce from your comments that you had killed the red-bearded man for changing your Whitefish tribe's customs, which eventually led to the disintegration and the decline of your people," Howkan concluded. "You had blamed *him* for corrupting your people with his evil ways!"

"Yes, what you say is true. And then soon, another white man that I later killed came into the village, and traded his dog, a short gun called a pistol, and ten-pounds of rice, and five-pounds of tobacco; and also, he traded a case of whiskey fire water for the six remaining good dogs the village men owned," Umber remembered and divulged in his native tongue. "And then my uncle Koo-So-Tee mocked me and the others for hunting moose with bows and arrows, and not using the pistol, which shot six black magic bullets at close range. But one day a grizzly bear approached Koo-So-Tee, and my dumb-ass braggart uncle shot the animal six times with the gun, but then my uncle was brutally and viciously mauled by the angry grisly grizzly bear, and soon Koo-So-Tee died. And so," Umber summarized. "My uncle was also killed by the white man's fucked-up evil medicine. So, you see. Koo-So-Tee's squaw and his family suffered badly, and became ill, since my stupid-shit uncle was dead, and could no longer normally hunt wild animals and bring meat to his tent."

"So, you're saying that the white man was responsible for Koo-So-Tee's death, because your uncle refused to use a bow and arrow as was the traditional method of hunting; and instead, your now-dead uncle used a pistol?" Howkan interrogated.

"Yes, that's exactly what the fuck happened!" Umber attested and verified. "Soon, the meat in the forest became less abundant with fewer moose, elk, and caribou around to hunt. And all the tribes of the forests and mountains quickly began to diminish in numbers, including the Whitefish and the Pellys. I discussed the white man invasions with the League of Elders and with village shamans, and the tribesmen all agreed with my disgust," Umber communicated through his erudite translator. "The fucked-up white men were a curse to the victim Indians, and they've corrupted our sacred ways with their greed and with their many evil medicines. I decided that I must begin killing the arrogant assholes in order for me and my people to survive as we had done in the past."

"Did you advocate or incite rebellion among your people?" the now-impressed Indian translator asked Umber. "Did you have any accomplices in committing your crimes?"

"The elders and the shamans were all weak and cowardly jerk-offs and stupid-brained assholes," the stubborn witness adamantly testified. "And so, I decided to take the law into my own hands to protect myself and to guard my dumb-shit people from extinction. I was hunting with my rifle along the big river that the greedy white men call the Yukon, when two white-skinned trespassers came ashore in their canoe," Umber recalled and stated. "I shot the first dumb-fuck encroacher in the heart with my bow and arrow to honor the old forgotten customs, and next, I blasted the second greedy bearded old fuck in the head with my white man's rifle. Then, I burned the dead assholes' canoe and all of the possessions inside, out of pure contempt for the white invaders, and out of scorn for their black magic medicine that had brought only misery to the diluted Whitefish people."

A buzz of whispers filled the courtroom, as the folks in the gallery gossiped amongst themselves about what peculiar explanations that had just been translated and revealed. Then, the well-composed and very confident Howkan continued his fascinating investigation into the essential facts.

"Let it be chronicled in the court records that the two men that Umber has just confessed to killing were Peter James and Matthew

Delaney, who were merely engaged in bringing the mail pouches upriver all the way to Le Barge to be delivered to recently arrived settlers. And furthermore," the conscientious law graduate student proceeded with his competent inquiry, "let it be noted that Umber here acted unilaterally, and was not part of any organized conspiracy. Now good Whitefish Warrior, tell us more details about your other sensational wanton killings."

Umber then described in his language how he had killed groups of white men near the Chilcoot Pass, and some others not far away from Caribou Crossing. All of those random murders were conducted to prevent the relentless invaders from confiscating land and destroying the Indians' forest food supply, and had been performed to protect the native lands from being abused and violated by the evil white interlopers and their diabolical magic, their sinful medicine, and their "evil fire-whiskey".

"Do you have anything else to say in support of your own defense?" the junior prosecutor asked the Whitefish Indian in *their* native language. "Now is your last chance!"

"I am old, and I'm the last true-blood of my tribe, and I wish to die as soon as possible," Umber pleaded. "I would prefer being shot by rifles rather than to be fuckin' hanged. It doesn't fuckin' matter what your white people in this room think; or what you Howkan think, or what the chief sitting-up there behind that large table thinks when he bangs his stick on the table! I just want to fuckin' die by shooting, for I have lived too long; and have seen too much sickness and suffering; and now, I simply desire to hunt in the Great Spirit's big forest in the sky where moose, bear, elk, caribou, and white fish are very plentiful!"

"Your Honor and Gentlemen of the Sexist Chauvinistic Jury, what is your verdict?" Howkan objectively inquired.

"Guilty!" thirteen elderly male voices yelled in unison. "Guilty!" all thirteen judiciously repeated and confirmed in compliance with the letter of the white man's inflexible laws and justice.

# "The Law of Life"

Old Koskoosh was near death, and the elderly codger was well-aware of the consequences defined by tribal tradition as interpreted among the Eskimos. The needs of those that contributed to the community, and to the clan's welfare, preceded the needs of the individual, particularly those of the faltering aged and infirmed. Over the years, Koskoosh's eyesight had diminished, his hearing was no longer acute, his kidneys were weak and dysfunctional, his skin wrinkled, his pecker shriveled-up, and his loins shrunken and dry. The ancient former chief's vibrant granddaughter Sit-cum-to-ha was harnessing the dogs to the funeral sled, and her thoughts were not on her withered and broken grandfather sitting alone in the snow, forlorn and defenseless. Her troubled mind was focused on other more important concerns. Camp had to be broken, and the long trail awaited their passage, since the short period of energy-giving sunlight would certainly be abbreviated. The 'law of life' governed Sit-cum-to-ha's immediate duties and responsibilities, but death was the only prospect that was predictably imminent to old, dependent Koskoosh.

The aged man's mind fondly reviewed his long history as a proud and honored hunter and revered village leader, but now, as his senses had declined, Koskoosh's terrible fate was predetermined. The elderly geezer gingerly felt the pile of wood next to his side, and realized that its existence would probably outlast his. His ears could faintly hear the women in the distance disassembling the hides that had constituted the temporary shelters of the nomadic tribe, and Koskoosh's decrepit mind vaguely visualized that it was time for the clan to follow the migration of the caribou, and move-on to a new temporary destination.

The shaman's voice could be heard barking guttural commands, and the cries of the recently born Koo-tee could also be discerned, the screaming child requiring food and nutrition, but in reality, an infant whose fate might in the future actually parallel old Koskoosh's. Koo-tee was besieged with welts, and the irritated bambino had a bad case of very large bug bites at that. In the bitter end, death stalked anyone and everyone, but its specter being especially imminent at present; the old man and the infant, both now thoroughly incapable of providing for their own personal needs, and thus, being dual burdens, affording little value to the traveling clan.

The whining dogs despised the work and the trail, at least that was Koskoosh's recollection of the past along with his present perception of reality. The hoary patriarch's ears heard the sleds departing one by one, as the 'sentenced by nature' grandfather sat motionless in the freezing snow. But much to the old fellow's comfort, his lone son loyally stayed behind to offer *his* last allegiance.

"Is all well with you?"

"As well as it fuckin' could be as death approaches and encroaches," Koskoosh, resigned to his fate, answered. "I was once in your role, ready to abandon my father, and I did so according to the fucked-up law of the wilderness clan. Now, I know exactly how the fuck my pappy must've felt at that moment, and my restless soul feels the same solitude and the same desolation. Why the fuck couldn't I have been born a rich white man?"

"I'll start your final fire, and I hope your wood lasts long," the compassionate son indicated. "The warmth of the fire will, for a short time, protect you from the cold as long as it lasts. The fire will remind you of your wife; my mother, who was your old flame!"

"Aye, it is snowing, and it is no wonder that my mind is flakey, if you fuckin' get my drift!" the old man attempted jesting to his son. "I remember my father saying those same fucked-up words before I left him behind to die; many meteors, asteroids, hemorrhoids, and also, many suns and moons ago!"

"I now hear the other men are summoning me to follow them," the son apologetically explained. "The hungry hunters have not feasted in a long time; the trail journey is long as *we* must travel fast without you holding back our progress. Such was true in your time, and I'm sure you understand the custom of clan necessity, no matter how fucked-up it all seems and sounds. But still, better you fuckin' perishing than me!"

"I fuckin' understand it, but don't fuckin' like it, when I know it's fuckin' happening to me," melancholy Koskoosh sadly replied. "Don't you get the idea, my son? I'm a degenerate leaf desperately clinging to its vine. Soon, I will fall, and nobody except me gives a shit. My voice is like a weak old woman's words, and my feet are heavy, and I'm more tired than a sex-starved whore after a night of intense humping and pumping. You'd better be on your damned way, to live and hunt another day, so that I can meet my scripted tragic end, with as much dignity as nature will fuckin' allow me."

The old, former tribal chief fathomed that his limited time would decrease in proportion to the duration of the fire's flames. Such was the overriding principal of *that* final inevitable phase of the law of life. Soon, the apathetic frost would take its toll with his feet yielding first, and then the cold and the numbness would dominate his other extremities; the old man's hands followed by his penis, his testicles, and then his head. 'It is easy. All men and women must die and maybe go to the great spirit in the sky, if that myth is not a lot of smelly moose shit; but the missionary people claim it is true, although I have my fuckin' strong doubts,' Koskoosh reasoned. 'But this death shit really hits home when it fuckin' has to happen to *you,* all alone in the frigid ice and freezing snow, and hoping that you die before the next Arctic blizzard fuckin' kills you! If this is the fuckin' meaning of life,' Koskoosh semi-rationally reckoned, 'then life has no fuckin' meaning or purpose at all!'

Koskoosh fully comprehended that nature had no sympathy for the individual, and that its laws in regard to man's existence were strict and unalterable. The laws of instinct and endurance valued the species and the clan over the person next in line who was distinctly designated to die. The strong survive, and the weak perish. The yellow leaf falls, but the green one thrives, but only during its ephemeral time.

The old men that Koskoosh had known as a boy had been acquainted with the old men before them. 'I'm now experiencing what generations of my dumb-shit people have known, honored and stupidly practiced for countless centuries,' the former tribal chief evaluated. 'I have produced a good son, and my name shall carry on through *his* deeds and exploits. I had been a skilled hunter in my youth, but am now being stalked and hunted by Death, and I now know how the prey feels before succumbing to a savage predator,' the dying man contemplated. 'And I had screwed several well-endowed women in my lifetime, but now can't even piss a yellow stream into a wide rock crevice. And those squawking squaws had been left behind with their wood and fires after famine hit the clan, and after their formerly luscious wet, pink cunts had dried-out. I, just like those lousy bitches from years ago, shall pass away like a summer cloud, with my descendants only to be replaced by the next moving cloud. Shit! Why's my memory so fuckin' cloudy?' the weary veteran questioned his mental alertness. 'Why is my fuckin' name Koskoosh and not fuckin' White Cloud?' the old man regretfully considered, as he placed another stick onto the fire and then resumed his lonely, futile meditating.

'Ah yes; the mosquitoes vanish each fall with the first frost, but what kind of brain could a tiny mosquito have? Does it even fuckin' know it's dying? The squirrel and the rabbit realize that they are old and slow, and can no longer outrace their famished enemies, but do those failing creatures have any concept of either death or dying?' And then the old man's thoughts became more morose and macabre. 'I remember leaving my father to die in a similar manner as my present predicament, yes, up in the Klondike Territory. But he passed on to that great hunting ground in the sky before camp was broken without ever fully digesting his last Eskimo Pie; and I had time to bury his body, but then, the hungry wolves dug him up, and consumed everything; flesh, blood, undigested Eskimo Pie, along with his bones! Shit, Great Spirit! Why the fuck was I ever born into this fucked-up world?'

And then the disconsolate, fatigued man thought about past famines, and the loss of his mother, and about how the salmon had not run the river that summer; and how the caribou never migrated through the territory that particular winter; and how only one in ten of the clan survived to hunt, to screw, to reproduce, and then to die. For what end? 'Ah yes,' Koskoosh logically concluded. 'The true meaning of life is to eat, sleep, screw, and reproduce. Now I fuckin' get it! Ah yes!' the aged philosopher seriously reflected as if trapped in his own dream. 'There were good times too when the meat was plentiful. I'm fuckin' glad I've not been a dumb-ass vegetarian all these years, or else, I would've died decades ago from either fuckin' starvation or malnutrition! And the dogs were fat and healthy *that* warm July, and the horny women had nice firm breasts and delicious juicy pussies that were very accessible during the entire summertime mating season!'

Other fleeting random memories raced through the apprehensive old man's mind. 'When the men of my clan were fat-stomached and healthy, we then waged war with other neighboring clans, and out of sheer greed, we killed each other for each-others' women to screw,' Koskoosh recalled. 'And then there was the amazing time when my friend Zing-ha and I witnessed a pack of hungry, ferocious wolves bring-down a colossal-sized moose, and then Zing-ha got so excited and disoriented that he fell into a deep hole, and when we finally dug him out six months later, my friend was frozen stiff; so, we had to thaw him out and eat him just so that we could survive the hostile winter! The zany son-of-a-bitch tasted pretty good though, I must admit. And I think I had acquired some of his hunting skills after munching on Zing-ha's delectable arms and shoulders! But that fucked-up story about Zing-ha's strange death doesn't seem quite so hilarious right now as it used to sound.'

Koskoosh's erratic psyche then reflected some more about his deceased comrade and trusty companion. 'Ah Yes,' the frail old man remembered as his fuzzy mind forgot all about all aspects of chronological order. 'Zing-ha and I had seen that old bull-moose that could no longer keep-up with the thundering herd, and the herd's patriarch was thus abandoned just like my worthless ass has been presently rejected and discarded. The wolves methodically separated the exhausted moose from his brothers and family, and then had him consumed for their dinner. Holy shit!' Koskoosh hypothesized and imagined. 'The same fuckin' thing might soon happen to me! I might be fuckin' wolfed-down by fierce snarling wolves! I hope I'm not greedily eaten alive just like Zing-ha was! And most of all, Great Spirit; I fear that my limp dick might be the first thing to be bitten-off and chewed right before my very eyes!'

The bloodstained moose had fought valiantly, going-down twice, and regaining its feet in the midst of the snarling and hissing wolves, two of which had been crushed to death by the weight of the falling animal, and subsequently, immediately consumed by their voracious peers. The entire episode had been carefully watched and followed by both Koshkoosh and Zing-ha. "The trail was red with the moose's blood," the two had told the dubious shaman, who in return succinctly declared, "I think both of you' juvenile assholes are hallucinating, because you've together eaten too much of the white man's stale 'chocolate moose' that we had luckily found in a village garbage dumpster."

'And now, after all of the great things I've done and accomplished for my ungrateful clan, the tribe leaves me out here to die like a sick animal!' Koshkoosh sorrowfully summarized. 'Such is the fucked-up Law of Life that I've helped to perpetuate!'

Then, the former proud chief pondered his adventurous youth and assessed his many contributions to the selfish clan. Koskoosh replenished his dwindling fire with fresh kindling and thought, 'If lazy Sit-cum-to-ha had only been more industrious and had gathered more firewood, I could survive out here on the frontier for another day and a half. But the arrogant, nymphomaniac whore is married to that relentless sex fanatic Beaver, the son of Zing-ha, who is an eager Beaver for my granddaughter's beaver, and every other goddamned hot beaver in the damned clan,' the faltering old man conjectured. 'But how could I envy, fault, or despise 'Eager Beaver', when he's only acting just like Zing-ha and I had done in *our* mutual 'hump and pump' every damned pussy' pasts.'

Momentarily, everything became still as the north winds seemed to cease. The old, shivering patriarch took a deep breath amidst the dreadful, all-encompassing silence. But hark! What was that very distressful rustle his still-perceptive ears were hearing? A great chill shot down his weakened spine. An all-too-familiar howl caught Koskoosh's attention, and the recognized distant noise further depressed his flagging spirit. 'Should I fight like a wild beast? Should I resist certainty as the bull-moose had ineffectively done? Or should I simply rationally accept my hideous fate and surrender to being torn apart and ravenously consumed?'

Soon, the inexorable circle of gray and white fur appeared, and the terrible sniffing and snuffling began, which was soon followed by the characteristic snarling, panting, and slathering dry mouths. Instinctively, the old Eskimo's hand shot towards the fire and grabbed a blazing stick; then desperately waving the contrived weapon in the face of the first suddenly-alarmed wolf, which promptly withdrew its nose from Koskoosh's throat. Several of the less brazen brutes retreated from the dwindling fire, but then soon again advanced, but this second time more audaciously. More fiery sticks were thrust forward and swirled about, but the determined, starving beasts refused to either scatter or disperse. The only inconclusive matter in dispute was which wolf would have the most flesh and muscle to rip apart and swallow.

The old man had now lost all of his desire to continue living. He dropped his burning stick and took one last sigh, voluntarily placing his head between his knees before being eagerly attacked. One last thought dominated Koskoosh's agony, and his anguish, before being devoured: 'I should not resist reality as the bull-moose had done.' Koskoosh accepted the principle of being conquered and defeated by the Law of Life; a covenant of nature that governed both man and beast in that remote Klondike Territory of northwestern Canada.

# "Lost Face"

Subienkow knew that the end of his life's adventures was near. The journeyman had traveled to the splendid capitals of Europe, and now on the frigid Alaskan Coast, his extensive trail was about to terminate. The condemned man impatiently sat in the snow, waiting for the brutal torture that was a hostage mercenary's destiny. A huge Cossack, Subienkow's servant Ivan lay in the snow fifteen-feet away, moaning and groaning from excruciating pain that had just been brutally inflicted. The calloused-local-clansmen had just completed their punishment of the defeated Russian giant, and to mock his manhood, the mean-spirited tribesmen now turned *his* master's fate over to a sadistic-minded cruel gaggle of garrulous woman.

Subienkow shuddered from observing the hideous spectacle, but was not afraid to die. His trail of exploits and escapades had gone from his native Warsaw all the way to the present Nulato Village. But the humiliation of being publicly tortured and ridiculed truly offended the world traveler's pride. The prospective victim did not dread the idea of pain, but Subienkow did not wish to die a mortified and humbled man. That ugly, alien notion was contrary to the disgruntled Pole's self-esteem, and to his sense of nobility.

'I refuse to die like a tormented beast; howling and screaming like a delusional asylum maniac!' Subienkow solemnly promised his dwindling ego. 'I have been playing the dangerous game, and this time, have lost. I should never have been fuckin' captured alive! If I had to fuckin' do it all over again, suicide would've been a much more desirable option!'

In the beginning, Subienkow, like other idealistic Polish countrymen, dreamed of a liberated and independent land free of Russian dominion. But fate had directed his odyssey from Warsaw to St. Petersburg; to the Siberian sweat mines; to the Kamchatka Peninsula on the eastern Pacific; to the fur boats of the ruthless sea thieves, and now to the bitter end game on the Alaskan Coast. Once upon a time, the romantic Subienkow was an aspiring poet; an ambitious young artist, and a fanciful dreamer. Now, the Pole was a cursed man, about to be maimed and mutilated.

'That's Ivan lying over there on the ground,' Subienkow sadly observed. 'The Russian was once a man of iron. But ironically, the human hulk has now been reduced to a quivering mass, suffering and agonizing like a wounded and abused beast. But Big Ivan is enduring his tremendous pain; a harrowing ache that is so terrible that even the formidable Ivan the Terrible would've felt pity for the giant's incredible anguish. I hate to see Ivan crying and writhing around like a worm. The giant deserves much better!'

And standing above Ivan was the belligerent clansman, Yakaga, who had just the week before been expelled from the fort by Ivan. The chief's son had betrayed Subienkow along with the Giant Russian for having *him* lashed, and now the vindictive Indian native sought revenge. A group of amused squaws huddled around and above the doomed Ivan, and mockingly chanted derisive remarks in their native tongue while rhythmically clapped their hands.

Attempting to stop the irksome demonstration, the tied-up Subienkow shouted and then hysterically laughed, and everyone stopped their activities and stared at the Pole in wonderment. As the natives gaped at the condemned man, Subienkow's mind reviewed his circuitous route from Warsaw to the Alaskan Coast.

'Ah yes, there was the little spotted-pony in my youth, a gift from my parents,' the captured man fondly remembered. 'And my gay French tutor had sneaked me a copy of Voltaire, which I soon learned to cherish. That's when I was inspired to become a revolutionary in my own country,' Subienkow recalled. 'Then, my two colleagues in rebellion were executed in St. Petersburg. And I luckily managed to escape *that* hostile city alive. A drunken jailer had beaten another friend to death. Savagery has been the theme of my lackluster life,' the about-to-be-executed Pole reminded himself. 'And then others and myself had been whipped into mincemeat in the fucked-up Siberian mines. In our daring escape, vile Cossacks had maliciously killed my remaining fellow revolutionaries, and only I made it safely to the Kamchatka Peninsula to eventually join fur thieves and traders, and then sail east to Alaska. I had used money and documents from a dead Russian traveler I had murdered to change my identity, and to later convince the demented captain and the lunatic crew that I should be accepted aboard the Russian ship.'

Then, Subienkow recollected some other memorable past events. 'I couldn't return to Warsaw, going back west into Russia, so my ultimate dream was to meet up with Europeans in Alaska; travel across America, and then sail the Atlantic back to Europe, thus entering Poland from the west instead of from Russia. But the fur thieves I was travelling with made enemies with the Eskimos, and with the native clansmen, and I soon became stereotyped as being one of them,' the Pole's mind reviewed. 'That's why Ivan and I had to build the fort, but regrettably, we were overwhelmed in battle, and betrayed by that no-good-bastard-scoundrel, Yakaga. So, here the hell I am; sitting with my hands bound behind my back and about to die. I must hastily contrive a plan to either escape my abominable penalty, or to manage to die like a nobleman; the aristocratic nobleman that I had always wished to become!'

It had been rumored that to the east, a vast river known as the Yukon was home to blue-eyed Europeans, the type of men that could lead Subienkow back to Europe, and to then join the revolution against Russia. 'If only I could've made it to the Michaelovski Redoubt, I could've eventually found the Yukon River. Then Ivan and another trader decided to build the fort at Nulato, and the local Indians helped construct it. But then, Yakaga's father and his repugnant, traitorous sons refused to pay the fur traders any tribute. And that's when the chief's son betrayed and captured Ivan and me, after heinously slaughtering and mauling the other fur traders, most of whom were unscrupulous thieves.'

'Shit!' Subienkow regretfully thought. 'True. I had lashed Yakaga on his shoulders and face with my whip, but the bastard intends to torture me to death while I'm being simultaneously belittled by his harem of cackling squaws. The punishment is too great for my crime. I wouldn't mind if the prettier bitches sat on my face and rubbed their hairy nude snatches against my mouth, and thus pleasantly suffocated me to death. But the type of indignity that they practice is absolutely inhumane!' the condemned man assessed. 'Oh Hell! Here's old Makamuk approaching now to further insult me. I'm glad that I had shouted and screamed to attract his attention. I've got to outsmart the clan's chief, or else suffer a similar fate as that of my loyal servant; the blatantly disparaged Ivan!'

* * * * * * * * * * * * *

"Oh Makamuk, your thinking is quite amok, and soon you'll be totally out of luck," Subienkow cleverly began his last-ditch defense. "I should not have to die, and it would be extremely foolish for you to have me die. I am superior to other white men in many, many ways." The Pole peered-over at the wriggling, semi-conscious Ivan lying on the ground, and then gazed-up directly into Makamuk's eyes. "I am too wise to die, for I am the possessor of great medicine knowledge; even much more powerful than your wise shaman understands," Subienkow maintained. "Now then, since I'm about to die, I shall exchange this magic potion secret with you, for it shall protect me from death."

"What is this great medicine?" Makamuk curiously asked. "Can it make my dried-up balls function again? Can it put new sperm in my worm?" The chief asked through his advisor and interpreter, his mentally challenged son, Yakaga.

Subienkow paused for a moment, pretending as if not wanting to part with his great secret. "It is indeed a strange and powerful formula that is not fucked-up like Ivan down there has been. Just a little bit of this wonderful potion rubbed onto the skin will make it harder than a rock, and no cutting weapon, including an arrow, a spear, a knife, or even an ax can penetrate the user's skin," the wily captive insisted. "A bone knife becomes like a piece of mud, and a harpoon becomes like a limp pecker. What will you give me to learn of this great medicine? It could make you the greatest chief with the longest, thickest and hardest dick in all of Alaska!"

"I will spare you your life," the impressed elderly chief answered. "Yes, I will give you back your life, but you shall be a slave in my house, and lick my asshole three times a day," the retarded interpreter replied after conferring with his father Makamuk.

The sentenced-to-death Pole laughed scornfully. "Look Makamuk. Untie my hands and feet, so that we can talk like honest men. I am not bound to tell you the truth when my damned hands and feet are strongly bound, also."

The chief gave a signal to one of his warriors, who then, using a sharp knife, freed the Pole of his tethers. Showing self-confidence, Subienkow rose to his feet, rolled a cigarette, and then lit it before resuming conversation with his captor.

"This is fucked-up silly talk!" Makamuk said through his trusted interpreter. "No such magic medicine exists anywhere on the fuckin' planet. But let me tell you foreign Asshole; my ax's cutting edge gives me the cutting edge *over you,* every fuckin' time, ha, ha, ha!"

But the wary chief recollected that his tribe had experienced cultural shock before, especially with the guns, cannons, and other weapons of the technologically-superior fur traders, devices that his clan had warred against in the past, and Makamuk had been astounded by the great inventions that other white men had utilized. "Okay Dumb-Shit," the chief said through his principal interpreter. "I'll spare you your life, and you will not be a slave."

Sublenkow played his debating game as if he were a fur trader bartering for a common fox hide. "This invincible medicine of which I speak has saved my life on many occasions," the Pole nonchalantly stated. "In addition, to my personal freedom, I also want a sled with six healthy dogs to pull it to the North Country. I also wish to have six of your best hunters to travel with me one day's sleep beyond Michaelovski Redoubt, and I want no doubt from you about my trip to Redoubt."

"That's a fucked-up request!" Makamuk strenuously objected. "You must stay here with my clan and teach us all of your deviltries. That is my condition for you to continue breathing. Your skinny, fucked-up neck will never leave this neck of the woods."

Subienkow shrugged his shoulders, and the accompanying delay was his strategic negotiating ploy. The adventurer casually and deliberately blew cigarette smoke into the air, and peered-down at the remains of the once mighty Ivan, who was never ever seen working on any railroad.

"Look at that scar on your neck!" Makamuk observed and noted. "Your dumb-shit medicine was not strong enough to prevent that from happening. Was your jugular surprised by an errant juggler's knife? Ha, ha, ha?"

"A very strong man, much stronger than Ivan down there, and certainly much stronger than you or your strongest hunter, had administered that very serious blow to my neck," the Pole melodramatically explained. "And also, at the time, the application of the medicine was thin and weak, for you must understand, where the incident had happened was in far-away Russia. There was an absence of an important berry that is plentiful here in your land. So, Makamuk," the shrewd captive continued his oddball narrative. "Don't rub me the wrong way, or you'll never once rub my magic medicine; a powerful medicine that could even make your dick hard, so that you would be potent enough to have many more children and produce, or should I say 'reproduce', many fine muscular warriors and retarded hunters like Yakaga into your fucked-up family."

"I'll allow you to have the sled, with six dogs, and the six hunters to go to Michaelovski Redoubt, where no doubt I will re-doubt my decision," the chief replied through his bilingual, moronic spokesman. "Now go before I fuckin' change my mind!"

"Well, Makamuk. You were too slow in replying to my demands, and also, your delay has offended my powerful medicine," the sly Pole accused the very superstitious chief. "You should've accepted my friendly terms sooner. I also now want a hundred furs to trade with other white men at my destination. I also wish to have a hundred pounds of dried fish that smell better than your clan women's cunts," Subienkow stipulated. "And furthermore, now I want two sleds; the second one being for my furs to be transported to Michaelovski Redoubt for me to sell there. And finally, you must also return my rifle to me so that I can be a big shot among my people. And if you reject my asking price," the hostage emphatically warned his captor, "my price will grow just as sure as your impotent dick no longer does."

Yakaga then yakked something of relevance into his father's ear. "But how do I know that this fantastic medicine of which you speak is real?" the all-too-skeptical chief-to-be demanded knowing. "This nonsensical shit of which you speak might be some kind of resourceful sorcery; perhaps an evil poison?"

"It is all very easy to comprehend," Subienkow declared. "First, I shall go into the woods to gather my goods; that is, my goods for creating the magic medicine, which will be a special mixture of berries, bark, roots, dried-up leaves, and other important shit like that. When I return from the woods with the six hunters that you will assign to me," the Pole pontificated, "my two sleds, and my twelve dogs, will be waiting for me, along with the hundred furs loaded onto the second sled, and my rifle and remaining ammunition placed on the first one. Either you or your strongest hunter can then strike my neck three times with your sharpest ax blade," the captive orally reviewed. "After you fail in performing your attacks, and you certainly will because the magic medicine will be smeared on my neck," the Pole loquaciously qualified. "Then my departure sleigh will be mine, since you could not slay my lily-white ass."

"Do you expect me to believe this obnoxious caribou shit?" Makamuk boisterously exclaimed through Yakaga, his exclusive idiotic interpreter.

"Well Asshole; there are more details to my statement," the haughty Pole verbally persisted. "Between each ax blow, I must be able to apply more coats of the medicine. Your ax will be sharp and heavy, and I want to live through your fucked-up ordeal."

"You shall be granted your wish, which can now be taken for granted," Makamuk communicated through his slow-learner offspring Yakaga. "Now go into the woods for your goods with six of my hoods."

"You have been too slow in again responding to my conditions and my strong medicine has been offended by you a second time," Subienkow arrogantly played his trump card to the hilt.

The Pole then pointed to the chief's ugly, snaggle-toothed daughter. "I also want your daughter to give me blowjobs all the way to Michaelovski Redoubt. And if the bitch becomes pregnant by me, and my *necking*, just think of all the strong medicines your children will inherit from *our* fabulous union. I mean to say, Makamuk. Who in your clan wants to pump and hump that ugly, hideous-looking bitch? I'm doing you a big favor by getting that buck-toothed witch away from your village for a couple of weeks. And besides," the loquacious Subienkow finished his incredible statement. "Your grotesque-looking daughter looks like she's growing a walrus tusk, and could be a twin to a dancing ballerina, lesbian whore I had once occasionally dated back in gay Paris!"

"All of your caribou shit demands shall be done if you'll demonstrate your medicine, and then share its special secret with me!" Makamuk answered through his treacherous son Yakaga. "But I predict that it'll be *I* who will have your neck on the chopping block, and I shall be using my best ax, and not fucked-up Chinese chopsticks to behead you!" the chief angrily elaborated. "Now here are the six hunters to accompany you into the dark forest. And while you're fucking around looking for ingredients in the woods, Yakaga here has told me he wants to rape and screw his ugly wolf-toothed sister one more time before she becomes your property on your lengthy excursion to Michaelovski Redoubt."

"My father will finish for me the punishment I had started with the Giant Ivan," Yakaga prognosticated. "His work with your neck will be easily completed in Chinese style, chop-chop! Ha, ha, ha!"

* * * * * * * * * * * * * *

"Listen to my words, Father," Yakaga said when the Pole and his assigned guards had disappeared into the nearby spruce and pine forest. "When you have learned the elements that go inside the magic medicine, you'll be able to destroy that white-skinned bastard. Then, your name will be famous all over this land!"

"But how can I eliminate him? By using the process of elimination?" Makamuk confused and challenged his mentally-deficient son. "The dangerous Asshole's strong medicine will not allow me to destroy him! Don't be a stubborn ignoramus all your fuckin' life!"

"There will be some part of his body like his eyes, his ears, his nose, his dick, and his balls, where he will not thoroughly rub the medicine," the detestable son related. "I'd get tremendous satisfaction from puncturing his testicle sac! Better still; I would love to stick a long hot metal needle straight-up the tiny piss hole in his pecker!"

"Sometimes you're very bright like the sun," Makamuk praised his exclusive interpreter. "Other times, you think out of your rectum, and that's when you act like a wise ass!"

Inside the nearby spruce and pine forest, which was not all-spruced-up as various Indian legends had often described, Subienkow wasted no time in gathering-up ordinary coniferous tree needles, willow bark, birch bark, dried-up pinecones, and a quantity of soggy moss berries. Several frozen roots complemented his meticulous items' selection. Thirty-minutes later, the strange entourage was making its way back into the clan's makeshift camp.

Makamuk and Yakaga crouched-down beside the Pole, mentally calculating the exact amount of each ingredient to be concocted into the innovative, supernatural magic potion. Each item was gingerly dropped into a small kettle of boiling water.

"You must be careful that the moss berries go in first," Subienkow imperatively stated. "You must remember to follow the exact sequence of ingredients, or else the entire experiment will result in failure. Oh yes; there is one matter that I had neglected to disclose to you imbeciles. The formula must include a man's finger, an index finger to be exact. Here Yakaga, you're a brave fellow. You can volunteer to offer yours!"

But Yakaga put both his hands behind his back and scowled in a bellicose tone of voice, "Find your damned finger somewhere else! How the fuck can I fully enjoy eating finger-licking-good seal meat if one of the suckers is missing?"

"Yakaga, give him your finger!" Makamuk ordered. "What the fuck kind of a coward do I have for a son? The Pole's not asking for your testicles, you know!"

"There're plenty of fingers, ten to be exact, lying on the Giant's hands down there in the snow," sagaciously answered usually dense-skulled Yakaga. "There's your ever-loving finger farm down there, just waiting for you to harvest one!"

"In order for the medicine to work, I must use the finger from a living man, and obviously Ivan is now dead," the Pole insisted. "At least he appears to be dead."

"The insane Giant is not yet dead," Yakaga declared as he wickedly kicked Ivan in the ribs, his newly inflicted injury resulting in a low groan. "I'm sure it'll be a good finger for you to use because it is quite enormous in size."

After Yakaga sliced off Ivan's index finger on his right hand, Subienkow dropped the bloody object into the boiling hot water. "Now listen carefully, you two knuckleheads. You must memorize the words to the French song 'Marseillaise' that I'm gonna' slowly sing. The magic lyrics will make the medicine work." And as the

Pole sang the notable French liberation song, the prevaricator vigorously rubbed the magical brew onto both sides of his neck.

"What's this fucked-up song all about?" Yakaga balked. "I don't know *that* asshole gay-sounding language you call French. I only know English to translate."

The Pole ignored Yakaga's protests, and turned his attention to the grim-faced Makamuk. "And please remember, Chief. You are to strike my neck with all of your' might, or else the women of your tribe will know that you're wimpy, besides being impotent. Soon, you'll be walking as erect as your limp dick hangs! But two violent strikes to my neck should do the trick, because in my country, three strikes and you're out!" Subienkow specified as he glanced around at the ring of fierce-looking savages, which reminded him of a circle of hungry vicious wolves.

"And Makamuk, one last paragraph of important advice," the hostage indicated. "Be careful that one of your asshole clansmen doesn't stand behind you when you raise your magnificent ax. And also, the ax might bounce off my neck, and go flying out of your hands, thus injuring or maybe even castrating Yakaga, or one of your more lethargic slow-footed tribesmen. In fact, Chief. I think that I'm *ax*-ually going to enjoy this entire bullshit activity!"

The audacious Pole then peered to his right, and admired the two sleds, the twelve dogs, the hundred animal pelts, the requested rifle and ammunition, and the snaggle-toothed ugly bitch standing next to his assembled supplies. Then, Subienkow gracefully got-down on his knees, and placed his head sideways on the stump chopping block, which his mind mused would certainly stump the tribal chief's effort.

"I laugh at your incompetence and at your squaw strength," Subienkow chided his already-aggravated avowed enemy. "Strike my neck with every ounce of energy you can muster, you pathetically dumb-ass Old Shit!"

The incensed Makamuk hastily lifted the awesome ax over his head, the sunlight gleaming off of its sharp-curved metal blade. Then, the weapon/tool was violently thrust down upon the Pole's exposed neck with the force of a French Revolution guillotine. The lethal blade sliced clear through the victim's flesh and bones, and in a flash, smashed against the huge tree stump's execution platform. The astonished clansmen that had witnessed the gruesome event saw the Pole's head bounce like a ball a full two yards away, while blood spouted out from the deceased man's trunk.

A great bewilderment and silence were soon followed by raucous laughter and cheers among the gossipy squaws, and their astounded warrior husbands. Everyone finally realized that the promise of great medicine had been a colossal hoax, and that Makamuk had been severely hoodwinked by Subienkow's imaginative canard.

"Father, because of your stupidity, the Pole has escaped *my* torture!" Yakaga disrespectfully accused his elder. "You've acted like an imbecile and a moron! Your fucked-up insanity has deprived me of my responsibility to torture the white-skinned jerk-off!"

Makamuk slowly retreated to his tent with his head crestfallen in shame. The woebegone chief had been deceived and tricked by a mediocre white-skinned fur thief. The tribal leader would be prodigiously ridiculed and belittled by even his lowly and inferior snaggle-toothed, ugly, incest-loving daughter.

'How fuckin' stupid could I possibly be!' the disgraced chief mentally concluded. 'I've lost face while the Pole has lost his head! My new name will be 'Lost Face', and my asshole brain-dead son, Yakaga, will soon be elected the new tribal leader. Why the fuck didn't I order that dopey moose-brain Yakaga to slice-off the fur thief's head? I can't live with this horrendous scandal. The record of my buffoonery will stay with me all the way to my grave!' Makamuk lamented. 'And my reputation will be marred and smeared all the way from the shores of Alaska out to the Aleutian Islands, which might also be invisible as a result of some other kind of fucked-up magical white man's medicine I know nothing about!'

# “A Daughter of the Aurora”

“You’re what’s known as a lazy man, a foolish lazy man that desires having me for a wife without offering me much in return,” Joy Molineau chided Jack Harrington. “I’ll never marry a lazy man, no matter how handsome his looks may be. If it’s a choice between being the Queen of Hearts or the Queen of Diamonds, I’m afraid Jack, that diamonds are gonna’ win out!” the voluptuous woman explained outside her village trading post. “I had mentioned the exact same thing last night to that other area bachelor-loser, Louis Savoy, who incidentally also is interested in asking me to walk down the church aisle with him!”

“You’re beautiful, and I don’t know one single guy in this part of Alaska that isn’t interested in courting ya’,” Jack attempted to flatter the extremely-alluring female. “Believe me Joy, when I say, it’s not only your gorgeous body and beautiful face that excites the hell out of me. You’ve got wits about you, and plenty of courage, and vim and vigor, too, that I greatly admire.”

“Why must I listen to the empty words of a lazy dolt such as yourself?” Joy Molineau admonished her principal suitor. “You hang around my cabin trying to woo me; make too many visitations, and yet, you accomplish next to nothing running around in monotonous circles. How do you intend to ever be able to support a family? Other men are busy staking claims and finding gold. How come you can’t be ambitious like they are?” Joy questioned Harrington. “And also, Jack. When you’re prospecting up the creek, it’s usually without a damned paddle at your disposal! Jack; you don’t know Jack!”

“My dogs are quite tired, Joy, but I’m still makin’ an effort to strike it rich and win you over,” Jack futilely uttered his standard excuse. “True; other men have been lucky findin’ gold deposits, but up to now, I’ve not been so fortunate.”

“Why the heck should I want to marry an unlucky man, even though you’re a lot cuter than that romantic rascal, Louis Savoy is,” Joy replied and challenged. “When that fellow Johnson, who had the Indian wife, journeyed-off to the Klondike and discovered gold, other men followed and became rich, too. But you, being a stubborn idiot, Jack; you went in the opposite direction and found nothing but hardship, toil, and futility! Not only are you an ass; you’re a damned lazy Jackass!”

Jack decided to use another type of verbal ploy, and not argue with his idolized woman. “Yes, Joy. I was prospecting and panning over on the head reaches of the Tanana River, and didn't learn about either the Eldorado or the Bonanza claims until it was too late," Harrington objected in defense of his wrong-weathervane direction decision. "And your other boyfriend, that unscrupulous rogue, Louis Savoy, followed me all the way to the Tanana and made the identical error in judgment as I had."

"The man who drove the stakes at Eldorado has disappeared and his claim is protected for sixty days until it expires," Joy Molineau reminded Jack Harrington. "Other men will race to jump the claim, and you can be one of the contestants, Jack! You'll be able to go and file the appropriate legal papers, and beat everyone else to the claims' office over at Fort Cudahy. Louis Savoy told me last night that the Frenchman was interested in racing to the Fort and staking his claim to a piece of the up-for-grabs Eldorado stake, and if you want to pursue my hand in marriage and rival Louis's," Joy stipulated and insisted, "then I strongly suggest and urge that you get your ass motivated, or else admit defeat in both love and money."

"Hang Louis Savoy! That scoundrel-bastard could be eaten by wolves, and I wouldn't give a rat's rectum! What else did that obnoxious pecker-head tell you, Joy?"

"Last night, amorous Louis asked me to marry him, and then told me that he planned to become sinfully rich, and that he had a team of strong dogs to easily win the race to Fort Cudahy. I think that Louis has the drive and the ambition to win the up-for-grabs gold claim, and to also win my hand in marriage, even though you're plenty more handsome and more well-endowed than he is!"

"And what if the rotten son-of-a-bitch skunk doesn't win his claim?" Jack asked. "What then Joy? Is he out of the picture? Am I still in the vital picture?"

"Then, Louis Savoy will not be the father of my children," the vivacious French blonde stated. "I don't give a crap how much quality sperm he has going for him. He'll be completely out of the picture."

"And what if I should work a miracle and win the race to Fort. Cudahy?" Jack inquired. "Would you then marry me?"

"You? Win the dogsled race! That'll never happen in three centuries, along with two dozen blue moons added on to the time line!" Joy laughed and belittled. "The damned Earth will stop spinning and end, and the sun will revolve around the moon before *that* impossible shit ever happens!"

Jack knew that Joy's style was to force all of her lovers to sacrifice and suffer in order to qualify for her highly coveted engagement promise. And the gorgeous blonde had a very capable dogsled team of her own with the most prized husky, Wolf Fang, as its esteemed and notorious leader. If Jack could only have Wolf Fang at the front of his team, the idle dreamer suspected that he would be almost-guaranteed to beat Louis Savoy, or any other determined prospector in the race to the claims' office at Fort Cudahy.

"What do you say about Jack Harrington winning the important race?" Joy Molineau affectionately asked her precious Wolf Fang. "If he gets there first and fills out the claims' papers, should I then break-down and marry him?"

Wolf Fang picked-up his ears and rendered a ferocious growl toward Jack Harrington's standing position. And if Joy were not restraining her favorite spoiled dog, then the fierce husky would have definitely made a thrust at Jack's tender loins.

"It is very cold Jack, and I must be on the trail, but I have to confess that I admire your patience and your persistence," Joy evasively and elusively said in one of her typical backhanded compliments. "Now listen-up, Wolf Fang! Mush on and lead my team away from this pathetic loser of a man!"

Jack sadly watched Joy Molineau's excellent dog team speed-down the icy snow trail in the heading of Forty Mile. Her sled halted in the road fork that crossed the river in the direction of Fort Cudahy, a full hundred miles away. Then, the knockout of a woman turned her head and shouted words of encouragement to the stunned Jack Harrington.

"Oh, Mr. Lazy Fellow standing back at the trading post!" Joy merrily screamed. "Wolf Fang says you're a winner now, and you'll be a winner in the big contest racing Louis Savoy and all the other dreamers wanting to stake a claim to the fantastic gold find!"

* * * * * * * * * * * * *

Word had gotten-out in that frigid section of Northwestern Canada about the impending hundred-mile-long dogsled race between Jack Harrington and Louis Savoy for the dual prizes of Joy Molineau's hand in marriage, and a prospective Eldorado gold claim worth at least a million dollars. The whiskerandos from Forty Mile all the way to Fort Cudahy were abuzz with discussing the thrilling scuttlebutt. Speculation, along with huge wagers and bets, abounded between the two opposing and ever-expanding gambling camps. A wild scramble among the partisans to obtain the best dogs ensued, and large sums of money were raised and placed on both Harrington and Savoy's behalf, the generous contributions dedicated to securing the finest canines available for each main participant.

"Jack Harrington's gonna' defeat that lover boy Louis Savoy, and go get his claim, and after becoming fabulously rich," one enthusiastic bettor said at the Forty Mile Saloon bar, "he's gonna' marry that blonde beauty queen Joy doll; travel down to San Francisco, and go stompin' at the Savoy! Ha, ha, ha!"

"That's what the fuck you think!" an old, inebriated alcoholic answered the first drunk's bragging statement. "I'm investin' my money in that fellow, Louis Savoy. He's a Frenchman, and Joy's French, too. And that lazy English bastard Harrington's gonna' meet his Waterloo! Ha, ha, ha! It'll be a reverse Napoleon, ha, ha, ha! Bartender, set-up another round for me, and my anonymous friend!"

The news of Johnson's discovery had spread like a timber-fire all throughout the region, and hundreds of inhabitants and potential gold prospectors became extra-excited about the Bonanza claim, along with the subsequent Eldorado find, where Olaf Nelson was reported to have laid claim to five-hundred-feet of virgin, gold-laced ground along the river, and then duly and mysteriously disappeared into oblivion.

Men from the Lower Country, and from Circle City, and Forty Mile all flocked in the direction of Fort Cudahy (and other relay stations along the race route) ahead of the scheduled event to gamble-away their savings on the imminent-upcoming dogsled race, and wager their gut instincts on either Jack Harrington or Louis Savoy staking claim to Olaf Nelson's phenomenal Eldorado piece; that is, once the sixty-day "grace period of Olaf's claim immunity" had expired.

Since the money was stacking-up quickly between Harrington and Savoy's camps in regard to securing the highest quality dogs, no other man had the adequate resources to compete with the two prime race candidates. The course was a difficult hundred-mile-long affair to the police barracks and to the assay office at the Fort, with fresh dogs to be awaiting the two major competitors at twenty-five-mile intervals.

As the feverish gambling and the colossal investments in the two leading contestants quickly escalated, the local conjecture turned to discussing Joy Molineau, and her fabulous dog Wolf Fang. Whoever was to acquire that sensational canine in the last twenty-five-mile relay leg would certainly be the favorite to win. But the beautiful woman had made no official announcement about which driver (if any) would profit from her personal endorsement.

But Joy Molineau was reputed to be “A Daughter of the Aurora”, whose coy father had been a prominent fur trader prior to any prospector ever showing-up along the Yukon River to try his hand at gold panning and mining, and to learn to appreciate the beauty of the evening “Northern Lights”. Yes, because of Joy’s relationship with her cunning and shrewd father, the enchanting female understood men better than men actually understood themselves, and being blinded by feminine beauty, the unassuming suitors never really fathomed wily Miss Molineau’s deftness and unparalleled wisdom in regard to her authentic comprehension of their motives, and also their obvious behavioral habits. But it was not until Joy sagaciously cast her final trump card that the gambling men and their natural instincts swayed, and then blatantly leaned in the direction of her scrupulous disposition of the one and only, incomparable Wolf Fang.

The temperature registered at fifty degrees below zero as the day of the widely anticipated great dogsled race showed-up, circled on everyone’s wall calendar. The race’s odds had been strongly influenced the week before when Joy Molineau drew aside Lon McFarland, who was the manager in charge of Jack Harrington’s four dogsled teams, and the blonde-haired goddess conferred with “the Lieutenant” inside the Forty Mile Saloon. Lon then unhitched the legendary Wolf Fang from Joy’s sled, and put the fantastic animal at the head of Jack Harrington’s team, and then skillfully mushed the string of animals onto the Yukon Trail.

“That woman’s decision definitely tips the scales in Jack’s favor!” everyone standing and seated inside the popular saloon concurred and gossiped. “That classical violinist Louis Savoy is now gonna’ be playin’ second fiddle in lovely Joy’s orchestra!” became the slogan for the fascinated barroom crowd. “Word’s gonna’ spread the entire hundred-miles between the start and the finish lines, and the money’s gonna’ mostly be put on Jack Harrington, and his lucky acquisition of that incredible Wolf Fang creature!”

* * * * * * * * * * * * * *

The aurora borealis had painted tantalizing colors on the night sky, as rosy and green waves glowed across the Arctic zenith. And the neurotic wolf dogs howled in the custom of their noble ancestors. Captain Constantine of the Mounted Police had stationed men along the prescribed race route to guarantee that all rules of fairness and courtesy would be honored and enforced. According to agreed-upon terms, the relay dogs had been strategically placed at the twenty-five-mile intervals on that clear and crisp morning, as the intrepid entries stepped-forward to their sleds, which were situated on the starting line. The eager contestants then gripped their claims' stakes, and next, the rivals confidently mounted their respective sleds.

A bearskin-coated policeman had been designated the official starter, and the rules-enforcer carefully and very deliberately gave the familiar instructions, "Ready! Set! Go!"

The sleds, pulled by dogs with bristling manes and shrieking fangs, shot-out across the frozen river, and then into the darkness of the overhanging banks. The sleds measured sixteen inches from runner to runner, and the formidable trail was a mere eighteen inches wide, representing little space for either error or passing. Soft snow blankets lay drifted on either side of the route, and any deviation from the established course would certainly slow the rider and his team to almost a standstill, with the restless dogs then becoming encumbered with resistance all the way up to their bellies.

The final fifteen-miles of the first leg was down to Dawson, the route following first the Klondike River in the vicinity of the recent Bonanza find to the Yukon River, where the first relay dog replacements would be encountered and performed. The Yukon passage was like a precarious slide across a slippery dance floor, and it was there that Jack implemented his clever scheme and passed the struggling Louis Savoy midway across the frozen-solid river's smooth expanse.

Louis Savoy's team valiantly attempted keeping pace with his lover boy adversary, and the determined Frenchman's lead dog's nose was precisely at the tail end of Harrington's swift-moving sled. The town of Dawson could be seen silhouetted in the distance, under the glow of the aurora borealis, and its entire population was loudly shouting screams of encouragement to the daring racers.

The temperature was now sixty degrees below zero, and Harrington and Savoy, both veteran sleds-men, amply knew that they had to exercise their lower limbs to assure that poor blood circulation did not lead to detrimental numbness and ultimately, muscle fatigue. Each knowledgeable man employed the traditional method known as "run and ride", alternating hopping-off their sleds, running ten steps along the icy trail, and then jumping back on again.

The race proceeded through the first seventy-five miles in a very similar manner of adherence to the basic established rules, with fresh dogs being exchanged for exhausted ones at the agreed-upon twenty-five-mile stops. But when Jack Harrington saw his loyal race manager Lon McFarland ready with Wolf Fang impatiently standing there at the interchange, the determined-but-astonished lucky participant thought, 'Holy polar bear shit! What a pleasant surprise! Joy wants me to win the race, to get rich, and marry her at the altar!'

Instantly, Louis Savoy realized that he was out of the competition upon getting a glimpse of the famous and supreme Wolf Fang going to his' talented opponent's jurisdiction and control. 'Joy has deliberately rigged the race, so that Jack gets the two coveted prizes!' Savoy sadly concluded. 'Oh, well. I guess all's fair in love and war, and I suppose I've just unofficially lost the goddamned war along with my goddamned love!'

* * * * * * * * * * * * * *

Joy Molineau waited impatiently at the finish line, wondering if she, the gorgeous blonde bombshell, had made the correct decision. Her four agents (who were also her trading post employees) had been circulating around the crowd of active bettors (at all four interchange locations), and taking any and all wagers *against* Jack Harrington, and *against* her beloved Wolf Fang at odds of ten to one, since everyone present believed that Louis Savoy didn't have "a snowball's chance in Hell" of winning.

'I've always been a foolish girl, just as Jack's always been a whimsical, dumb-shit, Asshole himself,' Joy pondered as her agents eagerly worked the assembled crowds. 'I've put all of my inheritance from my father, along with my cherished trading post, and other owned and mortgaged property, up as collateral to cover my risky bets. But if I lose, I'm financially ruined and basically bankrupt. Oh well. let's just call my rather-chancy economic experiment the roulette wheel of life!'

"Ten to one on Wolf Fang, and that Harrington feller'!" a recently successful Birch Creek gold prospector yelled to one of Joy's bettor aides. "No way that dog's gonna' lose and let me down! This is easy money, I say. The easiest damned money I'll ever make at automatic ten percent interest!"

"All bets are made and final! No more betting!" a lieutenant from the Mounted Police shouted above the din. "Here they come into town now! It's Wolf Fang and Harrington in the lead! No more bets are to be accepted!"

The two sleds came flashing around the bend, and Wolf Fang was definitely showing his resourcefulness, strength and prowess. Louis Savoy's reliable team was sustaining a pace closely behind, and the rider was making a valiant last-ditch-effort to catch his bitter rival.

But Wolf Fang had won so many races in the past, and was so remarkably dependable that this current exhibition was just one more mediocre contest to add to his stellar success repertoire.

The whips lashed as the awed spectators then became anxious and silent. But astonishingly, Wolf Fang abruptly left the established trail, and in so doing, the formerly invincible canine had tugged-along the remainder of the dog team, and simultaneously, the bewildered Jack Harrington tumbled from his sled, and speedily rolled into a side snow drift. Louis Savoy passed-by like a meteor, crossing the finish line, and much to the amazement of all witnesses, the underdog had won the grueling contest.

Joy Molineau, after acknowledging and briefly petting Wolf Fang, worriedly dashed over to see if her favorite beau Jack Harrington had been injured from his tumble, while the remainder of the stunned crowd gathered around the victorious Louis Savoy.

"What the fuck happened?" Jack asked, his foggy-mind still in a deep daze. "Joy; I was thinking about your luscious body and your fluffy blonde pussy, and the next thing I knew, I was heading towards defeat and disaster!"

"Well Jack," Joy joyously said with a wink of her right eye. "*Our* dreams are finally coming true! Wolf Fang had been trained to respond to my special dog whistle, and when my prized husky heard me discreetly blow into it, my obedient pooch recognized his command and veered directly over to me. That's why the hell you lost the race! And as you know Jack, the people in the cheering crowd couldn't hear the high-pitched dog signal, but Wolf Fang certainly did!"

"But if I lost the race, how could we ever get married and become rich?" Jack wondered and questioned. "I'm now doomed to poverty if I can't locate any gold on my own!"

"Well, you see Jack," Joy explained while still holding her love's head above the snowy ground, "I figured that a safe gamble was more reliable than any speculative gold prospecting contract. And so, I gambled everything I owned on this race, but instead of betting on you to win, at odds of ten to one," the charming female verbally conveyed, "I bet against you and then hit the absolute jackpot! We're rich Jack; without you ever havin' to go-out and panning, or mining for gold! And besides," Joy jubilantly summarized. "I've always thought that *that* flowery-talkin' asshole Louis Savoy is a damned big aurora *bore*-e-alis! Ha, ha, ha!"

“My word Joy! How lucky can a poor man like me get?” Jack marveled and exclaimed from his horizontal position lying upon the hard snow. “I’m going to marry both the Queen of Hearts and the Queen of Diamonds! Thank God that you had the wisdom to stack the deck against that connivin’ scoundrel Louis Savoy!”

# “The Heathen”

After I had become socially acquainted with the Heathen, I regretted that I had been a practicing Christian all my life, and every morning, I now vow to my conscience that I am a bona fide “Heathen Christian”. But maybe this vague introduction requires sufficient historical background, so perhaps I should start my exposition at the beginning, and then methodically proceed to the ending rather than tell my extraordinary story in reverse order.

The first time I had seen “the Heathen” was on the island of German Samoa, twenty-five years ago. The Heathen was not a pugnacious brawler, and the island native never looked for trouble or conflict, as I was later to discover, after fortunately befriending him. The Polynesian was an impressive six-foot-two-inches tall, and fantastically muscular in build. Although my sea chum was not an accomplished fighter, the brute was also not a coward as one prize fighting American boxer had found-out the hard way.

William King was a notable professional boxer, who had just arrived on the island with his entourage of admirers. Outside a German Samoa bar, the bully picked a fight with the Heathen, and soon regretted his egocentric audacity. William “Samson” King had been in his youth the heavyweight champion of the American Navy, a hairy brute of a man; and a hideous-looking cross between an ogre and a gorilla. King was a hard-hitting, highly-skilled, well-conditioned boxer. The “Hammer” was a basic roughhousing, two-hundred-and-thirty-pound monster, who was very adept with his fists, using a variety of punches to decisively punish his doomed ring victims. But when the obnoxious prizefighter chose the Heathen for an opponent, King, the boxer, met his match, and was indeed summarily crowned.

Bill King had too much whiskey in his gut, and felt motivated to pick a quarrel. The veteran boxer struck the Heathen twice in the mouth, and then savagely kicked him in the leg for good measure. And the aggressor kept pummeling his designated foe until the bland-spirited Polynesian felt it necessary to adequately defend himself. But Bill King was out of the boxing ring, and the bully and his chosen adversary were not wearing gloves. The heavyweight puncher was now involved in a no-holds-barred fracas that apparently constituted an unfamiliar environment for him.

The Heathen knew nothing of scientific boxing, and the gentle giant had never heard of important expert people-rules like the Marquis of Queensbury, but the Polynesian easily manhandled Bill King in less than four-minutes, giving the loud-mouthed pugilist three broken bones, a fractured mandible, and a ruptured forearm and, after the aggressor had gotten the feces knocked out of him, the heavyweight champ required three months of bed recovery time inside an island hospital ward.

But coincidentally, it was not until the Heathen and I were sailors aboard the schooner *Petite Jeanne* that I finally learned his true name. On-board the sailing vessel were eight Kanada seamen; a white-skinned captain; his first mate; a supercargo buying agent, and six cabin passengers, along with eighty regular travelers, mostly Paumotans and Tahitians, all going home from one island to the next. We were sailing from Rangiroa to Tahiti, and the itinerant passengers were voyaging back to their families because the annual and profitable pearl-diving season was then finished.

The other six cabin passengers were all competing pearl buyers. Two were Americans; one was Ah-Choon, a whitish Chinese who would sneeze incessantly; a German, and a Polish Jew. We were all satisfied with our shrewd purchases, and were contemplating making our handsome profits from reselling our splendid merchandise. Everyone was looking forward to having a good time celebrating our individual successes, once we would arrive on the shores of Papeete.

The *Petite Jeanne* was a ship of only seventy tons, and the vessel was overloaded with a cargo consisting mostly of pearl shells and coconut copra. Captain Oudouse would often-joke to the crew, "Please don't squeeze the bananas; squeeze the coconuts!" and then he would further amuse himself by grabbing and crushing somebody's testicles. Such was his sadistic sense of humor.

But in fact, the small schooner was so immorally overcrowded with passengers that the acrobatic crewmembers maneuvered about by swinging from guy wire to guy wire, and by climbing and walking across the side gunwale rails. And the mostly poor passengers were packed together like sardines; and had to sleep on the deck on blankets and mats, and their possessions were hung in baskets on various guys, along with myriad banana hands and coconut arrangements that had been temporarily placed and stored in hemp rope sacks.

Captain Oudouse was in a jovial mood the first day out of port, and had, on three different occasions, held a shot glass of rye liquor in his right hand, and with his left hand, the inebriated fool lifted-up the cargo trap and yelled down below to pissed-off crewmembers, "Down the hatch!" And after imbibing his addictive alcohol, Oudouse would indulgently and hoarsely laugh, and then slam-shut the trap lid tight.

The sea voyage from Rangiroa to Tahiti was supposed to take three days, but unfortunately, the southeast trade winds ceased their blowing. And soon, the breeze transitioned from fading to completely dying away. The silent calm continued all that second night, and worry began appearing upon the faces of the captain and his all-too-knowledgeable crewmembers.

But then, a thin passenger from the Easter Islands became sick on Good Friday, and it was soon learned that the traveling pearl diver had contracted smallpox. The very next morning, the formerly ill-diver was pronounced dead, and his body immediately cast overboard, quickly becoming a feast for the ever-present, ever-hungry ocean sharks. Within an hour, three additional cases of the dreaded, contagious smallpox disease had been identified and announced.

The sick couldn't be segregated or quarantined, because there was no room or space aboard to accommodate their agonizing needs. And naturally, protection of the rest of us (who remained unaffected) was paramount in Captain Oudouse's mind.

A secret conspiracy prevailed aboard the *Petite Jeanne,* and during the night, the supercargo agent; the Polish Jew; Oudouse's gay first mate, and four traveling pearl divers (experienced boat rowers) sneaked-away inside the schooner's whaleboat. The following morning, the vessel was still not making any significant headway, because of the lack of wind. So, Captain Oudouse ordered for the remaining two small boats to be scuttled for the explicit purpose of preventing any additional passenger or crew abdications.

That third day at sea, there were two more deaths; that night three; and the following morning, eight additional smallpox victims were reported, as the ship's population began to rapidly dwindle. A random thought had plagued my brain. 'If smallpox could do this much havoc, what the fuck could large-pox do to us?' I mused and wondered.

But our French captain's hands began to shake, and then he exhibited facial twitches, and drank whiskey more-heavily just to calm his nerves. Oudouse, Ah-Choon, the German pearl buyer, and I all smeared our skins with scotch whiskey from the storage hull cases, which we believed would be an adequate antiseptic killing-off any and all smallpox germs, and thus keeping our bodies safe from the alien microbe invasion.

And amazingly, the hot nautical temperature made steam billow-up from the dead bodies saturated with smallpox germs that, ironically, were still quite alive inside the corpses. So then, the sage crewmembers tossed the human remains overboard, and we all hoped that the carnivorous, swarming, frenzied sharks would also contract the dreaded disease and die off, too.

For a full week, the *Petite Jeanne* make no measurable progress towards Tahiti, and then much to our alarm, our whiskey supply had expired. The schooner's barometer, which ordinarily read 29.29, or thereabouts, had then registered a dangerously low atmospheric pressure reading of 29.60, indicating that a hurricane of major magnitude would soon be encountered. Captain Oudouse revealed to me that he had been noticing the declining mercury also, and that he had already crapped his pants trice from severe diarrhea.

Two hours later, the storm hit us with incredible force, and a huge wave smashed against the reeling vessel's port side, sending myriad luggage pieces and hanging personal possession baskets overboard. The more alert passengers latched onto stanchions, and others clung to the masts, but at least six were abruptly washed like helpless crabs into the turbulent Pacific.

Ten minutes later, a second gigantic wave crashed into the port side, and this time the water splashed high over the rails; and the schooner's stern sank-down, and her bow was instantly raised and tossed skyward, consequently making several surviving women, old men, and children disgustingly vomit their guts-out onto the already-slippery deck.

The thoroughly-battered man who had been standing next to me with his arms wrapped around the mast had had his head cracked open like an eggshell from the waves impact, but instead of yellow yolk oozing-out, crimson red was squirting all over the goddamned place, and especially into my exposed face. And then, the bruised and lacerated man, an elderly American, went flying through the air like a piece of balsam wood, and was soon hurled into the roaring, heartless sea. And next, after sneezing one final time, Ah-Choon went zooming over the rails, his trajectory instantly being followed by a three-hundred-pound pregnant Polynesian woman.

Miraculously, the two remaining pearl buyers and myself managed to lock ourselves inside the center cabin, and we noticed that all three of us were naked, for the strong monstrous gales had torn and raped the flimsy clothes right off of our frail bodies. Imagine tons of invisible sand hitting your face, and that is exactly how the pelting rain and driving wind had felt. But on second analysis, the downpour and the hundred mile-an-hour gusts had the force of invisible mud rather than of invisible sand. The phenomenon we had been experiencing was as if that entire section of ocean had directly been sucked-up into the maw of the colossal, swirling ocean storm.

The canvas sails had been ripped-off the masts and topmasts, as nature continued to act berserk. And the detrimental effect was made doubly sickening, because there was still hardly any air for us to breath, because of the low barometric pressure that seemed to dominate everything in, around, and aboard the rocking, canting, and rolling ship. All three of us inside the tiny cabin became extremely nauseous, and we all began involuntarily regurgitating upon one another. And when we ran out of sour intestinal and stomach puke to expel from our mouths, we belched dry heaves into each other's faces.

The relentless waves were over eighty-feet-high, and still the *Petite Jeanne* withheld all of the physical violence, as its well-designed construction had been tested to the maximum. It was as if the ship was in anarchy with itself, and when the sturdy masts snapped-off, and the cabin roof blew away, the three of us were well-aware that the *Petite Jeanne* had little time left sailing upon the high seas.

The helpless vessel was wickedly torn apart, section by section, and before I could evaluate anything further, I had been vacuumed-up right through the vacant cabin roof area, and mercilessly propelled into the choppy, oscillating waves. I tried desperately swimming, and as I gasped for oxygen to feed my lungs, I reckoned that I was already two-thirds drowned, and spitting deadly water out of my mouth like a Roman fountain. No sharks were circling about the vicinity, because of the vacillating, formidable sea waves. And when I instinctively turned my head sideways, I was shocked to witness that the noble *Petite Jeanne* was no longer in sight.

*************

While bobbing around in the choppy waves, I managed to smack into a hatch cover that had detached from the ship, which I immediately improvised into a small raft, after successfully sliding my abused body on top of it. A half-hour later, the rain had ceased, and my first mental reaction was that either the nasty storm had passed, or possibly, that I was presently situated directly in the eye of the inhospitable hurricane.

About twenty feet to my left was another floating hatch cover that was at that moment the source of a fierce verbal commotion. The half-intoxicated Captain Oudouse was having a loud argument with the Heathen, and attempting to push the generally mild-mannered Kanada away from the drifting cover.

"You, white son-of-a-bitch!" I angrily screamed in the French captain's direction. "You call yourself a Christian, you. selfish loathsome mother-fucker! You belong in fuckin' deep hell, and that innocent fellow you're kicking your feet at, who you call 'the Heathen', has already earned his lofty place in Paradise a thousand-fold! Stop kicking and punching at him; you dirty-drunken bastard!"

Feeling that I would certainly provide the Polynesian with less animosity than the incensed Captain Oudouse had been administering, the Heathen swam over to my bobbing hatch, and we shared its limited space. Upon initiating a conversation with the exhausted hatch-sharer, I learned that his name was Otoo, and that the island native had originated from the island of Borabora.

We took turns (of hour or so intervals) with one of us resting on top of the hatch-cover, while the other clung to the tiny rocking mass while his or my body was bobbing-up-and-down in the rough water. That particular alternating process continued for two whole days, until Otoo spotted a distant island, and pretending that we were hungry sharks, we promptly and desperately swam towards its alluring shore.

"I don't think it's a mirage, because I can see it, too," I confirmed as we swam. But fifteen minutes or so later, my strength had failed me. and the next thing I knew, I was waking-up on a white-sandy beach, and lying under the shade of a mango tree. Otoo and I drank plenty of coconut juice, and I honored one of his people's most valued traditions by agreeing to exchange names with him.

"We have shared near death experiences together," Otoo lectured and explained. "So now, we are like blood brothers to the end. You have saved my life by allowing me onto the hatch-cover, and I have saved you from drowning when you had gone unconscious while swimming to this island."

"I don't know if I oughta', Otoo," I said in regard to changing our names. "I've never heard of such bullshit! Are you sure you're not a Kanada from Canada?"

"My people do this practice all the time, because it seems that we're always saving each other from death in one way or another," Otoo indicated. "We are a hard-working, but stupid people; always having too many damned accidents both on land and at sea! When we aren't rescuing someone, we're being salvaged ourselves."

"So. how does this name-sharing stuff work?" I inquired. "That ritual is unheard of in places like Los Angeles, Buffalo, Philadelphia and Chicago."

"When you address me from time to time, you will call me Charley, and when I address you, sometimes, I shall call you Otoo!" the Kanada declared rather matter-of-factly.

As we eventually explored the small island, we were thrilled to discover that we had come ashore on Papeete. A week later, after I had somewhat-recuperated from my weak health dilemma, Otoo and I parted company. The Heathen returned to Borabora on a cutter to visit his family, while I stayed behind on Papeete to continue my slow rehabilitation. But then the unpredictable Kanada returned six weeks later, and informed me that his wife had been killed during the hurricane when her house collapsed on her, and truthfully, I was saddened to learn of the family tragedy.

"Where will you go now that you are recovered, Charley?" Otoo asked me. "To Los Angeles, Buffalo, Philadelphia or Chicago?"

"All over the fuckin' world, now that I feel quite-strong and adventurous again," I answered. "There's so much to see and explore, and so little sand left in my life's hourglass, so to speak." But every time I thought about an hourglass, my evil mind contemplated screwing another big-breasted, horny bitch.

"I will go with you, Charley," the amiable Polynesian insisted. "For you are part Otoo, and I am part Charley, and nothing will separate us now that my wife is dead and buried."

I never had a biological brother, so naturally, I welcomed our new relationship. And despite all of the Christian morality I had been indoctrinated with during my formative years, I became a much better human being, and a more moral man simply by being closely associated with the awesome Heathen, Otoo. If there was anyone besides Jesus Christ that I would voluntarily die for, it certainly was the extremely moral and decent Heathen.

Throughout our friendship, Otoo never criticized anything or anyone, and my better-half even tolerated my chronic cursing without ever uttering a foul word back. Whenever I said invectives such as "mother-fucker", or "cock-sucker", or "fuck", or "bastard," Otoo merely ignored my boisterous and emotional intonations, and simply shrugged his shoulders as if I was having a mental aberration of sorts.

And for seventeen wonderful years, Otoo and I sailed on various ships; together visiting remarkable places like Hawaii, Sydney Head, Torres Straits, Galapagos Islands, Louisiades, New Britain, New Ireland, the Gilberts, and also, the Santa Cruz group in the Fijis. We collected and shared exotic pearls, along with beautiful pink shells that reminded me of wonderful fresh wet, pink pussy. But the Heathen and I had one major difference: I was a materialistic capitalist with many bad behavioral habits, and Otoo cared little about money, and seldom drank alcohol, or smoked tobacco, or screwed foreign women. He exercised discretion and moderation at every opportunity, and I, a Christian, did just the opposite.

Thus, the Kanada's stomach was very much intact, his lungs were clean, and "The Heathen" never knew of a harmful scourge known as venereal disease. Yes; even though I had been raised a Christian, there were a multitude of wise, self-discipline characteristics I needed to learn from my new teacher/benefactor, the Heathen.

* * * * * * * * * * * * *

A major transformation in my life involving Otoo's sagacity started on sun-kissed Papeete. A certain rowdy beachfront bar in those days catered to boisterous traders, pearl divers, ship captains and South Sea vagabond-itinerant riffraff, all of whom were readily willing to part with their money. Gambling and excessive drinking ran rampant, but on the contrary side of extreme amusement, Otoo very discreetly believed in moderation, and my trusted friend never overindulged in betting or in imbibing liquor.

"Watch how much whiskey you carelessly swallow-down, and how much money you foolishly bet away!" the Heathen prudently cautioned me. "You never save anything you earn, and *that* very bad trait is one that will haunt you in later years."

"I don't need any nanny or governess watching over my every deed," I objected, feeling damned insulted. "I've gotten over my bed-wetting forty-seven years ago, and have learned that my precious dingle has another function besides pissing-out yellow fluid. If I want to spend my dough on wine, women, and song, then Otoo, that's *my* goddamned personal business!"

"Honestly, Charley. I don't know why you engage in all this sinful activity, because you'll surely go to your Christian Hell once you're dead," Otoo admonished me like a parent might do to a recalcitrant teenager. "As for myself, I believe that once a person dies, that is the end of everything for him. He has nothing to look forward to, other than to decay in the ground while being eaten inside the earth by dirty maggots, insects and worms. I will know nothing when I am dead!"

"I appreciate you being so thoughtfully concerned about my mental and physical welfare," I admitted with some rancor evident in my tone of voice. "But Otoo, I'll pal around with anyone I so desire to befriend. And I'll always tell you precisely what I think, Otoo. You want to control every fuckin' aspect of my fucked-up life. You're a friggin' control freak, that's what the hell you are!"

"Listen to me, Charley!" the Heathen imperatively stated. "That fellow Randolph Walters you've been talking with down at the beach bar is what your society calls a homo' faggot, who wants to shove his erect sex stick up your smelly rear end. But you don't have to worry about that gay creep flirting with you anymore. I beat the shit out of him this morning over near the dock, and Randolph Walters is now sailing on a fast steamer to Auckland with a black eye, with a bloody nose, with a fractured wrist, and with a twisted dick and ruptured balls!"

Another time when we had gone ashore on Malaita, one of the Solomon Islands, a group of fanatical headhunters had descended upon me while Otoo was collecting shells a hundred yards up the beach. Apparently, the crazed headhunters were having a contest about who could collect the first white man's skull as a trophy to be shrunken, and proudly display the noggin for all visitors to the winner's house to gaze-upon and admire.

Otoo dashed up the beach with his spear raised and saved my ass from being decapitated. Like a human machine, the Heathen systematically and violently killed three of the insane, wooly-headed assholes, and deftly wounded two other cannibals, who then managed to crawl-away from the scene with their massive injuries. As for myself, I had killed one of the savages with the butt of my Winchester, and wounded another of the deranged primitives by kicking him in the testicles a dozen consecutive times while vociferously screaming like an enraged maniac, "Fuck you, asshole! Suck my dick, but by all means, don't eat me!"

One day, while our schooner was anchored in Tahiti, Otoo mentioned something rather profound to me. "You spend all of your money, and then go out to sea to earn more to spend," my friend plausibly communicated. "But some day, you'll be too old to go out to sea, and your money supply will quickly run dry," the well-intentioned Heathen seriously emphasized. "In fifteen years, you'll be just like the old salts that hang-out around the island bars, and beg the young, sympathetic sailors for drinks and gambling money."

"What do you recommend?" I humorously inquired. "Should I enter a fucked-up monastery and become a pedophile minister, or a goddamned gay bishop?"

"I think you should save your money all next year, and I shall give you mine, also," Otoo brilliantly proposed. "Then with our combined savings, you can buy an old schooner and go into business for yourself. I say you should do this before you succeed in devastating yourself through all your bad, self-destructive behaviors!"

"Do you have any other terrific suggestions?" I asked, seeing some merit in the Heathen's correct-flawless logic. "You should've been a Harvard, Oxford or Cambridge college professor, you know!"

"Yes, Charley. I do have more words to say to you," Otoo vociferated as we stood as passengers on our latest schooner anchored in the placid bay at Tahiti. "On the island of Guadalcanal, there is a space of two-miles between the two main rivers. That land now is cheap, but it'll be worth much in five years. You can buy the land four-miles-deep from the old chief for ten thousand sticks of tobacco; ten bottles of rye whiskey; a set of Winchester rifles, and a dozen average-sized pearls. Start saving your money, and I'll help you acquire those things I've stated through shrewd bargaining and trading."

Well, *we* together purchased a schooner named the *Doncaster*, and although Otoo refused to be my business partner, we made a considerable amount of money, and soon negotiated the Guadalcanal land deal from the accommodating old chief.

After six subsequent financial gains through shrewd dealings, I was astonished upon comprehending that I had become a very wealthy man in such a short period of time. I offered the humble Heathen a fifty-fifty share in my prosperity, and in my flourishing properties, but the Heathen modestly declined his share of the bonanza; wisely claiming that money wasn't the root of all evil, but that greed was, and that money eventually led to the development of greed in a man's soul. And therefore, the acquisition of plenty of money would gradually lead to an unworthy, self-defeating pursuit.

Well, I finally convinced Otoo to become my legitimate and legal business partner, and we had the official documents drawn-up by knowledgeable island attorneys. One day, I opened the mail and reviewed our individual expense expenditures.

"Otoo; this statement says that last year you drew-out only eighty-seven dollars for living expenses, when you had clearly made tens of thousands of bucks on our lucrative business enterprises," I questioned my low-keyed partner. "When are you going to start enjoying your accumulated wealth?"

"It is all well and good," the complacent Heathen suavely answered. "You just tell the accounting clerk to keep an accurate tally of my assets. When I want or need cash," my partner expounded, "I'll ask him to get it for me. And if the accountant cheats me out of a single penny, then the difference will come out of his wages and commission, or else, I'll beat the daylights and brains out of his skull!"

Later, I had learned that the Heathen, having no living relatives, had secretly made me the sole beneficiary of his will and estate. The following summer month, Otoo and I were doing some exploratory land research to acquire some potentially valuable waterfront property on Florida Island in the Outer Solomons. My "silent partner" and I were particularly interested in obtaining pearling rights in the placid Mboli Pass area.

Not far from the region referred to as Mboli Pass is land known as Savu, where Otoo and I were casually lying on the beach discussing our recent business opportunities.

"Let's hop into our canoe and paddle back to the *Doncaster,"* I suggested to the mild-mannered Heathen. "It's already past noon, and we ought to set sail if we want to make our scheduled meeting tomorrow morning with the landholders and their lawyers."

The schooner had been anchored three-hundred-yards off the shore, and after Otoo and I had paddled a hundred-and-fifty-feet into the harbor, a large shark smashed into the side of our canoe and flipped it over. The wooly-headed sailors on *our* ship had observed the precarious incident, and began shouting that a swarm of voracious sharks had been circling the Heathen and me, the voracious group perceptively scrutinizing our every move. I began swimming, but being aware that any heavy churning motions would attract a lethal shark attack, I nervously kept a rather slow, deliberate pace.

'Don't these dangerous fish know that I'm part of God's creation, and that according to the sacred Bible, man is a special being who has been given dominion of the Earth and seas?' I philosophically questioned my religious beliefs during *that* existential moment of imminent danger.

I persevered and prayed as I swam in a steady, rhythmic pattern towards the *Doncaster*. My endurance was rapidly being sapped, as I gasped for adequate air to energize my already aching arm and shoulder muscles. A large shark approached me head on, and I used my hands to grab its snout and fend the creature off before the monster could slice any appendages off of my all-too-vulnerable body.

A second time, the same determined, enormous shark rushed me, but during that confrontation, its sandpaper-like skin scraped the left side of my chest, and I began bleeding through my white cotton shirt. The schooner was still over a hundred-yards out. My depressed spirit was swiftly giving-up hope, and my mind realized that my soul was not fully-prepared to die.

But then, my ears keenly heard a familiar voice coming from along my right side. "Otoo," my soul brother, addressed me using *his* name. "Swim some more towards the schooner. I know sharks! They are like brothers to me! I, Charley, shall trick them, Otoo! You shall see! Keep swimming towards the *Doncaster!"*

I struggled-on, and all the while, my eyes noticed that Otoo was keeping himself between me and the obstinate fifteen-foot-long hungry tiger shark. As I expended the last energies left in my extremely fatigued arms, I was now only twenty feet-away from the schooner, and also from the screaming sailors waiting to drag me aboard. The shark sensed that I might be escaping its appetite, and it commenced one final bold thrust in my direction.

"Don't worry, Charley!" Otoo confidently encouraged. "Keep swimming! I shall make the shark feel sick! Keep swimming! Go to the left! I see a line in the water thrown there from the ship, and it's just for you!"

At that time, I was barely conscious, and was swimming out of my raw instinct to survive. As my left hand clutched the rope, I heard divergent exclamations from the crewmen standing onboard. Some of the sailors were cheering, while others were loudly crying and shrieking-out, expressing their total shock and horror.

I turned and looked behind me, and my eyes perceived my soul brother, the Heathen, breaking surface with both hands sheared-off at the wrists, and with blood spurting-out from the two horrible stumps.

"Good bye, Otoo!" my partner exclaimed his farewell. "But please always remember, half of me still lives inside you, Charley!" And then the courageous, meek, wonderful man submerged into the deep harbor, never to be seen again.

And so passed the valiant Otoo, who I must confess, successfully made me into a penitent and appreciative Christian. We had met in the maw of a hurricane, and we had parted with my better half in the maw of a tiger shark. The Heathen and I had been comrades for over seventeen excellent years, and despite him being a pagan, I now pray that Jesus will accept the noble and good Otoo into His Heavenly Eternal Kingdom.

# “The House of Mapuhi”

The *Aorai* handled the waves quite easily, and the sleek schooner drifted smoothly to anchor just off the South Pacific atoll known to local mariners as Hikueru, which is a crude coral islet a hundred-yards wide, and approximately twenty-miles long in a horseshoe-shaped circumference. The atoll was known for its abundant pearl harvest, but even small cutters could not navigate directly into the shallow and treacherous channel, but instead those vessels had to anchor a hundred-yards out, and any subsequent trade had to be accomplished by means of small boats being rowed ashore.

Alexandre Raoul, half European and half Polynesian, stood aboard the *Aorai*, ready to be rowed ashore to perform some standard purchasing business. Raoul was the son of Marie Raoul, who affluently owned a fleet of a half-dozen trading schooners that specialized in pearl commerce and coconut oil.

Fifteen minutes later, the small rowboat made it safely across the lagoon where Alexandre Raoul met and shook hands with a familiar tall native, the man having several inches of his left white ulna protruding down from his elbow, with the injury serving as evidence of a shark encounter, and a shortened-career as a pearl diver.

“Have you heard the wonderful news, Alexandre?” Huru-Huru asked the new arrival. “Mapuhi has found an incredible, sensational pearl that’s unlike any other ever discovered in Hikueru, or anywhere else in all the islands for that matter. And please remember, Alec,” the garrulous beggar continued his narrative. “Mapuhi is a colossal fool, and you can get the enormous pearl from him quite cheap! Now then, Alec. Do you have any tobacco to compensate me for *that* vital information? Or, any comparable contribution to my general welfare would be amply appreciated.”

After giving Huru-Huru a pouch of fresh tobacco as the informant’s just reward, Alexandre Raoul headed up the beach to further investigate the recent news, and to search-out copra, valuable shells, and possible “perfect pearls” to increase his mother’s wealth, and to further expand his future inheritance. But Alexandre was rather inexperienced when it came to intense trading, with this voyage being only his second round of excursions among the gorgeous native islands. Upon seeing the huge, pigeon-egg-sized pearl that Huru-Huru had described, Raoul’s eyes widened, thus revealing the procurer’s immediate interest in the item to the very alert seller.

"Examine it closely with your magnifying glass if you'd like," Mapuhi amiably suggested. "The damned thing doesn't have a single flaw or observable blemish. It has a very excellent weight, if I may add, and the beauty is almost see-through! Notice that it sparkles and shines like the bright moonlight!"

"Well, what the hell do you want for it?" Raoul asked, feigning nonchalance. "It does look perfectly genuine. Just a trifle out of the ordinary, I would surmise."

Two avaricious-looking women and a girl (a wife, a mother and a daughter) stood directly behind Mapuhi, and the trio nodded their heads in support of the man selling his prized gem. Each encourager eagerly anticipated the acquisition of instant wealth and luxury, especially the pair of adult females.

"First of all, I want a new house that must have a galvanized iron roof, and an attractive octagon clock above the main door," Mapuhi insisted and specified. "The house must be six fathoms in length with a porch built all around. A grand room must occupy the center with a round dinner table in the middle," the seller specified with certainty. "Four bedrooms total will also be included in the construction; two positioned on either side of the grand room. Each bedroom will have an iron bed; two chairs, and a suitable washbasin on a stand. And in the rear of the home will be an adequate kitchen with a stove; a sink, and pots and pans. And *my* new home will be built on the island of Fakarava, and not here on Hikueru."

"Is that all?" Alexandre Raoul asked and smiled, shaking his head in sheer amazement. "Are you sure you don't want the Crown Jewels of England, Buckingham Palace, and the London Bridge thrown into the settlement, also?"

"There must also be a sewing machine," Mapuhi's wife, Tefara, spoke-up and demanded. "I definitely need a sewing machine."

"And don't forget the special octagon drop clock!" Mapuhi's mother Nauri insisted. "The clock must have eight sides, just like a damned octopus has eight arms. The clock will bring good luck to the new house!"

"Yes; and I want a bedroom all to myself," demanded Ngakura, Mapuhi's daughter.

"Yes, that is all!" Mapuhi exclaimed and verified. "Those wonderful things will make us all fully satisfied! We will be one big happy family."

Young Alexandre Raoul laughed indulgently while his mind did some comprehensive mathematical calculations. 'Let's see now,' the youthful trader considered. 'I gotta' fuckin' voyage all the way to

Tahiti to buy the materials to build the house on Fakarava; that is, after I first acquire the goddamned land. That's at least four thousand French dollars, which is fuckin' equal to twenty thousand francs. My mother will have me castrated if I fuck-up on this crazy deal. But I gotta' admit; the pearl is fantastic and most enticing!'

"Mapuhi; I think that your stipulations are entirely too tremendous and completely out of line!" Raoul diplomatically replied as calmly as the novice buyer could express his opposition. "Set a damned reasonable cash price, instead of giving me a long list of impossible-to-meet demands!"

But Mapuhi was adamant and shook his head in disagreement, with the three stubborn female heads in the background concurring with his negative assessment of the visiting trader's recommendation. "I want the house, and it must be six fathoms long with a…."

"Yes, yes. I know all about the dimensions of *your* exotic house with the grand room; and the four bedrooms, and the exceptional octagon clock," the frustrated prospective purchaser answered. "Look here now. I'll give you a thousand Chili dollars, and a hundred Chili dollars to boot as a fine bonus."

"I want the house built on Fakarava, and that's final!" Mapuhi repeated. "No house; no damned pearl!"

"Look, Mapuhi. The first hurricane that comes along will demolish your new house, and then you'll have nothing to show for your fabulous pearl," Alexandre Raoul unconvincingly argued. "Captain Raffy standing watch out on the *Aorai* says that it looks like a sizeable hurricane is coming this way, soon. Won't you change your stubborn mind? There's still time to hammer-out a decent compromise!"

"The land on Fakarava is much higher than it is here on Hikueru," Mapuhi maintained. "And the house must be six fathoms long and have a big porch around the front and a…"

Alexandre Raoul spent three difficult hours trying to persuade Mapuhi, and his obstinate family, to accept the cash payment and to forget about the new house, but to no avail. The pearl-finder kept adamantly-repeating his memorized litany of his fantasy dream dwelling in exchange for the wondrous pearl that the inflexible South Pacific native possessed.

A large squall was seen approaching the remote atoll. The first mate from the *Aorai* hopped from his rowboat onto the atoll's dock, and asked the idle, local gazette, Huru-Huru, where the young merchant could be found. After giving the beggar a shiny coin for his cooperation, the dispatched sailor knocked on Mapuhi's shack door, and had an extremely urgent message to deliver.

"Sir, Captain Raffy says ya' gotta' get the hell outa' here on-the-double, so grab your shell or pearl, or whatever you're bargaining after and head straight for the dock. The ship's barometer has dropped-down to 29.70, and if we want to avert a dire emergency storm situation, we immediately gotta' raise anchor and head west. Time is definitely of the essence."

A sudden wind gust unexpectedly ripped apart an overhead palm tree, and sent a half-dozen coconuts clattering upon the shack's tin roof. Then the first-wave of rain sheets came pouring-out of the dark sky, signaling the encroachment of a terrible tropical storm approaching. "A thousand Chili dollars cash, on your table, and two hundred Chili dollars bonus in trade," the young trader offered the native and his family.

"I want a house six fathoms long with a..."

"Mapuhi. You're a fucked-up idiotic fool of the highest and greatest magnitude!" Raoul yelled as the novice trading merchant then angrily exited the shanty without negotiating any deal.

"Did you buy the pearl?" Huru-Huru asked Raoul as the visitor and the first mate made it to the rocking and rolling rowboat.

"Mapuhi is a fucked-up fool, who thinks his pearl is the most precious jewel in the entire world!" the livid trader shouted-back. "He'd be twelve hundred Chili dollars richer if he wasn't such a hard-headed, fucked-up asshole!"

* * * * * * * * * * * * * *

A half an hour later, Huru-Huru passively stood under a palm tree on the north end of the atoll, and casually watched the *Aorai* with Alexandre Raoul aboard heading out to sea. But coincidentally, coming in on the wings of the squall was the supercargo agent Toriki, and *his* newly-acquired merchant ship, the *Orohena*. Huru-Huru was keenly aware that Mapuhi owed the disreputable Toriki money for trade goods, and for a high-interest cash advance that had been given the year before. By now, the phantom sea storm had passed, and the lagoon was again flat and smooth, reflecting a mirror-blue image.

"Have you heard the most recent news, Toriki?" chatty Huru-Huru greeted the atoll's newest visitor. "Mapuhi has found the greatest pearl ever on Hikueru and wishes to either sell or trade it. The silly jerk is a fool who still owes you money. Remember, Toriki.

I've confidentially shared this secret news with you. Do you have any tobacco to share for me?"

After giving the beggar *his* petty reward, Toriki sauntered-off to Mapuhi's lackluster shack, where the notorious loan-shark quickly snatched the pearl from its owner's hand, and instead of examining the jewel, plopped it into his pocket. "You're quite lucky indeed, Mapuhi. It's a splendid pearl. I'll give you adequate credit for it in my records."

"But Toriki. I want a house that is six fathoms long, with a…"

"Six fathoms your grandmother's fat ass and smelly cunt!" Toriki gruffly exclaimed. "Now listen carefully, you dumb shit. You had owed me twelve hundred Chili dollars, but now you owe them no longer. If the pearl sells well in Tahiti," the slippery-minded trader speculated and stated, "I'll give you credit for three hundred more Chile dollars, in addition to canceling your massive debt. But if I lose money on the deal, you'll still have a clean slate on my accounting assets and debits."

After Toriki exited the dilapidated shack, the former pearl owner sat silently with his head crestfallen, wondering why he had ever showed the jewel's magnificence to the infamous sea ruffian.

"You are an asshole!" his wife Tefara accused Mapuhi.

"You are a bungling asshole fool!" his mother Nauri directly insinuated.

"My father is a giant, bungling, asshole, fool jerk-off!" his twelve-year-old daughter Ngakura mimicked and creatively added.

"What was I to do?" Mapuhi grieved and sulked. "The loan-shark knew I had the pearl and asked to see it, before I could ever conceal or hide it. Somebody had told him about the valuable object, and as the three of you know, I happened to have owed that lousy thug Toriki lots of money. An honest man always pays his debts, and my conscience dictates to my heart that I must be an honest man."

The three females hysterically burst into tears, and continued to abundantly criticize the man of the shack, who, looking dramatically defeated and bewildered, held his head in his rough callused hands and openly sobbed.

Meanwhile, the always-vigilant Huru-Huru observed a third schooner entering the mouth of the lagoon, and then dropping anchor. The moocher recognized the vessel to be the *Hiri*, owned by the German Jew Levy, who happened to be the shrewdest and most successful pearl buyer in the entire South Pacific. '*Hiri* is named after Hira, the Tahitian god of fishermen, pirates and thieves,' Huru-Huru thought and smiled. 'Maybe I can scrounge some high-grade imported tobacco from that German Jew bastard Levy.'

"Have you heard the latest news, Master Levy?" the conniving beggar rhetorically asked. "Mapuhi has found a huge pearl; the greatest treasure ever discovered on Hikueru. It's perhaps the most fantastic pearl ever found in the whole damned world! Rumor has it that the dumb shit-head has just sold the rare trove to Toriki for fourteen hundred Chile. I heard them speakin' and negotiatin' the transaction myself. Remember, Master Levy that it was I that told you this big secret. Do you have any spare tobacco?"

"Where is Toriki, now? His ship is still anchored outside the lagoon!" Levy asked and stated. "Tell me, and you'll get your cherished, expensive tobacco."

"He's over in old Captain Lynch's house drinking absinthe, and boasting about his outstanding barter with the imbecile Mapuhi!" Huru-Huru respectfully answered. "I believe that the grand sum of twenty-five thousand francs had been loosely discussed for the sale of the unbelievably precious pearl."

Just then, the guns aboard both the *Orohena* and the *Hiri* began firing, signaling that their buying agents should seek shelter on shore, while the two schooners would be temporarily heading out to sea to avoid possible catastrophe, because of impending inclement weather and high winds.

"I reckon the mercury in the barometer has fallen some more," Captain Lynch said to Levy. "Last reading in my house was 29.20, so that's why Toriki and I came outside on the porch to look at the sea and the sky."

An hour later, the sound of the pounding surf was loud and menacing, as thick swells paraded to the coral beach in what seemed like a visual aquatic symphony. Toriki and Levy's schooners had again entered the lagoon's mouth, and soon, their rowboats came ashore to conduct them back to their respective ships.

But ironically, the *Aorai* had come back to Hikueru, also. And Alexandre Raoul, who was now reconsidering the acquisition of the valuable pearl from Mapuhi, and who did not know that the unscrupulous Toriki had already-confiscated it, was also being rowed to the dock by two husky crewmen.

"You're too late, Alec!" Huru-Huru declared with a fake look of disappointment expressed upon his suntanned face. "Mapuhi sold the pearl to Toriki for fourteen-hundred Chile, and Toriki then quickly sold the gem to Levy for twenty-five thousand francs. I heard it all with my own two ears. Levy will get a hundred-thousand francs for it at auction in France. Now then, do you have any more fuckin' tobacco to compensate for my valuable information?"

'I don't exactly believe, Huru-Huru, who does have a certain reputation for sometimes lying and stretching the truth,' Raoul determined. 'Toriki might've bought the glorious pearl for a debt owed by Mapuhi, but I doubt that *that* Jew prick Levy, an expert on pearls, would've ever paid twenty-five thousand francs to that unethical, reprehensible fuck-head Toriki. I'll interview old reliable Captain Lynch about the transaction!'

"This son-of-a-bitch barometer is readin' 29.10!" Captain Lynch told his new visitor. "I'll tell you straight-up, Mr. Raoul; I've never before seen the pressure indicators registerin' so goddamned low! But just look your eyes out the window. Your boat the *Aorai* is sittin' calm outside the lagoon's perimeter, still all safe and sound."

"But the wave surges are becoming too strong for me to leave the dock," Raoul excitedly replied. "I should've never left the *Aorai* in pursuit of a fucked-up whim! I think it's best if I stay here with you tonight, Captain Lynch. I'll tell the two crewmen to haul the rowboat out of the water, to securely tie it down, and then to seek their own shelter somewhere on the atoll."

"Now the pressure's an unbelievable 29 flat!" Captain Lynch reported. "And strangely enough, the sea is constantly rising into a surge, I mean, Alexandre; there is little wind, yet such a powerful incoming tide exists! The wave impact will be like a fuckin' earthquake blastin' into this tiny atoll! It'll have the effect of a fuckin' major tsunami!"

"But there is no wind!" Raoul marveled and exclaimed. "It's like a summer afternoon in San Diego!"

"I moved to this remote atoll because of my chronic asthma condition," Captain Lynch stressed and explained. "I was afraid I would die anywhere else. Now I'm fuckin' scared out of my wits that I'm gonna' die pretty damned soon, right here on Hikueru. Make sure that if we're both knocked onto the floor, be sure to fart in my face so that I'll have something to breathe."

* * * * * * * * * * * * *

It was three o'clock in the afternoon, and the cloud-laden low sky was dark with the outer-fringe winds picking-up velocity. Families whose homes had already been swept into the lagoon came to the coral beach in the vicinity of Captain Lynch's residence to pray and endure the storm's fury. And if necessary, the village's members would lash themselves to coconut trees. Ironically, the highest spot on the atoll was the safest area, for the great sea surges had already breached and impacted many sectors of the narrow sixty-fathom-wide islet, whose population had recently tripled because it was the height of the pearl diving season.

"There're twelve hundred men, women and children now on Hikueru," Captain Lynch informed Alexandre Raoul. "Many will be dead tomorrow if the fuckin' storm grows in magnitude, which I fear it'll do! I've seen tempest disasters happen before, and from my experience, I predict that another one will soon occur here again!"

"But how come the wind isn't blowing that severely?" Raoul asked the old salt. "This weather pattern seems to be some kind of fucked-up nautical anomaly!"

"Don't worry, Alexandre!" the captain replied as a massive wave smote the beach, making the women and children scream in alarm as nervous chickens and cats neurotically scampered around in three-inch-deep sea water. "It'll blow like nothing you've ever seen or felt before, so fuckin' prepare for the worst, and hope for the best!"

In heightened panic, apprehensive natives climbed the sturdiest coconut trees with their most valuable possessions kept in baskets and sacks, while other inhabitants used thick hemp to tether themselves to the bases of the largest palm trees.

Captain Lynch and Raoul briefly studied the *Aorai* bobbing and pitching in the distant sea, and immediately decided to flee to a safer spot inside the house. "Twenty-eight-sixty!" the captain read and yelled from reading the wall barometer. "That's the lowest fuckin' numbers I've ever seen in my eleven years living here! I've witnessed this terrible bullshit before! Soon, even the strongest trees will splinter, and the debris will be lying all over the eroded beach like scattered matchsticks!"

Immediately, Lynch cut a long rope into two-fathom lengths and gave Raoul one half. "I think we're gonna' need this hemp to lash ourselves to trees, because this house isn't goin' to sustain the heavy winds and storm surges to come! Holy fuck!" the captain exclaimed with alarm. "It's now reading 28.20! We gotta' find a good sturdy tree in a hurry," the resident instructed as the house started to vibrate, and its foundation began to shake with two panes of thin glass loudly shattering. "It's too bad that tall oaks and tulip trees can't grow out here in the South Pacific!"

In a moment, another strong sea wave struck the house, and rotated the foundation six feet off its footings, as the frame tilted-downward at a ten-degree angle. The two exasperated men departed the doomed dwelling and whirled around several times in the swirling winds, desperately trying to locate an unoccupied coconut tree.

Captain Lynch managed to climb-up a tall, sturdy palm, while Raoul elected to tether himself to the base of an adjacent one. Another forceful surge breached the vulnerable atoll, and the water blast came-up to Alexandre's knees. The rain felt like dense pellets striking his exposed face, as the torrents began falling in vertical sheets from the darkened sky. The natives looked (to Raoul's vivid imagination) like human fruit suspended from and clinging to the tops of nearby palm trees. From sheer anxiety and instinct, the Tahitian-born merchant clasped the palm-tree trunk with his hands, and adroitly shinnied-up, and to his surprise, discovered two women and two children seated on flimsy limbs towards the top, literally holding on for dear life.

Off in the distance, Raoul could hear the Mormon missionary and some worried members of his congregation chanting prayers, and then nervously singing a solemn hymn. Without any warning, a tree, thirty feet to Raoul's right, snapped. And its unlucky occupants were flung to the beach, with their bodies instantly being washed into the lagoon by a powerful surge of frenetic water. Alexandre's own tree was swaying and vacillating in the perilous wind, as he, a non-religious person throughout his young life, began praying intently.

In the distance, the Mormon Church, with its small steeple, collapsed to the ground in one violent thud. And then its remaining structure was gradually moved into the lagoon's center by a very potent wave burst. People were being blown from, and falling out of the surrounding trees like overripe coconuts, while other victims were writhing about and squirming like worms upon the coral beach sands. The limp bodies of other less fortunate natives were being floated out to sea via the lagoon.

And then Raoul saw Captain Lynch's tree abruptly snap, and its three occupants being hurled into the sea like three separate rockets traveling at least fifty-yards in the air before splashing into the deeper section of the lagoon.

Surrendering to overwhelming fear, Alexandre Raoul impulsively left the company of the traumatized palm tree dwellers hanging-on for dear life just above his head, and carefully keeping his rope tied around the palm's trunk, along with around his waist, the drenched merchant slowly slid-down to the tropical tree's base.

'It's now around eleven o'clock at night, and the people that are still living are either howling like dogs, or crying like infants. I can't stand much more of this fucked-up misery!' Alexandre evaluated and gasped. 'I wish I was fuckin' dead like Captain Lynch, and the two sailors that perished with him! And the only way I can breathe is to press my lips against the goddamned tree bark! If I were a fuckin' dog, I'd be wishing that I was an elephant instead!'

At three in the morning, during the absolute height of the hurricane, the tall tree that had been holding Mapuhi and his family was severely uprooted, and everyone was tossed from a height of twenty-feet into the lagoon. Mapuhi surfaced, clutching his daughter Ngakura's torso. The other members of Mapuhi's family were presumed to have not survived the terrible plummet, and subsequent water crash. Mapuhi courageously emerged and staggered from the lagoon, but Ngakura's left arm had been broken, with the fingers of the girl's right hand being mangled, and her split forehead bleeding profusely. But still, the brave native managed to clutch a tree with one hand, while embracing his semi-conscious, in-shock daughter with his other appendage.

At five in the morning, the hurricane winds had gradually diminished, and just after sunrise, a dead calm persisted with the sun's rays finally refracting through the dense overhead clouds. Mapuhi left Ngakura leaning against a palm tree; located his wife Tefara, lying on the beach, and amazingly, the woman was barely breathing, but still alive. And Tefara was one among the three-hundred that had survived the incomparable storm; yes, three-hundred out of the twelve-hundred that had been living on the atoll, for the entire lagoon was cluttered with corpses, and neither a hut nor a house remained intact.

On the third day after the hurricane's wrath, the survivors buried and mourned their dead. Such was life in paradise when it occasionally turned hellish.

* * * * * * * * * * * * * *

On the fourth day after the savage hurricane, old conflicts and disputes arose between Mapuhi and his salvaged wife, Tefara, who now felt emotionally obligated to express her dissatisfaction with her "foolish husband".

"If you had followed my thorough and explicit directions," Tefara contemptuously yelled at the henpecked fellow, "you would've hidden the giant pearl, and you'd still be in possession of it now as we speak."

"But that blabbermouth Huru-Huru was with me when I had first examined the shell, and the tramp would've announced my discovery to anyone and everyone willing to listen to his rambling bullshit," the inconsolable spouse lamented. "He's got a mouth that's much bigger than the goddamned lagoon maw!"

"And kind Mr. Raoul told me yesterday evening that if you had not given-away the valuable pearl to that miserable thief Toriki," the incensed wife continued her verbal tirade, "the nice supercargo agent would've bought it from you for five-thousand French dollars, which translates, I think, into ten-thousand Chili! His mother Marie would've even paid more than her son had offered; that fact, I am sure."

"Look, Tefara. The great pearl paid my twelve-hundred-dollar debt with Toriki," Mapuhi attempted to justify his already-condemned action. "And that's important to me and to my conscience. Can't you forgive me for what I had done without *your* approval?"

"Toriki is dead, and his schooner along with the *Aorai* and the *Hiri* are probably also forever lost," the livid wife rehashed. "Will Toriki ever pay you the three-hundred-dollar credit he had promised you? No; because that rotten son-of-a-bitch is now stone-cold-dead! And let's say for argument's sake that you had never found any damned pearl in the first place. Would you today owe Toriki twelve-hundred-dollars? Toriki is dead, you stupid-Asshole, and you cannot pay a debt to a dead shit like him!"

"But the Jew Levy did not pay Toriki," the now-agitated Mapuhi defiantly answered in self-defense. "He merely exchanged with Toriki a piece of paper with *his* signature, good for receipt of money in Papeete. And now, Levy is dead, and cannot pay Toriki, and that devious scoundrel Toriki is dead, and the contract paper is gone with him, too. And the accursed pearl is also totally lost with that swindler Jew Levy dead to boot! You're absolutely correct, Tefara! I am a moronic asshole, because I've lost the pearl and got nothing for it! Now let's go to bed and have some hot sex, if you don't mind sleeping with a total ignoramus!"

Then, there was a noise coming from outside the ramshackle enclosure that was once part of Mapuhi's shack. "Holy shark shit!" Mapuhi exclaimed. "It's Nauri banging on the partition! I recognize her loud rap! Is that *you,* mother?"

"It's a ghost! It's your crazy mother's ghost that might be even crazier than she was!" Tefara screamed. "Husband. I'm scared shit-less, and have no more crap in my intestines!"

"Good woman spirit," Mapuhi said in a nervous voice as the superstitious pearl discoverer separated the flimsy partition to allow entrance into the roofless, makeshift living area. "Where do you come from?"

"From the damned sea!" came the woman's emphatic reply. "Where else would I have been blown into by the goddamned hurricane winds?"

Then Ngakura sat-up from her position in her new sandbox bed and started crying, but her moans were ignored because her parents were still astounded to witness Nauri standing there with her chubby arms folded in front of her massive chest.

"You might at least offer your old mother a drink of water!" Nauri demanded of her still-flabbergasted son. "That should prove to you that I'm not a fucked-up ghost as you believe, you superstitious Asshole! You've always been a very stupid, neurotic, foolish Asshole, ever since you began to speak at age seven! God; was I glad when Tefara married you and got you off my hands!"

"What is that in your closed fist?" Mapuhi curiously asked his mother. "I've always known you to be tightfisted."

"It's *your* damned expensive pearl!" Nauri matter-of-factly replied. "The Jew Levy lay dead on the north end of the atoll, and I intelligently removed the pearl from his pants' pocket. Now it is mine, and I call the shots around here!"

"And how will the pearl be spent?" Mapuhi incredulously wondered and queried. "Fairly, to all our family, I hope."

"First of all," Nauri declared in an imperative tone of voice. "The pearl will be sold to the supercargo merchant Raoul for…"

"Ten thousand Chile dollars," Tefara finished her mother-in-law's declarative sentence. "And the money earned will be used for a house that'll be six fathoms long, with the octagon drop clock in the wall, and the round table in the center of the grand room; but most of all, we'll have four bedrooms with iron beds in each, and the house will have a galvanized iron roof and also…"

"A modern sewing-machine!" Nauri euphorically yelled, triumphantly raising her bruised and lacerated hands up into the air. "That's what the hell kept me alive throughout the whole entire damned hurricane! Call it a dream come true, but throughout every wicked incessant wind gust, all I kept thinking about was operating that wonderful new imaginary sewing machine! Thank goodness that honest Mr. Alexandre Raoul has survived the terrible storm!"

# “The Pearls of Parlay”

Ordinarily, the South Seas are tranquil and serene, and an easy pleasure to navigate. But during hurricane season, the normally placid waters can be treacherous. One ship, the *Malahini,* was fortunate to escape the wrath of a devastating storm with its helmsman still-alive at the wheel. All seemed copasetic as the headsails emptied, and the boom tackles were shifting, when the *Malahini* reeled-over and glided away on its opposite tack. The early morning wind was brisk, but the captain and crew believed that everything was under control.

Five scantily-clad, sun-tanned men were lounging on the deck. David Grief, the ship’s new owner, and his guest Gregory Mulhall, an Englishman, were still in their pajamas, with their toes protruding through Chinese slippers. Captain Wakefield and his Holland mate Hermann were wearing thin undershirts and casual, un-starched, duck trousers, while the chief sailor stood with sweat beads upon his forehead with his muscular chest thrust forward in an indifferent wind that didn’t cool any particular part of his anatomy.

“Pretty muggy weather for a breeze like this one,” the husky sailor complained. “I hope this isn’t a bad omen for things to come. I have faith in this fine schooner, but even faith has its limitations.”

“And look to the west,” David Grief pointed-out. “I’m no goddamned Horace Greely, but look to the west, young man. There seems to be a vacuum of air, a terribly vacant spot in the atmosphere, if ya’ ask me.”

“I’ve seen this sort of shit before,” Hermann the Dutchman added, his arms and broad shoulders wind-milling around. “Sometimes the weather pattern just passes by, and other times it’ll blow the clothes right off your ass. Depends on fate and circumstance, mostly so. A little chance and coincidence thrown into the mix, too.”

“Something sinister is out there, mates,” Captain Wakefield assessed and opined while rubbing his bushy beard with the fingers of both hands. “Weather’s been crazy like a March Mad Hare for two whole weeks now. And we haven’t had the proper trade winds to trade anything for a full month. And the barometer has been dippin’ and risin’ as if the mechanism is governed by some supernatural forces, a struggle between devils below and angels above,” Wakefield strangely commented. “I saw this same sort of weird atmospheric pressure shit when I was an apprentice aboard the *Lancaster* before she went-down on *her,* and *my,* first voyage. My

Pop was the captain, and the ship's sinking broke his heart. Dad died the following year, never psychologically recovering from the disaster, which amounted to his great loss. Let's hope that my man Hermann's right, and that these ominous conditions are just a passin' fancy."

"The extreme heat's rather stifling, wouldn't you say?" the Britain, Gregory Mulhall, observed and remarked. "I've been to the Sahara once, and this is what the humidity felt like. Thank goodness I had a decent camel and a smart guide; or else I wouldn't be here tellin' ya' about my fucked-up desert adventure. But it bein' so hot and the sun havin' difficulty shining through the scant clouds, well gentlemen; that odd combination's definitely a very bad omen that can't be fuckin' ignored."

Captain Wakefield ordered the skilled Polynesian sailors to quickly adjust the head sheets and the boom tackles, as the sturdy and dependable *Malahini* rolled gently into the wind.

"This sucker maneuvers more like a yacht than a schooner," Gregory Mulhall commended the captain. "I didn't know that South Seas traders sailed yachts."

"This schooner was a Gloucester fisherman's boat in the beginning," David Grief interrupted and academically explained to his guest. "And the Gloucester boats are very similar to yachts in design; construction; rigging, and sailing capability. And if ya' don't believe me, Greg, just ask the Gloucester fisherman, ha, ha, ha! Now Captain Wakefield will show ya' in a fine demonstration exactly how a decent lagoon entrance is accomplished on a strong ebb current."

The *Malahini* smoothly-entered the narrow sea passage, with the mouth of the atoll constituting no problem at all. Coconut palms randomly grew on several sandy shoals, and the schooner had to maneuver around the obstacle islets that the lagoon's channel presented. The tidal entrance was challenging to the talents of the crew; indeed, with the outflow of water seeming like the rapids of a raging river in several areas, as the sea appeared to boil; whirl; surge, and swirl on either side of the gracefully approaching schooner. Several times, the *Malahini* headed towards the coral edge and had to be deftly steered back into the lagoon's central channel.

"Captain, now's the time to employ that new expensive engine of yours," David Grief suggested to Wakefield.

"Good grief, Mr. Grief!" the captain exclaimed. "That engine will pay for itself, but I don't need to fire it up just now. I gotta' admit; it's much better than insurance, especially when the waters become turbulent. I know my ship, David, and I assure you, when the proper time arrives," Captain Wakefield promised, "I'll let the engine do its work. But right now, everything's runnin' smooth and predictable, although *you* might not think so."

David Grief then pointed to a small cutter churning through the entrance. "I'll wager you Captain Wakefield five francs that the little *Nuhiva* over there beats us into the harbor and anchors before we do."

"Well David, she has ten horsepower, and we've got forty. But we're like an ocean liner compared to her tiny size," Wakefield noted and expressed. "But the *Nuhiva* can't buck the ten-knot current that she's up against. I'll accept your wager, David, because I know my ship's ability. And I also know the plusses and minuses of the *Nuhiva.* We'll most certainly beat her into Parlay."

"Why do ya' call her Parlay instead of Hikihoho as it appears on the maps and charts?" David Grief wanted to know.

"My brothers dive for Parlay for four summer months, and Hikihoho is a good place to find pearls," one of the Polynesian sailors (who didn't have four or more knees) stated. "Yes, the natives still call the atoll Hikohoho, but the bossy, stubborn white men call it Parlay."

"And the pearl divers have never gotten Mr. Parlay to part with one of his sacred pearls," Captain Wakefield explained with a frown. "I suppose that *that* avaricious fellow Parlay wants to parlay his precious pearls into a gigantic fortune. At least that's what the island scuttlebutt around these parts is!"

"Not exactly knit one, *purl* two," David Grief joked and laughed. "Any other pearls of wisdom about this Parlay fellow, Captain?"

"Well, old man Parlay had a hatful of the gems for his daughter Armande when he had set sail for Tahiti a decade and a half ago," Captain Wakefield revealed. "And the old codger's been adding to his vast collection ever since. Natives claim that this infertile lagoon has been fished clean of clams and pearls. Maybe that's why Mr. Parlay's recently announced his special pearl auction. The old gent wants to move-on to another location, perhaps goin' to find bigger and better pearls somewhere else."

"What's so damned secretive about this man Parlay and his pearls?" Gregory Mulhall inquisitively asked. "This old geezer Parlay is a beachcomber that struck it rich, so what? I've seen plenty bigger deals occurring in major casino poker and blackjack card games!"

"Hikihoho, the lagoon, and everything else here belongs to old Parlay," Dutchman Hermann informed Gregory Mulhall. "He's accumulated a tremendous fortune in pearls that's unrivalled anywhere throughout the South Seas. See all those eight schooners lined-up and anchored over there in the harbor. They're all here for Parlay's announced pearl auction, scheduled for tomorrow morning, and I presume that's why the hell the *Malahini's* here, too!"

"And we're ship number nine," Captain Wakefield verified. "Over there is Narii Herring, a half-caste Jew who owns the tiny *Nuhiva* that's tryin' to beat us into the harbor. That son-of-a-bitch Herring owes everybody money that the asshole has borrowed over the last six years, and every lender around looks-out for *his* welfare because that prick owes them all plenty of cash. As for me," Captain Wakefield continued his woeful monologue, shaking his head in disgust. "I owe no one anything, so the goddamned creditors don't give a shit whether I live or die. But as for that cock-sucker Narii Herring, even though his fucked-up name sounds a little like him bein' a scaley fish, he's their pride and joy, along with being their debt-owing poster boy."

"This fellow Parlay is a Frenchman, so I suppose Parlay parlais vous Francais!" David Grief, the enterprising new owner of the *Malahini* bantered.

"Well, what's this Narii Herring chap have to do with this whole pearl-seeking expedition, anyway?" the unfamiliar Englishman Gregory Mulhall asked his friend David Grief. "What's all this Parlay pearl nonsense? And David, please start your intriguing narrative straight from the beginning, so that I have sufficient background to be fully knowledgeable in future conversations."

* * * * * * * * * * * * *

David Grief paused for a moment, his mind organizing in chronological order the precise story he wished to communicate to his personal guest on the *Malahini*, Gregory Mulhall. "From what I've seen and gathered from observation, old Parlay is at least partly insane," Grief shared with Mulhall, with Captain Wakefield, and with Hermann the Dutchman, who only seemed to give a damn about Amsterdam and Rotterdam. "Parlay's a full-blooded Frenchman, originating from Paris, where his ancestors had sold plaster; the maniac used to brag that he was a descendant of D'Artagnon, Alexandre Dumas's fictional fourth musketeer, which leads me to believe that Parlay can't distinguish between fantasy and fuckin' reality."

"Mr. Parlay sounds like an interesting character himself," Gregory Mulhall, an avid novel reader, commented.

"Anyway Greg," David Grief continued. "Parlay learned to be an accomplished trader, and soon became familiar with Hikihoho, particularly with its fabled exotic pearls. The atoll had around a hundred inhabitants and eventually, Parlay, wanting to be royalty in his fucked-up mind, married the native Queen."

"What happened next?" Gregory Mulhall curiously asked. "This fascinating tale sounds like the preamble to a grand novel just waiting to be fuckin' authored."

"A measles epidemic came through the vicinity, and only a dozen natives survived," David Grief related to his close friend. "But months before the Queen died, she gave birth to a daughter Armande. Now the way I understand it, Parlay was too busy making his colossal fortune to raise a child, so when Armande was three, Mr. Parlay sent her to the convent in Papeete. And when she was eight, the girl was transferred to a much more famous convent supported by altruistic and humanitarian aristocrats over in France."

"What eventually happened to this girl, Armande?" Gregory Mulhall asked. "Did she stay to live in Paris?"

"According to the version of the story that I'm familiar with," David Grief recalled and stated, "Parlay sent for Armande when the girl turned eighteen, because by then, the jerk was the richest man around on any of the nearby islands and atolls. He had built his mansion on Hikihoho, and also owned a well-constructed bungalow over on Papeete. But that same year, the fiercest hurricane on record hit the South Pacific when Mani-Huni was swept clear, and over eleven hundred inhabitants drowned."

"I was a crew member on the *Magpie* when that turbulent storm invaded this region," Captain Wakefield contributed. "And the ship, along with the cook and me, wound-up inside the coconut trees situated a quarter of a mile inland. And the head peninsula of Taiohae Bay was reputed to be hurricane-proof! So much for legends and historical traditions!"

"Well, Mr. Parlay did land on a neighboring island just before the storm struck, and the greedy fellow had in his possession a hatful of pearls," David Grief articulated his recollection of events. "But the old fossil-faced geezer had to refurbish his damaged schooner, and then build a long half-mile of rails to launch her back into the ocean, because of the sea destruction that the hurricane had wrought."

"But what the hell ever happened to Armande?" Greg Mulhall verbally probed. "She was there all alone staying on Papeete, and how was she treated?"

"Armande, who was used to being treated and pampered as a princess back at the French convent, was basically ignored by everyone on the island," David Grief informed Gregory Mulhall. "A handsome sailor fell in love with her, but then shipped out to sea without ever saying a word of farewell. Armande felt alienated and became disenchanted with her South Seas' existence, and ultimately killed herself with a stiletto to the heart, before her father ever returned to take her back to Hikihoho. According to island gossip, the crazy fucker had a giant pearl in his possession worth sixty-thousand francs, but upon learning of his daughter's untimely fate, Parlay had to be put into a straitjacket for two days until he overcame his mania."

"That's the true essence of the story," grim-faced Captain Wakefield confirmed. "And now here's a little addendum. While grieving and angry on Papeete, the insane shit-head Parlay then pumped three bullets into a lieutenant, whom he had gotten into a verbal altercation with, and the belligerent old fogey also insultingly flung a glass of wine into the governor's face."

"Sounds like Armande's suicidal death turned Parlay into a raving maniac!" Gregory Mulhall remarked.

"Why yes," Captain Wakefield verified. "It's also reported that incensed Parlay viciously beat-up three native servants, and maliciously and deliberately wrecked the entire west wing of the island hospital. The reprehensible bastard absolutely pulverized a male nurse, breaking three of the innocent fellow's ribs, and then the vile prick dared the Chief-of-Police and three gendarmes to arrest him as he held the four men at gunpoint before setting sail back to Hikihoho. And fifteen years later," Captain Wakefield pontificated, "old Parlay has stayed put on his private atoll, and has never again ventured-out to the other islands. All the old codger does, according to island rumor I've heard in several saloons," the captain qualified, "is keep adding to his pearl fortune; that is, until tomorrow morning when Mr. Parlay plans on having his grand auction. To tell you all the truth, the jerk-off makes my flesh creep; such a fanatical dangerous lunatic he was and is!"

"Legend has it that this monster Parlay bosses and controls the weather around his atoll," Hermann the Dutchman added to the conversation. "Hey you, Tai-Houtauri. What do you have to say about Parlay and the weather on Hikihoho?"

"He's the weather devil!" the superstitious native claimed. "If Parlay wants no wind, no wind comes! But if he wants hurricane, it's just around the bend of the atoll ready to fuck everybody up!"

"He's a warlock; an evil wizard of sorts!" Mulhall marveled and exclaimed. "A sorcerer of the worst kind!"

"Them many pearls, no good luck," Tai-Houtauri blurted-out. "Parlay say he sell, and plenty schooner come here. Then Parlay make big hurricane and fuck everybody up; either dead or injured! Don't need that shit! Don't need that fuckin' shit!" the Polynesian reiterated.

"Well, just coincidentally, it *is* hurricane season right now," Captain Wakefield morosely noted. "Confidentially, gentlemen. I'd feel much better and safer if the *Malahini* were two-thousand-miles away from this infernal place! A wicked hurricane, manmade or otherwise, could really take a toll on this atoll!"

David Grief was quick to provide his oral evaluation. "I have a general theory. Parlay must blame the white men on Papeete for killing Armande, even though she had actually killed herself out of being rejected, and out of her father not being able to make it to her over a reasonable period of time because of the great hurricane," David Grief summarized and orally concluded. "Armande had definitely felt so trivialized that she took her own life. But I suspect that Parlay's insanity must be temporary, coming and going according to his many vacillating whims. And also, the old man's manic behavior is in conjunction with his various vacillating degrees of mental and emotional depression."

The overhead sails were empty of wind, and Captain Wakefield expressed his dissatisfaction at the impending bad luck omen. The oxygen in the air suddenly became noticeably rarified, and the men struggled to inhale their next breaths. Disappointment abounded among the now-worried passengers and crew aboard the classic ocean vessel.

"Here comes the *Nuhiva* skimming towards us!" David Grief indicated with an extended index finger. "She's got her engine churning at full speed and wants to beat us to the docking area!"

"All ahead full!" Captain Wakefield bellowed-down to the mates in the engine room. "We can't let that piece of shit beat us into the mooring docks!"

"That's that distrustful scoundrel Narii Herring steering the *Nuhiva* with that fucked-up wide sneer evident upon his puss," David Grief conveyed to his pal Gregory Mulhall. "He's the most audacious, conniving rogue in this sector of the South Pacific!"

"Look at the *Nuhiva!*" Captain Wakefield boomed and then chuckled. "She's popped her engine! I guess we're gonna' beat that despicable son-of-a-bitch Herring into the dock after all, and without much of a contest, too!"

"Look over yonder!" Hermann the Dutchman pointed-out. "There's Isaacs up on the *Dolly;* Jeffries on the *Lama,* and Peter Gee standin' on the *Roberta's* deck. Guess a potential storm generated by an evil sorcerer couldn't keep those greedy bastards away from an announced pearl auction. All the big buyers have arrived for the opening bidding. I suppose that Parlay will get his sought-after prices for his exotic pearls!"

"The *Nuhiva's* crew hasn't gotten their temperamental engine goin' yet!" Captain Wakefield noted with a smile. "Maybe they should start squeezin' the oil from the copra seeds inside those coconut trees sittin' over on those barrier islets. Better yet! That fuck-head Narii Herring could choke to death while chuggin' down the thick coconut oil!"

* * * * * * * * * * * * *

Parlay's remote atoll mansion was a sturdy two-story structure constructed of California lumber and sporting a gray galvanized iron roof, highlighting its external appearance. The fabulous house appeared as a distinct monstrosity, overshadowing and overwhelming the nearby coconut palms, and the surrounding atoll and lagoon. After anchoring the *Malahini,* Captain Wakefield and his principal passengers paid a courtesy visit to the picturesque Parlay residence, where other captains and prospective buyers had already assembled inside the grandiose parlor, and the fascinated attendees' eyes were conscientiously examining large pearls exhibited in glass cases.

Various servants carried trays around the vast room with glasses, ice, and several types of whiskey balanced on each one, while the sinister Mr. Parlay maneuvered in and out of groups of fascinated guests, the mogul occasionally cackling, and randomly engaging in cynical banter. But everyone inside the grand chamber observed that the old man's eyes appeared sunken, and his face gaunt and cavernous, with his gray hair patchy and unkempt.

"Goin' to buy a few of my terrific gems!" Parlay s encouraged, acknowledging newcomer David Grief's presence. "You must be a pearl connoisseur to have come to my island on this day. Ya' might be better experiencin' Mt. Vesuvius eruptin'!"

"They're worth risking Hades for," Grief jested as the mansion's guest admired Parlay's magnificent collection. "They're indeed well-worth the trip over here!"

"Check this gorgeous sucker out!" the old mariner exclaimed, picking up a pearl the size of a small walnut. "I was offered sixty thousand francs for it, and then declined its sale over on Tahiti. This pearl was found by my cousin in marriage, who later became a thief and tried hiding it from me," related the egocentric, paranoid owner. "His cousin, who was also my cousin by marriage, killed the pilferer to obtain it, and then fled in a cutter to Noo-Nau. But after I followed *him* there, the chief had that other cousin of mine killed, and I then acquired the item from *him*. Just remember, Mr. Grief, that when you inspect these magnificent fuckers, there're many dead men represented on display here. Each of the largest pearls has either a homicide or a suicide story behind it, ha, ha, ha!"

"I never thought there'd be so many stunning sea jewels in one place," Gregory Mulhall casually remarked to Peter Gee and Captain Robinson, both of the *Roberta*. "What do you think the entire collection is worth?"

"About sixty to seventy thousand pounds," Peter Gee estimated. "But that's in London. In Paris, a lot more, I believe."

"Yes, yes, and perhaps even more," old-withered Parlay added, cunningly eavesdropping on the conversation. "This one here was gotten by a diver from Easter Island. But the following week, a hungry shark fuckin' disposed of his ass. This one over here was retrieved from a depth of twenty-two fathoms, and a diver from Rarotonga broke all records to fuckin' grab it from the bottom. But a minute after the big-chested native surfaced with his astonishin' prize, his goddamned lungs burst from the bends, and the shit-head died gasping and bleeding profusely from the mouth, nose and ears! And then no sooner had *that* horrific tragedy happened when an immense hurricane hit the island, and destroyed virtually every fuckin' person and thing in sight!"

"Oh, hush your loud braggadocio, Parlay," chided cynical Captain Robinson. "A hurricane ain't gonna' blow anywhere in the vicinity, and your precious pearls ain't gonna' increase in price as a result of your excessive bravado!"

"Even if I was a young sailor of twenty-one years of age, I couldn't hop on a schooner and get the fuck outa' here soon enough," Parlay emphatically warned his somewhat-dubious guests. "But I also fuckin' understand that I can't drive you gluttonous buzzards away from my carrion! Here, have some more drinks! Whiskey is on the house, I say!" Parlay yelled as he motioned for a Paumotan servant to carry over a tray full of rye, scotch, and bourbon full glasses.

"Auction is at ten sharp, tomorrow morning. That is, if you're still alive and have managed to survive the torrential winds and rain!"

"That son-of-a-bitch is a vile old beast!" Captain Wakefield whispered to Peter Gee. "I'll swear he's a villainous, demonic son of Lucifer himself!"

"What if the old shit's correct and the winds do wildly blow, and the heavens empty their stored-up liquid?" the captain of the *Dolly* asked. "But then again, Hikihoho's never been directly assaulted by a savage storm's ferocity; at least not in the historical records."

"If a severe tempest does hit, I'd hate to jeopardize my new engine to ward-off the heavy winds!" Captain Wakefield confidentially uttered in a low tone of voice. But all dialogues in the enormous chamber ceased when Parlay pointed at a wall barometer and made a loud, foreboding prediction.

"Take a gander at this very accurate son-of-a-bitch!" Parlay exuberantly yelled. "A big sea is beginnin' to set, and this infallible gauge has already-dropped ten measures on this very scientific instrument. All of you greedy mother-fuckers are doomed! Just gaze-out at the beach and surf through my large bay window, or should I say enormous 'Lagoon Window,' and you'll soon fully grasp the goddamned gravity of your demise!"

All in attendance stared through the mammoth-sized window, and their eyes peered through the spaces between the sparse coconut trees, everyone peering at the sea. An orderly procession of large swells rolled-upon the white coral beach, and within a minute, the waves were increasing in size, in frequency, and in power.

"Ya' targeted assholes have just enough time to climb into your vessels and get the fuck outa' here!" Parlay derisively cackled. "You can tow across the lagoon while ya' still have fuckin' time to salvage your own butts!"

"It's all right, Old Man," laughed Darling, the chief mate of the *Cactus*. "The wind's blow is to the south side, and it's passin' this atoll. We're all safe from its fury. We certainly won't feel its brunt! No one's ass will be devoured by voracious sharks!"

"That's right. All you fucked-up, covetous capitalists and weather authorities!" Parlay scornfully evaluated and remarked. "And since when have children like you, Mr. Darling, become experts on the goddamned tropical weather? I sailed these warm seas long before most of ya' ever popped-out of your mothers' vaginas! I know the curves and angles of every storm that's ever hit the South Pacific in the last fifty-years, and I'm sayin' that this one that's comin' will knock your balls all the way to Tahiti, and remove your goddamned colons straight-out of your fuckin' assholes!"

A heavy, hard crash then jolted the side of the house as a tremendous wave shook the foundation. Several copra sheds on the north side had instantly been devastated, and the frail buildings quickly disintegrated into splinters from the incredible impact.

"Twenty-nine seventy-five!" Captain Wakefield read from the wall barometer. "It's growin' dark on the horizon, and I think a big blow is on its way! Before it's too late, I recommend all in my company to hurry aboard the *Malahini!"*

"It's ten o'clock in the morning, and it's like twilight outside!" Gregory Mulhall frightfully declared. "This whole incident is like a terrible Shakespearean tragedy. The stage lights have been dimmed, and someone in the end will die! May Heaven forbid the developing evil that just might be happening! Hamlet, King Lear, and Macbeth be damned! Let's hustle and get the fuck back onto the schooner before we all perish!"

Then a second rumbling crash smashed onto the atoll, and the intense wave blasted the side of Parlay's vulnerable mansion. The entire assemblage of guests panicked and rushed to the front door as Parlay laughed incessantly at the cowardly men's pandemonium.

"What's your haste, Assholes!" Parlay chided his evacuating visitors. "Have a final drink, you pathetic fools! Have a final drink before the auction tomorrow morning at ten, or else all of you dumb-ass cunt-lappers might die in the meantime! What the hell's this shit? I had thought you were all decent, brave men, when I had invited you to attend my spectacular pearl auction!"

* * * * * * * * * * * * * *

At the beach and near the dock, boat after boat was hastily manned, and then the crews shoved-off into the lagoon. The clouds became darker, and the wind gusts were more intense. Beach sand eddied into the air, and made the departing sailors and passengers squint their eyes. Meanwhile, Narii Herring, accompanied by three native sailors, and the mercenary Tai-Houtauri (formerly of the *Malahini* crew), hustled along the beach amidst the spiraling sand swirls.

"Get into the boat so that we can row back to the anchored schooner!" Captain Wakefield ordered Tai-Houtauri. "Get the hell into the boat and take an oar, I say!"

"I work no more for you!" Tai-Houtauri yelled-back. "Fire me skipper, but I don't care! I now fuckin' work for Narii Herring!"

"Get into the boat you devious swine!" Captain Wakefield hollered, raising his clenched fist. "Get in or I'll knock seven bells outa' ya' skull the next time we meet!"

"I now work on the *Nuhiva* for Narii Herring!" Tai-Houtauri reiterated. "I'm tired of obeying your stupid bullshit!"

"Come back here, or else you'll be sorry, you' stubborn horse's rear end!" Captain Wakefield futilely screamed.

"He's a free man!" Narii Herring yelled-up from the windswept coral beach. "Tai's sailed with me in the past, and now my friend wants to come aboard with me again; that's the long and the short of it!"

"Come on Captain; we must get back to the schooner as quickly as we can," David Grief urged Wakefield. "You can get your sweet revenge later-on in calmer weather!"

"I'll settle with you two rebels, yet!" the incensed captain boomed out at Narii Herring and Tai-Houtauri. "Are you hard of hearing Herring? You're the only damned skipper in this harbor that steals other captains' crewmen! You're both condemned brothers in the devil's sin, if ya' fuckin' ask me!"

The rowboat finally came alongside the *Malahini,* and Hermann the Dutchman praised the Lord that everyone (with the exception of Tai-Houtauri) made it safely aboard.

* * * * * * * * * * * * *

"Bottom has fallen out of the barometer!" Hermann shouted as the Dutchman addressed Captain Wakefield aboard the *Malahini*. "Remaining two anchors are bein' dropped to keep us right the hell where we are without bein' ravaged. Big storm comin' this way! Big enough to kick the shit out of all of us!"

"Lower the small boat to the deck and lash her tightly down!" Captain Wakefield yelled to his semi-shocked crewmembers. Soon a great clanking of chains could be heard from every schooner in the harbor as the crafts attempted dropping their anchors to offset the extremely powerful wind gusts that were rapidly-enveloping and endangering them.

One of Parlay's grass-thatched sheds was ferociously smashed by a white-foamed wave, and the fragile building was soon elevated into the air and transported by the water's force clear off the atoll.

"My throat feels as hot and dry as a goddamned stovepipe!" Hermann exaggerated. The burly Dutchman then took a machete and chopped open a ripe coconut, draining the contents within thirty seconds of serious gulping. The barometer was registering 29.50 when Hermann mercifully sliced-open three additional coconuts for milk for the other parch-mouthed men aboard to drink; one each for the Captain, for David Grief, and for Gregory Mulhall.

"I was never through the eye of a hurricane before, so this is a novel experience for me," David Grief loudly confessed. "According to that barometric reading that keeps on fallin', we're in for big trouble, possibly fuckin' life-threatening trouble."

"There she comes headin' this way from the southeast," Captain Wakefield yelled and indicated as the ship's main crewmember peered through his long spyglass. "Holy shit! Look at the *Roberta* bein' thrashed around like a mere toy boat over on the other side of the lagoon! She'll be a goner, soon!"

The *Malahini* vibrated under the men's feet, as Mulhall and Grief briefly lost their balance and tumbled onto the deck, rolling around like a pair of ball bearings. "It's absolutely incredible! I can't inhale any goddamned air!" Grief yelled as the affected passenger finally got to his knees. "And look at the *Roberta!* She's bein' dragged right by us, and the crew can do nothin' about that frightening shit! Her stern has just missed us by less than forty-feet! Captain Robinson and Peter Gee have no fuckin' control of her!"

The *Cactus* and the *Misi* had also been anchored in the harbor, and the force of the wind gales made the two vessels collide, despite each schooner being securely anchored-down as precautions. In less than a minute, each ship crashed ashore upon the atoll's beach.

Meanwhile, Hermann and the stouthearted native mariners put more gaskets on the sails to guard from being ripped-open, and as the crew toiled and labored against time, the blustery winds tore their thin undershirts right-off their backs. Mulhall pointed towards Parlay's mansion, which seemed to rock and sway in response to nature's awesome wind symphony. Helpless natives, with nowhere to run or hide, lashed themselves to the healthiest-looking coconut trees as the roaring breakers made their way from the lagoon, splashing high onto the formerly tranquil atoll.

"Captain, fire-up your engine!" David Grief begged Wakefield. "Ya' need something to counterbalance this raging typhoon-in-progress! Sorry to outrank ya' as the owner of this ship!"

"Good idea!" the captain reflexively agreed. "Start the engine! Start the fuckin' engine! Let's change this noble schooner into a stationary tub! Holy fuck!" Wakefield exclaimed. "Look at the tiny *Winifred* over yonder! She's friggin' breakin' up onto the coral rocks! Soon, she'll be nothin' but toothpick material! Look at her, will ya'! She's overmatched with her foremast and bow already-crumpled like a cardboard box!"

Of the five remaining vessels, only the *Malahini* had a functional engine, with the *Nuhiva's* power motor then being temporarily disabled. The *Dolly* and the *Mildred* headed toward the mouth of the lagoon, followed by the smaller *Moana*, looking much like a sea cripple chasing after two blind-captained wounded rafts.

Then suddenly, Parlay's large house was elevated by the winds, and forcefully thrust off of the atoll, and the edifice was hurled into the inhospitable lagoon; the still-intact part of the swiftly drifting residence passing by the *Malahini,* and moments later, crashing into the helpless *Papara*. And then on the shore, a coconut tree with three screaming natives attached to it was uprooted and unbelievably flung into the air. Two of the three desperate men detached themselves and somehow splashed into the raging water, and managed to miraculously swim to the shore. But the third unfortunate victim never surfaced and was presumed drowned. But then, quite remarkably, the third man surfaced and everyone aboard Wakefield's schooner was amazed to discover that the lucky survivor was none other than their ship's defector, Tai-Houtauri.

"Narii kill Parlay and try to steal pearls," the gasping survivor coughed-out between saltwater spews. "Now, I think Narii dead, too. Blown-off second tree and drown five minutes ago! Not sure, but I think so!"

"How about the pearls?" David Grief shouted and interrogated the panting man. "Have they been lost?"

"Still tied to tree. Wind at least a hundred mile an hour," Tai-Houtauri related. "Don't know how long fuckin' rope or coconut tree last! Pearls not fuckin' worth risking life!"

Five minutes later, Captain Wakefield climbed-up the steps from the engine room to announce that the schooner's engineer had breathed in a quantity of motor oil fumes, and that the loyal operator had become so dizzy that he had fainted. David Grief then bravely descended the rickety steps before Wakefield ordered the hatch to be battened-down.

The owner did a yeoman's job keeping the overtaxed engine running, while the industrious crewmen poured buckets of sea water out of the bilge, which they had earlier gotten to through a narrow hole that the men had punctured into the downstairs' cabin floor, using a pair of reliable axes. During the tense ordeal, the schooner's whaleboat and galley had disappeared, and together were lost to the turbulent lagoon; the objects obviously being detached from the vessel by the potent wind gusts and swirls.

By midnight, the engineer had recovered from his breathing-in the toxic fumes, and the crewman volunteered to relieve the valiant and grease-smeared David Grief down in the engine room. Meanwhile, most everyone aboard was becoming seasick from being violently tossed and buffeted about the main deck, despite their strong tight lashings keeping their bodies tethered to weatherworn posts and masts.

A surge of seawater then relentlessly battered the schooner, nearly separating the already-punished men from their lashings. Four bodies had been washed aboard during the most recent tidal upheaval. The first was Narii Herring, whose torso was instantly flung-off of the cabin's roof into the lagoon, as the large schooner canted to the right. The other three forms rolled-off of the cabin's roof, and in seconds, fell upon the *Malahini's* deck. The three deceased figures were identified as Parlay and his two native servants. Captain Wakefield freed himself from his tethers and instinctively rolled the three bloody, naked bodies down the steps and into the engine room, which was to serve as a makeshift morgue.

Ten minutes later, the wind ceased blowing, and an eerie calm prevailed. Gaining his senses, David Grief perceived what had happened, and the owner had the wherewithal to announce his theory to his shell-shocked companion, Gregory Mulhall.

"The barometer on the cabin's outer wall reads 29.32," Grief revealed and stated to his somewhat-traumatized friend. "I think we're in the dead eye of the storm."

And then astonishingly, like a resurrected ghost, old Parlay climbed the wooden steps and the crazed figure said, "My brave comrades. Please don't forget. My splendid auction is at ten tomorrow morning!" And upon uttering those bone-chilling words, and loudly cackling one final time, the old bleeding miser collapsed to the schooner's deck, finally dead as a window frame.

Almost simultaneously, to Parlay's queer last words, Captain Wakefield gave the command, "Lift anchor and let's have propellers full speed ahead! We'll head northwest while there's still a chance to escape the storm's second more deadly wrath! With a bit of luck, we'll be able to skirt around the back end!"

"We'll never get across the goddamned lagoon in time!" David Grief hoarsely screamed. "But if we don't give it the old college try, worse luck awaits us, because we'll be sittin' ducks for imminent disaster from the leeward side of the lagoon; once the second act of this fucked-up Shakespearean tragedy begins!"

* * * * * * * * * * * * *

The wind diminished as the barometric pressure increased. But the schooner's engine failed under the strain, and with a last convulsive effort of its forty-horsepower motor, the apparatus ceased functioning. A spray of seawater from the bilge sizzled over the defunct manifold, and clouds of engine room steam were spiraling about the tiny chamber. Meanwhile, on deck, David Grief freed himself of his tethering bonds and quickly rendered assistance to the remaining crewmembers that had almost-magically survived the gruesome ordeal.

Captain Wakefield used his trusty binoculars to survey damage on the opposite side of the lagoon, and observed that the *Papara* and the *Tahaa* were no longer occupying space there. "Not a stick or a trace of either of them," the captain sadly noted. "Sails alone cannot endure a hurricane. That's what the fuck happens when ya' have no engine aboard to counteract the deadly wind gales!"

And then, as the fortunate survivors surveyed the devastated atoll, all vestiges of palm trees and of Parlay's former excellent mansion had been scoured-out and washed-away, and remaining was a vacant space of three-hundred-yards that now existed in their place. But then, the ever-vigilant Captain Wakefield felt quite disturbed upon seeing a familiar, detested, and despised figure sauntering along the half-destroyed coral beach.

"Hello Skipper!" the seemingly immortal Narii Herring greeted with a haunting smile upon his tanned-but-bloody face. "Can I come aboard and gobble-down some delicious breakfast?"

Captain Wakefield's neck swelled, and his complexion suddenly turned purple with anger. Finally, the appropriate words came-out of his mouth to express the man's overall animosity towards the notorious scoundrel. "For two cents, Herring, I'd cut your throat, esophagus, and stomach right-out of your fuckin' body! And for four lousy cents, I'd incinerate your ass on a goddamned luau bon fire!"

# “The Wit of Porportuk”

In the Indian culture along the Canadian Yukon River, the verbal abstractions “wit” and “wisdom” are often intertwined; not only in common understanding, but also in definition. This exceptional anomaly-type-word-relationship is quite evident in what has been aptly chronicled as “The Wit of Porportuk”.

El-Soo had been an obedient honor roll mission student. After the Indian girl’s mother had died when El-Soo was a mere toddler, Sister Alberta quickly saw academic and religious potential in the intelligent girl’s acumen, and had her admitted into the Holy Cross Mission School. And throughout her later childhood, El-Soo had been raised in the adjacent convent. In her studies, the highly-self-motivated and keen-spirited El-Soo outperformed (in all of the subjects taught) all other students, including the very competitive half-breed along with the quarter-breed girls.

The girl’s father was the effervescent Klakee-Nah, a village chief who had an explicit passion for life, and also a need for clamorous revelry. But El-Soo had acquired from her flamboyant father a zest for life, and that quality was reflected in her singing, writing, artistic, and mathematical abilities.

Sister Alberta and her religious faculty colleagues at the Holy Cross School, who preached and practiced spiritual cleanliness and virtue, were conscientiously grooming El-Soo to join their order and help perpetuate the Catholic brand of Christianity throughout that pagan region of Northwestern Canada.

Eight years had elapsed with much progress being evident in El-Soo’s scholastic development, and now the girl was sixteen, and well-past puberty, or well past the time when hairy situations start happening in teenagers’ lives.

“El-Soo,” Sister Alberta said one fine spring morning. “We’re thinking about sending you to one of our high achievement schools in the United States to complete your formal education. But who was that dirty scruffy old Indian that had just visited you? Your acquaintance looked like an absolute unkempt vagrant to me.”

“He’s a servant of my father, and a bearer of bad news,” El-Soo directly replied. “I’ve just learned that my sixty-seven-year-old brother has passed away from some obscure venereal diseases, and now my father, Chief Klakee-Nah, wishes for me to immediately return home and help take care of managing his large empty house. Even though I think it irrelevant, my father is also suffering from those same lethal sexual diseases, and it's realistically feared that he too soon will rot away and die."

"But El-Soo, your father's residence is often called a raucous house of prostitution where fur traders, sailors, merchants, and other undesirable people hang-out and have roisters while eating oysters," Sister Alberta vociferously objected. "I urge you to stay here at the convent and keep your sacred virginity; by *that* nomenclature, I mean to say, protect your bearded clam."

"I'm sorry Sister Alberta," the girl politely apologized. "But my allegiance must first be to my *father,* who incidentally does not have a *son* or any *holy ghost* living with him, either!"

Klakee-Nah had recently borrowed a thousand dollars from his old business partner Porportuk and used the new revenue to clean-up and refurbish his huge "feast and party house", which many local outsiders gossiped as being a full-fledged brothel. Indeed, the elderly father was a rather-peculiar Yukon Indian in his recreational habits. Twenty years earlier, Klakee-Nah and Porportuk had struck it rich by discovering a terrific gold deposit on the Koyukuk River.

Then, the ambitious entrepreneur Porportuk bought-out his naïve partner's share of the claim, and the party animal chief kept on entertaining guests arriving to his enormous house, thus gradually blowing his entire fortune. And the all-too-cunning Porportuk kept on lending his old business colleague more money, until the shrewd capitalist had owned virtually everything in Klakee-Nah's possession, including his vast residence and the adjacent Circumcision Teepee. And so, as the one prominent friend's wealth proliferated, the other frivolous man's fortune dwindled-down to a very pathetic level. Indeed, Porportuk was now the richest and most successful Indian in the entire region.

Upon returning home, El-Soo did not attempt to reform her fun-loving father into the Christian ways, and the daughter only admonished him when the frivolous chief became excessively drunk and boisterous. 'Let my father enjoy himself in the only way he knows how,' the liberal-minded girl reckoned. 'If and when he should die, I'll then go back to Sister Alberta, and soon attend school down in San Francisco as she had promised me. There has to be a big world on the other side of Tanana Station, and I'm going to explore it once I get-out of this miserable trap I'm temporarily stuck in! My doomed and bankrupt father will leave me nothing. Damn it to hell! He has the fancy lifestyle of an aristocrat, and the bank account of a lousy pauper!' El-Soo lamented. 'And that son-of-a-bitch, black-hearted bastard Porportuk owns everything in this house except my failing father's immortal soul, and my virgin pussy!'

But with every additional advance of fresh money, Porportuk looked more greedily upon El-Soo, even though the ancient bastard hadn't had a decent erection in over twenty years. The mannerly girl ignored the old coot's flirtations, and firmly believed that her father should die as he had lived, extending hospitality and good cheer to any and all visitors to his famous home.

'Ah, if only my true love Adoon had Porportuk's money,' El-Soo dreamed, wished, and regretted. 'But handsome Adoon has nothing to his name, and if I should foolishly marry him, I'll be a loser in life just like he is. But I immensely despise Porportuk, and hope that the greedy-shit dies before father does. Porportuk has no family, so all of the accumulated debts my father has amassed would be erased.'

Adoon too loved El-Soo, but in a romantic-idealistic way, unlike the lust that dwelled within Porportuk's avaricious heart. Adoon was an adventurous young fellow, who had sailed on merchant ships to Siberia and to Japan, and who had even voyaged as far south as California. But the muscular mariner now piloted a steamship up and down the Yukon River, just to stay close to Tanana Station, so that the young man could visit Klakee-Nah's raucous house of merriment under the guise of telling the chief all about the outside world's spectacles, while incidentally, trying to gain the individual attention of beautiful El-Soo.

Klakee-Nah sat at the head of his extensive table, and was attended to by four old servants, slaves that the affable chief had inherited from *his* father during more prosperous times. And whenever the rowdy patriarch would begin choking from swallowing too much food and imbibing too much drink, the four old coots would aggressively and incessantly pound Klakee-Nah on the back between his shoulder blades to revive him from either gagging or dying.

It was an April night at the wild country party house, with many revelers in attendance, including the youthful Adoon and the parsimonious old codger, Porportuk, who overtly disapproved of being exposed to the loud festivities, wine drinking, whore strippers, and inharmonious song singing. But when the old curmudgeon gazed upon El-Soo standing at the other end of the feast table, a throbbing occurred inside his penis, unlike any sensation the financier had experienced in the preceding two decadent decades. Klakee-Nah insisted that a special place be set-up next to his "throne seat", so that Porportuk and he could reminisce their past exploits.

"Here, Friend! Swallow-down some wine!" the chief urged his former partner. "It isn't exactly vintage wine like in the old days, and quite frankly it tastes like polar bear piss, which I once drank when I was desperate and quite lost out in the wilderness. Drink Porportuk," the withered old chief insisted. "What the fuck am I saying? Why would anyone want to drink Porportuk, ha, ha, ha!"

"I will sample a few ounces of your cheap beverage just to be sociable," Porportuk diplomatically answered. "But Old Friend; the wine is killing your ass, slowly-but-surely. We're both the same age Klakee-Nah, but I am still alive and strong, and your rambunctious lifestyle has finally caught-up with you."

The old chief began wildly coughing and choking as the crowded banquet room suddenly became silent. The four decrepit servants began punching and pounding Klakee-Nah upon his back to revive him from the jaws of death. After the patriarch endured his close-call spell and began speaking again, the guests in the room resumed their joke-telling, drinking, gambling, and eating.

"You cheap bastard," Klakee-Nah deliberately berated Porportuk. "All these cold years you've spared the use of wood in your stove because you say it costs too much. Your fucked-up life is like a cabin with no fire in the hearth, and with no furry animal rug on the floor. I've lived a life abundant in warmth and happiness, and you've lived one devoid of either of those things," the notorious party-giver asserted. "My nights have been short, and I've slept warm all these years, while your nights have been cold, and you've slept short. So therefore, Fine Friend," Klakee-Nah summarized, "my wealth can be measured in pleasant memories, and yours in piles of old, cold gold coins stacked on your lonely kitchen table!"

The inebriated chief then raised his glass to recite a mock toast to the humiliated Porportuk, but the object fell from his grasp, and none of the four lethargic old geezer attendants had the reflexes to catch it in midair before it shattered onto the wood-planked floor. "Now then," the dying chief said to his former business associate. "What is to become of my massive debts that I owe you? Tell me, how great are they, first of all?"

"You owe me the grand sum of fifteen-thousand-nine-hundred and sixty-seven-dollars and seventy-five cents," Porportuk accurately communicated without even blinking an eyelid.

"Odd numbers like *that* positively bore and perplex me," Klakee-Nah argued. "Let's make my debt an even sixteen thousand dollars. Make out the note, and I shall sign it. You'll be paid your money in the next world, when we'll both be sitting at the enormous feast table of the Great Father Spirit in the Sky, who'll decide and explain who had led the better life: you or me!"

"Are you fucked-up Old Man, or what? Do you take me for a complete idiot?" Porportuk yelled. "I have no dealings with the fuckin' next world! I live in this one! I want my money now!"

"Where is your reverence? Have you no thought of meeting me at the table of the Great Spirit?" the dying chief asked, further breaking his old friend's testicles. "I'll surely be sitting there entertaining and being entertained."

"I know fuckin' little about the next world," Porportuk conceded. "I only know that you owe me plenty of debts in this real one!"

"Okay. Take my house, and then burn the debt paper in yonder candle," Klakee-Nah requested. "My house is your house, in either *ours* or in anyone else's fucked-up language."

"It is an old dump in which you live and worth only a fraction of the money you owe me," Porportuk realistically evaluated. "And don't even begin to mention your three worthless mines on the banks of the Twisted Salmon. Those fucked-up shabby caves on the Twisted Salmon aren't even fuckin' worth a pound of bent fish."

"Well then, you can have my shares in the steamboat *Koyukuk*," the dying patriarch facetiously proposed. "I'm half owner of that beautiful yacht, and that property ought to fully satisfy the remainder of my debt, in addition to my house and my three gold mines."

"That fucked-up ship sank a year ago, and lies at the bottom of the Yukon," Porportuk strongly objected. "Nothing in it can be salvaged!"

"It seems then that I owe you an enormous sum of money that I cannot repay," Klakee-Nah expressed with little regret or remorse. "Apparently, Porportuk, despite your many successes, you're a very poor businessman after all. You lent me more money than I can possibly repay."

"Well, Asshole Friend. There remains one major security in your possession that has not yet been introduced or discussed," the wily investor declared. "Your daughter El-Soo will represent sufficient compensation to me to completely eradicate your staggering debts. Give me her, and I will, with pleasure, burn the debt contract in the candle's flame!"

"What a fucked-up joke your mouth has hatched! Ho, ho, ho!" the palsied chief guffawed as his hands trembled, spilling wine all over his fur clothes. "Your now dead daughter would presently be old enough to be El-Soo's mother if Kliska were still alive."

"This is no fiendish joke that I am relating to you. It is my only provision that I demand in order to have you die a happy man with a debt-free clear conscience," Porportuk articulated before sipping a bit of vinegar-tasting wine. "My speech has been sincere and should be interpreted as such!"

The entire room became still and not a sound could be discerned throughout the vast chamber. Then Klakee-Nah raised his new glass high above his head and with a scowl upon his scabby face, commanded his twenty guests, all seated in parallel rows across from one another, "Take this rotten mother-fucker outside and roll the arrogant son-of-a-bitch in the snow down the steep side hill. Then all of you having full kidneys must urinate on the dirty prick's ugly face, because as we all know, it is far better to be pissed-off than to be pissed-on!"

And when the riotous mob re-entered the mammoth room, Klakee-Nah again raised his glass and suggested, "A salute to the short night when all good drunken men sleep warm in their beds!"

* * * * * * * * * * * * *

Tommy, the diminutive-sized clerk at the area trading post, was selected by El-Soo to settle the deceased Klakee-Nah's impoverished estate. Notes and mortgages abounded, most of which were held by the obstinate and covetous Porportuk, whom the short Englishman Tommy described as "a first-class pirate thief who capitalized on the troubles and mistakes of others". That afternoon, the ruthless loan shark confronted El-Soo outside the aforementioned trading post, and received a good dose of the girl's ire.

"I shall tell you two things that you must remember," the poor girl said to the unscrupulous, sanctimonious lender. "First, I shall never be your wife under any circumstances, so don't go there with your asinine, simpleton rhetoric. Second, you shall be paid the last cent of my father's sixteen-thousand-dollar debt he owes to you."

"It was fifteen-thousand-nine-hundred and sixty-seven dollars and seventy-five cents," Porportuk clarified. "You, my Sweetheart, don't owe me a penny more."

"Look, Idiot King! If my father said it was sixteen thousand, then that's what the hell it's going to be!" the pretty girl yelled. "And that's the exact amount I intend to pay you!"

"How are you going to obtain the money? Rob a bank, or a train, or a steamboat?" the cruel lender asked.

"I don't know how," El-Soo genuinely answered. "Now walk away and bother me no more, or else this time I'll get my father's friends to roll your fat ass down a snow-covered mountain, and not simply over a snow-covered hill! And this time, in addition to pissing on your face, the crowd will be instructed to shit on your face, also!"

In late May, El-Soo surprised the residents in and around Tanana Station by publicly announcing in front of the trading post that in early June at the commencement of the annual salmon run, that she would sell herself at auction to satisfy the outstanding debts her father had owed to Porportuk. Sister Alberta tried to dissuade the girl from transacting herself into slavery, but to no avail.

"Only debts owed to God are settled in the next world," El-Soo declared to the bewildered nun. "But the debts of men are to be settled in this world! Don't worry, Sister Alberta. Porportuk will never get to my bearded clam, although the dumb-shit eats a lot of imported un-bearded oysters!"

And then the obsessed girl was later encountered by Adoon, who was astounded to hear her say, "I do love you Adoon. But honor exists on a much higher plateau than love does. My dead father now wanders in the Great Spirit's thick dense forest, totally lost and confused. All because he still owes that skunk bastard Porportuk huge sums of money. He's not out of the woods yet, and it is now up to me to show him the escape route by erasing his earthly debts. To some," the charming girl sadly philosophized, "the next world may be angels, clouds, halos and harps, but to my party-animal father, it will be the large mansion of the Great Spirit where Klakee-Nah will wait sitting at the huge banquet table. Yes, Adoon; he'll be sitting there patiently waiting for his old friend, Porportuk, to show-up and feast."

"Are you sure the Great Spirit really exists?" Adoon skeptically questioned his girlfriend. "Some educated Indians think that He's nothing more than a mound of bear shit!"

"The Great Spirit of Indian culture might be the same entity as the Holy Ghost of Catholic teachings," El-Soo wisely replied. "And I don't ever want to see either of them insulted. Just look, Adoon, at what the Holy Spirit did to the Virgin Mary. He knocked her up, and you wouldn't want to see that sort of nasty crap happen to me, would you Adoon?"

"Shit no!" the boyfriend loudly exclaimed. "I want to knock you up all by myself!"

The June morning of the auction finally arrived on the white men's calendars, and the event was to be conducted on the bank of the Yukon River at the south end of Tanana Station. Hundreds had gathered for the annual salmon run, and the auctioning of El-Soo added a new carnival-like dimension to the fish running spectacle. Interest in the highly-anticipated bidding event was reaching a crescendo. But jealous Adoon circulated among the crowd, wielding his rifle and vowing that whoever was to buy his favorite girl would be promptly shot and killed by him.

At El-Soo's request, the midget Tommy stood on a chair and asked for the bidding to begin. After silence prevailed with no one shouting an offer, El-Soo stood on a second chair and courageously addressed the restless crowd.

"Who will buy a faithful devoted wife?" the worried girl began her solicitous narrative. "I pledge to be a good spouse to the noble man who generously purchases me. If I'm bought by a white man, I shall dress like a white woman does. And if I am acquired by an Indian man, then I shall dress like a squaw," the girl sincerely promised. "I know how to make my own clothes and can wash, sew, and cook, too. I can read and write English, and have learned all of the curse words in that language should I need to use any of them. I know mathematics well, and a little algebra also. But I have plenty of trouble doing basic geometry, which is pretty damned useless up here in this barren remote part of the world, anyway. I weigh a hundred-and-thirty-pounds, and am a virgin," El-Soo elucidated. "And finally, my father is dead, and I must pay off his debts. Now, who the hell wishes to buy me?"

The four palsied and arthritic male servants that were the last human remnants of Klakee-Nah's bankrupt estate surrounded El-Soo as she spoke while standing upon the rickety-wooden chair. The principal members of the auction audience consisted of Eldorado and Bonanza claims' kings that were lucky to have struck it rich along the northern riverbanks. And also, there were French Canadians from the northern areas, along with prospectors from Lake Le Barge. And of course, the entire population of Tanana Station was in attendance, in addition to rural residents Adoon, and the contemptible Porportuk.

The sound of myriad flocks of wild fowl could be heard flapping their wings across the Yukon, when suddenly, an Indian boat pilot from Tozikatat started the bidding at one hundred dollars. And then, a white old-timer from Dawson raised the ante to two hundred. Up stepped Porportuk, as confident as ever, and elevated the offered amount to five hundred dollars.

Tommy the auctioneer noticed that El-Soo was becoming disconsolate because the bidding for her was so unacceptably low.

The self-appointed auctioneer boldly stated that he was eligible to bid too, despite the fact that he was the designated price-determiner, so he yelled-out at the top of his lungs, "Thirteen-hundred-dollars," which drew a mild reaction from the crowd, and noticeably infuriated both Porportuk and Adoon.

Soon the bidding war narrowed-down to a wealthy Bonanza Gold Mine King, and the shrewd and diabolical miser, Porportuk. The sum of fourteen-thousand-dollars had been reached within fifteen-minutes, and the crowd was becoming extremely nervous as the suspenseful oral offers continued to escalate.

"Seventeen-thousand-dollars!" screamed-out Porportuk; his bid exceeding the substantial debt that Klakee-Nah had amassed.

"Eighteen-thousand!" yelled-out the enthusiastic Bonanza Mine King. "This cute little Indian bitch must be something hot if someone like that old fart Porportuk wants her that badly!"

The oral competition continued for ten more tense minutes, until Porportuk obstinately blurted-out "Twenty-six-thousand-dollars!" and then the disgusted gold mining mogul decided to drop-out of the contentious bidding contest.

"Going, going, gone!" Tommy declared. "Sold to the man known as Porportuk!"

The very efficient auctioneer made-out the "Bill of Sale", and had El-Soo and Porportuk sign the official document. Then the greedy, old, miserable miser attempted to outsmart the gullible Indian girl.

"The money that I've just signed to deliver was for *you,* and not for your father's myriad debts to me," Porportuk said to El-Soo. "As long as you stay with me as my wife, I won't pressure you for your father's accumulated expenses."

"You are right!" the Indian girl laughed after she realized her foolish mistake in logical judgment.

"Come home with me, now!" the villainous old fart impetuously demanded. "I need you to perform some special services for me! Maybe you can make my loins function properly again, as they once did in my youth!"

"Remember what I had explained to you outside the trading post several months ago," the academically smart girl reminded the old impotent sex maniac. "I told you that I would not ever marry you and be your wife, and I also vowed you would be fully compensated some day in the future."

"But I own all of you now, Bitch!" Porportuk bellowed, much to the elation of the curious eavesdropping crowd, and much to Adoon's chagrin. "Just like I own a mongrel dog, I also now own you, and you must obey my every demand. And just like when I tell my dog to follow me," the nasty old curmudgeon stated, "the canine obeys, and so too will you comply; you stubborn, sassy little Witch!"

"Not so damned fast, Porportuk!" El-Soo disagreed. "What if you buy a dog, and then it runs away, because it abhors your vile commands. Do you then still own the animal if it escapes to freedom?"

"As the owner of the dog. I should beat it into obedience, and so too I will do to you if you dare give me any more of your insolent and defiant verbal shit!"

"Then, you'll have to first catch me, before you can violently pummel me into submission!" the pesky girl hollered as El-Soo swiftly darted-away, and anxiously scampered towards the timber woods. "Try and catch me, you Old Fart Asshole!" El-Soo shouted back as the captivated audience let out a loud roar of approbation.

In his tender youth, Porportuk had been the quickest racer in the entire valley, but now that his weak flimsy legs were swollen with arthritis and phlebitis, the former sprinter/athlete lacked the stamina and the endurance to deftly pursue the Indian girl through the forest for more than a half-hour.

The speedy Indian doll sprinted and scampered along obscure trails and paths that were quite familiar to her, and El-Soo soon demoralized Porportuk's spirit. The frustrated and distraught old geezer had to exit the woods with his head crestfallen, as the three-hundred excited spectators cheered wildly in recognition of his humiliating defeat at the hands of "a young rebellious squaw". The population of Tanana Station and vicinity had been treated to a wonderful episode of slapstick comedy, and the witnesses loved every precious second of the impromptu, satirical scene.

* * * * * * * * * * * * * *

Tired of being ridiculed at the Yukon River auction scene for not taking vengeful action against Porportuk, Adoon trekked a half-mile to the local steamboat landing. In the meantime, Porportuk wasted no time in selecting and recruiting a half-dozen scouts and trackers to capture El-Soo, to bring her to his custody, so that the brutal creep could teach the girl an indispensable lesson in physical discipline.

The following morning, the steamboat *Seattle* pulled into Tanana Station to obtain wood for fuel. Adoon boarded the ship, upon which he often worked, and climbed up the stairs to enter the pilothouse.

"Captain Jensen," Adoon respectfully said. "I'd like to navigate the *Seattle* for the next several hours. I've worked for you and for

Captain Sullivan on the *Oregon,* and for Captain Montross on the *Eskimo,* and I know this river like I know your name."

"Sure thing, Adoon," Captain Jensen instantly agreed. "I was drinking and partying all last night at a downstream bordello, and could use several hours of nap time. And if you fuckin' know Mr. Sandman, you can tell him I don't require his services, because I think I can easily fall asleep all by myself!"

A mile downstream, Adoon spotted a familiar, small, birch-wood canoe leaving the shore with one person aboard. The astute pilot steered the *Seattle* closer towards the shore, but did not anticipate that Captain Jensen would awaken from his slumber and enter the pilothouse to interrogate him.

"What the hell are you doing?" Jensen angrily questioned Adoon. "I didn't know you grew-up in Texas! Why are you giving everyone on this ship a bum steer?"

Adoon grunted upon noticing a large canoe leaving the riverbank with seven occupants, that apparently were in hot pursuit of the Indian girl frantically paddling in the first smaller boat. 'That's that ogre Porportuk and some hired goons chasing after my girl, El-Soo!' Adoon realized. The pilot's concentration was interrupted with a critical comment from his ship's superior officer.

"It's only a lousy squaw!" Captain Jensen observed and stated. "You'll be aground on top of a shoal if you don't steer back into the center of the channel. Here, give me the wheel Adoon, or I'll have to send you to the brig!"

But Adoon held fast to the helmsman's wheel and threatened to stick the old captain's head between two of its wooden spokes, and then rotate the circular object in the direction of the Yukon River channel if Jensen gave him any more sass.

"Okay Captain," Adoon replied when the small canoe finally reached the starboard side of the *Seattle*. "I'm going to rescue my girlfriend and help her clamber aboard. After I do that, go full speed into the channel and head on down to Fort Yukon where she and I will gladly disembark."

"Why the hell didn't you tell me *that* bullshit in the first place!" Captain Jensen exclaimed. "I haven't had this much excitement in my life since I took my first shit inside my diaper!"

At Fort Yukon, Adoon quickly outfitted a small poling boat, and with his improvised device, the boyfriend and El-Soo alternated paddling-up the Porcupine River. The brave beau had traveled that river before, exploring deep into the interior wilderness, where the headwaters of the swift-flowing river led into the northernmost peaks of the Rocky Mountains.

"We will reach a river known to the white man as the Mackenzie," Adoon told his rescued girlfriend. "Then we next travel south ahead of the winter winds. We'll spend the cold months in the sunny land where there isn't any snow, but soon thereafter, we'll come north again to live in *our* land."

"And I will faithfully teach you how to read and write, because I don't wish to be married to a primitive, illiterate, savage," El-Soo joked. "For all the hell I know, you Adoon might somehow, someday become the next James Fennimore Cooper."

Upon reaching the Mackenzie River, Adoon and El-Soo got into a skirmish with a band of local Indians, and the boyfriend was wounded in his right arm from an errant rifle bullet. El-Soo had learned basic nursing skills when the girl had attended the Holy Cross School, so she performed some rudimentary surgery on her lover and set Adoon's elbow bones back into place. Then, the pair peacefully rested by the fire, so that the smoke would keep the flitting mosquitoes away from Adoon's injured arm. The itinerant duo found the delusional elders (unlike the hostile, rebellious young warriors) of the Mackenzie Indian village to be most-accommodating to them.

The next morning, Porportuk and his six Indian henchmen arrived on the scene, and Adoon appealed to the tribal elders to protect his girl and him from the "troublesome evil intruders". A council meeting was scheduled for noon, so that the elders could determine what fair judgment should be rendered in regard to El-Soo's disposition. Porportuk was acting as if he were an accomplished regional prosecutor, and also the trial plaintiff.

"And I paid for this skinny squaw a heavy price," Porportuk emphasized towards the termination of his lengthy complaint. "If you esteemed councilmen were to sell all of your spears, knives, canoes, skins, furs, dogs, rifles, arrows, tents, and women, you would maybe have a thousand-dollars to show for it. Multiply that sum by the number twenty-six, and you elders will then realize how much I have paid for this disobedient, puny, undisciplined squaw."

"Why would anyone pay such a fantastic price for an ordinary squaw such as her?" an alert elder asked Porportuk. "She must have at least three cunts in her crotch for you to be that interested in her!" the questioner pithily added as the old-timer spat a red bloody lunger onto the ground, and then coughed incessantly. "Is this talk of yours true?" the old-fart finished his analysis before choking-up another bloody mass of mucus. "That scrawny bitch, El-Soo, looks like the spitting image of my fucked-up, dirty-faced, daughter-in-law, El-Soot!"

"It is true that this old-fart Porportuk had a daughter who was old enough to be El-Soo's mother," Adoon voluntarily contributed to the heated debate. "But, if El-Soo has three cunts, as has been jested, then I wouldn't be surprised to learn that Porportuk has three dicks, as minuscule as they may be!"

"Watch your fuckin' language, Young Wounded Brave!" a second agitated elder petulantly reprimanded Adoon. "This venerable council consists of five elderly fucks, just like this self-righteous old-shit-Porportuk happens to be!"

The four other mentally-deficient elders sitting on the council nodded their heads in agreement and lacking teeth, the uncouth deciders all simultaneously chomped their gums.

"I told this old coot that I'd never marry him and be his wife," maintained El-Soo. "He was my father's best friend, and has always wanted to rape me, but now his bowels are almost as slow as his running ability."

"Yet you took from him twenty-six times all that we as a tribe own!" the blood-spitting chief codger argued. "Is this fact fuckin' true, or isn't it?"

"It is quite true," El-Soo regretfully admitted. "But I will run-away from this cruel and deranged old fuck bastard again, and again, until his legs and dick fall off!"

"What price did *you* pay for her?" the chief blood-spitting elder asked Adoon. "And please, Young Asshole; don't tell me it was a full load of sperm juice!"

"No price," Adoon sincerely answered. "I love this lovely woman El-Soo very much, and *that* glorious affection I have just described cannot be measured in tents, dogs, guns, arrows, furs, gold dust, or in white sperm juice."

"Porportuk has indeed paid a heavy price for the skinny unmanageable squaw," the jealous, impotent, and biased senile tribal leader announced. "And it is the verdict of this council that El-Soo belongs to this distinguished rich freak, Porportuk."

"I will kill you, Porportuk!" Adoon shouted and promised in direct English. "Your obese scabby body will be butchered and thrown to mongrel dogs!"

Joyfully receiving his favorable verdict from the Mackenzie Indian council, Porportuk stood-up and commended the dysfunctional elders for exercising wise discretion. "I'll reward you five exceptionally kind men with five pounds of tobacco, so that your sons can lose their teeth too, just as you five wise men have lost yours by chewing tobacco and by eating infected pussy. There is a direct correlation between wisdom and having no teeth, you know!"

"Sit there at my feet and listen carefully to my sage polar bear shit!" Porportuk commanded El-Soo. "Now then; it is true that I am an old fart as has been alleged. Yet, I was once young, and I presently understand the wild sensational feelings that you and Adoon share with one another. Now, I am old with much intestinal gas, and realize that I cannot chase your cute, little, firm ass through the dense forests each and every day. You *run from* me El-Soo, yet I fathom that you are always *running to* your asshole boyfriend, Adoon!"

"Make your damned story shorter before we all fuckin' die without knowing its dramatic ending," the blood-spitting, tobacco-chewing chief council elder demanded.

"When a dog runs away and is captured and then beaten, it will run away again," Porportuk logically concluded. "But El-Soo does not run like a dog. She runs like a fuckin' elusive deer. So, therefore, not wanting to run my ass and balls off chasing this young bitch through each and every neighboring forest, I ask for one of you eminent elders to buy her from me."

The five old council farts sitting with their legs crossed, coughed, spit-up blood, chewed more tobacco, but said not a single word in response to Porportuk's unexpected solicitation.

"Now, the young impulsive fool Adoon here would buy her, but the juvenile moron has no money," Porportuk convincingly declared. "So, therefore, my Friends. I'll give this skinny squaw bitch El-Soo to Adoon at no price, but only on one condition."

"And what is that one condition?" the about to go to sleep chief elder asked before prodigiously yawning.

"The young spoiled squaw has the bad habit of running away whenever she doesn't like something," Porportuk eloquently elaborated. "If she runs away from me now, this unbridled doe will certainly run away from Adoon in years to come, when the ephemeral love between them wears-off, and the arguing segment of their relationship predictably begins. But my guarantee to you, Adoon, is that *she* will never flee from your clutches and authority!"

"And how is that amazing feat to be accomplished?" Adoon asked. "Are you a shaman, or a fucked-up magician of sorts?"

"It's all a simple matter when you have the wit of Porportuk working in your favor," the demented old curmudgeon/miser lectured. Stooping down, Porportuk carefully crossed El-Soo's feet. Then he quickly lifted his rifle and discharged two bullets through the girl's ankles.

"That was a fuckin' just solution!" the chief elder marveled and yelled. "Why the fuck didn't I think of it? It sure looks like El-Soo's running days are over!"

El-Soo sobbed, as she sat and stared at her bloodied, shattered ankles. The squaw realized that she would be crippled for life, and would never again be able to run into the forest. "That son-of-a-bitch Porportuk's ruined my whole fuckin' life!" the girl cried. "Now I'm out of the running for your love, Adoon!"

"Your sad eyes are like deer eyes!" Adoon romantically said to El-Soo. "I shall marry you, despite your severe handicap. I shall marry you because I still love you!" the young stud exclaimed with a sparkle in his eye. "But from now on, your name will no longer be El-Soo. It is my expressed wish that you'll now be known throughout all of Canada as Broken Ankles!"

"Was my solution just?" Porportuk asked the impressed old fart council elders.

"It is just!" all five geriatrics answered in unison. "It is just!" the five nincompoops reiterated before chewing more chaws of tobacco.

"Where the hell do you live Porportuk?" the chief council elder requested knowing. "This wonderful chewing tobacco of yours is really fuckin' delicious!"

# “To Build a Fire”

Dawn had broken under a cloudy sky, and the self-confident man deviated from the Yukon trail, and climbed up the steep, rocky bank to a higher, but less used pathway that led eastward through the spruce timberland. After ascending the incline and walking along for several hours with his wolf dog trailing behind him, the man inspected his watch and observed that it was already nine o’clock. The absence of the sun made the entire physical environment seem drab and gloomy. But still, the man was determined to persevere.

‘In a few more days, the sun will be visible on the southern horizon,’ the cocky trekker believed from past experience witnessing similar atmospheric phenomena. ‘My fuckin’ retarded wolf dog has no concept of the sun, of its function, or of its necessity! The stupid beast is probably much better-off being ignorant of nature and its laws! Basically, it’s really all the old reason-versus-instinct college bullshit propaganda, and conversely, I possess the goddamned knowledge, and my dunce-dog does not!’

Looking beyond from his lofty vantage point, the observant man saw the mile-wide Yukon River frozen solid with three-foot-thick ice, and several-foot of snow had drifted upon the hard surface. The river’s course wound its way around several spruce-laden islands in the same direction as to where the man would meet up with friends later that afternoon, and together, then continue their journey southward. The newcomer to the North stubbornly believed that the icy, fifty-degree below zero temperature was fairly tolerable, and not potentially dangerous to anyone with any element of courage in his character, and any spark of self-reliant determination in his spirit.

‘Mittens, ear muffs, warm moccasins, fur hat and coat, flannel shirts, thick socks, and woolen underwear will insulate me from these abnormal elements,’ the obstinate man rationally thought. ‘But how the freakin’ Eskimos ever have wintertime sex up here is far beyond my limited comprehension!’

The man spit some green mucus from his mouth, and was amazed that a sharp explosive crackle occurred when the liquid solidified in the freezing air before ever hitting the snow. ‘The boys will be meeting me at Henderson Creek at six o’clock as has been planned,’ the tundra ambler recollected. ‘In an hour or two, I’ll take out a biscuit and have it for lunch. But I’ll have to eat that son-of-a-bitch in a hurry before it hardens, just like the spit did in the air. I don’t want the hard bite to break my teeth. There aren’t too many fuckin’ dentists up here on the desolate trail, so I'd better be careful how I use my damned choppers!' the adamant man concluded.

And each biscuit was rich in fatty grease and wrapped in a nourishing slice of bacon. 'Not exactly a meal fit for a king, but up here in Northern Canada, it sure beats fuckin' starvation! Although I'd rather eat pussy, the *bacon*-covered biscuits are definitely more nutritious! I'll just pretend I'm eating Sir Francis, and then the delicious bacon will taste all that much better! Too bad I couldn't be devouring the Earl of Sandwich, too!'

He and his wolf dog maneuvered along the deep snow trail as the man occasionally rubbed his masked nose and cheekbones with his right hand's mitten. 'It's a little uncomfortable out here, but I'll endure,' the determined traveler haughtily convinced himself.

But the wolf dog knew that it had been too cold to be traveling anywhere, even though the animal lacked the arithmetical knowledge that the temperature was actually approaching seventy-five degrees below zero. and not fifty-degrees-below as his master had erroneously believed. A hundred and seven degrees below the "frost-point" is an unbearable condition that is hostile to the survival and sustenance of human life. The trailing animal instinctively knew from past experiences with humans that its master should either seek shelter or enter a camp to get warm, and the canine's pea-brain mind wondered why the supposedly more-intelligent human that the animal was following persisted in struggling his meandering journey through the fierce harsh winds.

Every time the man attempted to expel juice from his chewing tobacco, the fluid would freeze and attach itself to his dangling red beard, because the brown liquid would not shoot-out over his chin onto the ground. In fact, an amber-colored icicle was forming between the man's mouth and chin from the extremely cold Arctic weather. 'This is not the time to give my boots a spit shine, or even a fuckin' brown spit shine!' the audacious fellow thought in an effort to amuse himself. 'Christ! If I was born in Belgium, I'd be even more fuckin' 'phlegm- ish' than I am right now! And this phlegm I'm discharging from my mouth can't possibly remind me of my old kinky girlfriend back in Fairbanks because she was a real spitfire!'

Several miles ahead, the trekker stumbled down a slippery snow embankment and reached the foot of Henderson Creek, a mere ten miles from 'the forks', his next intended rendezvous point. 'Let's see now,' the anxious fellow considered. 'If I average four-miles an hour, I'll arrive at the forks by around two in the afternoon. I'll hold off my stomach pangs until then, and enjoy swallowing-down my bacon-flavored biscuits. Then between six and seven o'clock, I'll meet-up with the boys at the camp and can finally examine some of their wonderful porno' magazines. Shit, I hope they've gotten some new nude centerfolds! Oh well. I'll just keep my current pace and extend the length of my amber icicle beard. Shit, the thing's already twice as long as my dick has ever been! But I can't wait to lick it, and see if it's root beer flavored.'

But then, the encumbered adventurer noticed that his nose and his cheeks were numb, and that his facial skin no longer felt the sensations of warmth, touch, or pain. 'I'll put-up with these frosty, numb cheeks and numb nose for six more hours. A little discomfort never killed anyone! Shit!' the sufferer realized. 'How will I ever know if I piss myself if my dick becomes numb, too! Oh well; I'll just think about those porno' periodicals over at the camp. They'll keep me movin' on. It's amazing how the power of pussy can motivate a guy to ignore terrible things like fifty-to-sixty degree below zero temperatures out here in the bitter wilderness. If worse comes to worst, I'll just start singing the lyrics to 'Frosty the Snowman' to myself!'

* * * * * * * * * * * * *

The man's locomotion was not seriously impeded, despite the frigid cold and the high snow accumulation in his path. His awareness knew that although no deep-water creek could avert being frozen over, still, pockets of springs bubbled-out from the warmer hillsides, and the reality existed where the trekker could accidentally fall into a pool of water and drown. Such a horrifying misfortune would mean immediately building a fire to dry-out, and also changing his thick woolen socks to prevent getting frostbitten toes. The covered pools might be three inches deep, or perhaps three feet deep; the latter representing a life-threatening situation to certainly be avoided.

'I must be careful, because if I fall into a pool of water,' the man thoughtfully evaluated, 'I might as well be authoring my own self-destruction. And I don't need the delay of building a fire, if I could instead use my intelligence and my savvy to avert having to do it. And besides, I strongly desire to continue living, so that I could go back to Fairbanks down in Alaska and hump and pump my old spitfire girlfriend. Now that I've evaded the soft-snow water pool traps, I can resume my four-mile gait. I'm not going to allow nature's obstacles to fuckin' stymie my progress, so sir!'

Two hours later, the advancing man encountered another patch of soft snow that he recognized might be hiding unexposed water pools, so honoring an inspiration, the on-a-mission wanderer decided to make his wolf dog go first, but the beast refused to take an unaccustomed leadership role in the expedition. The man forcefully pushed the dog forward, and its weight suddenly broke through the thin ice, instantly wetting its front paws.

Immediately, the canine licked its paws and instinctively bit-out the ice between its pads; a natural reaction to its need for self-preservation. Fearing a loss of time, the man ripped-off his mitten and quickly helped the animal scrape-off and remove the remaining embedded ice chunks. Realizing that his right hand had become numb in less than a minute of exposure, the man quickly put his mitten back onto his fingers, and then pounded his chest thirty consecutive times to get vital circulation flowing again back into his wrists and knuckles.

At one-thirty in the afternoon, the fatigued trekker arrived at the designated forks to stop and consume his bacon-flavored biscuits, which had been strapped inside a pouch that was concealed underneath his warm fur coat. Again, his exposed fingers became numb at locating and removing his precious food. He then struck his hand two dozen times against his knee to get the circulation and his feeling sensation going again. Now, the beleaguered traveler realized that his feet were wet, his nose, cheeks and fingers numb, and that perhaps starting a fire would be not only advantageous, but also fully necessary.

'That son-of-a-bitch old geezer back at the lodge at Sulfur Creek knew what the hell he was bullshittin' about when he said that it gets unbearably cold out here in the open country,' Jim Monahan recollected as the trekker continuously stomped his feet and thrashed his arms about as if performing improvised gym class calisthenics.

Using twigs and small branches from nearby spruce trees, the man built a fire to sit beside and then swallow-down his three biscuits while the obedient wolf dog sprawled-out just far enough from the roaring flames to not get its fur singed. After warming his hands and briefly smoking his pipe, the pathfinder speedily pulled on his sealskin mittens, adjusted the flaps of his fur cap over his tender ears, and then proceeded up the left fork trail that paralleled Henderson Creek. But as the middle-aged gent and his dog advanced onward, the canine knew that it was far better to dig a hole in the snow and curl its body into a semicircle to keep warm rather than to be walking along a creek in such hostile weather conditions.

'Ah, no signs of underwater springs on this left fork!' Monahan gratefully assessed. 'I should be able to maintain my schedule and meet the guys before seven. I hope the fuck those zany assholes don't wanna' play strip poker! Oh shit! I've just broken through down to my goddamned knees! That's what the fuck I get for losing my concentration for a second and letting my fucked-up imagination run amok! It's imperative that I lose another damned hour to build another fire, or else risk freezing my fingers, toes and dick off!'

At the top of a rocky hill, the frustrated man industriously gathered grasses, twigs, sticks and branches, for time was of the essence. Monahan removed a piece of treasured birch bark from an inner pocket, scraped a match, and fortunately managed to ignite a fire. The Prometheus imitator very methodically fed the flames with dry twigs and grass, and much to his utter elation, the sparks and flames became greater, and soon began to roar.

'When it's more than fifty-degrees-below-zero, there's no room for error,' Jim plausibly concluded. 'If my feet are dry, I can run in the snow for a half a mile and get my blood flowing in my extremities again. But if my feet are wet, I gotta' build a fire and expose them to heat; otherwise, I'll be even worse-off than that famous Venus de Milo statue, having no legs in addition to no fuckin' arms! I must complete my scheduled route without any further complications! I can't get cold feet! Ha, ha, ha,' the man mentally laughed at his moronic cliché. 'No way Joseph; er, I mean, 'No way, Jose'!'

* * * * * * * * * * * * *

The encumbered man was not used to such severe adversity and realized that he should have adhered more diligently to the old-timer's advice back in Sulfur Creek. 'I gotta' act fast and not fuck-up again!' Jim frantically conjectured. 'It's early March, and I can't be as slow as molasses in January, because damn it, it's even colder now than it fuckin' was two months ago!'

To build his second fire to an appropriate level of heat and power, the pathetic struggler had to remove his mittens, and utilizing his overtaxed brain, Monahan promptly comprehended that his hands, in addition to his fingers, were completely numb; and also, his feet were now objects simply attached to his body. The full force of the swirling wind added more harsh reality to his treacherous dilemma.

'It's so fuckin' cold that I won't know if or when I shit my pants or freeze my balls off!' the perplexed man comprehended while persistently shivering. 'My blood is staying in the center of my body and my arms, legs, and head are feeling the hellish consequences. My skin can feel the loss of blood, and all sensation has diminished, but let's hope this fire flourishes, because I don't know if I have the wherewithal to fuckin' start a third one!' Monahan lamented and regretted. 'Now I know. The next time the temperature drops under fifty below, I should stay the fuck under the covers in my bunk bed. Hell, my uncooperative gloved hands can't even feel the twigs that I'm feeding into the fire. Forget screwing my kinky girl down in Fairbanks! Oh, if I could only be alone in my bunk and be jerking-off one final time!'

The man attempted untying his ice-coated boots; however, the strings seemed like rods of straight steel, but upon acknowledging the folly of his actions, the desperate victim of nature drew his sheath knife to sever the strings. But then, an unanticipated fate occurred that would send shock waves from his brain down his spine. Jim had made the crucial mistake of building his fire under a large spruce tree, thinking that twigs and wood would be readily available.

The tree had a tremendous weight of snow upon its boughs. While yanking the fifth twig from the tree, that minor agitation precipitated disaster as a load of heavy snow descended from the top branches, until virtually all of the accumulated debris had descended into a mini-avalanche, and in five seconds had extinguished the fire that the determined man had labored so assiduously to ignite. A foot-deep mantle of snow now occupied the space where the benevolent fire had existed, just thirty seconds before.

'The old fuck at Sulfur Creek was absolutely right. I should've been travelin' with another trekker. It's as if my death sentence has just been cruelly announced,' Jim Monahan hypothesized with disgust. 'I'm never gonna' read those porno' magazines at the camp, or ever get laid again by my spitfire bitch back in Fairbanks, or by any other horny whore anywhere else! I gotta' try one more time to build this fuckin' fire, but even if I succeed, I'm certain to lose a few fingers and toes to apathetic frostbite!'

Monahan gathered some twigs using his two hands, behaving like a primitive machine, but that next endeavor was performed out in the open away from any snow-laden tree branches. Jim could not separate the trigs from the worthless green growth around them, because of the lack of available dexterity in his fingers. All the while, the confused dog sat in wonder at the incompetence of the desperate man, who was ordinarily the skilled fire provider. Monahan then fumbled in his pocket for his second and last piece of birch bark to start the flames, but the gold prospector lacked the motor skills to effectively clutch the hanging tree limb. Realizing that his feet were now also frozen, the man's mind entered a panic-state frenzy.

'I gotta' beat my hands against my sides to get some feeling back into my fingers,' Jim worriedly thought. 'Just look at that dog peacefully lying there, all fuckin' curled-up in a ball; still warm and vibrant! Believe it or not, I would trade places with that dumb animal in a Seattle minute. I think that all-too-comfortable beast has more of a future than I fuckin' do! I can't believe it. I actually envy that furry, complacent son-of-a-bitch, who in reality, was basically really only a little son-of-a-bitch when he was born!'

"For an ephemeral minute, the overwhelmed man enjoyed with satisfaction an excruciating ache in his left hand, briefly indicating that a marvelous sensation again existed there. Jim was able to remove his pack of matches, which unfortunately then fell into the deep snow. Unable to pick the matches up with his numb fingers, Monahan devoted all of his energies on how he could ignite a fire.

Jim again used his two hands as an improvised machine/shovel to grab the elusive pack. Wearing his thick mittens, the poor fellow was able to again manipulate his hands like two shovels. Monahan managed to get the entire pack between his palms, and then he awkwardly raised his mittens up to his mouth, which had difficulty in opening because his lips had been ensconced in ice. Then, the overmatched man succeeded in lighting one flare, which then set the entire pack on fire, and burning brimstone soon ascended-up into his nostrils and down into his lungs, causing the man to excessively cough. The burning pack of matches plunged into the snow, and then its accompanying flames quickly faded-out.

* * * * * * * * * * * * *

Jim stared avariciously at 'Czar', his curious-but-defensive minded wolf dog. 'You must think that I'm a total asshole if you have any fucked-up concept of what the hell a total asshole is!' Monahan thought during a moment of self-serving amusement. 'Once you realize that I'm dying and am no longer your personal fire provider,' the master visualized and considered, 'you'll sure as taxes and death abandon me as if I was a hard turd that had just dropped-out of your furry asshole.'

The battered man peered again at his bewildered dog, and the master's faltering mind successfully manufactured a fleeting idea. 'That's it!' Jim imagined as he again briefly glanced at Czar shifting his weight back and forth with anxious wistfulness, as the animal rested in the snow. 'The old-timer back at Sulfur Creek had once told me about a man caught in a blizzard who had miraculously killed a caribou, and then crawled inside its partially gutted-out carcass to stay alive until someone accidentally discovered him. That's exactly what I'll have to fuckin' do to survive! I'll try to kill Czar, and then stick my hands into its warm body to get the sensation of feeling back into them. It's my only chance of survival in this goddamned surreal, supernatural, life-or-death raffle that my accursed name has been entered in! I must fuckin' live at Czar's fuckin' expense!'

Monahan beckoned to Czar to come close to him, but the skeptical animal was used to listening to stern, distant commands, and the dog detected fear in Jim's weak voice. The canine's suspicious nature also sensed that ordinary things were out of kilter, and that his relationship with his master had somehow drastically transformed from dominant man and subordinate beast to something else more primitive.

Czar's ears flattened as the dubious animal ignored the man's feeble solicitations. Jim then got-down on his hands and knees, and very slowly crawled towards his furry companion, but again becoming wary and apprehensive, Czar slowly sidled away. The thwarted master then became cognizant of one important fact: he must rise to his feet and tower over the wolf dog if he expected Czar to obey his commands in any way; thus, rendering his allegiance to his master. 'If I don't watch myself, I might somehow weirdly become a serf to Czar in a power-structure reversal of roles!'

After achieving the arduous act of standing erect, Jim had to wait a moment to verify that he was indeed in a vertical position, perpendicular to the ground; for his energy reserve was rapidly sapping, and Monahan had no distinct feeling in his legs, feet or toes. The exhausted man attempted clutching the dog's neck, but instead, Jim collapsed upon the animal, endeavoring to either strangle or smother Czar beneath the weight of his body. All the while, the surprised dog snarled, whined, and struggled.

'If only I had the coordination and the strength to stab Czar with my sheath knife,' Jim thought during his mental and physical mania. With virtually all of his stamina expired, the physically spent man released the wolf dog from his greedy grasp. The creature wildly plunged away with its tail curved between its hind legs, panting heavily between snarls. Then Czar, with his ears pricked forward, halted a safe distance of forty feet away from Jim to then survey the man and his miserable plight. The dog's keen instincts detected weakness and craziness, and Czar did not value either strange entity.

Jim looked-down at his gloved hands in order to accurately locate them, and was surprised to see his wrists still attached to his dangling arms. 'I've never before had to use my fuckin' eyes to find-out where my goddamned hands are located,' the grieving man's mind fancifully thought. 'I'm just as doomed as the last asshole standing at the Alamo had been doomed!'

For five whole minutes, Monahan violently pounded his hands against his knees, and his heart was able to eventually pump enough blood to temporarily make his persistent shivering cease. But still, his extremities remained frozen and numb. 'Even my hard head is feeling no damned sensation. I'm truly the epitome of a human *numb*skull!' Jim mused. 'I'm no longer afraid of having my damned fingers and toes amputated! I'm now dreading the thought of losing my whole friggin' life! I swear there is no paradise, but I fuckin' pray there isn't any goddamned hell!'

Out of sheer desperation, Jim attempted to jog toward the logging camp, situated several miles distant, and the now-cautious Czar reluctantly and subserviently followed his trail. As the disoriented man floundered and staggered forward, his eyes perceived certain familiar objects that gave him renewed strength: the banks of the creek, the timber jams, the leafless aspens, the spruce trees and finally, the dull gray sky. 'Fuck. If I'm not careful, I might soon be stiff and dead, just like I want my useless pecker *not* to be!' Monahan poignantly assessed. 'I must make it to the camp before some carnivorous, nocturnal animal finds and attacks me. Even if I lose part of my face, hand, feet and ass,' the man decided, 'I don't honestly give a diarrhea shit! I gotta' somehow endure this awful mess and write a goddamned novel about it!'

Jim was both astonished and confused that his heavy legs could run at all on feet that were so terribly abused and so horribly frozen. The weight of his body was now indiscernible to his mind's perception. Monahan's feet had no relationship to the solid earth and thick ice, as his tottering body advanced, skimmed and slid ahead.

'I must not fall!' his stressed-out brain kept registering and reviewing. 'I wonder if that winged-helmeted Greek god Mercury could move as fuckin' swiftly as I'm moving now! And as for that fucked-up son-of-a-bitch bastard Prometheus, where the fuck is *he* when I really fuckin' need his services the most!' Jim illogically hallucinated. 'Why the fuck couldn't I be lost in the steaming hot Amazon jungle! At least I wouldn't be fuckin' freezing to death up here in nature's gigantic ice box! Shit!' Monahan realized during a moment of elevated frustration. 'I gotta' make sure I don't lose my balance tripping-over a goddamned crocodile or giant anaconda! Jesus Christ!' the hallucinating trekker imagined. 'I'd rather be nailed to a cross on Calvary than to mentally and physically suffer like this! I don't have the endurance to survive another mile!' the defeated man sobbed. 'My only fuckin' hope is to be miraculously found by the boys! But they're all egotistical, self-indulgent assholes! I'll bet they're all reading their fucked-up porno' magazines in their warm bunks, and looking at pictures of nude crocodile and anaconda centerfolds! Am I becoming fucked-up, or what?'

Then, the negative, pessimistic thought of his frozen arms and legs extending their numbness that was advancing to his chest and abdomen horrified Jim as the victim valiantly staggered onward. 'I'm more fuckin' afraid of panicking than of fuckin' dying!' the brave man concluded. 'I want to walk, but actually I need to run! Shit! When I used to play baseball in my youth back in Portland, Oregon, I used to walk all the fuckin' time!'

Jim abruptly fell to the ground with a thud, and Czar parked his gray and white furry body ten-feet in front of the frenetic victim, as if deliberately taunting him and his futility. The warmth and security of the animal angered the jealous man, now wishing that Czar was a ferocious crocodile or a ravenous anaconda seeking to devour a near-frozen human being.

'I'm gradually losing my battle with the frost!' Jim academically reckoned. 'Why the fuck couldn't I have been a soldier at Gettysburg, or a frontiersman at the Alamo, and died battling other humans rather than being defeated by a goddamned, relentless, mean-spirited bitch named Mother Nature?'

Then, a certain peculiar simile entered the disenchanted man's distorted and disarrayed mind. 'I must sit-up and meet death with some degree of dignity. No sense in running around like a chicken without a head, because I'm not a goddamned chicken, even though I can't feel or even touch my goddamned head, or even the head of my limp and shriveled dick!'

Monahan stoically decided that he must encounter death decently and peacefully by going off to sleep, and then subconsciously surrendering his will to live. That imagined scenario appeared to be the best solution: to use sleep as an anesthetic, since the sensation of pain had been reduced to a mere conceptual fantasy, devoid of reality. Jim's last thought was his ghost accompanying his concerned friends, and together, the quartet discovering his frozen body lying motionless upon the uncaring tundra. The man's spirit had been persuaded by his diminishing will to abandon its imprisonment and exit his body in pursuit of its predestined place in the invisible Universe.

In his final thought, Jim's erratic mind conjured-up an image of the old-timer at Sulfur Creek being the immortal God-the-Father sitting upon his Olympian-like golden throne inside His marble palace in the center of Heaven. The dead man's initial words to his omnipotent Deity would be, 'You were right, Old Boss! I should've had a strong fellow along with me on the wilderness trail. You're always right and quite truthfully, omnipotent God; Your damned ubiquitous, eternal wisdom makes me want to puke!'

Gradually, Jim dozed-off into the most comfortable and satisfying sleep that is humanly possible, lying on even the softest and most desirable bed mattress. The puzzled dog sat restlessly, waiting for his master to awaken, and to remember to ignite another warm fire. But the man's soul, half-Mercury and half-Prometheus, had peacefully journeyed into the afterlife. As the twilight drew closer, and dusk was imminent, Jim Monahan did not stir from his sitting position, all-the-while having his head loosely bowed between his knees. The silence was quite extraordinary, and particularly alien to the confused animal's prior experiences.

A half-hour later, Czar wined loudly, and then aggressively yawned. The furry creature crept closer to its former master, and its nose smelled the scent of death. The baffled animal instantly bristled its fur, recoiled, and then backed-away in momentary confusion. A short interval of time elapsed, and then Czar howled under the canopy of night stars that had appeared overhead, coincidentally and inadvertently growling-up at Canis Major.

And finally, out of despair and disappointment, Czar turned and trotted-up the trail in the direction of the camp that his limited brain had memorized in a sort of biological map. From its knowledge of the local terrain, the wolf dog knew exactly where the other fire providers could be easily discovered.

# "The Story of Keesh"

When I first heard the name Jack London (1876-1916) as an eighth-grade student attending a Levittown, Pennsylvania parochial school, I naively believed that the famous author was from England. London was born and raised in abject poverty in San Francisco. Although he resented formal education, Jack London was an avid reader and a frequent visitor to the local public library. As a roving teenager, Jack lived a rather unorthodox lifestyle where the adventurer was an oyster pirate, a sailor, a tramp, and the itinerant youth eventually wound-up in jail on vagrancy charges.

Jack London ought to be admired as a role model for young people, because he turned his life around full circle. He took night courses at the *University of California*, studied literature, and developed a respectable vocabulary. The reformed young man soon got caught-up in the Alaska gold rush fever. The avid reader didn't find gold nuggets up in the Klondike and in the Yukon, but he found something as good as gold if not better than the precious ore: Jack London discovered a wealth of material, settings, themes, and characters to construct and support imaginative plots for wonderful novels and novellas.

The versatile author refined the writing technique known today as "Realism", and that very evident quality is reflected in his major novels like *The Call of the Wild* and *White Fang*. Most of Jack London's tales are about strong men, or animals, and their instinct to survive in very harsh environments. Realism is also definitely apparent in London's classic short fiction works such as "Love of Life," "To Build a Fire" and "The Story of Keesh".

Keesh was an Eskimo boy, who never in his life made or sold an Eskimo Pie or a Klondike Bar to anyone. Through courage and wisdom, the audacious youth ascended to the position of village chief, despite opposition from senile village elders, and from jealous village rivals and hunters. By demonstrating steadfast virtue and an indomitable will, the lad was able to advance from the most-humble igloo in the village to becoming the most prosperous clansman. Here's how this incredible bullshit all happened.

Keesh was a bright boy, who sometimes glowed in the dark. At age thirteen, the healthy, strong lad had seen "thirteen suns", but not all at the same time during the same year. That's the terminology his Eskimo clan used in their native village to describe thirteen years, so naturally, the inhabitants probably also must have called the sun "a year", if they called a year "a sun".

Keesh's Eskimo elders were totally fucked-up. That's why he had to straighten all of the stupid assholes out, so that the proper things could be called the proper words and names; some of which might also have been proper nouns that were *commonly* used, and common nouns that were *improperly* used.

Keesh's father Bok had been a valiant fellow that had died during a *grave famine* when all the burial plots in the icy cemetery had also become frozen. Bok sought to save the weaker members of the village by setting-out to hunt and kill a great polar bear, but unfortunately, the great dark beer drinker never came *bok*.

Keesh was Bok's only son, and over the years, the people forgot about Bok's bravery, so the proud boy and his poor indigent mother were demoted in rank to live in the village's smallest and most shabby, dirty-iced, small-assed, ghetto igloo. The igloo was made out of ice cubes from an ancient icebox, rather than constructed out of traditional large, carved, rectangular ice blocks as was the norm according to Eskimo construction codes. Keesh was pretty pissed-off about his relegation to the lowest social and economic echelon in the Eskimo community, which incidentally, also included the fucked-up Eskimo gay and lesbian community.

A council meeting in the big igloo of Chief Klosh-Kwan was rudely interrupted by a complaint from an angry upstart sitting in the rear. Keesh rose to his feet, showing the strong dignity of an elder, and demanded to be heard amidst the babble of a chorus of critical condescending voices.

"Oh, great Klosh-Kwan," the acne-faced juvenile began his oratory. "The meat my mother and I have been apportioned has entirely too much fat, too much gristle, and too many bones. Hell, I demand better quality meat, and make 'no bones' about it. Know what the frig' I'm bitchin' about!"

The grizzled, elder, veteran hunters were appalled and aghast at Keesh's confident attitude, which the senile idiots interpreted as brash brazenness. The council lawmakers were perturbed that an audacious punk pretending to be a man was attempting to arbitrarily break their balls in front of the entire Eskimo community, which included the fucked-up Eskimo gay and lesbian sub-community.

"Who is this impudent child that talks like a man?" one councilman asked. "He has absolutely no reputation as a skilled hunter, nor any track record as a proven scout. Sit-down Macho Boy, before we throw your ass out of the big igloo, and ostracize you from the entire Eskimo village, including banishment from the influential gay and lesbian village people, along with other less powerful heterosexual village idiots!"

Keesh was undaunted by the sudden outburst of criticism directed against him, so the lad stubbornly continued with his grievance. "I've heard from many of you demented charlatans that my father Bok was a fantastic hunter. It's said that Bok brought back to the village twice as much meat to share than any two other hunters combined. And it's also reputed that my father also knew how to beat his meat better than anyone else in this clan," Keesh reminded his disinterested listeners. "And Bok would then generously give his meat to the old toothless women of the village to suck on!"

"Nay, nay!" the old prune-faced men on the council *neighed* like discontented horses. "Put the disrespectful delinquent out of our company!" and "Send the infant wanna'-be back to his crib!" is what the incensed crowd boisterously yelled. "No man would ever insult the long graybeards as this lazy, juvenile punk delinquent is attempting to do!"

Keesh patiently waited for the assembly's clamor and the elders' protests to calm-down. Then, the determined lad incisively continued his critique, much to the chagrin of his already-peeved adult audience. "Ugh-Gluk," the Eskimo adolescent said to one of the humiliated hunters smugly sitting on the council. "Thou hast a wife, and for her do you speak."

"That's right!" The old man sitting in the assembly hollered-out. "Ugh-Gluk has some *ugly luck* with both married and unmarried squaws. Ha, ha, ha!"

"The old coot's insulted wife punched him squarely in the face as Klosh-Kwan banged his two hunting spears together to reestablish order above the hoots and jeers of the assembled crowd inside *his* huge igloo. Then, the wise old chief motioned for Keesh to continue his brazen oratory.

"And thou, Massuk, you have a mother, and for her do you speak. My mother has no one to speak on her behalf, except me, so that's why the hell I'm here," Keesh boldly declared. "Bok is dead because he hunted too fanatically for the benefit of others, who have now regrettably forgotten his glory," Keesh emphasized for everyone's consideration. "So based on my father's great contributions to this community, including the fucked-up gay and lesbian sub-community," the teenager cautiously proceeded, "I insist that my mom Ikeega and I be given better meat as long as this tribe has a plentiful supply. I, Keesh, the son of Bok and of Ikeega, have spoken. I say this just in case some of you deaf sons of bitches seated on the other side of the igloo, and some of you deaf and dumb sons of bitches whose smelly asses sit on the council, were wondering what the hell I was doing when I was moving my mouth and jaws!"

The brash kid sat-down in a huff with his ears perceiving the abundant dissension and commotion that his stinging words had generated. Keesh then alertly absorbed the intense, malignant harangue being channeled in his direction.

"That ungrateful boy talks disease out of his ass and shits out of his unwise mouth!" Ugh-Gluk mumbled to Massuk. "Let's face the music Massuk. Keesh is a sick, young, walrus pup trying to *seal* an easy life for his big fat cow mommy, and also for Keesh'! Ha, ha, ha!" Ugh-Gluk robustly laughed. "Massuk; tell that ambitious roughneck to fuck-off and quickly leave the council's igloo, so that we can conduct our important business!"

"Fellow Eskimos, shall the babes in arms tell us veteran experienced men how we must distribute meat?" Massuk implored those parents still grumbling in the general attendance. "If Keesh was to have more meat, tell him to live in a 'porterhouse' instead of in the smallest igloo in Alaska! Ha, ha, ha!"

The entire assemblage. with the exception of saddened Ikeega, mocked and jeered Keesh's brashness. After order had again been restored, Klosh-Kwan commanded Keesh to bed to have 'white dreams' of delicious polar bear carcasses. "You shall have scheduled beatings administered to you by the council's administrators!" the livid Chief thundered at Keesh. "You're a most rambunctious, presumptuous, little tyrant, whose all-too-thin hide needs to be tanned! Have *you* no modesty or humility?"

Keesh's eyes flashed with heightened anger, and the blood within his veins, arteries, and capillaries promptly boiled. The defiant young prodigy/progeny jumped to his feet to challenge the council's supreme adult authority, all happening before the entire appalled village population. "Hear me speak elderly retards and pedophiles!" the youth hostilely replied. "These are my last words to you. Bok was a great hunter. I, his son, shall prove to be a great hunter, also. I shall go and hunt the meat I shall eat without your goddamned, unjust welfare system, and I shall divide my meat and apportion it fairly," the agitated lad boldly stated. "First, I shall share my meat with widows whose husbands have been killed. Secondly, I shall share my meat with the mothers whose sons are dead; and thirdly, I shall give my meat to the impotent old men that sit on council and can go longer get erections or shoot an ounce of sperm juice. And I predict,"

Ikeega's son loudly communicated, "that in the days to come, the gluttonous, fat old men that arrogantly sit on this sham council shall know the meaning of the word 'shame' without the aid or use of a dictionary! I, Keesh, have spoken."

"You ain't gonna' screw me up the ass, you arrogant, piss-ant mother-fucker!" Massuk yelled at the audacious upstart like a raving maniac. "Just come over here and suck my dick to see exactly how *impotent* I am in this damned village!"

Keesh did not answer Massuk's degrading insult, because the youth had told everyone at the meeting that he had spoken all he had wished to say. Jeers and abundant scorn filled his ears as the mocked lad abruptly left the meeting with his head raised high. Keesh's jaw was set tight, for the teen Eskimo looked neither left nor right as he silently battled his sudden lockjaw attack.

The next morning, the determined boy trekked along the coastline where the sea's ice met the hard frozen land. Several elders had witnessed him leaving the village with his bow, a handful of bone-barbed arrows, his father's enormous hunting spear, and a bulging hard-on sticking out from his thigh-length fur coat, which was made from the skin of Bok's last polar bear kill.

Never before had a thirteen-year-old fledgling gone-out to hunt, let alone gone out to hunt all by his lonesome. Many horny women stared with pity in their hearts at Ikeega, whose facial expression reflected both grimness and melancholy. "He'll be back before long, Ikeega," the considerate women encouraged their disconsolate, grieving friend. "He'll become tired, and return to the village, and eventually learn to curb his rash tongue. Your obstinate son is rebelling against a gross injustice, and blaming it all on adult authority."

"Let the junior jerk-off go; let him learn the meaning of 'disgrace' *without* the aid of an elementary school dictionary," the hunters laughed while mimicking Keesh's council meeting presentation. "And the callow wise-ass will come back soft of tongue and meek in speech, and he'll finally respect the wisdom of his sage elders; that young punk double-fuck!"

And three days passed with strong gales and ten inches of snow, but there was no sign of Keesh. Ikeega pulled-out her hair and smeared soot all over her face as tokens of sorrow, symbolically telling everyone it was better to do that than to smear soot onto her scalp, and to pull her face off. The village women all openly criticized their husbands for mistreating the haughty, naughty boy at the council meeting, and the clever wives had cut-off their spouses' sex lives, and no longer sucked their partners' dicks, telling their husbands that those practices would only be resumed when the women could eat and enjoy Keesh's meat. The men of the village felt guilty, and were totally pissed-off by the stubborn women's statements, so the adult males reluctantly organized search parties to track-down and find the adamant, opinionated "lost boy".

On the fourth morning, Keesh entered the village, but the boy was wearing a cheerful, confident face. A bountiful supply of freshly-killed meat was carried across his scrawny shoulders. Ikeega's son had triumphantly returned, and his success gave his militant personality a new-found cockiness.

"Go ye' men with your dog sledges, and travel my trail for a full day," the "Macho Boy" commanded the astonished residents, which included the gay and bisexual village people. "I've left much meat on the ice. A she-bear and two cubs."

Ikeega was filled with happiness at her son's apparent good fortune, and at his safe completion of his daring one-boy expedition. "Come Ikeega; let us eat meat inside our tiny little igloo. After that, I shall sleep, for I'm quite exhausted from beating my meat out there on the cold ice!" Keesh suggested and confessed. "In the future, I'll have that ugly bastard Massuk pound my meat so that I can conserve my energy for future hunting expeditions!"

'Oh boy,' Ikeega proudly thought. 'Now Keesh will become rich and will give me enough money to open a village furniture store!'

Much discussion and debate abounded throughout the small tribal village concerning Keesh and his "lucky hunting foray". The killing of a she-bear attending to her cubs was very dangerous, considering *her* inbred maternal instinct to protect her young. The men could not believe that Keesh was a better hunter than *they* were, but the knuckleheads were glad that the youngster had come back, because now the jerk-offs could again receive decent sex and stimulating blowjobs from their sometimes-faithful wives, who actually preferred lesbian homosexuality to heterosexual activity with their marital partners. So, the grumbling men departed the village to retrieve the polar bear kills, remembering their wives' memorable, familiar refrains, "No sex or blowjobs until you retrieve and finally return with Keesh's fabulous meat!"

In northern Alaska, it was imperative that the polar bear carcasses be located as soon as possible. Wild animals in search of scarce food might discover the remains, or the exposed meat could freeze so solidly that it could break even the sharpest cutting knife. A three-hundred-pound polar bear is not easy to lift and deposit onto a sled when it is frozen-solid *dead weight*. But when the recovery team eventually reached the dead animals' location, the searchers observed that Keesh had already neatly and impressively quartered the prey in true hunter practice.

Keesh's mysterious hunting prowess became more and more evident with the passing weeks. On his second mission, the wonder boy killed a nearly adult-sized male bear, and on his third expedition into the Alaskan wilderness, a male and its female companion were slain. Both of those remarkable exploits had been condensed into rather short three-or-four-day journeys that Keesh had conducted into the snow-covered, frontier barrens.

"How does he do it?" the very concerned Massuk asked Ugh-Gluk. "He never takes dogs with him, and certainly, dogs can be of great assistance. I believe that Keesh is possessed."

"Daaa, I don't know!" the over-challenged Ugh-Gluk replied. "Daa, I don't know!" the old senile fool reiterated.

"Let's ask the lucky punk about this good-luck skein he's been on!" Klosh-Kwan chimed-in. "And let me do all the talking, you two old stupid jerk offs!"

The three decrepit council members ate humble pie (which is not as tasty as hair pie), and approached the valiant Keesh standing outside his humble igloo. "Why do you hunt only polar bear, Keesh?" Klosh-Kwan curiously asked. "Why not also go after Christmas and Easter Seals, and also sea lions?"

Keesh contemplated Klosh-Kwan's motivation for wanting to ask such a silly, damned, asinine question, and then the lad illustriously responded, "Are you three, ancient, cretin, stupid assholes, or what?" the teen scolded his elders. "Every Eskimo from here to the North Pole knows that there's more meat on a polar bear than on a seal, or on the kind of sea lions that frequent this God-forsaken part of the known world!"

"I think you practice witchcraft!" Massuk openly accused Keesh. "You hunt with evil spirits that gladly help you in exchange for selling your soul! You are an evil sorcerer!"

"Maybe the spirits that help me are good ones and not evil ones," Keesh alertly challenged. "Maybe my noble father's spirit is expertly guiding me, and allowing me to attain excellence and tribal reward through *his* fine example and wisdom."

"I think you beat and have pounded your meat too much!" Massuk criticized his young adversary. "That's exactly your fuckin' problem! You beat your meat too much! Ha, ha, ha!"

"At least I have meat that can be pounded!" Keesh smartly answered his narrow-minded opponent, whose last valid erection was on his eightieth birthday three decades before.

Keesh's accumulative kill production was quite prolific by Eskimo standards. The lesser skilled hunters were kept busy going-out and hauling in sleds full of polar bear carcasses. Just as Bok had done before him, Keesh's distribution of the meat was fair, and the village elders became extremely pissed-off when the popular boy became the first official Eskimo meat distributor getting advanced orders from neighboring villages.

The teenager was both just and democratic in his allocations, providing the least of the women and the weakest of the grandfathers (not on the council) with abundant portions. The lad was achieving great prestige and honor from his peers, along with recognition from the women, and many knowledgeable gossipers predicted that Keesh would replace ancient Klosh-Kwan as the village chief. But the obstinate boy remembered his promise, and never returned to the village council until Keesh would be invited by the bullshitting ruling elders to share *his* unique experiences, his expertise, and his precocious philosophy about village affairs. The sanctimonious, bureaucratic, senile elders were too proud and too ashamed to publicly compromise, relent, and invite the impetuous boy to address them in council.

One morning, in the center of the icy village, Keesh confronted Klosh-Kwan, Ugh-Gluk, and Massuk, who were eagerly looking for a fourth member to sing bass to form a sort of un-harmonious Eskimo barbershop quartet.

"I'm considering constructing an igloo," Keesh began his oral statement. "And it shall be a very tremendous igloo to accommodate my mother Ikeega, and also my super-big ego. In fact, you wrinkled old farts, it will definitely be the largest and most spectacular igloo in the whole damned village."

"Ay!" the three nodded in amazement. "Ay!" they hypnotically repeated and nodded.

"Ay! Ay! Ay!" Klosh-Kwan exclaimed. "Ay, Ay, *I* wish I was in *Dixie,* hooray, hooray, In Dixieland I'll take my stand, to live and die in *Dixie*!"

"Away, away, away down south in *Dixie!*" Massuk and Ugh-Gluk idiotically joined-in with Klosh-Kwan, to further aggravate their principal nemesis.

"Stop this crazy nonsense right now!" Keesh indignantly yelled. After silence reigned supreme, the boy continued his braggadocio-type monologue. "But I have no time to build my igloo because of my scheduled commitment set aside for hunting polar bear meat for the entire village," Keesh boastfully maintained. "I recommend that the old men and widows that eat my meat should construct my huge igloo during my absence."

And much to the council elders' humiliation, a week later the giant iced edifice was almost completed and being constructed to Keesh's strict specifications, and the huge structure was especially designed to be three times as massive as Klosh-Kwan's meeting hall. The spacious home was the first material comfort Ikeega would experience since the death of Bok, who according to village scuttlebutt, only came *bok* as a benign spirit, assisting Keesh in *his* celebrated hunting exploits.

Keesh's mother also earned admiration and recognition from the other village women, and Ikeega became the First Lady of the settlement, despite the fact that the place had no President, and that her husband was deceased. Many squaws asked the matriarch's sage advice on sensitive female matters like dealing with menstruation, and having multiple sex partners, and Ikeega competently showed the other women how to masturbate like crazy using both hands, and how to use a whalebone dildo to achieve multiple orgasms when not engaged in formerly forbidden lesbian sex.

One day, Klosh-Kwan, Massuk, and Ugh-Gluk accosted Keesh in front of the youngster's work-in-progress, almost completed igloo. The three elders appeared rather annoyed and in prosecutorial moods, despite the fact that the trio had recently found a talented bass singer to complement the correct rhythm for their inharmonious Eskimo barbershop quartet.

"What's this shit about a new culinary sensation being attributed to you?" Klosh-Kwan jealously asked the Eskimo boy prodigy. "Stop stealin' our fuckin' thunder!"

"My new eating delight is when a person puts seven slabs of polar bear meat on a skinny stick, and flame broils the flesh over a fire," the now-famous young hunter gloated. "Ikeega calls the new fabulous dish Eskimo *Keesh-ka-bob!"*

"It is charged," Ugh-Gluk yelled, deliberately changing the topic of conversation, "that thou Keesh dealest with an evil spirit; wherefore thou hunting expeditions are rewarded by dead demon shamans with plentiful polar bear meat."

"There is 'spirit' involved," Keesh readily acknowledged, "but it's not an evil spirit. When I see a polar bear about to attack me, I simply *spear-it!* Ha, ha, ha! Get it! Spear-it, ha, ha, ha!"

"Don't give us any of your polar bear comedy shit, or we'll excommunicate you from the village!" Massuk sternly warned his young formidable enemy. "Your new ice house is probably held together by E-glue because types A, B, C and D glue were ineffective."

"Is not the meat good that I give you?" Keesh objected while getting back on subject. "Has anyone in our village taken sick from eating it? Is your accusation of witchcraft being involved in my skill a slick cover-up for the envy and jealousy that consumes your black, selfish souls?"

"That's enough out of you; you disrespectful, insolent, walrus pup!" Klosh-Kwan admonished the proud youth. "Keep your nasty fucked-up thoughts to yourself!"

"You three senile, deranged, stupid shits can *Keesh* my smooth, white Eskimo ass!" the boy-prodigy/genius contemptuously answered his mortified superiors.

And the three elder councilmen fearfully withdrew from Keesh's illustrious company with their hands trembling, and the gossipy eavesdropping village women intensively snickered at the "three charlatans" failure to effectively intimidate the emboldened lad. At a council caucus meeting, the trio of embarrassed elders asked for "suggestions from the ice" on how to deal with Keesh's blatant defiance of their authority.

After much discussion, it was finally decided to send four scouts out on patrol to spy on Keesh, and to see if witchcraft was indeed associated with his sinister hunting activities, or if skill was the dominant factor responsible for the boy's uncanny success. Four crafty hunters, Bim, Brim, Baum and Bum were assigned to trail the boy wonder into the icy wilderness, and then report back to the pissed-off council elders precisely what they had witnessed.

Five days later, the four fatigued spies re-entered the shabby village and addressed a closed-session of the council. Their eyes were bulging out of their sockets, and the neurotic men's hands were shaking as if each spy had contracted Parkinson's disease during the five-day absence. Klosh-Kwan requested that one of the four hunters step forward to the front table, and then orally review exactly what the spy had personally observed.

Bim reluctantly approached the elders seated behind a rudely fabricated table made from timber imported to the northern tundra from the Alaskan taiga forests. "Aged Brothers; the four of us had done as commanded by the council. We cunningly trailed Keesh, and we did it so secretly that he never suspected our furtive presence; our eyes scrutinizing his every move," Bim prefaced.

"Get to the point, or we'll have Bum tell us what the fuck happened!" Klosh-Kwan characteristically chastised the all-too-vociferous, gossiping villager. "You have a shit-mouthed tendency to prevaricate and equivocate!"

"Well, midway in the first day, Keesh encountered a ferocious large bear with teeth longer than Bum's dick!" Bim cockily asserted.

"I've never seen such a gargantuan bear in my entire life!" Baum verified. "But the amazing thing was that although provoked by Keesh's spear, the monster refused to fight him. It all was quite fuckin' extraordinary to witness, to say the least."

"And what transpired next?" Massuk demanded to know. "Make it short and sweet, just like Bum's abbreviated dick. I gotta' leave the meeting soon, Bim. It's almost time for my ugly wife to give me my nightly enema."

"The strange-acting bear turned and moped slowly over the ice," Bim elaborated with mild excitement. "And Keesh chased after the beast, which became very much unafraid. And the obnoxious boy shouted insults at the great brute, which just ignored the dumb kid's nasty comments. Some jerks get all the friggin' luck!"

"And then," Brim enthusiastically interrupted Bim. "The bear became so antagonized that it stood-up on its hind legs and growled fiercely. But Keesh stepped right up to the giant polar bear as if it were a baby seal pup."

"Next," interrupted a very nervous and stuttering Baum, "Keesh ran-up to the enraged ferocious bear, and prodded him with his father's magical spear. I thought that the asshole must be insane to be acting so aggressively!"

"Ah, witchcraft!" Ugh-Gluk surmised and exclaimed. "The little bastard was using witchcraft! The spear is bewitched! I knew all along that *he* was fuckin' communing with evil spirits!"

"Perhaps!" Baum continued and acknowledged. "Keesh then ran away, and the aggravated mammoth bear took-off in pursuit of his ass. But Keesh then dropped a little red round ball upon the slippery ice, and the mammoth bear amazingly stopped, smelled it, and finally chewed and swallowed the circular sphere!" Baum exclaimed. "And then Keesh dashed-away some more, and dropped his balls all over the ground, and the irate bear continued to devour them."

"What are you four fucked-up simpletons expecting us to believe?" Massuk incredulously asked. "Are you four assholes fuckin' delusional or what? I think the four of you neurotic, imbecilic cunt-lappers are infected with evil spirits, too!"

"We all saw it with our own eyes!" Bim confirmed.

"With our own eyes!" Bum corroborated.

"With our own eyes!" Brim affirmed.

"With our own eyes!" Baum verified.

"Fuck your own eyes!" Klosh-Kwan boisterously derided. "Your eyes can only behold evil witchcraft, and nothing else!"

"But eminent elders," Baum facetiously answered. "This red-ball activity continued until the immense polar bear stood erect, cried-out in agony, and then thrashed its forepaws wildly about as if it was going absolutely crazy. The lunatic bear paid no attention to Keesh as it growled and groaned in excruciating pain," Baum added. "The goddamned polar bear became very weak and exhausted, rolled over on its back, and then seemed to beg Keesh to kill it, which he soon accomplished with his father's bewitched, supernatural spear."

"The spear was a charm! It was an evil object not intended for Eskimo use in this accursed world!" Ugh-Gluk exclaimed. "The spear definitely belongs to an evil sorcerer! A fuckin' shaman of the forbidden black arts!"

"Exactly what happened after Keesh killed the bear with Bok's haunted spear?" Klosh-Kwan insisted on learning.

"When we left the incredible scene," Bim summarized almost out of breath, "Keesh was preoccupied skinning the bear, so we came sprinting back to the village in record time to accurately reveal the unearthly truths that we had witnessed."

"All four of you shit-head clowns, get the fuck outa' here right this instant!" incensed Klosh-Kwan nastily screamed. "Besides sucking Keesh's dick, you four assholes must also eat his little red balls, too!"

That afternoon, the humble women of the village all earnestly pounded Keesh's meat, while their aggravated husbands attended an emergency council session in Klosh-Kwan's igloo, now the second largest ice building in the whole damned village. A courier was dispatched to Keesh, ordering the vernal hunter to attend the important meeting, and of course the young man considered and then declined to go, even though he believed "the order" was "an invitation" by the elders to formally address the council. "I'm too tired and hungry this time," the polar bear killer told the shocked and disappointed messenger. "But my new igloo is the largest in the village and can easily accommodate all of the councilmen, along with the gay and lesbian sub-community," the kid just entering puberty shrewdly answered, effectively breaking everybody else's testicles and tits.

Klosh-Kwan and the others were so curious about inspecting Keesh's new igloo that the ignoramuses all got their asses up and paced over to the recently-constructed "Ice Palace". Keesh was busy eating his one-man banquet, but he took the time to welcome the elders and the rest of the 'rank' and file clan, and next seated them according to their positions of importance. Ikeega was proud of her son's evident haughtiness, and the loyal mother became the hostess, going around the tremendous-sized igloo and cordially serving everyone delicious Eskimo pies without any pubic hairs in them.

During the formal council meeting, Klosh-Kwan presented the testimonies of Bim, Brim, Baum and Bum. "So young Keesh," the tribal chief concluded and articulated, "I believe that an explanation of your fantastic activities is indeed warranted. Describe to our village people, Macho Boy, your secret method of hunting polar bears. Is there any witchcraft or evil spirits involved?"

Everyone listened intently for Keesh's explicit accountability. "Nay, old Klosh-Kwan," the lad nonchalantly answered. "A boy, such as I, knows little about witches or about the forbidden black arts. I have but cleverly developed a means to successfully kill ice bears. I assure you, Mighty Assholes perched on the council, my genuine hunting methods involve good head-craft, and not evil witchcraft as you presume."

"And may any hunter perform the same method?" Massuk inquired. "Could I be able to kill a polar bear?"

"Yes, even you Massuk!" Keesh amusingly responded as the other men in the audience loudly heckled and jeered the village's old codger. "If you can still pop a load into a hairy pussy, you could kill a polar bear with my proven strategy."

"And will thou share with us this wonderful hunting secret?" the aged Ugh-Gluk pleaded. "I'd love to kill more polar bears if the process could be made easier, and if it didn't involve any fucked-up satanic witchcraft!"

"Yes, I'll tell thee now that the council has had the courtesy to assemble in *my* igloo!" Keesh lectured and stated. After sucking on a rich marrowbone, the lad stood on a crate and again spoke to the astonished Eskimo community, including the influential gay and lesbian Eskimo sub-community. "It is all quite easy and simple to comprehend, you asinine simpletons!"

The lad picked-up a thick strip of whalebone cartilage and showed it to his captivated audience. The ends were honed like sharp needle- points. Keesh then meticulously coiled the cartilage strip until it released and sprang open in the palm of his hand. He next picked-up a piece of red blubber, and made the mass hollow on the inside.

"Then, I place the coiled whalebone cartilage inside the blubber, add another layer of red meat, and next form the mass into a rounded red ball," the young hunter orally described and demonstrated for all to see. "Next, I take the Eskimo 'meatballs' and allow them to freeze outside. The bear swallows the red ball, thinking that it is delicious food, which in a way it is," Keesh convincingly explained. "But it happens to also be deadly food. When the blubber melts, the whalebone cartilage either uncoils in the bear's throat, or in its stomach. The polar bear becomes ill, chokes incessantly, suffers from internal bleeding, and when it's too weak to fight, I kill it with my father's trusty spear that is not haunted, as *you* especially fucked-up idiots on the council falsely presume."

And Ugh-Gluk exclaimed "Oh!" and Klosh-Kwan yelled out "Ay!" and old Massuk boomed-out, "You conniving smart-assed little bastard!"

Soon, Keesh became the eminent chief of the remote village, located on the rim of the great polar sea. His loyal hunters practiced good head-craft instead of evil witchcraft, and the Eskimo village was soon the most prosperous on the entire Alaskan coast. Neither widow nor weak grandfather clamored for fresh food, even during the fiercest winter blizzards.

Keesh instituted a tradition in the village that is still practiced today. The new teen Chief declared the warm month of July "Polar Bear Month", and every resident was required by law to crawl around stark naked on all fours inside his or her igloo in imitation of the great white animals whose flesh and meat sustained the village's population. The horny men would sniff their wives' hairy asses and crotches all day long for that whole warm summer month, and every calendar period between March and April of the following year, the village was blessed with many new baby Eskimos.

The promulgation of surplus Eskimos trained in the art and skill of "head-craft" led to the tribe's great prosperity, and vastly expanded the clan's already-renowned reputation. Even some of the avowed village lesbians surprisingly became pregnant, and reproduced their own kind, thanks to wonderful Keesh's incomparable genius and indispensable wisdom.

# "Love of Life"

The two very fatigued men hobbled-down a steep embankment, and staggered across rough jagged rocks. Each was heavily encumbered with blanket packs strapped to his shoulders. while having head-straps across the forehead, used for stabilizing and supporting cumbersome camping paraphernalia. The very tired men both wished they were situated in a more pleasant and less hostile natural environment.

"I wish we had a couple of those cartridges in that cache of ours," the second man disgustedly stated to his traveling colleague. "Then, we could either shoot an animal and live, or pop a few slugs into our brains and get the fuck outa' this goddamned cruel world."

The man's disgruntled tone of voice was very mechanically spoken without evident emotion or motivation, and his utterance was completely ignored by the second man, who was thinking about getting laid on a tropical island, and not about trekking across the worst, desolate part of Alaska.

Soon, the two gold prospectors splashed and staggered through a stream of icy cold water, making their feet and ankles even more numb than they already were. The trailing man slipped on a smooth, underwater rock and uttered a sharp expletive.

"Fuck!" the follower exclaimed and objected. The trailing trekker reeled around and attempted to balance himself from falling over into the icy water. "Thank God the ice will make the goddamned swelling go down!" the staggering gent yelled as the man thought about his throbbing ankle, and not about his throbbing dick penetrating the lead man's gorgeous native princess on the ideal tropical island. But the lead man was still thinking about getting laid on the tropical island paradise, and ignored the following man's loud cry for assistance.

"I say Bill; I've fuckin' double sprained my right ankle!" the second injured victim hollered. But the man in front again ignored his companion's entreaty, as the leader awkwardly stumbled onward through the icy-cold, shallow river. The first fellow's eyes were like those of a dazed, wounded deer, as his distracted mind pleasurably imagined experiencing a wonderful sperm ejaculation. Then Bill ascended up the stream's embankment without ever looking back and acknowledging his faltering companion. 'I'll now think about my next fuckin' sexual fantasy!' the lead hiker selfishly considered. 'Yes, fantasy! That's really the only fuckin' thing that's keepin' me alive,' Bill concluded, trudging ahead.

The man left stranded in the stream still had sufficient energy to give his abandoner a stiff middle finger. His lips were trembling from his pain and from his general exhaustion. A rough mustache and a thatch of brown hair encircled his quivering lips. The beleaguered man's tongue moistened his mouth, and the fellow was pretending that he was licking the imaginary native princess's hairy beaver on that wonderful, fanciful tropical island.

"Bill!" the left-behind man yelled with all of his strength. "Don't leave me out here all alone, you fuckin' degenerate!"

But Bill never turned his head to recognize his friend's desperate plea. William kept on lurching forward up the embankment toward the dull gray skyline, where his sex-starved mind now imagined that a dozen horny babes on another tropical island were wildly masturbating and waiting for him to arrive. 'I hear the bastard callin' me, but I don't give a shit about Jack!' Bill thought. 'I don't care Jack about Jack. I'm gonna' keep all my gold, and sail from Tahiti out to Samoa, so that I won't have to dream about *some moa'* goddamned pretend sex! I want the real fuckin' thing!'

The deserted man stared ahead in the direction of Bill, and Jack observed his friend's form passing through the mists and vapors as if he had entered an atmospheric portal into another weird dimension. While placing his weight on his good ankle, the abandoned man standing in the frigid stream still possessed the wherewithal to pull-out his watch, which faithfully indicated four o'clock.

'It's just about the First of August, and the damned sun is in the northeast,' Jack perceptively reckoned. 'The Great Bear Lake is to the south, and then after that lies the Canadian Barrens. I wanta' fuckin' stay away from that desolate place. And this stream I'm in feeds into the Coppermine River, which flows into Coronation Gulf near the Arctic Ocean. God, I'm sure glad I won that shitin' Geography Bee in elementary school!'

The man again surveyed his bleak environment of low-lying hills that were devoid of vegetation. 'No damned trees, shrubs, grass or ladies' bushes,' Jack regretted. 'And Bill still has two good legs, and the determined bastard is liable to eventually make it back to civilization and to the nearest whorehouse, way before I do. Fuck you Bill, even if ya' gotta' be sodomized! Fuck you I say!' Jack mentally repeated in what constituted an introspective rage.

The abandoned man stood shivering in the icy water, cowered-down, and then examined the empty gun in his hand. His shaking allowed the gun to fall from his grasp into the cold stream, and the almost-delirious fellow groped in the water until his searching hands finally located the weapon. Then, Jack weakly trudged-out of the stream onto the solid, hard, frozen land. 'Why the fuck did I ever leave San Diego?' the prospector wondered and regretted. 'Now I remember. I wanted to find gold up here in Alaska. I'd rather die of venereal disease recalling fond prostitute memories than drown is this lousy, scumbag creek, and wind-up being polar bear food,' the wincing man mused.

Next, the determined stream escapee struggled-up the rise and gradually reached the hill's crest. Jack noticed no trace of Bill limping forward, anywhere. Instead, the fellow's weary eyes perceived a shallow valley showing no signs of life, so Jack stubbornly lurched forward thinking about how Bill had left him in *his* moment of dire need, even though his fiendish friend was hallucinating and didn't know what the hell he was actually doing.

'Jack and Bill went up the hill, to fetch two sacks of gold,' the man from sunny California recollected and laughed. 'Jack fell-down and sprained his leg, and Bill never heard his partner beg! Fine partner I've been fuckin' associated with!'

The valley's basin was extremely soggy, and moss-covered rocks were prevalent in that God-forsaken sector of the Alaskan Tundra. Each time the man struggled a step forward, the muddy water squirted out from under his boots, causing a sucking sound, which immediately made the survivor fantasize about getting the best Samoan blowjob of his life. Jack slowly meandered through the muskeg *marsh,* looking for delicious marshmallows to eat, and then sampled the disgusting mint-green moss, only to spit the foul-tasting slime out of his mouth. But Jack was as doomed as Biblical Abel.

'I'm not lost, even though I'm all alone,' Jack pensively and hopefully pondered. 'Pretty soon, I'll be south enough to reach the dead, stunted trees on the shores of the little lake the Eskimos call the *titchin-nichille*. That means 'little sticks', and logically, they're the only kind of erections the damned Eskimos could achieve in this fuckin' frigid temperature. I'll locate the stream and follow it to the Dease River, where *our* cache of supplies is hidden under the overturned canoe. I'll be able to find my gun bullets, fishhooks, lines, a small net, flour, bacon, beans, and my treasured porno' magazines,' Jack remembered, enjoying a brief moment of felicity. 'Yes; the memory of those fuckin' porno' magazines; *that* is really the only goddamned thing keepin' me alive. There aren't any boondocks out here to be out in the boondocks, and there are no sticks around here to be even out in the goddamned *titchin-nichille!'*

‘When I regain my full strength,’ Jack reckoned, ‘I’ll locate the hidden canoe and paddle-down the Dease to the Mackenzie River, and successfully race south ahead of the encroaching winter. Next, I’ll finally reach the Taiga, where the frontier Hudson Bay Company post had been constructed in the northernmost coniferous tree line. Food will be aplenty, and after being rejuvenated, I could then use my precious gold to hire the myriad services of several enterprising, itinerant Eskimo prostitutes.’

And meanwhile, Jack still possessed some semblance of distorted reality. ‘Bill will probably be waiting at the cache with Tippycanoe and Tyler, too,’ Jack’s inventive mind fabricated. ‘I haven’t eaten for two days, and for the first time in my life, I actually desire chomping on food more than eating juicy, succulent pussy!’

So, the man stooped-down and picked-up a handful of bitter-tasting muskeg berries and carefully chucked them into his mouth. And as Jack chewed on the sour-flavored vegetation, he imagined that even dingle-berries would taste better than a handful of friggin’ mushy muskeg berries.

The distracted trekker seriously stubbed his big right toe on a protruding rock at nine o’clock. Jack faltered and then toppled over in response to the pulsing excruciation inside his big right toe, which augmented the pulsating pain in his double sprained right ankle. He knelt-down on the permafrost and roughly slipped off his backpack straps, wishing that he could convert to being a Muslim, die, and then shack-up in heaven with a minimum of seven virgins eager to lose their virginity. As twilight settled in the eastern sky, the man built a fire out of dried moss, and then heated a tin pot of water to drink in the absence of good hard whiskey.

Jack next unwrapped his pack, and with his mind in a bewildered, fuzzy state, meticulously counted his remaining matches, and twelve consecutive times the counter reached the sum of sixty-seven, wishing he had two more so that he could contemplate ‘sixty-nine’. Bill’s paranoid, left-behind companion divided the matches into three piles, and then placed one pile into his empty tobacco pouch, the second handful in his pants’ pocket, and the third batch inside his battered and tattered hat’s headband.

‘I can’t remember how many matches I have,’ Jack thought while doubting his own judgment. So, the perplexed survivor counted his three sums an additional time to verify the validity of his former mathematical determination.

Jack placed his wet boots next to the smoldering fire, and then he briefly removed his socks and examined his abused feet, which were pallid, lacerated, and bleeding. 'I'm glad my dick and my ass aren't in the same condition,' his twisted mind considered. 'Then, I would need four socks. Two socks would cover my tender feet, and another pair for my dick and my ass to wear. And my ankle's' now the size of my knee, and my knee looks like a baby watermelon. Christ! I must have *water*melon on the knee!' his warped, exhausted, deteriorating mind deducted. 'And this fuckin' swollen big toe is really aggravatin' my excruciating gout condition.'

The gold prospector tore the seam strips from one of his two blue blankets and recklessly bound them around his severely injured right ankle. The rest of the strips Jack ingeniously used to wrap around his feet to serve as suitable protection until his saturated socks would dry near the gentle fire. Next, Jack poured the hot water into a tin cup and greedily drank, pretending that the bland liquid was powerful rye whiskey. He next wound-up his watch, momentarily studied the heavens, crawled between his blue blankets, and finally dozed-off.

The Land of the Setting Sun had only brief darkness around midnight, and soon, the Earth's nearest star rose in the northeast, and the flickering object was discernible amidst ominous gray clouds. Jack woke-up hungry, and realized that he required nutrition to continue his arduous journey to the hidden cache stashed under the hidden, inverted canoe. He turned over and then shrieked to the barren wilderness, "Holy shit! I need a delicious fuckin' sizzlin' steak!"

A nearby bull caribou had been inspecting with curiosity Jack sleeping, tossing and turning on the cold ground. The nervous man heard snorting and then fully awoke. 'That bastard animal probably wishes he was a wolf rather than a weak grass eater,' the man suspected. 'I sorta' wish that he was a goddamned wolf, too!' "Eat me, you son-of-a-bitch!" Jack futilely screamed, scaring the bull caribou into thinking about flight and about sex with its mate, rather than wasting time studying a stupid, silly, sleeping human stranded many miles from civilization.

Jack instinctively reached for his gun, pulled the trigger, but no bullet was released from the chamber. The bull caribou soon had escaped the desperate man's range of vision. At that moment, the lonely human wished that he did have a bullet in his pistol's chamber to blow his own brains out, and escape to Muslim heaven and start pumping the poop out of those seven gorgeous, horny virgins.

In sheer contempt of his hostile environment, the miserable fellow groaned and finally managed to stand and assume an erect posture. The commonplace task of standing required a full minute to complete, because Jack's joints felt like rusty door hinges needing lubrication, and his tender ass felt like it weighed the equivalency of a ton of bricks. Next, the aggrieved prospector attempted taking a leak, but that simple process required a full half hour to perform, mostly because of faulty internal plumbing, along with a bad case of bladderwort infecting his aching bladder.

The weary survivor stumbled and crawled up a small knoll, and still had the presence of mind to survey the distant scenario. Everything appeared gray, including the prospect of *his* returning to the overturned canoe. The lakelets, sky, moss, rocks, streams and distant caribou all were gray, symbolizing stark uncertainty, old age, and the encroachment of death. 'I've lost my fuckin' sense of direction!' Jack eventually realized. 'But now, I remember! I'll just proceed in the opposite direction from which I came! I say, how many fuckin' matches do I have left! I'd better count the suckers again just to make sure I'm in control of my sanity!'

After carefully tabulating and double-checking his matches, Jack seriously considered having 'sixty-nine' instead of '67' with the bull caribou, but then immediately exited his peculiar delusion when the beast (in his mental manifestation) started kicking the man's face with its hooves as it started to orgasm. 'Christ! My mind is really fucked-up now!' Jack concluded. 'I gotta' use-up another match, burn and singe my numb finger, and get this friggin' sixty-nine bullshit fixation out of my goddamned head!'

Then, the delusional prospector assessed his moose-hide sack containing fifteen-pounds of gold nuggets. 'Should I discard this precious ore?' Jack wondered and evaluated. 'It's fuckin' weighin' me down, and it means nothin' at all to the goddamned caribou and wolves in this most secluded part of Alaska. Oh well, I'll take it with me in hopes that I can reach the Hudson Bay outpost and buy some sixty-nine with a decent hooker rather than dream a nightmare of doin' it with a fuckin' male caribou! Damn it! I gotta' use up one more of my freakin' matches, or else I'll fuckin' go insane!'

Hunger pangs gnawed-away inside Jack's stomach as he fancifully craved all sorts of food, and would even kill and cannibalize a weak vegetarian caribou if one were within choking range. He haphazardly descended into the ugly-empty valley, where rock ptarmigan rose with flapping wings, pecking away at the scattered muskeg berries. "Ker, ker, ker" the birds squawked as their beaks picked at the tart berries randomly growing between rocks and ledges. Jack pathetically stalked the bad-tempered birds on his knees, just as a hungry cat might hunt a family of yard birds (outside a prison). His abused legs left a blood trail as the hapless man squirmed and wriggled over wet moss and rocks, futilely attempting to clutch and strangle an unwary mother ptarmigan nesting its young.

"Ker, ker, ker," the disturbed birds mocked as they communicated danger to one another.

"Fuck! Fuck! Fuck!" Jack answered in frustration, repeating in his language what he had interpreted "Ker, ker, ker!" had meant to the apprehensive wary ptarmigans.

Almost in tears, the thwarted man crawled-upon what must have been a sleeping deaf bird. Jack impetuously grasped at the suddenly surprised creature, which quickly regained its consciousness, and frantically flew-off. Only three gray tail feathers were present in the man's dirt-smeared palm. "Come back and retrieve your ass-end steering feathers!" Jack yelled to the escaped ptarmigan flying overhead in a circle. "Come back you fuckin' birdbrain, and I'll surely kill your ass the second time around!"

The dazed man rose and clumsily tripped his way forward. In the afternoon, the disoriented fellow entered a valley of marshes where animal life was more abundant. Twenty caribou played peek-a-boo with him, and aimlessly ambled and grazed a hundred yards away. 'If only I had a loaded rifle,' Jack thought. 'I would easily take-down the biggest of the herd. And if I could sprint, I could surely catch the swiftest of the pack. Holy Christ! Are my totally angled thoughts fucked-up, or what?'

A black fox accidentally came ambling toward the incoherent man, and it was carrying a squealing ptarmigan in its mouth. "Drop that fuckin' bird!" Jack shouted at the sly fox, which quickly and skillfully leaped-away onto higher rock ledges, and then hastily disappeared over a hill's crest. 'Even sloppy seconds from a wily fox seems tantalizing,' the desperate man supposed in self-sympathy.

Jack then glanced-down at his dungaree zipper. 'The next thing I gotta' prevent from happenin' is to keep that freakin' fox away from *my* damned bird, especially since *he* carries his cherished food away to eat and enjoy in secrecy!'

The overwhelmed man came upon a milky, lime-colored stream that flowed through multi-shaped patches of green grass. Jack pulled the grass rushes up from their roots, which to his jumbled mind, reminded him of onion sprouts, hardly the size of a pinky fingernail. The fibers were tough and stringy, and the small bulbs were hardly as palatable as the famished man had wished.

And next, the tenacious struggler got-down on his hands and knees and wildly foraged and munched the grass like a distraught bovine would, even though Jack hated everything about cows, including their sweet milk. 'I'd much rather have a nice juicy *Porterhouse* and chew the fat with a homosexual friend, rather than to suffer the indignity of lying here in this isolated marsh imitating a lowly cow chewing its cud!' the weary wanderer decided. Then, another basic consideration surfaced in the all-too-frustrated prospector's troubled cerebrum.

'Damn it; I wanna' find some nourishing food,' Jack lamented. 'I need meat! I'd even eat live frogs, or squiggly worms, if I could only find them!' the pathetic wanderer thought as he aggressively dug away into the muddy marsh grass with his fingernails. 'I'd even eat a horny toad! God, how I really love frog legs! Shit! No frogs, toads, or worms live in this far-northern wasteland, but I'm gonna' keep on diggin' for reptiles and amphibians, anyway!'

Jack searched every shallow water pool hoping, to see a small fish. And then, almost miraculously, the fanatic spotted a tiny old *minnow* that, to his warped mind, looked like it was a carryover from the ancient Greek *Minoan* civilization. The starving fellow plunged his arm up to his shoulder into the cold pool, but the daylight had been refracted, going from the medium of air to the medium of water, and the slippery minnow eluded his frantic lunge. The incensed man then used both hands exploring the depths of the pool, trying to use tactile sensation to locate the tiny old fish, which nearly had died from fright during its most recent misadventure. The unfortunate human fell and splashed into the murky marsh, getting wet up to his chest.

'I have to wait until the sediments settle so that the water is clear again,' he concluded. 'I must stay on task and not lose sight of my *mission!'* the food searcher thought as his destitute mind conjured-up an image of the *Alamo.*

After the muddy water became somewhat clear again, Jack attempted capturing the evasive minnow, which again wildly avoided his frenetic effort. The encumbered man anxiously began bailing water out of the pool with his tin cup, while boisterously screaming, "Everybody out of the pool! Everybody out of the fuckin' pool!" the asshole shrieked as if he was a maniacal lifeguard. His freezing hands were shaking, and his heart was rhythmically pounding inside his chest cavity. In a half hour, the pool was nearly empty. The tiny fish had managed to squeeze itself though a tiny crevice between two stones, and had escaped to a larger adjoining pool that was big enough for a small whale to swim in.

'Damn it!' Jack mentally cursed. 'If I had known of that fuckin' crevice, I could've plugged it up.' Then, the famished fellow's attention was directed toward his rusty zipper. 'Shit!' he realized. 'My limp pecker will never again plug-up any damned female crevice, diminutive or otherwise, unless I fuckin' find some food fast!'

The virtually-defeated, lost rambler slowly climbed out of the freezing-cold pool and rolled over upon the wet ground. Jack cried loudly to the apathetic and heartless marshes, mountains, hills, and dull gray sky. His soul felt as desolate as his insensitive surroundings seemed to be.

In a moment of sheer inspiration, the stubborn survivor managed to build a campfire and warmed several quarts of hot water, which he indulgently gulped-down to keep his fragile body warm. Jack next conscientiously checked his supply of matches, and ascertained that they were still dry. 'Now I think I only have sixty-five.' he sulked. 'How the hell do you do sixty-five with a naked woman?'

Jack's blue blankets were moist and clammy, and his right ankle, knee, and big toe ached with incredibly intense pain. He again wound his watch and eventually fell asleep, dreaming of Viking feasts, of huge wedding banquets, of exotic Hawaiian luaus, of cheap Eskimo smorgasbords, and of fast-food brothels. The dozer awoke from his disturbing slumber feeling physically cold and emotionally irritated.

'What the fuck's goin' on?' the lost gent thought in disgust. 'Snow flurries are ornamentin' the hills, makin' them pure white; and a heavy wind is blowin'. The dampness from the larger flakes has put out my fire! Why the fuck was I ever born!'

The poor soul carelessly packed his wet gear, awkwardly strapped the blankets to his back, and proceeded onward. 'Fuck the land of the little sticks, and the cache under the canoe on the bank of the Dease. All I wanna' do is eat some grub. I can't believe I'd rather eat broccoli or celery than savory wet pink pussy! I must be turnin' into either a goddamned lame wimp, or a fuckin' gay son-of-a-bitch! One thing's for damned sure!' Jack irrationally decided. 'I'll never follow Bill into the goddamned wilderness again, gold or no goddamned gold nuggets!'

The pessimistic adventurer again stared at his heavy moose-hide sack of gold. 'This sucker's weighin' me down,' the trekker assessed. 'It's worth a fortune anywhere in the Klondike or the Yukon, but it ain't worth shit out here with the various hungry animals. No creature would accept a fuckin' ransom for me, that's for damned sure! But I'll try and preserve my strength to carry the sack to the damned Dease. Then, the gold will be worth something again!'

Jack re-cinched his ankle with his blanket strips, and blood oozed through the fabric. The hilltop snow had partially melted, and after identifying the position of the morning sun, the man valiantly set-out on his quest to reach the secret cache. 'I gotta' go about five degrees to the right,' the left-behind man roughly estimated. 'I believe I've gone slightly off course. I don't want to wind-up somewhere in shitin' Siberia or fuckin' Antarctica.'

The man's tongue felt dry and enlarged as he trudged along. He frequently paused to rest, and his heart was irregularly palpitating, going "thump, thump thump" as if it was a big brass drum lodged deep in his thorax. 'My goddamned parched tongue feels like it's growin' hair!' Jack thought. 'Could it be that it's turnin' into a woman's fuzzy beaver?'

The woebegone trekker came upon a fairly large marsh pool with two minnows darting about in it. 'This damned basin is too large to bail-out!' the observer accurately determined. Showing less excitement at finding a marsh pool than he had exhibited before, Jack slowly pushed his tin prospecting bucket through the water's surface and (through noteworthy perseverance) managed to isolate and catch several of the small creatures. And then after taking a deep breath, he thrust the wiggling fish into his mouth, and avariciously chewed them raw, all-the-while imagining that he was enjoying a wonderfully delectable baked flounder dinner.

That evening, Jack successfully caught three more minnows and saved them for breakfast. 'I gotta' cover at least ten miles a day,' the prospector reckoned. 'I gotta' stay strong. The goddamned wolves are huntin' the old and weak caribou. I can hear the carnivorous critters howlin' in the distance. Fuck breakfast! I better *wolf* down these three squiggly fish before those friggin' wolves wolf both me and my arrogance down.'

The perplexed man had a tough decision to make, and finally rationality triumphed over greed. Jack divided his gold nuggets into two piles. He stashed half into a crack in a prominent ledge inside some blanket material, and the remaining half he returned to his *moose-hide* sack, which entirely was too small for even a baby moose to hide inside of. 'I'll keep my gun for as long as I can,' the grim-faced struggler convinced himself. 'I can get ammo' when I finally reach the overturned canoe. I might even need bullets to kill Bill, that fuckin' dirty, faggot prick!'

Jack was overwhelmed from giddiness that had been caused by a lack of nutrition and plenty of weariness. His bewildered and befuddled brain was as befogged as the strange-looking atmosphere. He stumbled and fell five times, got-up, and continued his weird one-man procession. His bedraggled body stumbled a sixth time, falling squarely into a well-concealed ptarmigan nest. Jack's blurred vision detected four squealing, newly hatched chicks, little day-old specks of life. The man honored his impulse to act quickly.

The desperate human eagerly hi*jacked* the tiny birds, flung them into his mouth, and chewed them ravenously (ptarmiganly), his teeth crunching them as if they were shelled peanuts. 'These little critters taste much better than those tart minnows did,' the starving trekker reasoned and appreciated. 'I can't wait to find and catch a warty frog, or a couple of earthworms, and see if I like the taste of them better!'

The alarmed mother ptarmigan returned from scavenging food, tried protecting her nest, and chirped and squawked all about, just managing to elude Jack's wild lunges. The prospector endeavored using his gun as a suitable club, but the annoyed bird dodged his erratic thrusts. He then hurled stones at the protesting bird, one of which injured her right wing. The distressed mother ptarmigan forgot all about her maternal instinct, entered a survival mode, and subsequently always maneuvered to stay several steps away from Jack's incessant clutching and smashing.

'Those chicks have whetted my appetite,' Jack realized. 'A bird in the hand is worth two in the bush!' the crazed Californian concluded as he lustily rubbed his limp *Johnson* while pursuing the thoroughly agitated 'lady-bird'.

The chase brought Jack across several swampy swales in the bottom of the valley where his fertile mind conjured-up a half-dozen valley girls masturbating like crazy. Then, amazingly, the dazed pursuer discovered recently formed footprints. 'Those suckers look like Bill's,' Jack theorized. 'They must be Bill's. That snot-nosed bastard must not be far ahead. I know the six valley girls are safe from molestation, because my buddy Bill's a goddamned, impotent, one-balled, homosexual.'

The mother ptarmigan lay exhausted ten feet in front of Jack's grasp, but the exhausted predator lacked the stamina or the will to leap and land upon her. But the man and the bird required rest, and both existed only ten-feet apart from one another. 'No more smorgasbords!' Jack mused in despair. 'And when the guy mustered-up sufficient power to lurch forward, the petulant-but-frightened mother bird also had reserve energy to elude his exaggerated effort by nervously fluttering and hopping forward. Jack tripped and fell flush on his face, cutting his pallid cheeks and chin between two sharp-edged stones. The courageous man did not move a muscle for an hour. Then, he diligently wound his watch, shit his pants, and went to sleep.

The following foggy morning, a nasty wind and a light drizzle had completely obscured Bill's footprints. By midday, the weight of the backpack became too oppressive, so Jack discarded the balance of his gold nuggets, and blatantly cursed man's proclivity toward valuing avarice. Starvation was setting in, so the temporarily lost soul also threw-away several items of necessity, and carried only his blanket, the tin sifting bucket, his knife, and his gun.

'I'm so goddamned hungry I'd even eat a smelly Eskimo hair pie,' Jack whimsically reflected for a moment. 'I believe I have one bullet remaining in my gun.' He industriously checked the weapon and was dismayed that his hope turned-out to be a mere fantasy. Jack next plodded and tramped ahead in disappointment, trying to ascertain how reality and his imagination had merged into one entity.

During the next two hours, the plodder fancifully inspected his gun six times, searching for the indispensable bullet that his undependable mind had created. The serious hunger pangs were increasing in severity and in frequency. The man robotically advanced southward, acting like a strange automaton devoid of compassion, self-sympathy, or other common human feelings. Suddenly, a fierce sight caught the trekker's immediate attention.

'Holy horseshit!' Jack's mind thought. 'It's a giant bear lookin' for its next meal!'

The ferocious carnivore was studying the pathetic hiker with bellicose scrutiny. 'I must do something before the animal goes into an irreversible attack mode!' Jack decided. 'If I run, I'm dead meat; and if I fight; I'm dead meat! I'm about to get my ass kicked and eaten! This is all ironically fuckin' un*bear*able!'

Jack remembered that he had not thrown away his trusty hunting knife that remained fastened to a leather sheath strapped to his belt. He touched its pointed blade, making certain that it was sharp. The worried gold rush participant's strained heart again began beating irregularly, and he felt as if his knees were wobbling and about to buckle. 'I'm going to pass out!' he frightfully thought.

In a gesture of total desperation, the dumb-ass man rushed forward with his raised knife and screamed as loud as he could, 'I'm gonna' kill you, you fuckin' ugly brown bastard!' The bear reared-up in a defensive, combative posture, considered its circumstances, and then retreated back three steps. Jack's grisly eyes met those of the big grizzly, and the man menacingly growled as the shouter crazily gestured with the raised knife. His startling animation had effectively intimidated the fierce predator, which was momentarily stunned by the mysterious human's uncharacteristic antics. Jack stood still as a statue, and then commenced roaring in imitation of a vicious circus lion he once saw as a boy. The gigantic, brown bear scampered-away on all fours, figuring that it would judiciously select a less insane and more predictable prey for its next meal.

The man wept and sobbed for a full half-hour; his psyche had been completely overwhelmed by his latest bizarre ordeal. 'I don't give a flyin' shit about dying like a man!' Jack contemplated and wept. 'I don't want to be violently ripped to shreds and then devoured by a fuckin' wild, ferocious Alaskan bear, or consumed by a pack of savage wolves. Oh, dear God; isn't my troubled soul deserving of a more favorable fate?'

Over the next several hours, full-bellied wolves crossed his path in packs of three and four, but the wily predators steered clear of the vertical creature weeping and screaming like a mental patient escaped from an insane asylum. The carnivores were hunting and feasting off of old, weak and young caribou, which did not stab, or scratch, or bite like the weird human standing and shouting crazy expletives in a threatening, erect, defensive stance.

An hour later, Jack discovered scattered caribou *calf'* bones. The backpacker felt the rear of his knees and thought, 'I'm fuckin' lucky to still have my two *calves* attached to my legs. Look what the fuck those carnivorous wolves have done to this poor, innocent, grass-eating animal!'

And then, the unstable man did something grotesque and unthinkably primitive. He solemnly touched the bones and thought, 'Is this what the fuck I'm gonna' look like tomorrow? These remains can't be Bill's dismantled skeleton!' And then an additional thought brought some consolation to *his* chaotic mind. 'There is no pain or suffering in death! Only the desire to live brings about misery, hurt, and anguish! Heaven, please help me! I'm not ready to fuckin' die!'

Jack was soon squatting in the damp moss, and sucking on a pink bone, biting off every savory shred of flesh and available sustenance left behind by the already-satisfied wolves. The sweet meaty taste sent Jack's mind into a mild ecstasy. He chomped-down on the bone with his weak jaws. Sometimes the caribou's bone broke exposing its rich marrow. Sometimes the intense crush broke several of Jack's molars.

Then, the almost-vanquished man had an inspiration. He smashed the bones against the nearby rocks, pounding them into small fragments, and then Jack swallowed the almost-pulverized remains. His fingers were bleeding from the times his descending rock missed the bone, or when the white femur or clavicle broke, scraping the skin off of his exposed knuckles and wrists. 'I'm livin' like a freakin' caveman!' the man sobbed and anguished in languish. 'Neanderthals had more dignity than I have right now. At least those primitive assholes had the security of bein' with their moronic family upon leaving *this* life!'

The next two days featured a mixture of snow, sleet, and rain, and Jack behaved like a machine that was not synchronized with its environment. His sleeping patterns were irregular, with him traveling both during the day and at night. Sometimes, the despondent man gingerly walked, and other times, he irresponsibly crawled and groveled. Jack was unwilling to surrender his soul to death's beckoning. He repeatedly made, and then quickly broke camp at whim, and did not honor any standard practice or regular habit.

The desperate survivor carried in his pack remnants of the caribou calf's bones, and he actively sucked and crunched them whenever he felt a need to react to his biological compulsions to eat and live. Jack now loyally followed a wide, fast-flowing stream, and his hazy mind was filled with exotic visions and mirages, none of which were entirely comprehensible.

The following morning, the tormented nomad awoke; his body lying on a rocky ledge. The wanderer felt the sun's rays shining upon his countenance, and heard the sounds of curious caribou calves to his left. 'I want to live, and I also want to die!' he ambivalently thought as his disoriented mind grappled with fathoming the significance of the two extreme alternatives. 'But if pain, anguish, and suffering are all that fuckin' life has to offer,' the lost fellow regrettably pondered, 'in the final analysis, I would prefer dying.'

But the warm sun reflected off his bearded face, and provided the obstinate man with encouragement to continue his intrepid travail. He rolled onto his side and perceived the wide fast-flowing stream, the identity of which challenged and puzzled his memory. Jack observed the dismal, bare, distant hills devoid of vegetation. Only the river valley had grass and caribou feeding off the vegetation supply, and eager wolves feasting off the healthy, captured caribou. The worried man's emotional state was very melancholy, and quite apparently, now lacked interest, motivation and enthusiasm.

As the pitiful human gawked into the distance, he believed his mind was playing cruel tricks on him. 'There's a ship out there on the shining sea,' Jack interpreted and comprehended. He closed his eyelids, opened them, and then rubbed his face to confirm his recognition of the familiar object outlined on the horizon. 'It is a ship anchored in a bay, and several small islands are surrounding it. I wonder if they're the friggin' *Illusion Islands* between Alaska and Siberia!' his giddy mind mused. 'I gotta' get my bearings straight!'

The hopeful vision persisted, and did not fade into oblivion, and *that* particular realization (mirage) energized Jack's spirit and afforded his weakened heart the far-fetched prospect of being rescued.

But then, the obstinate trekker's soul plunged into despair. 'There's no bullet in my friggin' gun,' he sadly remembered. 'And also, no ship on the shining sea. What a fuckin' living nightmare those goddamned lousy illusions are!'

The vanquished explorer soon heard a snuffle behind him, that was actually a combination cough and pant. He shifted his body weight and witnessed a most despicable companion. Jack noticed the gray head of a wolf, and its primitive-looking jade eyes were greedily peering at him through several jagged rocks, twenty or so feet away. The predator's green eyes were glassy and bloodshot, and its head was drooping, and almost crestfallen. The animal blinked as if it too was witnessing a terrible mirage.

'What the fuck's this shit?' Jack thought in total consternation. 'A fuckin' sick wolf! And the goddamned bastard is waitin' for me to expire so that it could enjoy its last meal. What a travesty of justice if a dumb abstraction such as justice exists in this survival-of-the-fittest animal world!' the giddy man neurotically considered. 'If there's justice anywhere in this fucked-up misadventure of mine, it must indeed be a freakin' miscarriage of justice!'

Jack turned his bloodied head left toward the nebulous ship upon the shining sea, and then rotated it right toward the very real diseased wolf, and the befuddled observer attempted to plausibly distinguish between the 'dual mirages'. Then, the suffering man chuckled. 'A weak dying wolf! What utter irony! What a fuckin' appropriate fateful conclusion to a goddamned, meaningless human life!'

The whimpering sufferer closed his eyes and reviewed the dramatic events of the past few days. His difficult journey had been heading south by southwest, moving away from the Dease Divide in the direction of the fabled Coppermine River. His unexpected destination was well-defined on the wall map at the Hudson Bay Company outpost. 'That damned shining sea is the majestic Arctic Ocean!' Jack hypothesized. 'And there's a damned whaling ship anchored in Coronation Gulf! God save both the Queen of England and my lily-white ass!'

The hope of deliverance gave the temporarily defeated man additional emotional energy. He carefully felt his aching feet, which were now deformed lumps of raw meat. 'My fuckin' gun and knife are now several miles behind me,' Jack reasoned. 'I still have matches in my pocket. It's eleven o'clock,' his brain realized and stared blankly at his still-ticking watch. 'I've been through too much to simply give-up and sacrifice my life and my body to a goddamned, sick, gangrened, lustful wolf!'

The beleaguered man attempted remaining calm and prudent. All awareness of pain had now disappeared, and even his lips and fingertips had little sensation. Jack thought of swallowing food, but that ignorant idea made him feel nauseous, and his stomach felt like vomiting. The unfortunate gold prospector re-cinched his swollen ankle, causing blood to drip upon the surrounding rocks. 'I still have my tin cup and my matches,' he doggedly considered. 'I'll be able to drink boilin' water and kill off the bacteria. I wonder if I could set the wolf on fire? That's one fuckin' advantage I still have. The wonder of fire is my staunchest ally over that repulsive, sick animal.'

Jack's hands now shook as if he was afflicted with a palsy. He gathered dry moss into a heap to ignite into an improvised blaze. Man's mastery of fire could be used against the filthy offensive wolf. 'He's probably been abandoned by his pack, just like Bill had abandoned me,' Jack accurately concluded. 'How terribly merciless and inhumane could nature be?'

The brave man inched forward toward the diseased wolf and peered directly into the creature's glassy, bloodshot eyes. The animal was still fearful of Jack's unorthodox behavior, and the wolf reluctantly yielded territory to the crazed, strange-behaving human. The wolf greedily licked the sides of its mouth, contemplating food (once Jack would die), but the man noticed that the revolting beast had hardly the strength to curl its flaccid tongue.

'Jesus H. Christ!' the dejected man thought. 'The goddamned enlarged tongue isn't even red! It's yellowish-brown, and coated with a layer of thick, germ-infested mucus! I'm not goin' to be this hideous, diseased animal's next son-of-a-bitchin' meal. No way!'

After Jack drank nearly a liter of hot water, the injured prospector found that he still possessed adequate strength to rise-up on his abused feet and stand almost erect. 'If I die, it'll be with a man's dignity, and not with a sheep's cowardice!' Jack proudly thought. 'I can walk at least four-miles toward the ship anchored on the bay, even in this debilitated condition. I hope the ship's not an illusion created by my horribly stressed-out psyche!'

All night long, Jack habitually blinked his eyelids and could not fall asleep. The sick wolf's coughing and wheezing, along with the squawking of distant ptarmigan and caribou, kept him awake. 'I am this sick wolf's only hope of living,' Jack pragmatically evaluated. 'If I live, it fuckin' dies! If I die, it fuckin' lives! Fuck philosophy! The basic formula is so amazingly simple, yet at the same time, so terribly brutal!'

The repulsive creature stood on its four legs, assessing Jack's every movement, including his most recent bowel movement. Its mangy tail was tucked between its legs in a subordinate, defensive position, and the sickly animal lacked the strength to even snarl or moan. It very deliberately and slowly skulked in a circle around the frightened human, who now regarded the dying beast as a mutual companion in suffering. The infected wolf even seemed to broadly grin at Jack's rueful face, when the shocked human orally addressed the disgusting, sick animal, using sarcastic and obscene language.

That afternoon, the weak man's legs dragged his vulnerable frame three-miles forward, but fatigue rapidly set-in, and soon Jack was slowly advancing on all fours, just like the sick wolf that was avariciously trailing him. 'Thank God it's an Indian summer day. If it were three weeks from now, my Caucasian butt couldn't be distinguished from an icicle's asshole in broad daylight!'

As Jack slowly progressed on all fours toward the glittering ship on the shining sea, his form came across a small pond where he triumphantly captured four minnows in his tin cup. "Here," he declared to the diseased wolf while tossing the smallest of the fish before the creature's maw. "Eat to your goddamned heart's content. You've been officially reduced to a lousy, goddamned scavenger, just like me, but I see that you don't give a shit!"

Jack crawled along for several-hundred-yards, following the trail of another man that had also crawled that doomed path. A heap of fresh-chewed bones was surrounded by wolf footpad marks that had been imprinted in the soggy moss. The recent arrival observed a moose-hide sack, similar to the one he had been carrying, and Jack automatically theorized that the skeletal remains were those of Bill. "These pinky, white bones are yours, Bill," Jack acknowledged and sobbed with tears forming in his eyes. "But don't worry, good buddy! I will not suck your bones. I'm not a fuckin' cannibal, or any goddamned fuckin' civilized queer, either. I'll never suck another man's bone! Never I say!"

An hour later, the distraught, paranoid man arrived at a deep pond of water where the deflected sunlight reflected his wretched-looking face. He spotted three minnows swimming inside the pool, and thrust his arm inside the cold water in an unsuccessful attempt to acquire his next snack. 'I'm afraid that if I accidentally tumble into the pond, I'll certainly drown,' Jack regretted. 'And I know that I could easily friggin' drown in only six inches of water if I was lyin' on my face. Tell me, bitter destiny; explain to me, fate; how the hell did I get to be so totally fucked-up in this totally fucked-up world?'

The next morning and afternoon, Jack was able to exhaustively stumble and crawl three-additional-miles towards the tantalizing gleaming ship upon the shining sea, and the following day, his labor gained him two-more-miles. 'This is how Bill expired,' Jack remorsefully thought. 'He was crawling, and fainting, and sleeping, and inching his way, but his labor was all in vain. Who needs this raunchy crap? Who needs this fuckin' Alaska Tundra shit?' the man's addled and cluttered mind questioned.

And then, as Jack turned his head, his pupils observed the lugubrious-looking, infected wolf diligently licking *his* trail of crimson with its gruesome, enlarged, yellowish-brown tongue. But the defiant man was adamant about persevering and enduring, so he pulled and dragged his abused carcass across the desolate ground with the wolf scavenging and licking-up his recently shed blood.

'If the wolf were a healthy one, I would gladly surrender to death,' Jack contemplated. 'But since the ugly bastard is diseased, the thought of him eating my flesh is absolutely repugnant. I'd prefer sucking Bill's raunchy dick when *he* was alive rather than have this son-of-a-bitchin' loathsome disgrace of its breed biting my tender ass and sensitive balls off!'

Jack's intervals of lucid mental activity now alternately appeared into, and then quickly faded from his addled mind, in more rapid succession. Hallucinations perplexed his perception and cognizance, and doubt plagued his sensibilities, especially his misgivings about the 'artificial glistening ship on the shining sea'. Late that afternoon, the man was awakened from a deep slumber by a faint sniffle at his ear. When Jack reflexively moved his head, the rancid-furred wolf leaped back and stumbled, exhibiting an almost ludicrous, awkward demonstration of its current pathetic plight.

'I guess that the glowing ship's only about four-miles away now,' Jack estimated. 'That is to say, it's four-miles away if it's really a ship anchored in the bay.' The survivor rubbed his eyes so that his peepers could focus with more clarity. 'It has white sails; but fuck! I can't even crawl a half-mile, let alone four wicked miles! Why the fuck didn't I join the navy like my parents wanted me to do!' his wild madness sarcastically concluded. 'Then, I'd be a safe, contented sailor, standing at attention aboard that gleaming ship on the shining sea!'

The grief-stricken man closed his eyes and visualized his existence speeding toward a tunnel's entrance with a small intense bright light glowing at the other end. 'I'm dying!' he happily thought. 'Thank God I'm fuckin' finally dying!'

As Jack lay on his back gasping for his next breath, his left hand felt the sick wolf's putrid-smelling breath wheezing against his left cheek. Next, the petrified fellow felt the sick wolf's huge, discolored tongue pressing against his mud-smeared face. It's persistent lapping had the horrible feel of sandpaper grating against his almost-numb skin. 'I'll not move until the exact right moment!' Jack promised his in-flux conscience.

The wolf showed tremendous cunning and patience, but Jack's stubborn attitude was equal to his adversary's resolve. The man lay still for a whole half-day, allowing the wolf to gain confidence and to begin initiating its disrespectful feast. Jack dreamed of a spectacular beautiful blonde whispering in his ear, only to awaken to the despicable wolf's harsh, coarse tongue caressing his face and lips. 'This must be a gay fuckin' wolf that only wants to eventually lick my dick!' Jack conjectured during that very traumatic moment. 'I'm still vulnerable in the neck, and this scumbag scavenger is liable to accidentally puncture my throat and sever my goddamned jugular!'

Soon, the infected dying wolf's tongue began lapping at Jack's bleeding right hand. The animal's fangs pressed against the man's palm, and the diseased creature attempted to penetrate the already-lacerated skin. Jack wrapped his left arm around the wolf's neck, and the prey's mouth was soon full of flea-ridden, stench-smelling, dark, gray fur. 'I can't choke him to death, but I think I can sever the gross creature's throat with my teeth!' he hoped. 'Maybe I can smother the damned carnivorous wolf. Take that; you mangy, ugly, foul mother-fucker!'

Five-minutes later, the pathetic man's entire weight had pinned-down his immobilized adversary, and thirty-minutes thereafter, Jack felt a very unpleasant warm trickle rolling down his throat. 'He's dead!' the man realized and concluded. 'The mother-fucker's dead! My will has prevailed!' Then, the victor slowly rolled over, closed his bleary eyes, and dozed-off.

* * * * * * * * * * * * * *

A whaling ship, *The Bedford,* had brought a contingent of scientists to northern Alaska to expertly conduct pertinent experiments, and to assiduously record observations of polar flora and fauna. The alert sailors on the ship's main deck had binoculars, and noticed a large, strange creature moving like a crippled crustacean along a riverbank. The mariners instantly climbed into 'a whaling harpoon boat', and set-out to discover exactly what they had seen. Jack was squirming forward like a mammoth worm. He then was writhing and twisting about, wrangling and wrestling with an imaginary sick wolf in his volatile, semi-conscious mania.

Three weeks later, Jack sat-up in his bunk bed on *The Bedford* to disclose to his fascinated audience the elements of his incredible tale, which the listeners regarded as mostly bunk being told from a *bunk* bed. Tears cascaded down the man's cheeks as he recalled and vividly described each episode of his extraordinary adventure. Intermixed with his revelations about caribou, a bear, the gold, the ptarmigans, the sick wolf, and Bill's morbid fate, were recollections about his mother, his family, and sunny California. Somehow, orange groves got blended in with muskeg berries, and semi-tropical flowers were intermingled with lichens upon hard Arctic rocks, which added a certain dimension of implausibility to Jack's disheveled presentation.

The following morning, the rescued man sat in the ship's galley, and he gobbled-down his hardy breakfast as if he had just survived a horrendous famine. 'They're goin' to steal my fuckin' food!' the distrustful eater imagined and believed. 'These fuckin' surreptitious sailors and scientists are no different than that black fox and that bastard dying wolf! The scumbag bastards think my story's a gaudy lie!'

After breakfast, the rescued man briefly toured the ship, and paid particular attention to where all of the food had been stored. And he voraciously ate like a hog in heat, stuffing every available morsel into his mouth, making each bite swiftly disappear into his esophagus before any crumb could be stolen by his 'jealous and envious ship mates'. In three weeks, Jack had added four inches to his waist, and began exhibiting a most prodigious girth.

All the way from Alaska to San Francisco, Jack hoarded hardtack biscuits, filled his pockets with the crunchy crackers, and ate with suspicious eyes. He clandestinely hid and stuffed biscuits inside his mattress and also inside his bunk bed. Jack steadfastly guarded his 'highly coveted food supply' from the *Bedford's* 'less intelligent crewmembers'.

‘I must take precautions so that no one pilfers my goddamned food,’ Jack greedily imagined. ‘All of these treacherous son-of-a-bitches are ruthless! I must and will survive for the sake of my love of life!’

## About the Author

Jay Dubya is author' John Wiessner's pen name. John is a retired New Jersey public school English teacher, having diligently taught the subject for thirty-four years. John lives in Hammonton, New Jersey with wife Joanne and the couple has three grown sons.

Counting *London: Lashed, Lacerated, Lampooned and Lambasted,* along with its companion books *Twain: Tattered, Trounced, Tortured and Traumatized, Poe: Pelted, Pounded, Pummeled and Pulverized* and *O. Henry: Obscenely and Outrageously Obliterated,* John has written and published sixty-two total books. *Pieces of Eight, Pieces of Eight, Part II, Pieces of Eight, Part III* and *Pieces of Eight, Part IV* all contain short stories and novellas that feature science fiction and paranormal plots and themes. *Nine New Novellas, Nine New Novellas, Part II, Nine New Novellas, Part III, Nine New Novellas, Part IV, One Baker's Dozen, Two Baker's Dozen, Snake Eyes and Boxcars and Snake Eyes and Boxcars, Part II* are short story collections all written in the spirit of the *Pieces of Eight* series.

Other Jay Dubya adult-oriented fiction are the works *Black Leather and Blue Denim, A '50s Novel*, and its exciting sequel, *The Great Teen Fruit War, A 1960' Novel. Frat Brats, A '60s Novel* completes the action/adventure trilogy. Jay Dubya also has produced two irreverent Biblical satires, *The Wholly Book of Genesis* and *The Wholly Book of Exodus.* A third satire *Ron Coyote, Man of La Mangia* is a parody on Miguel Cervantes' classic novel, *Don Quixote* published in 1605. *Thirteen Sick Tasteless Classics, TSTC, Part II, TSTC, Part III* and *TSTC, Part IV* are satirical works that each corrupt thirteen classic stories from American and British literature and from Greek mythology. *Fractured Frazzled Folk Fables and Fairy Farces* and *FFFF & FF, Part II* satirize and corrupt famous children's literature stories. *Mauled Maimed Mangled Mutilated Mythology* is an adult-oriented satirical/parody work that pokes fun at twenty-one famous classical myths. Finally, *Shakespeare: Slammed, Smeared, Savaged and Slaughtered* and *Shakespeare: S, S, S and S. Part II* lampoon the famous works of the great playwright.

The author has also penned a young adult fantasy trilogy: *Pot of Gold, Enchanta* and *Space Bugs, Earth Invasion. The Eighteen Story Gingerbread House* is a collection of eighteen new children's stories. And last but not least, two Jay Dubya non-fiction works are *So Ya' Wanna' Be A Teacher* and *Random Articles and Manuscripts.*

## Author Biography

Born in Hammonton, NJ in 1942, John Wiessner had attended St. Joseph School up to and including Grade 5. After his family moved from Hammonton to Levittown, Pa in 1954, John attended St. Mark School in Bristol, Pa. for Grade 6, St. Michael the Archangel School in Levittown for Grades 7 and 8 and then Immaculate Conception School, Levittown, Pa. for Grade 9. Bishop Egan High School, Levittown Pa was John's educational base for Grades 10 and 11, and later in 1960, the aspiring author graduated from Edgewood Regional High, Tansboro, NJ. John then next attended Glassboro State College, where he was an announcer for the school's baseball games and also read the nightly news and sports over WGLS, GSC's radio station.

John Wiessner had been primarily an English teacher in the Hammonton Public School System for 34 years, specializing in the instruction of middle school language arts. Mr. Wiessner was quite active in the Hammonton Education Association, serving in the capacities of Vice-President, building representative and finally, teachers' head negotiator for 7 years. During his lengthy teaching career, John had been nominated into "Who's Who Among American Teachers" three times. He also was quite active giving professional workshops at schools around South Jersey on the subjects of creative writing and the use of movie videos to motivate students to organize their classroom theme compositions.

John Wiessner was very active in community service, being a past President of the Hammonton Lions Club, where he also functioned for many years as the club's Tail-Twister, Vice-President and Liontamer. John had been named Hammonton Lion of the Year in 1979 and in 2009 received the prestigious Melvin Jones Fellow Award, the highest honor a Lion can receive.

John also was a successful businessman, starting with being a Philadelphia Bulletin newspaper delivery boy for two years in the late 1950s in Levittown, Pennsylvania. After his family moved back to New Jersey in 1959, John worked at his grandparents and his parents' farm markets, Square Deal Farm (now Ron's Gardens in Hammonton) and Pete's Farm Market in Elm, respectively. He later managed his wife's parents' farm market, White Horse Farms in Elm for three summers.

Also, in a business capacity, for 16 summers starting in 1967 John Wiessner had co-owned Dealers Choice Amusement Arcade on the Ocean City, Maryland boardwalk and also co-owned the New

Horizon Tee-Shirt Store for eight summers (1973-'81) on the Rehoboth Beach, Delaware boardwalk. In addition, “Jay Dubya” was a co-owner of Wheel and Deal Amusement Arcade, Missouri Avenue and Boardwalk, Atlantic City. And then, for 18 summers beginning in 1986, John had been the Field Manager in charge of farm crew-leaders for Atlantic Blueberry Company (the world's largest cultivated blueberry farm), both the Weymouth and Mays Landing, New Jersey Divisions.

After retiring from teaching in 1999, writing under the pen name Jay Dubya (his initials), John Wiessner evolved into the author of 62 books in the genre Action/Adventure Novels, Sci-Fi/Paranormal Story Collections, Adult Satire, Young Adult Fantasy Novels and Non-Fiction Books. His books exist in hardcover, in paperback and in popular Kindle and Nook e-book formats.

After retiring from teaching in 1999, writing under the pen name Jay Dubya (his initials), John Wiessner became the author of 62 books in the genre Action/Adventure Novels, Sci-Fi/Paranormal Story Collections, Adult Satire, Young Adult Fantasy Novels and Non-Fiction Books. His books exist in hardcover, in paperback and in popular Kindle and Nook e-book formats.

In January of 2022, John Wiessner (Jay Dubya) was nominated into Marquis Who’s Who in America, and in April of that same year, was one of nine distinguished Who’s Who in America members honored with Lifetime Achievement Awards, all nine sharing an article of recognition appearing in the Wall Street Journal.

Google: Jay Dubya books

www.ingramcontent.com/pod-product-compliance
Lightning Source LLC
Chambersburg PA
CBHW070501120726
47910CB00003B/1079

* 9 7 8 1 5 8 9 0 9 6 9 7 4 *